On The Run

As the son of a bookshop owner, Max Luther grew up immersed in literature, reading the likes of Roald Dahl and the Biggles books, before discovering crime fiction in adulthood. A lover of fast paced stories, whether on the screen or the page, he decided to try his hand at writing one of his own. *Nowhere to Hide*, a crime thriller starring private bodyguard Alex Drayce, is the first.

Also by Max Luther

Alex Drayce

Nowhere to Hide
On The Run

ON THE RUN

MAX LUTHER

CANELO

First published in the United Kingdom in 2024 by

Canelo
Unit 9, 5th Floor
Cargo Works, 1–2 Hatfields
London SE1 9PG
United Kingdom

A CIP catalogue record for this book is available from the British Library.

Print ISBN 978 1 80436 582 3
Ebook ISBN 978 1 80436 588 5

Cover design by Andrew Smith

Cover images © Shutterstock

Look for more great books at www.canelo.co

Printed and bound in Great Britain by Clays Ltd, Elcograf S.p.A.

1

For my father.

Prologue

Friday night

Bunnies was as busy as Jeanette had ever seen it. It had taken her a solid hour to get the queue at the bar down to an acceptable level, every table in the tired venue occupied now that everyone had enough drinks to keep them happy for a while. The rundown old strip club on the outskirts of Las Vegas appeared as though it had been standing there, unloved, since the mafia era of the Fifties and Sixties, when Bugsy Siegel and Meyer Lanksy had first discovered the city's potential to make, hide and launder money for organised crime. In truth, the building was constructed in the Nineties as a hardware store, before being purchased and converted into a strip club in the early 2000s by Jeanette's boss, Mr Conrad McAuley: a man who loved nothing more than to spend money on himself, but when it came to the business, was less than generous.

The conversion had been carried out on a shoestring budget and he hadn't spent a dime on it over the twenty plus years it had existed. A scruffy stage, scuffed by a thousand stiletto heels, snaked out into the room from a curtained area like a catwalk, chrome poles fitted at various points, with tables surrounding the entire structure. There were no windows, the entire scene lit by disco lights on the ceiling and shaded lamps that sat on each table. The once black awning over the entrance was now more of a greyish colour, having been bleached by the sun over the years, and the dirty-white render that coated the outside of the building was crumbling in dozens of places. There wasn't a metre square uncracked, the bricks underneath exposed where dinner plate-sized chunks had fallen off. But then, Jeanette supposed, men didn't spend their money in Bunnies for the chance to admire the architecture; they had other, more basic desires in mind.

She walked along the bar, bottle of Jack in hand, the stiletto heels on her knee-high boots *clipp-clopping* across the floorboards, and caught the eye of George, Bunnies' head bouncer, stood square on to anyone who dared approach the curtains where the stage appeared from, his white shirt stretched tightly across his jacked physique, black hair swept back, watching the crowd of oglers. She stopped where she'd lined up the glasses a moment ago, went to pour the measures of Jack, but was distracted by the entrance doors swinging inwards.

Kelly and Adriana hustled inside, the inseparable pair hurrying into work. Both wore comfy tracksuits – Kelly's pink; Adriana's blue – their 'outfits' for the night hidden underneath. Their hair and make-up were already done – both young women dolled up to the nines. Adriana's olive skin and long black hair stood in contrast to Kelly's short blonde bob cut and pale complexion, making them the perfect double act on stage: *something for everyone when they're up there*, Conrad had often said. On their feet were comfy white trainers, the high heels they'd wear on stage tucked into the handbags that swung from their forearms. Jeanette rested the bottle of Jack on the bar, put her hands on her hips, cocked her head to the side, and frowned at them.

'You're both late!' she said as they sped past.

'Not by my watch,' Kelly fired back with a grin. That firecracker always had a goddamn comeback for everything, Jeanette thought. 'We're not due on stage for another five minutes.'

'Better get a move on, then. Conrad'll take it out of your tips if you ain't swinging on those poles by the stroke of midnight.'

'Relax, Jeanette,' Adriana said as she walked towards George on her way to the dressing rooms behind the stage curtains. 'You ain't the boss.'

Jeanette felt her jaw clench in response to the sassy Latina's attitude. 'Just get your ass on stage and do your job!'

Adriana ignored her as she strolled out of sight backstage. Kelly turned, smiled, and strutted through the curtains, the last part of her to disappear her middle finger, which she held aloft proudly for Jeanette to see.

Jeanette sighed. 'Cheeky bitch,' she said under her breath.

She poured a healthy measure of Jack in each glass and topped them up with Coke. The bleary-eyed revellers in front of her took their drinks, handed over their cash, and shuffled back to their table. Before she put the cap back on the bottle of Jack, Jeanette poured a triple into a tumbler nestled just out of sight under the bar, squatted, and necked it while no one was watching. Cap back on, she wiped her lips with the back of her hand, stood up, replaced the bottle on the rack, and scanned the vicinity, happy she hadn't been seen.

Bunnies always attracted the same type of people, who created a consistent kind of atmosphere. In the day, truckers would come to watch the girls over lunch and coffee; at night, Bunnies was full of the types who wanted to see naked women dance on a stage, but either couldn't afford, or didn't want to pay, the entrance fees for the glitzy venues on the Strip, with their guest lists, dress policies and expensive drinks. Jeanette surveyed the delinquents who occupied the tables that surrounded the stage. Tonight was no different, she thought.

The atmosphere changed when a group of six men walked in.

There was an aura about them, Jeanette thought, the moment she laid eyes on them. The way they carried themselves, their swagger, as they burst through the entrance and marched over to the bar, was an entire galaxy away from the types she was used to serving. Their black suits looked insanely expensive, the glint of diamond encrusted watches peeking out from their cuffs. She felt a chill as they got closer, their presence evidently having the same effect on the customers, several of whom clocked their arrival and turned away, the intimidation factor causing them to be wary of making eye contact with these men. They were all Latino, and had the hard bodies, jagged facial features and wary eyes of men who had seen and done things most others hadn't. Their confidence gave them the appearance they got what they wanted in life, by doing whatever was needed to come out on top, legal or not. They set Jeanette's nerves on edge. She felt vulnerable for the first time in a long time. When the guy at the front of their group put his elbows on the bar and leaned forwards, Jeanette looked into his eyes, and instead of the creepy feeling she experienced with their usual clientele, she felt a whole new sensation.

Danger.

'Six bottles of champagne,' the man demanded, the words spoken with a heavy Spanish accent. 'And I want the best you got.'

Jeanette put him somewhere in his fifties, but he had the strong body of a man twenty years his junior. He was clean shaven, his hair jet-black, slick with gel, and swept back like a Wall Street character from an Eighties movie. His blue silk shirt was open at the collar, the V shape sagging three buttons down. Jeanette spotted a tattoo in Spanish on his muscular chest: *El Jefe*.

The Boss.

'Six?' Jeanette asked. She wasn't used to serving champagne; she was used to pouring Jack and Cokes and giant pitchers of beer. Wasn't even sure they had any.

The Boss nodded as he took out a packet of cigarettes from his pocket, tapped out the tip of one, and pulled it free with his lips. Marlboro Reds, Jeanette noticed. Old-school cowboy killers.

'Tiago!' The Boss barked at one of his men.

Tiago leaned over with a chrome Zippo lighter and lit the tip, which glowed bright red as The Boss took a long drag. Smoking was prohibited inside Bunnies, but Jeanette wasn't going to say anything to this man. He blew a cloud of smoke in her face and spread his arms out wide to encapsulate the men around him. 'Six bottles for six men.'

The other five who were with him had fanned out in a protective semi-circle, facing outwards, hands hidden within sharp suits, their keen eyes watching the room. The Boss was the only one who appeared to have been drinking, his eyelids lazy, words slurred, his posture softened and movements uncoordinated in the way of a drunkard. He was the only one who would be drinking, of this Jeanette was certain, and he wasn't getting through six bottles of champagne by himself, so most of it would surely be wasted.

Not my problem, Jeanette thought.

She shrugged. 'It's your money, pal, but I'll need to check to see if we've got some.'

He waved at her dismissively. 'Then go. Hurry! I'm thirsty.'

Jeanette bristled. Such words spoken by regular customers would see her flash a look George's way, who would know to make his presence felt immediately; it was important you nipped disrespectful behaviour in the bud in a place like Bunnies. But that didn't strike Jeanette as a sensible option with these men. Best to let it slide.

'You boys Mexican?' she asked.

The Boss's eyelids narrowed as he regarded her with contempt. 'You got a problem with that, *Guera*?'

A flutter of fear scurried up her spine. 'No, not at all. Just making conversation. I noticed your tattoo…'

He glanced at his open shirt collar, then flicked back up again, staring into Jeanette's eyes, his own awash with an intoxicated glaze as he squinted from the strobe lights that flickered across his face. 'You been gazing at my chest, Chica?' He pulled on his cigarette, flashed a wide smile her way, and leaned further forwards, leering at her. 'You like what you see?'

Jeanette blinked the smoke out of her eyes and forced a smile onto her face to keep him on side. 'Excuse me while I go check if we've got some champagne in the back.' She turned her back on him, walked along the bar, and pushed through the door into the Staff Only area. She peered into the storage room. A twelve-bottle case of Crystal sat in the corner. She took a step in, paused,

6

thought better of it, and turned around. Seconds later she knocked on McAuley's office door.

'What is it?' he called out.

She opened the door. A giant TV was mounted to the wall straight ahead of her, the screen separated into multiple squares for the feeds from the numerous cameras dotted around Bunnies. Conrad was to the left, sat at his desk, tapping away on his keyboard, cooking the books. The sleeves of his pink shirt were rolled up to flaunt the giant imitation Rolex on his wrist, the top three buttons undone to show off the fake gold chain around his neck. His iPhone was tucked into his chest pocket, the weight of which made the garment sag, exposing more of his saggy man-breasts than anyone wanted to see. Jeanette fought the urge to gag. She took a step into the room and cleared her throat; he didn't even look up at her. Arrogant son of a bitch.

'We've got a customer who wants six bottles of champagne, and it's got to be "the best you got".' She rolled her eyes as she quoted him. 'Am I okay to use the Crystal we got?'

Conrad's head whipped around to face her, his concentration broken at the thought of being ripped off by a bunch of bums. 'Hell no! Are you crazy? I bought that in for a special event I'm hosting next month.' He pointed a bony finger her way. 'And you must be stupider than you look if you think he's for real. None of the cockroaches who come in here on a Friday night can afford six bottles of the world's most expensive champagne. They must have counterfeit bills or something. Tell him to take a hike further into the city and try ripping off one of the casinos if that's his game.'

Jeanette put her hands on her hips. She wasn't in the habit of answering McAuley back; he'd been violent in the past, and she knew of at least one illegal firearm he kept on the premises, so it was always a good idea to keep him sweet. But the men at the bar were unequivocally more dangerous than her pink-shirt-wearing boss.

'Maybe you want to come tell him yourself.' She rubbed the back of her neck, her eyes flicking to the CCTV feed that covered the bar area. 'I don't like the look of these guys. They're not our usual clientele.'

Conrad followed her gaze. As soon as his eyes met the screen, his whole body stilled. Once he'd snapped out of it, he stood up and moved closer to the screen.

'It can't be,' he said.

'It can't be what?'

He turned to face her. His expression had dropped, a look of worry infecting his entire demeanour. His forehead glistened as though he'd instantly broken into a sweat.

'Not *what*,' he said. '*Who.*'

She gazed past him to the screen and focused on the man at the bar. 'Who is he?'

Conrad pushed past her and marched to the storage room, ignoring her question.

Jeanette followed. 'Hey! You gonna tell me who this guy is or what?'

He stopped dead, his head snapping around to stare at her. 'That "guy" is Luis Vasquez.'

Jeanette scratched her nose as an excuse to cover her mouth with her hand as she spoke: a poor attempt to block from McAuley the smell of Jack Daniels on her breath. 'Who the fuck is Luis Vasquez?'

8

'He only runs the most powerful cartel operating on the West Coast.' Conrad rubbed his forehead and continued to stride down the corridor. 'Jesus Christ. Of all the bars in Vegas, he has to walk into mine.'

'Will him and his boys cause trouble?' Jeanette called out after him, lowering her hand now he was a few strides away. 'Shall I get the shotgun?'

Conrad stopped in his tracks so fast it was like he'd hit a forcefield. He spun around. 'Jesus Christ, no! Are you crazy? They'd kill us. And even if we managed to escape the bloodbath we'd have started, we'd soon be hunted down and buried in the desert.' He continued to the storage room. 'We just give them what they want and keep them happy until they leave. Now make yourself useful and help me with these.'

Jeanette reluctantly followed him in. A minute later they both made their way back to the bar with a bottle of Crystal in each hand and another tucked under an arm. They lined them up in front of Vasquez, who was too busy watching Adriana and Kelly dance to notice.

'Your champagne, gentlemen,' Conrad said, wide-eyed and grinning. 'My apologies, though. I'm afraid it isn't chilled.'

Vasquez turned to face Conrad, slowly, surveying the man as a snake might a mouse.

'Jeanette,' Conrad said, keeping his eyes on Vasquez, smiling at the intimidating Latino man like a pathetic fanboy. 'Fetch six champagne flutes for these gentlemen.'

A step further and you'll be the one giving him a lap dance tonight, Jeanette thought.

Vasquez looked Conrad up and down disapprovingly. Finished with his assessment of Jeanette's boss, he turned his head to the side. 'Miguel. *El dinero.*'

Miguel stepped forwards with a bundle of cash in his hand, far too much there even when you considered the insane price of the champagne. As he reached over and placed the entire wedge on the bar, the sleeve of his suit jacket rode up, revealing the tattoo of a black hand on his forearm. The long fingers edged out from his cuff, their tips reaching all the way to the heel of his palm.

Vasquez tossed the stub of his cigarette to the floor, snatched two bottles off the bar, and sauntered off to an occupied table in a prime position to watch Adriana and Kelly dance. His goons took the remaining bottles and followed their boss. Jeanette noticed another black hand tattoo on the neck of one of the others, the fingertips rising above the collar of his white shirt, as though a prisoner was trying to escape from under his clothing. She couldn't hear if anything was said because of the music, but it didn't appear as though many, if any, words were necessary to make another group vacate their table and shuffle off, heads bowed, to stand and watch at the back.

Jeanette turned to the racks of glasses under the bar, hooked six flutes between her fingers, and walked over to the Mexicans, praying they weren't going to be a problem.

Unfortunately for Jeanette, there was evidently no one there to hear her.

–

The sound of breaking glass was the first warning Jeanette got that trouble was brewing. It was one of the champagne bottles, elbowed off the table by Vasquez, the distinctive *ting-smash* audible above the music. Most of the content had been drunk, but the floor was now covered in razor-sharp shards dancing amongst the fizz of the champagne.

Customers at the surrounding tables upped and left in response to Vasquez's increasingly reckless behaviour. He was on his feet, waist pressed into the edge of the stage as he leaned forwards with a fist-full of dollars, a wide, gormless smile on his face, trying to reach Adriana. With his free hand he beckoned her forwards, his anger growing by the second as she refused to go near him. She backed off, hugging the pole, fear evident on her expression. Kelly noticed and walked over from another area of the stage to come to her friend's aid. She caught George's eye and flicked her head towards the rowdy Mexican. George nodded and walked towards their table.

Shit, Jeanette thought. *This is going to get messy.*

As George approached, the entire group got to their feet and faced him. Suit jackets were swept aside. Jeanette spotted the grips of at least two pistols amongst them, the weapons tucked into their belts. The temperature in the room seemed to rocket, the entire scene reminding Jeanette of the kind of western films her dad liked to watch, the sheriff barging into the local bar to deal with the outlaws, the whole confrontation a powder keg about to explode.

Conrad came running out of the back, having plainly witnessed the proceedings on the CCTV feed in his office. 'Wait! George, wait!' He scurried over to the brewing melee and stood between them. 'It's okay, George.'

The giant bouncer shrugged, turned, and walked back to his post, oblivious to the danger he'd been strolling towards.

Conrad faced the Mexicans. 'Sorry about that, gentlemen.' He glanced at the broken glass. 'Let me get this cleaned up.'

He eyed Jeanette, the command obvious. She turned to get the dustpan and brush, but spotted Vasquez eyeballing the two thugs who had moved to the front to stare down George. 'Gabriel! Raul!' Once he had their attention, he raised a hand, palm down, patting it in the air as a way of telling them to settle down. 'I'll handle this.' Gabriel and Raul covered their pistols with their jackets and stepped back. Vasquez walked forwards, squaring up to McAuley.

Jeanette turned her back on the skirmish, walked through the Staff Only door, and grabbed the dustpan and brush. On her return, Vasquez was in Conrad's face, their noses inches apart. Angry words were thrown at Conrad, a finger pointed in his face for emphasis. Vasquez turned to Adriana, his arms waving as though demanding she come over to him. Jeanette couldn't hear what was being said from where she was, but it seemed he wanted more from Adriana than she was willing to offer. Conrad was evidently trying to calm the man down. Kelly had come to the edge of the stage and was stood between Adriana and Vasquez, clearly trying to protect her friend. Raul drew his gun. Kelly and Adriana both stiffened, the former's confidence vanishing in an instant.

As Jeanette scurried over to them, dustpan and brush in hand, Kelly reluctantly stepped aside. Adriana walked to the curtains, resigning herself to whatever it was she'd previously been resisting. Raul put his gun away, the arrogant smile of a victor plastered across his face. Conrad put an arm around Vasquez's shoulders.

The entire group of men followed Adriana backstage.

1

Monday morning

The weapon he'd chosen for the job was an M2010 Enhanced Sniper Rifle, chambering a .300 Winchester Magnum. Made in America, both the rifle and the bullet were two of the most popular in the country. Rare fire-arms and ammunition used in crimes are easy for the law to trace; common ones aren't – an important factor for any criminal to consider, especially one who planned to send a round across the skyline of one of the busiest cities on the planet, into a designated area roughly one square foot, on a moving target. Quite the challenge, even for a man with his skill.

He moved his cheek away from his rifle's stock, rolled his head from side to side to relieve the stiffness in his neck. A headache introduced itself in his left temple, the pulsing throb an indication the worst was yet to come. He squinted against the Los Angeles sunshine, torturously magnified through the telescopic sight, and glanced side-ways at his watch. The convoy would be en route by now. He took a deep breath.

Nearly time.

He grimaced, a tight feeling having crept into his lower back. He contracted his abs and glutes a dozen times to get the blood flowing, altered his prone position slightly, then opened his eyes, adjusted his earpiece, and checked the connection to the team radio. He needed to be ready for every single update. He'd get one chance at this.

There was nothing to suggest the convoy – a black Cadillac SUV and a silver Isuzu – would be early, but it was important he be prepared. In position for over an hour, he was ready and waiting to take advantage of his narrow window of opportunity. The pride he took in his role within the team meant he'd planned everything with meticulous detail. While the others learned the protection team's routine, he'd scouted the city for a week, searching for the best urban hide, which he'd narrowed down to an empty office unit on the fifty-second floor of the Wilshire Grand Center: a huge skyscraper set within the financial district of Downtown LA. One of the tallest skyscrapers in the city, he hadn't been able to open a window to give his bullet a clear trajectory to the convoy. Instead, he'd been forced to think outside of the box.

He'd fixed a breaching device to the pane of glass he was aiming through. A simple frame charge, it was packed with just enough explosive to shatter the thick glass window, giving his bullet a clear path to the target. He'd run electrical wire from the bomb to the detonator in his left hand: a simple trigger mechanism with a safety cover over the switch. When the convoy rolled into view, he would blow the window out, allowing him to take the first shot without the glass deflecting the round. A tactic he'd used numerous times in the past.

He examined his range card: a piece of white paper, six square inches, propped up against his rifle's bipod. On it, he'd marked every building and road in his field of vision along with distances and elevations. The most important landmark was the Harbor Freeway, which snaked away from his position just the other side of the Wedbush building: the route the convoy planned to take.

A crackle erupted in his ear, followed by surveillance commentary from his team. The target convoy had just passed Dodger Stadium on the 110. Three minutes away. He reached for the wire that ran from his earpiece and pressed the transmit button.

'Over-watch received. Ready and waiting.'

He settled his crosshairs on the middle of the freeway, just as the asphalt appeared from around the corner of the Wedbush bank. As the convoy came into view, the vehicles would be facing away from his position, meaning there was little to no chance of the protection team spotting his muzzle flash and identifying his position. But it wouldn't matter if they did. The first shot would do the bulk of the damage.

He paid close attention to the speeds and lane positions given by his team. The convoy was making ground; seconds now, not minutes. This was it, what all the planning and preparation had been for. He took a steady breath, slipped his index finger inside the trigger guard, flicked the safety cover off the detonator, and rested his thumb on the switch.

He was ready.

—

Alex Drayce took one hand off the armoured Cadillac's steering wheel and adjusted his sunglasses. Three weeks into this contract and his eyes still hadn't adapted to the LA weather; they'd become accustomed to the grey skies in London. He shifted in his seat, uncomfortable in the plate carrier body armour he'd sourced at short notice.

A Sig MPX carbine was strapped to him on a single point sling, resting across his chest where he could have it in play in an instant if required. His secondary weapon was also a Sig, the P226 pistol, holstered on his chest – the ideal place to draw from whilst seated inside a vehicle. He wore black Mechanix tactical gloves, which as well as being ideal for handling weaponry, were also perfect driving gloves, giving him absolute control of the Cadillac's steering wheel. The fierce LA sun reflected off the giant glass buildings that surrounded the freeway. He dropped his visor to block the glare, the little mirror bringing into view the two guys in the back.

Nelson, the leader of their close protection team, was sitting behind the front passenger seat, having been unable to fit behind Drayce. They were both big men and the laws of physics didn't allow two objects to occupy the same space at the same time. The Pauli Exclusion Principle, Drayce had once read. He was north of six foot six and two hundred and eighty pounds, and his team leader was a big, strong Mexican guy, who despite being in his early fifties, wouldn't have looked out of place throwing men around in a Lucha Libre ring. According to his tattoos he was a former member of an aggressive task force in Mexico City – the Policia Federal – and judging by his physique he killed most of his free time lifting weights. Like Drayce, he had a thick neck, wide shoulders and strong arms, and although he might get lost in Drayce's shadow, he nonetheless took up most of the space in the back.

Nelson didn't have a surname, or at least not one he wanted to share with Drayce. Drayce had managed to coax out of him that after several years with the *federales*, he'd been employed by the DEA's El Paso office, helping him on his way to earning an American passport. After a few years passing back and forth across the border, he'd got a taste for the American way of life and decided to set up his own company on the West Coast, called SIPS: Security, Investigative and Protective Services. Three weeks ago, he'd thrown an offer out to all the top bodyguards on the international circuit as a last-minute thing to help cover the protection needed for this client. Drayce had been chosen from the shortlist, unsurprising when you considered his experience. After serving eighteen years in British law enforcement, first on the Armed Response Vehicles in Manchester, then as a Counter Terrorist Specialist Firearms Officer in both Birmingham and London, before finishing his career as a bodyguard in Scotland Yard's Royalty and Specialist Protection unit, his skills were always highly sought after on the circuit.

He'd been contracted for four weeks, so this job would soon be coming to an end. He didn't need to know Nelson's surname because it wasn't important. In a week's time he'd be back in the UK where he had some personal matters to attend to, and they would likely never meet again. If a first name was enough to get the man's attention when it came time for Drayce to collect his pay cheque, then that was all he needed to know.

On the other side of the rear seats was the client, Mr Stephen Vanderbilt, his expensive pinstripe suit forming wrinkles as he was forced back by Drayce's seat and squished up to his door by Nelson's brawn. He tapped away on the screen of his phone, engrossed in his digital world. He ran one of the top consultancy firms in Los Angeles serving a select list of high-net-worth clients, specialising in digital media and marketing – information

Drayce had sourced online once he'd arrived in LA. He was glad he'd done his research beforehand, having got very little out of Vanderbilt – the man had said all of five words to him while he'd been protecting him these past three weeks. Drayce could forgive his silence, though. Vanderbilt had a hell of a lot on his mind.

Two months ago, a business associate of Vanderbilt's was kidnapped and tortured by a highly trained team of criminals and was only released once he'd transferred several million dollars into an untraceable numbered account. The FBI were investigating it, assisted by the LAPD, but they weren't making much ground, and Stephen was understandably petrified he might be targeted next. Beyond the other passengers, Drayce could see the support vehicle through the back window: a silver Isuzu truck, about four feet off his rear bumper. It was driven by Geoff, the third member of the protection team: a fit, wiry, forty-two-year-old from Florida, who for some reason didn't have much time for Drayce. Drayce wondered if maybe he was the unsociable type, or perhaps just insecure. The fact Drayce had been introduced onto the protection team as extra support after the contract had already got underway, could be seen as Nelson bringing Geoff's ability into question. Drayce wasn't particularly bothered about why the guy didn't like him; he wasn't there to make friends. He was there to get paid doing what he does best.

Drayce didn't know much about Geoff's background, but the guy seemed fairly switched on. No doubt he'd spent some time in law enforcement before getting into the private security game. Drayce had seen an old, slightly frayed, FBI Hostage Rescue Team badge sown onto his kit bag at a morning briefing a few days ago, which he'd been leaning on as he'd taken notes. Drayce remembered looking at him as he'd scribbled away and had wondered why he bothered. Note-taking was a waste of time in their game. It's not as though you could pull them out and have a read to remind you of what to do whilst the shit's hitting the fan all around you. Personally, Drayce preferred to keep things simple, and had chosen to narrow this job down to a seven-word summary, played over and over in his mind.

High speeds; tight positions; stop for nothing.

Everything else would be dealt with spontaneously using whatever tactics he deemed to be suitable at the time. He wasn't a fan of working everything out in meticulous detail beforehand. Plans were always too fragile. As Joe Louis once said: everyone has a plan until they've been hit.

Drayce focused on the road ahead. His eyes strained against the glare of the sun off the shiny concrete freeway, its surface polished over the years by the obscene amount of traffic. He'd been assured by the locals that spring was coming to an end, but from what he could tell, seasons weren't much of a thing in LA. The weather these past few weeks had been glorious and today was no different. It was like another planet compared to what he'd left behind in the UK. The weather reporter on the car radio told listeners not to worry, because summer would soon be breaking through with the promise of even hotter weather to come.

It was a shame Drayce had to return to London next week.

He cruised the convoy along at a steady ninety, only moving out of the fast lane if they needed to overtake something, which if they did, they did as one: a single entity, snaking through traffic as though joined together. The imposing financial district towered above them on the left as they flew under a series of bridges. As their path was darkened by the shadow of the Wedbush building, they hit traffic. Nelson studied the GPS tracker on his phone.

'Looks like it only gets worse from here, sir,' he said to Vanderbilt in his thick Spanish accent. 'We'll just have to suck it up for a few minutes. Shouldn't be long before we make the next exit. We're on track to get you to your meeting on time.'

Vanderbilt didn't say a word in return. He just nodded his head without looking up from his phone, his overly styled black hair flopping up and down. As the convoy was forced down to twenty miles an hour by the traffic build up, Nelson opened his jacket, freeing the grip of his short-barrelled, compact M4 carbine, which was slung to the body armour he was wearing. Slow movement was a protection team's nightmare; it made them sitting ducks for anyone who might be planning an attack.

Drayce followed Nelson's lead and swept aside the lapels of his ThruDark jacket, parting the lightweight grey material to fully expose the grip of his carbine. Forced to slow the Cadillac down, he scanned the traffic build up and examined people in the vehicles around them. As they came out the other side of the Wedbush building's shadow, a blaze of light flashed in the rear-view mirror. Drayce hadn't been looking directly at it, but it had caught his eye, somewhere in the corner of his peripheral vision, registering on his threat perception. It had come from a mid-level floor of a building behind the bank. A small explosion of some sort. So small nobody else had noticed it.

Drayce felt his adrenaline spike. He parted his lips to tell Nelson of his fears just as another burst of light flared from the same window. Not as obvious as the last, but far more concerning.

Muzzle flash.

–

The sniper breathed out.

His focus stayed on the sight, watching the Cadillac closely as the round hit the centre of the target. Other than his chest, the only part of him that moved was his right arm as he worked the bolt back and forth, spitting out the used cartridge and chambering a fresh bullet. He moved his right hand back to the grip and settled his index finger inside the trigger guard.

Breathe, hold, squeeze.

The second shot landed high and right but was only a few inches out, nothing too drastic. He exhaled, worked the bolt, and repeated, sending the third shot an inch low and left; an over correction, but nothing to worry about. All three were devastating hits. He'd done his job perfectly.

The sniper broke down his rifle like the well-practised expert he was, packed it all away in its case along with his range card and detonator switch, then quickly zipped it up and threw it over his shoulder. He took the ski mask out of his pocket, slipped it over his face, then walked out of the room, headed straight to the elevator, and hit the button for the ground floor. On the way down he removed his backup weapon: a Beretta pistol. He knew he'd see other people on his way out, like hotel staff, guests and security, but they didn't concern him. They'd be stupid to interfere with an armed man wearing a ski mask. As long as they didn't mess with him, he wouldn't mess with them. He'd just run straight past and carry on out of the building to get involved with the next part of the plan.

He knew the alarm would be raised by the hotel staff because of his appearance, but a 911 call didn't really matter because he'd be long gone before the cops arrived. As for the building's cameras, they wouldn't be much use to them. He'd worn completely different clothes when he'd walked into the building, and now his face was hidden as he left, so they'd never be able to link the two and figure out what he looked like. As always, there was very little he and his team hadn't considered.

As the elevator dropped like a lead balloon, the sniper racked the top slide of his pistol to chamber a round, and listened to the rest of the team through his ear piece. The next part of the plan was unfolding: they were moving in. Once the elevator doors opened, he would sprint out of the building and cover the distance to the freeway on foot in less than a minute; plenty of time to join in on the vehicular assault the rest of his team would soon be carrying out. He smiled under the ski mask, his eyes turning to the floor counter.

Seven. Six. Five. Four...

He held his pistol down by his thigh and stared at the thin vertical crack in the doors in front of him, readying himself for when they would open. He was excited and a little jittery, but that was to be expected. No way would he be able to hold back and act calmly once he was out of that elevator. He'd explode through those doors, running as fast as he could. A clammy, nervous sweat introduced itself underneath his ski mask. He planted his feet, one in front of the other, an athlete on the starter block, then looked back at the floor counter, gripping his pistol tightly.

Three. Two. One. Zero...

A fraction of a second after spotting the muzzle flash, Drayce heard the round impact the Cadillac's hood.

'Get down!' he shouted.

Nelson was already moving, forcing Vanderbilt's head between his knees before throwing his giant frame on top of him. Drayce changed down a gear just as the second round landed near the same spot on the hood, and punched the throttle as the third one hit home.

'Get us out of here, Alex!' Nelson shouted.

Which was easier said than done. The traffic in front was clearing, but the Cadillac's throttle wasn't having much effect any more. Drayce saw three neat holes in the vehicle's hood that hadn't been there a moment ago, steam pouring out of them as the vehicle rolled slowly forwards, with nothing powering it except for what little momentum it had retained from crawling along with the heavy traffic. The engine was making a hideous, crunching, grinding sound. He didn't know much about car mechanics, but it sounded exactly like the noise an engine might make as it died a painful death. A couple of seconds later there was no noise at all. The engine cut out and their momentum quickly ran out, bringing them to a complete stop.

'Fuck,' Nelson said as he pushed Vanderbilt's head further down and climbed on top of him. 'Not good.'

Drayce agreed. They were stuck in the middle of a busy freeway with a high value client, they were being shot at, and they were inside a vehicle that was now totally un-driveable.

Basically, they were sitting ducks.

'I see smoke,' Geoff said over their radio. 'You guys having vehicle problems?'

'Shots fired from a building, seven o'clock from our position,' Drayce replied. 'Our engine bay's destroyed. Geoff, I need you to pull up along our nearside to give us cover from the shooter while we move the client into your vehicle.'

While Geoff moved the Isuzu into position, Drayce quickly analysed the attack. His initial instinct told him the three shots had been aimed at the cabin but had gone wide, but as he looked at their tinted windows, the shooter's plan became clear. Firing through the glass would have been a shot in the dark, and no sniper worth his salt aimed at something he couldn't see. Furthermore, the only parts of the Cadillac that were armoured were the doors, which gave the passengers in the cabin some protection, but left the engine bay vulnerable. Consequently, the shooter had decided to fire at their Achilles heel, with the intention of disabling the vehicle. All of which likely meant one thing.

An assault team was coming.

Drayce gripped his MPX and checked the mirrors, knowing an attack would most likely come from the rear.

He was right. There were four of them: two pairs, approaching either side on foot. Dressed in black tactical clothing, with body armour on their torsos and ski masks on their faces, they worked their way through the lines of stationary traffic that had built up, each figure with an assault rifle on aim as they closed the Cadillac down.

'Contact rear,' Drayce said to Geoff over the radio set. He turned around in his seat, aimed his MPX through the Cadillac's tinted rear window, flicked off the safety, and spoke directly to Nelson and Vanderbilt. 'Keep your heads down. Vanderbilt, cover your ears.'

The client let out a gentle whimper from underneath Nelson, but then did as he was told, cupping his hands over his ears because he was the only one who wasn't wearing advanced ear protection.

Drayce tracked the four-man assault team. Inevitably, chaos ensued in their wake as people reacted to their presence, a wave following their progress as hordes of terrified motorists abandoned their vehicles and ran off in the opposite direction.

Drayce ignored the carnage and aimed at the gunman on the far left. He was bobbing up and down and side to side, weaving through the traffic, making good use of cover. Drayce took his time. He watched the man go out of sight behind a large truck and tracked his MPX along the length of the wagon, keeping in time with the speed of the man's movements. Moments later he saw the figure's head and shoulders reappear. He settled his sight picture square on the man's face, held his breath, and pulled the trigger.

The gun shot was a monstrous presence inside the Cadillac, the air displacement like that of a miniature explosion. The round punched through the glass, shattering the entire window. The gunman dropped like a lead balloon, but the others instantly returned fire as they moved into cover, bullets thudding into the Cadillac's bodywork. Drayce resisted the urge to duck out of sight, instead returning fire with rapid trigger pulls, sending enough hot metal down range to stall their attack. He hurriedly stalked another figure with his weapon, opening fire as soon as his sight picture settled, aiming for centre mass due to his target moving sideways. His rounds hit the attacker's body armour, knocking the wind out of him and forcing him to cower behind a vehicle.

As Drayce reloaded his MPX, a barrage of bullets shot through the Cadillac's windows, forcing him to drop down. The assault team had raised their point of aim, having realised the armoured doors were impenetrable. Drayce turned around in his seat and slouched as low as he could, using the mirrors to get a view behind. The figure he'd forced into cover was now back up, closing the Cadillac down as he let rip with containing fire. The others were keeping Geoff pinned down in the Isuzu. Drayce tried to twist around in his seat to get into a position to shoot back, but it was no use; every time he went to lift his head, a bullet came whizzing through the cabin.

He clenched his teeth and fought hard for an idea. If he didn't think of something before the attackers got to his vehicle, they wouldn't survive.

Painful moans from the back seats provided Drayce with some tactical inspiration.

'Who's making that noise?' he said, keeping his head down.

'Me,' Nelson grunted.

'You been hit?'

Drayce could hear him patting himself down, searching for the injury.

'Yeah, I think so.' There wasn't even a hint of panic in Nelson's voice. Just annoyance.

'How bad is it?'

'Hard to tell.'

'Find it quickly and get a close look. How's Vanderbilt?'

A moment's pause while Nelson checked him over. 'Alive and well.'

Drayce watched the Cadillac's mirrors. The gunmen were starting a flanking manoeuvre from less than twenty feet away, running with their weapons on aim. The nearest was close enough for Drayce to see his eyes, wide with excitement, a wolf who'd smelt blood.

'I've found it,' Nelson said through heavy breathing. 'It's okay. I'm fine. Looks like a round only clipped me.'

'Where?' Drayce asked.

'Top of my right shoulder.'

'How badly is it bleeding?'

'It's making a mess but it's not as bad as it looks. Doesn't need a tourniquet. I can still fight. I think… Argh! What the fuck are you doing?'

Drayce had reached between the seats and clamped his hand on Nelson's upper right shoulder, exactly where he'd told him his injury was. He pulled his bloody hand back, smeared it across his forehead, and checked the wing mirror again. The closest gunman was now all of ten feet away, changing the magazine on his weapon – a final assault position. In seconds he would be pointing his muzzle through the front passenger window, right in Drayce's face.

'Keep screaming, Nelson,' Drayce said.

'What?'

'Just keep screaming!'

While Nelson let rip with his hearty Mexican voice box, Drayce lay his MPX across the centre console and slumped forwards in his seat like a dead body. He drew his pistol and held it across his chest in his left hand where it would be hard to see, with the barrel pointing at the passenger door. He relaxed his neck muscles and hung his head, resting it on top of the steering wheel. His jaw slackened and his tongue hung lifelessly between his teeth. Nelson's blood dripped down his face. His eyes glazed over, a thousand-yard stare into nothing. To all intents and purposes, he was a dead body. No threat to anyone.

The passenger door flew wide open.

Two rifles were aimed at Drayce. The world paused, everything slowing to a standstill. Drayce's surroundings morphed from the noise of a battlefield to the quiet of a graveyard. He could feel the pulse in his neck, his heartbeat so loud he worried the gunmen would hear it. Muzzles hovered inches from his face, the gunmen assessing the body laying before them. Drayce knew what they were thinking: the driver was dead, ignore him. No use pumping bullets into a corpse. Through the corner of his lifeless gaze, he saw both men glance at the rear seats. Their rifles followed, their priorities changing as they shifted their point of aim away from him and towards Nelson's screams.

Bingo.

Drayce's pistol kicked up into his chest, a double tap splitting the heads of both men. He shouldered the driver's door open and turned the pistol on the man who was keeping Geoff pinned down. Two rounds to the man's centre mass rocked him backwards, but it was Nelson who ended it for him, rearing up from the back seats and sending a flurry of bullets through his skull with the M4.

Silence fell on the freeway.

–

The sniper sprinted to the 7th Street Bridge, pausing once he had sight of the freeway. The two vehicles his team had attacked were at the front of a huge block of stacked traffic, the road behind them a parking lot. He tore a pair of binoculars from his pack as he moved to the bannister, perched his elbows on the railing to steady himself, and zoomed in on the scene.

Something had gone horribly wrong.

His teammates were scattered around the concrete, pools of blood interlinking their ruined bodies. There was no movement from any of them, not even the slight expansion and contraction of working lungs. The sniper felt a sudden rush of anger, sweat now pouring down his face under the ski-mask. His grip tightened around the binoculars as he panned from side to side, searching for the man they'd come for.

Movement in the Cadillac caught his eye.

The protection team, and presumably Vanderbilt himself, were still alive, manoeuvring inside that vehicle. The Cadillac's engine was evidently broken, hence why they hadn't driven off, but if they made it to the Isuzu, they'd be able to escape.

The sniper could not allow that to happen.

He ditched his binoculars, unslung his rucksack, and began assembling his rifle.

–

Drayce holstered his pistol and then collected his MPX from the centre console. He leapt out of the Cadillac and shouldered the weapon, scanning the area for any further threats. The freeway was in total chaos behind them. Hundreds of vehicles had been abandoned in a traffic jam stretching back as far as he could see. The far-off screams of motorists could be heard as they ran for their lives, but there was nobody in the immediate vicinity and the traffic in front of them had cleared. Drayce faced the Isuzu.

'You alive in there, Geoff?'

A breathless voice responded, tinny and dull from within the truck, as though he was hunkered down in the footwell. 'Yeah. I'm still here.'

'You hurt?'

'Nah, I'm good.'

'The immediate threat has been dealt with, but there could be more. We're coming to you and then we're getting out of here. On me, Nelson.'

Drayce heard one of the rear doors of the Cadillac open behind him, followed by the sound of a scuffle. A few seconds later Nelson was stood next to him, manhandling Vanderbilt.

'Cover's on,' Drayce said. 'Get our man inside that truck.'

Nelson dragged Vanderbilt over to the Isuzu, pushing his head down the entire way. Drayce scanned the vicinity with his weapon as they moved, only relinquishing cover when he saw Nelson bundle Vanderbilt into the back seats and climb in after him. Drayce opened the front passenger door and jumped in next to Geoff.

'Let's go,' Drayce said.

As Geoff hit the throttle, Drayce heard the *ting* of a high-velocity round impacting the front of the truck. He turned in his seat and tried desperately to get eyes on the shooter, spotting him a second later, hunkered down on the other side of the road, halfway down the concrete steps that gave access from the 7th Street Bridge to the freeway, resting a sniper rifle on the handrail to steady it while he took aim.

'Heads down!' Drayce shouted to the other men in the truck, as a bright flash of light erupted from the rifle's muzzle. The bullet hit the vehicle's bodywork a split second later, the sound of the gunshot echoing around the tall buildings that surrounded them. The armoured doors stopped the bullet from penetrating the cabin, but Drayce knew they wouldn't stop many more because of the size of the calibre.

He steadied the barrel of his MPX against the side of Geoff's seat, pointed it over the top of Nelson's and Vanderbilt's heads, took aim at the sniper on the steps, and squeezed his trigger. The shot was a little rushed and it deflected fractionally on impact with the back window, sending it high and right, whizzing over the sniper's left shoulder and kicking up dust on the bridge. With the window now obliterated, the following shots were more accurate, forcing the sniper to drop low to avoid being hit. As Drayce continued firing, he felt the Isuzu begin to move, despite the large calibre bullet embedded in its engine block.

'Punch it, Geoff! Punch it!'

Geoff didn't need telling twice. He stamped his foot on the throttle and sent them flying forwards, directly towards the next exit a hundred metres ahead.

With the sniper still ducking low, Drayce took careful aim and fired a succession of shots in his direction. Shards of glass flew everywhere as he tracked his aim with the movement of the truck, sending round after round through the windows. The flames spitting out of his muzzle set fire to Geoff's headrest. A burst of red mist sprayed into the air from where the sniper was cowering, his lifeless body collapsing into view as he slumped to the side of the barrier. Drayce carried on shooting regardless, putting another five rounds into him, on the off-chance the guy was still capable of getting up and returning fire.

When the bolt in his weapon locked back, Drayce turned in his seat to face the front. He dropped the magazine and reloaded with a full spare, just in case they weren't out of danger yet. A strong wind blew through the smashed windows and swirled around the cabin, extinguishing Geoff's smouldering headrest. Drayce patted it down with a gloved hand to be sure it was out, then checked all around them for signs of a further threat. As they covered more distance along the freeway, it appeared all the gunmen had been dealt with.

Geoff turned sharply for the exit, maintaining a high speed to get them out of the area. They may have survived the attack, but it wasn't a smart idea to hang around. The training manual for close protection teams was clear on this matter. They needed to put distance between themselves and the killing ground they'd just escaped from, as quickly as possible.

The road signs they'd just passed said twenty miles per hour for the exit.

Drayce glanced at the speed dial.

They were doing five times that.

2

The road forked up ahead. Drayce told Geoff to go right, the tyres on the nearside squealing against the concrete as he took the bend at speed. Drayce reached up and gripped onto the handle above his door as the truck teetered dangerously close to either oversteering into the line of palm trees on one side of the road, or understeering into the row of tents that occupied a large gathering of the city's homeless community on the other. He breathed a sigh of relief as the road straightened out. Seconds later his ears picked up the sound of crying coming from the back seats.

'You guys all right back there?' he asked.

'Yeah, we good,' Nelson said.

Drayce released his grip from the handle and checked the mapping app on his phone. They were on 8th Street, heading west. After a few seconds he turned to Geoff to give him some instructions. Nelson was the leader, but after what had just happened, Drayce couldn't help but continue to take charge. It was his nature.

'Stay on this road,' he said. 'When we get to Koreatown, head north on the 258. Got it?'

Geoff nodded his head, a little reluctantly in Drayce's opinion. 'No problem. But this thing ain't gonna run all day.' He leaned forwards as though he wanted to inspect the dials more closely. 'The engine's already overheating.

Won't be too long before we run into problems and need to stop.'

'It's probably leaking fluids from the gunshots it took. Don't worry, we're not going far.'

'I'm not worried.' With shaky hands, Geoff pulled out a pack of cigarettes stuffed between his chest and body armour. 'I don't worry. Was just letting you know the situation with our transport, is all.' He shook out the tip of a cigarette and pulled it the rest of the way with his lips. His hand delved back inside his body armour, presumably searching for a lighter, until Nelson's hand appeared from the back holding a chrome, storm-proof Zippo. Geoff took a few deep tugs and then exhaled. The wind blowing through the smashed windows whisked the smoke out of the cabin. As the nicotine flooded Geoff's system, his hands stopped shaking and his body settled. Apart from his right foot, that is.

'You can ease off with the speed,' Drayce said. 'We're clear of any immediate danger.'

Geoff glanced at Nelson in the mirror. 'What do *you* say to that?'

Drayce sighed. He didn't take Geoff's attitude personally. In the heat of battle, when you're terrified, you take orders from whomever steps up. But now he was no longer in fear of his life, it was only natural for him to revert to the original hierarchy.

'Just do what he says,' Nelson snapped.

Drayce turned to his window so Geoff couldn't see the smile on his face. He focused on the wing mirror, checking the vehicles behind them, searching for signs of a tail.

As soon as they made it to the 258, they headed north. Drayce directed Geoff to turn off into the side streets, wanting to take them on a long route back and forth and round in circles to make sure they weren't being followed. Eventually they found themselves on Beverley Boulevard.

'Take the next left,' Drayce said.

Geoff did as he was told. They turned onto North Windsor Boulevard: a quiet residential street lined with palm trees, behind which were modest, well-kept houses, with beautifully manicured lawns. Californian middle class at its finest.

'This'll do just fine,' Drayce said. 'There's definitely nobody following us.'

Geoff came to a stop in the shade of a palm tree and killed the engine. It continued to tick and hiss even though it was no longer running. Drayce stashed his Sig in the footwell and climbed out. He walked to the back of the vehicle; a long line of fluid marked the route they'd just taken. He crouched low and saw a puddle of the same stuff pooling underneath the truck. Steam escaped from somewhere underneath the hood. Both Nelson and Geoff climbed out and shut their doors, leaving Vanderbilt on the back seat. All three of them walked over a grass verge and stood together on the pavement.

'Everyone okay?' Nelson asked.

Drayce nodded.

'All good,' Geoff said.

'How's Vanderbilt?' Drayce asked Nelson.

'Not a scratch on him, but a bit traumatised.'

'We need to call the police.'

'We will.' Nelson took a closer look at the wound to his shoulder. 'Question is, will you still be here when they arrive?'

Drayce regarded him sternly, wondering if he'd heard him right. 'What's that supposed to mean?'

'Yeah,' Geoff said as he took the cigarette out of his mouth. 'What *is* that supposed to mean?'

Geoff appeared to notice the look Nelson was giving him. He shut his mouth.

'What it means,' Nelson said as he turned back to Drayce, 'is that maybe you should consider taking your money and walking away right now.'

Drayce didn't say a word. He eyed up Nelson, assessing whether he was serious.

'I'm throwing you a lifeline here, Alex,' Nelson said. 'You've got less than a week left in this country. If you hang around to talk to the cops it'll drag out for months, and it'll cost you big with bail money and lawyers. You name it, you pay for it. Everything will be an expensive, uphill struggle as a foreigner. Doing things my way avoids all that.'

Drayce stayed silent.

'What do you say?' Nelson asked.

'Spell it out for me,' Drayce said. 'Just so I know you're saying what I think you're saying.'

The leaves of the palm tree they were under began to waft slightly in the breeze. Dappled shade danced over the three of them. Nelson squinted and blinked every time the sun hit his eyes.

'All right,' he said. 'I'll spell it out for you: I pay you in cash, right this minute, for the entire job, and you walk away a week early. I never breathe your name to anyone, neither does Geoff, nor Vanderbilt. Not that the filthy rich *puta* will ever be able to recall a single detail of what's just happened. The long and short of it? You were never here, Alex. I took the shots; I saved the day. It'll be much less work for me to take the rap. Probably just involve a quick statement down at the Sheriff's office explaining how I saved Mr Vanderbilt's life, ending the careers of a highly organised gang of kidnappers and extortionists. It'll do wonders for my reputation. Business'll soar. Shit, a DEA vet like me? They'll probably give me another medal.'

Drayce's steely expression didn't falter one bit. 'Why?'

'Because without you, we wouldn't even be having this conversation. Instead, Geoff and I would be swapping places with the ski mask brigade, bleeding to death on a goddamn Los Angeles freeway, while those *concha-de-tu-madres* back there kidnap our client.' He scrutinised Geoff. 'Alex here saved our lives, didn't he, Geoff?'

A humble nod of the head was all he got in response.

Drayce ran it through in his mind one last time. It certainly sounded like a good deal, that was for sure. With the hardware strapped to the dead bodies of the men he'd killed, he was sure he'd be able to prove he was acting in defence of both himself and others. However, as Nelson had said, it would be a long and expensive road to take, whereas with this deal, he could get paid and make his flight back to London at the end of the week. No stress, no cops, and most importantly, no lawyers.

He held out his hand.

'Hold that thought,' Nelson said.

Drayce watched him walk back to the truck, pop the trunk open, and spend a few seconds rummaging around inside his kit bag. He returned seconds later with a stack of bills in his hand. He slapped them into Drayce's palm.

'Twelve grand, as agreed,' Nelson said.

Drayce stuffed the stack of bills into his rucksack then returned his hand to where it had been. Nelson shook it but kept a tight hold.

'One more thing before you go,' he said.

'No such thing as a free lunch.'

'You got that right, kiddo.'

Drayce smiled. 'Let's hear it.'

'I took a call first thing this morning from a guy wanting my help. I told him I'd get back to him, but with what's just happened, it looks like I might be a little too busy to give him the help he needs.'

'What kind of help is he after?'

'His nineteen-year-old daughter's gone missing. Says she's been going off the rails the past few months, hanging out with some bad crowds, doing some bad things. Usual story, I guess. He wants her found.'

'You do that sort of work?'

'From time to time. I was a bounty hunter for six months while I got SIPS up and running. If you can find bad guys who know how to hide their tracks, then a bratty teenager is nothing but light work.'

'How long has she been missing?'

'A couple of weeks.'

'What have the cops done so far?'

'That's the thing. He hasn't called them. Doesn't want them involved. He's worried she's off with that bad crowd I mentioned, doing bad things. Drugs, I think, and maybe selling her body as well, from reading between the lines. He doesn't want the cops finding her and locking her up. He just wants her found.'

Drayce thought about it. 'I'm a stranger in this country. I don't know the different cultures and communities like you do. Not sure I'd be the best person for the job.'

'I've seen your résumé, remember? I know the kind of things you've done as a cop back in England. People are people, same the world over. You can find this girl. It'll be easy work to see out the rest of your days here before your flight back home at the end of the week. Plus, you'll be doing me a favour. I don't want to let this guy down. I've got a daughter myself, so I feel his pain. I want him to get the help he needs.'

Drayce nodded, slowly, mulling it over. After the offer Nelson had made him, he could hardly say no.

'What do you say?' Nelson asked. 'We got a deal?'

'Sure. It's a deal.'

Nelson smiled as he let go of Drayce's hand. 'It's been a pleasure.'

'Pleasure's been all mine.' Drayce turned and smiled at Geoff. 'Wish I could say the same to you, you grumpy son of a bitch.'

Geoff opened his mouth to respond but was drowned out by Nelson's laughter.

'I'll need your weapons and your body armour before you go anywhere,' Nelson said to Drayce once he'd finished laughing.

'No problem.'

They walked to the back of the truck where Drayce laid it all down in the trunk. Still hot from the shootout, he took off his gloves and jacket and stuffed them into his rucksack, wafting the front of his white T-shirt to help cool him down. Nelson opened a first aid bag and pulled out some bandages and sterile solution to treat his shoulder. He handed a couple of vials to Drayce along with a gauze pad, which he used to wipe the blood off his face.

'Keep my name and number close by,' Drayce said. 'I owe you for this, so if you ever find yourself the other side of the pond in need of some help, you give me a call.'

Nelson nodded. 'I appreciate that. Thank you.'

He took out a small notepad and pen from his kit bag, scribbled down a name and a phone number on the top sheet, then tore it off and handed it to Drayce.

'That's the guy,' Nelson said. 'Give him a call. I don't think he can pay you big money, but it'll be good enough for nothing more than a couple of days' easy work.'

Drayce closed his big hand around the note. 'Consider it done.'

Nelson took off his jacket and body armour and started cleaning his cut. Drayce lifted his rucksack from the back of the truck and fed his arms through the straps. Once it was secure on his back, he noticed Geoff holding out his hand. Drayce shook it firmly.

'Take care of yourself, Alex.'

'You too, Geoff.'

'While it's nice to finally see you two getting along,' Nelson said, 'you need to leave, Alex. Right now.'

Nelson had his phone up to his ear. He was making the call to the police. Time to leave.

Drayce gave Nelson the thumbs up, glanced at the note in his hand, and walked away. Maybe Nelson was right, he thought, as he stepped out from under the shade of the palm tree and quickened his pace. He had another week left until his flight back to London from LAX, and he wasn't the tourist type, so spending his money on hotels and sightseeing wasn't really for him; he'd get bored within a few hours. What he needed was an objective. He read the phone number on the piece of paper. Perhaps it'd be nice to earn a little extra money on this trip.

Why not? he thought to himself as he wiped the rest of Nelson's blood off his face.

After all, it had been such a breeze so far.

3

After a short walk through the neighbourhood, Drayce found himself back on a busy main road. His ears picked up the sound of sirens, somewhere off in the distance. He told himself it was nothing to worry about; this was LA, where sirens were a part of daily life. But nonetheless, it made him want to get off the streets, at least for a short time. If the police had his description from a witness to the shootout, he didn't want to be on the sidewalk when they drove past.

He considered his options. A sign informed him he was on Larchmont Boulevard. He looked left and saw nothing but a long line of big, beautiful houses. To the right he could make out a stretch that appeared different. Signs hung from buildings and there were rows of parked cars either side of the boulevard, all of which were facing in towards the kerb, as though the planners had wanted to fit in as many parking spaces as possible to make it easier for the customers. All of which told him it was a commercial strip, full of the kinds of things residents wanted close by. Such as a cafe, Drayce hoped, or a restaurant, or perhaps a food hall of some description, where he could spend time out of sight of any LAPD black and whites passing by. He checked his G-Shock watch: 12:30 p.m. Lunchtime in anyone's book.

The walk through the neighbourhood was beautiful. The houses he passed were grand structures, set a good distance back from the road, with front doors wide enough to drive a car through. Their gleaming white facades stood proud behind giant gates and tall green hedgerows, regularly and carefully manicured. The sidewalk was wide enough for four people to walk shoulder to shoulder, but Drayce hadn't seen a single other pedestrian since he'd left the others back at the broken-down Isuzu. Apparently walking wasn't a thing in LA.

Warning bells rang in his ears; the sirens he'd heard earlier were getting closer. Up ahead he could see movement: people jumping in and out of cars, jogging up and down the sidewalks, walking in and out of shops. He picked up the pace, wanting to be hidden amongst the organic movement up ahead, not the lonely pedestrian at risk of catching the eye of a police officer when the black and whites flew past.

The first building he came to that wasn't someone's home belonged to the Bank of America: a concrete fortress with big red signs out front. Beyond that there was a parking lot, a real estate business, and then, finally, the shops and restaurants he'd been hoping for. The boulevard itself was lined either side with giant ficus trees, underneath which was a decent footfall on the sidewalks. Couples were walking hand in hand, families were shopping, and there was even the odd loner like Drayce. Perfect camouflage.

A flicker of red and blue lights in the distance made him turn sharply into the first cafe.

It was cooler inside than he'd expected. Noisier too. The chatter of other customers hummed throughout the space, soft music played in the background, and the sound of pressurised steam fired out of the espresso machines. It had the same presentation as every other coffee shop Drayce had ever visited that was part of a chain. There were cakes on display behind glass, and shelves full of coffee related products with the company name plastered all over them. He joined the queue and studied the menu boards while he rummaged in his rucksack, trying to use just one hand to work a single fifty out of the stack of bills Nelson had given him. He didn't want to get the entire bundle out in the middle of the cafe. It would have looked suspicious and drawn attention to him. Paying in cash was bad enough on its own because everyone else in the queue was simply touching their bank card or their phone to a machine. But making it obvious he had thousands of dollars on him would have made him stick in the cashier's memory, which he didn't think was a good idea under the circumstances.

The queue shuffled along. By the time Drayce got to the cashier, he'd slipped a bill free. He bought a latte and an egg and cheese sandwich, found a table, and dumped his rucksack on the floor. As he took a seat next to the big glass windows, three police cars hurtled down the boulevard, heading in the direction from which he'd just come, responding to Nelson's call, no doubt. The scene on the freeway would be swarming with local and federal law enforcement by now, and these cops were clearly competing to be the first one to detain the security detail that had won the gun fight.

The other customers seemed shocked when they heard the sirens screech past, craning their necks to get a view, their eyes wide with curiosity. Judging by what Drayce had seen of the area, it perhaps wasn't the type of neighbourhood accustomed to police responding in that fashion. East of the 110? Sure. South of the 105? Definitely. But perhaps not around these parts. Drayce was the only person in the cafe not gazing out of the window. He had more important things to be doing.

The coffee was good and the sandwich wasn't too bad either. He ordered another of both just to be sure, then he bought dessert: something big and round with icing on top. When his second coffee was down to a quarter full, he took the note Nelson had given him out of his pocket, laid it face up on the table, and read the name and number to himself.

Carlos Garcia. 877-254-3634.

He wondered for a moment if he should plan what he was going to say, but then he remembered his long-held opinion on plans, took out his phone, and dialled the number. It was answered on the first ring.

'Hello?'

'Mr Garcia?'

'Yeah. Speaking.'

There was only the slightest hint of a Spanish accent, barely detectable underneath the American. He sounded as though he'd spent most of his adult life in California. His voice was high-pitched, full of emotion.

'Mr Garcia, I'm calling on behalf of Nelson…'

It was at this point Drayce remembered he didn't know the man's surname. Luckily, Mr Garcia saved him.

'The bounty hunter guy?'

'Former bounty hunter. He now runs the private security and investigation company you recently contacted regarding your daughter's whereabouts.'

'Yeah, that's right. I've been waiting for his call. And please, call me Carlos. I'm not used to being called "mister".'

Drayce drained the rest of his coffee and smiled. 'No problem. Well, Carlos, I've got some good news and some bad news. Bad news is Nelson has had to extend his work on another job, so he won't be able to take your case on. Good news is he's outsourced it to me. My name's Alex Drayce. I'd like to help you find your missing daughter.'

4

After exchanging details with Carlos, they agreed to meet in person. Drayce left the cafe and walked to the nearest car hire company. He rented a black Ford Expedition SUV because there was no chance of walking this one. Turns out Carlos didn't even live in LA. His home was in a small community called Baker, carved out of the desert wilderness towards the border with Nevada. It would take Drayce three hours to drive there before he could sit down with Carlos and get started with some enquiries. He was beginning to think it was no wonder Nelson had been so quick to offload this job onto him.

After signing a couple of documents with the rental company, he threw his rucksack into the back of the SUV and got on the road. The vehicle's navigation system took him north to Pasadena, then east on the 210 until Fontana, where he headed north-east on Interstate 15. It was only at this point, having driven at freeway speeds for over an hour, that he felt as though he was finally leaving the sprawling mass of LA behind. The bustling communities made way for the San Gabriel mountain range, drawing a dark silhouette in the sky ahead of him. He stayed on I-15 for the rest of his journey, snaking through the mountains, before breaking free across the dusty desert landscape of San Bernadino County.

Drayce arrived in Baker just before four o'clock that afternoon, and straight away saw there wasn't much to the place. As he turned off I-15 he came to a crossroads, on the four corners of which were a gas station, a Taco restaurant, a country store and a trucker's cafe. He took a right because the Expedition's GPS told him to and drove past four or five more fast-food restaurants and not a great deal else. Everything seemed to be geared towards serving truckers and Death Valley tourists. They probably didn't get many other people coming through town, other than those who got hungry on their way to or from Vegas and needed somewhere to stop for a bite to eat.

The road he was on was the main drag. There was asphalt under his tyres, but it didn't seem there would be for very long. Just when he was beginning to think the GPS had made a mistake, it told him to steer onto a sandy track that headed off into the desert. He cautiously did as he was told and took the turn, the wheels churning up dust behind him as he followed the coordinates. Aside from the main road, Baker consisted of maybe a dozen others, carved out of the desert by little more than tyre tracks alone.

After bouncing along the soft sand for a short time, the front wheels of his SUV hit asphalt again, the surface of which was not kept smooth for the truckers and tourists but had instead been left to form the cracks and pits that were an inevitable consequence of living a neglected life in the blistering sun. There were a few dwellings scattered either side of the road: white, single-level structures, made from plastic and wood – trailer park homes with no foundations, which could be loaded onto the back of a lorry and moved elsewhere at any point in time.

Drayce sighed. If this was where Carlos lived, then this job was not going to be a good earner. He wondered if he'd even be able to cover his expenses for the drive out there.

Damn it, Nelson.

A few seconds later the GPS told him he'd arrived at his destination. He pulled all four wheels to the side of the track, crushing a couple of small brown creosote bushes on the way, then turned off the engine and climbed out.

He considered getting his ThruDark jacket out of his rucksack, but even on an afternoon in late May, it was too warm to wear an outer layer. He'd only worn it on the Vanderbilt job to hide his weapons and body armour, and had been sweating in it all day, every day. After all, he was a big, light-skinned Englishman. His ancestors had spent generation after generation learning the hard way how to survive in freezing cold northern climates. In the desert, he was a fish out of water, so the jacket would stay where it was. He stretched his giant frame, releasing the knotted muscles from the long journey, then shut the door and examined the home of the man he'd come to see.

It was on the corner of a set of crossroads, in the middle of a small plot of sand, no more than maybe a thousand square feet, the border of which was denoted by chest-height metal fencing, chain-linked and ugly. The house itself was just like every other he'd driven past in Baker: small, white and single level. It was raised on concrete blocks a couple of feet off the ground with wooden boards blocking access to the crawl space. Steps led up to a porch. Mesh screens covered the door and windows, presumably to keep the sand out on a windy day. A rusty old Ford pick-up truck, red paint faded from its harsh life in the desert, was parked on the driveway.

Drayce strolled up to the front of the trailer. The door opened wide before he'd even got close enough to knock. A middle-aged gentlemen stepped out confidently.

'You the investigator?'

The voice was the same as the one on the phone.

'That's me,' Drayce said.

Carlos moved aside and held out a hand. 'Please, come in.'

Drayce climbed up the steps onto the wooden front porch and went inside. Even though he ducked, his messy brown hair still bristled against the ceiling. He found himself standing inside a small kitchen, with just enough space for a sink, a cupboard and a microwave oven.

Carlos closed the door behind him. 'Thank you for coming so quickly. Please, come this way. We'll take a seat through here.' He skirted around Drayce and walked into another room. 'That accent of yours. What is it? Australian?'

'English,' Drayce said as he followed him.

'An English PI in California?'

'It's a temporary thing. I was doing some work for SIPS for a few weeks, but that ended prematurely, so Nelson asked if I'd take your case on. He didn't want to let you down.'

In the next room, Drayce ducked so he didn't rub the top of his head across the ceiling. He found himself in a living room with a fabric sofa and an armchair, both beige-coloured, and facing a wooden coffee table with an old television on it. Fitted bookshelves covered an entire wall, each volume neatly stacked side by side. A large metal lamp towered over the armchair. In the corner of the room was the fridge freezer that wouldn't fit in the kitchen. Its persistent humming was one of the few sounds in the quiet trailer.

Carlos sat in the armchair; Drayce took a seat on the sofa. Despite the cheap furnishings, the place was immaculate; even though he was demonstrably not a wealthy man, Carlos was evidently proud of his home. Sunlight shone through the windows directly onto Carlos. Drayce examined his brightly illuminated figure properly for the first time.

He was older than Drayce had expected; probably somewhere in his late sixties, at a guess. He appeared frail – his limbs little wider than rakes. He wore blue jeans and a bright white polo shirt, the loose fabric hanging off him the way it might a skeleton, accentuating his bony frame. He was slumped forwards in his chair, his posture that of a man close to giving up; clearly his daughter's behaviour was causing him a great deal of stress and worry. His hair was a mop of grey, and salt and pepper stubble covered his cheeks and neck. Dark bags of skin drooped underneath his eyes; a product of his age, no doubt. What was undoubtedly *not* a product of his age, was the large cut across his left temple, deep and nasty. Drayce eyed the wound. From his experience in hand–to–hand combat, it presented as the product of a vicious downward hook from a right–handed assailant. It was likely there had been something large and heavy in the attacker's hand at the time. Certainly a point of conversation.

'What happened to your face?' Drayce asked.

Carlos reached up and touched it delicately with nothing more than fingertips, as though this action might help rejuvenate the memory.

'My daughter,' he replied. 'I went to her apartment to try to talk. She is living a...' Carlos paused, moving his fingertips away from the cut. 'A dangerous life. She wouldn't listen. She wanted me to leave, but I couldn't.' He eyed Drayce as though assessing the man in his home. 'Do you have children, Mr Drayce?'

'No, I don't. And please, call me Alex. Or just Drayce. But not mister. I'm not used to that kind of language either.'

Carlos nodded as he glanced at Drayce's wedding ring. 'Married, though.'

Drayce kept his eyes on Carlos, his thumb moving to the ring, turning it gently around his finger. He pushed memories of Lily to the back of his mind; this wasn't the time or the place. 'Not anymore.'

'Divorced?'

Drayce took a deep breath. 'Widowed.'

It was a few seconds before Carlos spoke again. 'Sorry to hear that. As a father, all you want to do is keep your child safe. It is the one job you have in life: do your best for them and keep them from harm. I couldn't go on letting her make such bad decisions. I had to do something. I went to see her, to talk, to try to make her understand how much danger she is putting herself in with her lifestyle. But as usual, she wouldn't listen to reason. She just wanted me out of her apartment and out of her life. When I refused to leave, she pushed me towards the door, and when I stepped forwards, she hit me.'

Drayce watched him closely. He gently touched the cut with his fingertips again, his eyes drifting to the floor.

'I left shortly after, deciding I'd give her time to cool off. When I went back to her apartment the following morning, there was no answer. The front door was unlocked, so I went in, and saw she'd already packed her things and left. I need to find her. I need to apologise.

I need to make things right.' The words rushed out of his mouth almost too quickly for his lips. Tears built in his eyes, his voice nearly cracking under the strain of his emotions. Drayce got the impression he was normally a calm and gentle man, used to taking his time and speaking with ample consideration, but the turmoil of his current situation was forcing him to act a different way. Each syllable felt panicked. 'I need to know she's okay. I need to get her away from the people who are controlling her life.'

'And who are those people?'

'They're criminals!' Carlos's glistening eyes locked onto Drayce's. 'Criminals who call themselves my daughter's friends, but who have done nothing but corrupt her life.'

'What are their names?'

'I don't know.'

'Well, what *do* you know about them?'

Carlos looked off into space as though he was thinking hard.

'What about the area they live in?' Drayce asked. 'Or any gangs they might be affiliated to?'

'I'm sorry, I don't know.' Carlos shrugged. 'It's hard for me to find these things out. My daughter tells me nothing.'

Drayce fought the urge to sigh away his frustrations. 'What's your daughter's name?'

'Adriana.'

'Is her mother still in her life?'

'No. She passed away many years ago. I'm the only family she has.'

Drayce eyed him closely. 'Looks like a nasty cut she gave you.'

Carlos took his hand away from his temple and nodded his head.

'Still pretty fresh,' Drayce said. 'Looks as though it's only just started to dry up.'

Carlos gazed at his feet, avoiding Drayce's eyes.

'You told Nelson your daughter has been missing for the past two weeks,' Drayce said. 'Yet that wound you say she inflicted is perhaps only a day or two old.'

Carlos's eyes flicked up towards Drayce's face and then straight back to his feet, quick as a flash, guilty as hell. When Drayce next spoke, his voice had dropped an octave or two, each syllable like the burble from a V8 engine.

'Shall we start again? And this time, I want nothing but the truth.'

Carlos raised his head slightly, turning his eyes up towards Drayce's. 'The fight at her apartment happened on Saturday.'

'Two days ago?'

Carlos nodded.

Drayce rubbed his face with his hands. The sigh he'd been holding back suddenly burst out between his fingers.

'I'm sorry I lied before,' Carlos said. 'But I couldn't tell your boss the truth. If I'd told him I had a fight with my nineteen-year-old daughter two days ago, and that I need to find her to make things right, he would have laughed and then hung up on me.'

Drayce nodded his head. When he took his hands away from his face, his expression was thunder. 'Yeah, maybe, and do you know why he would have hung up?' Carlos shook his head. 'He would have hung up because he wouldn't have wanted to waste his time on a silly domestic fall out. It sounds as though your daughter's going through a tough time with whoever these people are, and I'm sure it's hell for you to witness, but we're talking about an adult, alive and well, who by the sounds of it just wants to be left alone. I'm not sure what you expect the end game of this to be, but—'

'I need to know where she is. I don't want her with those people. I don't want her doing those things. She's my little girl!'

Drayce's expression softened. 'I sympathise with you, I really do. But let's say I do find her for you. What then? If she wants nothing to do with her father, I'm pretty sure she'll want nothing to do with the man he's hired to track her down.'

'All I need is an address. That's all. Just an address for where she's moved to. I just want to see her, to make sure she's all right. She wasn't herself on Saturday. Never in her life has she lashed out at me like that. I think something happened to her recently. Something that shook her up. That terrified her.'

Drayce thought through his options. 'Where's her old apartment?'

'It's in Vegas, not too far from the Strip. 4610 West Sand Creek Ave. Apartment two.'

Drayce considered how much he'd spent to travel to Baker, and how much extra it would cost to drive to Vegas. Car rental; fuel; hotel bills: expensive stuff. He stood, bumped his head on the ceiling, and growled as he rubbed his crown.

'I think it's time I left. I've already driven a hell of a long way on the back of a lie. I'm not sure it's going to be worth my time going even further, all the way to Vegas, to make enquiries about the location of an adult who is not missing, and who is not in any real danger. All for nothing more than some loose change.'

Carlos stood up in a flare of emotion. 'She *is* in danger!'

'No, she's not, Carlos. Not in my book. Only in yours, because you're her father, and for you it's personal. But I'm sorry to say that a person making bad life choices, and that same person being in imminent danger to the extent they need to be found ASAP, are not the same thing.'

'The things she does for money, the people she associates with, are all a danger to her, and I have a job to protect her.'

'Maybe she's just avoiding you for a few days while she cools off. I'm sure she'll call.'

'I need to know she's safe!' Carlos put a hand to his mouth, plainly holding back tears. Eyes glistening, he removed his hand and spoke again. 'And who said anything about loose change?'

Drayce examined his surroundings. 'Just an assumption I made.'

'Well, you're wrong. I can pay you good money to find my daughter.'

Drayce sat back down. 'Show me.'

Carlos walked out of the living room towards where Drayce assumed the bathroom and bedrooms would be. He came back a minute later with a stack of cash and set it down on the wooden coffee table. It thudded as it hit the surface; more than just loose change.

'It's all I have,' Carlos said, calmer now.

'You're really that concerned about her?'

'Absolutely. I must find her. Nothing matters more to me.'

There was something else in his hand: a photograph. He placed it gently on the table for Drayce to examine. It showed an image of a beautiful young Latina woman with a broad smile on her face. She'd taken the shot herself, at arm's length, at just enough of a distance to capture her head and shoulders. There were bright lights in the background, taken somewhere in Vegas at night.

'Adriana?' Drayce asked.

Carlos nodded. 'And I want you to see this.' He placed a piece of paper he'd had clamped in the palm of his hand down onto the table and unfolded it. It was Adriana's birth certificate. 'As proof I'm her father. Her next of kin.'

Drayce read it. It appeared to be legit: a certified document to show Adriana was born in California and that Carlos was her father. He picked up the stack of cash and flicked through it. There was a mixture of denominations, but he estimated there was probably north of five thousand dollars there. Maybe Nelson was right. Maybe this job *would* be easy money.

'Okay,' Drayce said. 'I'll find out where your daughter's moved to.' He counted out enough money from the stack to cover the cost of the rented SUV and the fuel, plus some spending money for accommodation and food in Vegas, and stuffed it into his trouser pocket. He put the rest back on the coffee table and noticed the surprised look on Carlos's face.

'We'll discuss a final payment once I've found her,' Drayce said as he tapped his trouser pocket. 'This is just for initial expenses.' He picked up the photograph of Adriana. 'Am I okay to take this?'

Carlos nodded. 'But I want it back.'

'Of course. Stay close to your phone. I'll call you as soon as I know something.'

The two men shook hands. Drayce let himself out and walked down the porch steps to his Expedition. As he climbed into the driver's seat, he turned back to the house to see Carlos stood at his open door, arms folded as though comforting himself, eyes gazing down at the ground, focusing on nothing, his mind lost in the anguish caused by concern for his daughter.

Drayce started the engine and drove off, blanketing his sight of the broken figure in the window with a giant cloud of dust.

5

Drayce hit rush hour as he arrived in Vegas. He struggled down Interstate 15 into the city, passing by the iconic venues on the Strip, with its representations of architecture from New York, Paris and Venice. When he eventually turned off I-15, he looped around Spring Mountain Road, heading west, and after a few minutes took a left and weaved around the back roads. He kept a close eye on the car's navigation system. By the time he pulled onto West Sand Creek Ave, the sun was setting behind the rocky landscape, the top of its curve peeking out above the mountain range. Its diminishing light made the city glow like gold, a stunning background. Unfortunately, the foreground in Adriana's old neighbourhood was far less impressive.

Drayce examined the long row of double-storey apartment blocks, each one as poorly maintained as the last. The plaster was thin and crumbling, the colour a dull, greyish brown, as though nobody had ever bothered to paint it. Bags of rubbish lay next to the sidewalk. The contents spilled into the road, the sides torn open by a scavenging animal. Drayce judged it had been gathering for a while.

He parked in the lot for Adriana's block and climbed out. A staircase zig-zagged up the outside of the building, at the bottom of which a man lounged on a deck chair.

He was balding, with tufts of grey hair along the back and sides, the top of his head as tough as weathered leather. He wore frayed sandals, old jeans badly bleached from years in the sun, and a long-sleeved grey T-shirt, all of which sported a variety of holes and stains. He drank from a can of beer. Not a cold one at the end of a hard day's work, but something he'd been doing all day. Something he did most days, in all probability. Drayce flashed him a smile as he approached. He didn't get one back.

'Evening,' Drayce said.

'Is it?'

Drayce stepped over a pile of discarded fast-food packaging and climbed the stairs to the first floor. The man's eyes were barely open. Drayce suspected there was more than just alcohol in his bloodstream.

Apartment two was the second door on the left. If it was locked, Drayce would have a real problem getting inside: all the entrances and windows had a framework of iron bars forbidding access to anyone without a key. He reached for the handle. Carlos was right: it swung open with a *creak*.

The curtains were all closed, the occupant having left for good after an argument with her father. The room was cast in a red glow from the dying sun that shone through the material. Once his eyes adjusted to the poorly lit interior, Drayce noticed the mess. Items of clothing and toiletries were scattered across the floor, the aftermath of a frantic pack-up as a young woman left her home in a hurry, taking with her only what she needed. He walked inside, stood still, and listened. An unlocked, abandoned apartment in this part of town would be an attractive proposition for squatters, and with squatting being such an unstable and dangerous way of life, most people in that community carried knives and other improvised weapons. Drayce didn't want to take anyone by surprise and risk a violent encounter.

'Anyone home?' he called out, loud and full of authority.

No response.

He began the search.

The living room and kitchen made up the bulk of the space, a narrow counter separating the two. There was a single sofa in the middle of the living room, and a wooden table with a couple of chairs in the corner. He wasn't sure what he was looking for as he worked his way through the apartment, but he'd know once he found it. He checked under each discarded item for clues, aware you could track a person down from the smallest, most ostensibly meaningless piece of information. He lifted the sofa cushions. A leaflet drifted to the floor, having been wedged behind one. He squatted down to examine it: a membership flyer for a local gun range.

Could be useful.

He folded it in half and slipped it in his pocket.

He moved to the bedroom, which, thanks to the dying sun, was darker than the rest of the apartment. He hit the light switch. A dull, bare bulb that hung from the ceiling slowly flickered to life and revealed an even sparser space than the living room. A bare mattress lay sprawled on the floor, next to which was a wardrobe, the doors wide open. Inside were empty drawers in the bottom half. A couple of dozen plastic hangers dangled lifelessly on a rail above. He flipped the mattress. Nothing.

As the ceiling light warmed, the room brightened. Something caught his eye on the floor, over by the window. He moved closer. It was a picture frame, lying face down. A clear patch on the dusty window ledge above was presumably where it had lived before being knocked off at some point, perhaps when Adriana rushed around gathering her belongings. The back of the frame was dark brown, the same colour as the laminate flooring. An easy thing to miss if you were in a hurry.

Drayce bent down, picked it up, and flipped it over. The glass front was broken. He carefully picked the shards out of the way, pinched the edge of the photograph, and pulled it free from the frame.

Adriana.

She appeared to have been in her mid-teens when the image was taken, unmistakeably the same person as the young woman in the photograph Carlos had given him. She had an arm around another woman, the pair smiling to the camera on a sunny day in a busy park. A picnic was laid out at their feet. A silver bracelet dangled from Adriana's wrist, its love heart charm catching the sun, making it sparkle. The woman she embraced was an aged version of herself.

Adriana and her mother.

Drayce put it in his pocket, alongside the flyer.

Half an hour after entering the apartment, he was happy there was nothing else there of any use to him. He walked back down the staircase and passed the professional beer drinker in the deck chair at the bottom. His eyes were closed, his head slumped forwards. Drayce stopped to watch him, his eyes focused on his chest. It moved. Happy the man was asleep, not dead, Drayce turned away and carried on to his SUV.

The sun had set completely whilst he'd been inside the apartment, no longer a delicate golden tinge shining over the mountains. The street lights were now on, casting everything in a whole new light. The temperature had dropped substantially. Drayce strolled to the parking lot, catching early sight of his Expedition. He frowned.

Four men were gathered around it, all Latino males in their late twenties, early thirties. Their faces were partially obscured by baseball caps and bandanas in pretty gang colours, a few neck tattoos on display. One wore a bright yellow jacket, another a blue bandana wrapped around his throat, tied off at the back of his neck, the V of the material pointing down to the middle of his chest. They were the local neighbourhood tough guys, Drayce surmised, come to check out the stranger in the shiny new SUV to see if he was worth robbing. Drayce growled; he didn't have the time nor the patience for this.

He stopped six feet away: far enough to avoid an immediate reaction; close enough to be intimidating. He stood tall, clenched his hands into fists, rolled his shoulders to loosen the muscles. The group examined their intended victim, confidence dwindling as they took in his size: a neck as thick as a cruise liner's anchor rope, mounted above a body packed with muscles waiting patiently for the violence to start. The war-torn knuckles and cauli-flower ears, moulded during two decades of training in boxing, catch wrestling and jiu-jitsu, plainly caught their attention. But it was the look in his eyes that seemed to hold their focus. There was no flight in this man, only fight. And plenty of it.

'Nice whip,' one of them said as he stepped forwards. He appeared to be the oldest of the group. His maturity and self-assured body language made him stand out as their leader. His neck and wrists were stacked with gold jewellery, a teardrop tattoo under his left eye. He smirked at Drayce. 'Driving with rental plates in this neighbourhood marks you out as a tourist, dummy. Big mistake.'

'Perhaps for some,' Drayce replied.

'Perhaps for you, motherfucker.' He looked Drayce up and down. Slowly. Menacingly. 'Keys.'

Drayce sighed, rubbed his forehead, aware of how bored he was coming across. 'Really?'

'You think I'm playing with you?' He turned to glare at the man on his shoulder, a short, swift nod of the head enough to communicate the instruction. The man stepped forwards, a gold tooth visible in his cocky smile as his bloodshot eyes appeared from under the peak of his blue cap. On closer inspection, this man was younger than the others, perhaps only in his late teens. His hand delved into his pocket and reappeared with a lock knife. He unfolded the blade and pointed the tip at Drayce.

'Keys,' the leader repeated.

Drayce held out his hands, palms facing the group: a posture simultaneously non-threatening and ready to defend. 'You sure it's worth it?'

The leader smiled. 'A brand new ride for the price of a conversation?'

'Might cost you more than that.'

The leader stuck his chest out, bristling against Drayce's attitude.

Goldtooth switched his weight from one foot to the other, eyes darting between his boss and Drayce. 'We doing this or what?'

'Keys!' the leader barked. His fierce eyes bore into Drayce, his tone suggesting he wasn't going to repeat himself again.

Drayce shrugged. 'If that's what you want.' He slowly reached into his pocket, pulled them out, and tossed them on the ground, equidistance between them.

'You playing games?' the leader asked.

'If you think I'm letting him come near me with that knife,' he nodded at Goldtooth, 'think again. You can pick the keys up off the ground, take the vehicle, and leave.'

The leader caught Goldtooth's eye and motioned for him to go get them. He set off, an arrogant swagger to the youngster's step, the precious metal glinting in the street lights as he smiled, his confident demeanour demonstrating he perceived no risk from Drayce while that knife was in his hand. Drayce watched him like a hawk. The keys were two steps away for your average adult male; a single bound for Drayce. Goldtooth kept his eye on Drayce as he bent down for them, but glanced away as he reached out to gather them in his free hand.

It was all Drayce needed.

He took a big step and swung his right leg at Goldtooth's torso. Ribs cracked under Drayce's shin, the air forced out of Goldtooth's lungs making him wheeze loudly as he rolled violently towards his friends. The knife left his grip, clattering across the tarmac. The leader spotted it and made a move. Drayce ran at him, ducking low, tackling him with a double leg takedown and dumping him on his back before he could get to the weapon.

Slow off the mark, the other two ran at Drayce, hands slipping into clothing, undoubtedly for concealed weapons. Swiping the knife off the ground, Drayce hoisted the leader to his feet, pressing himself to the man's back with an arm around his neck and the blade to his throat, using him as a barrier to the advancing horde.

They halted at the sight of a lethal threat to their boss. Drayce felt the rhythm of the man's heavy breathing, a sheen of nerve sweat breaking out across his skin, no doubt pondering how his plan to rob the Expedition had collapsed so spectacularly. A silent tension thickened the air amongst the standoff. Goldtooth stood up, clutched his ribs, and staggered to the front of the group.

'Let him go!' he said.

'Or what?' Drayce replied.

'You'll find out.'

'Take note of the situation, young man.' Drayce nicked the leader's neck with the tip of the blade. He winced. A trickle of blood cascaded down his gold necklace. 'You are in no position to be issuing threats.'

Panic infected Goldtooth's expression. He locked eyes with his leader, their non-verbal communication evidently concluding the SUV wasn't worth it.

'All right,' Goldtooth said. 'You can let him go. We're leaving.'

Drayce released the leader and shoved him in the back, sending him staggering into his friends. The four of them walked off without saying another word, slowly at first in a poor attempt to save face, no doubt. Once they were a safe distance away, Drayce dropped the knife in a drain, collected the Expedition's keys off the ground, and climbed inside. He started the engine with one hand, buckled up with the other, then locked the doors, paying close attention to his mirrors.

Once the gang were out of sight, he took a deep breath, exhaled loudly, then switched on the interior light, pulled the gun range flyer out of his pocket, and tapped the address into the sat nav.

6

The parking lot at the range was huge, the building shiny and new. There were big signs out front telling everyone it was *the* place to shoot a *real* machine gun. Drayce sighed. Places like this were meccas for tourists; stupid, loud, ignorant tourists. And this was Vegas, a place where the tourists were as blissfully stupid, loud and ignorant as anywhere on the planet. He parked close to the entrance, told himself it was a necessary enquiry, and walked through the glass doors.

The lobby was an open plan, brightly lit affair, with shiny polished floors reflecting everything back. Several banners hung from the ceiling, advertising a variety of major gun manufacturers. On his way to the reception desk, Drayce walked down aisles full of ear defenders, safety glasses and other items the regular shooters might want to buy, along with the hordes of junk designed to be flogged to tourists, such as T-shirts, caps and barbeque lighters in the shape of miniature AR15s.

At the desk, he waited his turn behind a group of lads in their twenties who appeared to be in Vegas on a stag do. They were being served by a pretty woman who was a similar age to them, with curly black hair, held up by a grip cast in the shape of a pink flower. The badge on her shirt said her name was Betsy. She had the group of lads eating out of the palm of her hand. Drayce hoped her desire to please customers would help him get the information he needed.

The group were acting as though they had more than a few beers in them, pushing each other around and giggling as they showed off in front of Betsy. They were behaving like giddy children at a fun fair, struggling to contain their excitement at the prospect of getting their hands on a *real* machine gun. Drayce looked away when he heard one of them speak: they were Brits. Embarrassing.

When the stag do sauntered off to the range, Betsy toddled off and was quickly replaced.

Damn it, Drayce thought as he took a step forwards and pulled the flyer out of his pocket.

The woman who replaced Betsy didn't say anything at first. She was busy filling out paperwork on the other side of the counter. Drayce scrutinised her body language, weighing up his odds of getting information from her she wasn't supposed to divulge. Perhaps in her mid-forties, and looking good for it, she had the square shoulders and strong arms of a person who trained, beneath the watchful eyes of someone with a military or law enforcement background. The no-nonsense type. There was no name badge on her shirt, and she did not look as though she would be susceptible to bullshit.

Drayce wanted Betsy back.

Knowing he would need to tell the truth, or at least something close to it, he leaned his forearms on the counter, smiled his face off, and switched on the charm.

'I was wondering if you could help me with something?'

The woman with no name badge inspected him from head to toe. She did not return the smile. 'Well, that depends on what you want.'

Great start, Romeo.

'I'm helping a father track down his missing daughter. I found this in her apartment and thought it was worth coming to speak to you guys.'

He put the flyer down on the counter, face up.

'Yeah, maybe,' the woman said. Her face contorted into a thoughtful expression as she examined it.

Drayce assessed her reaction. He was waiting for her to continue, but as she looked up from the flyer, all he got back from her was an empty smile, her mouth making the right shape but her eyes clearly not echoing the sentiment. Tough nut to crack, as expected. He noticed a colourful bracelet on her wrist. It had the build quality of something a child might make at Sunday school; perhaps her own daughter. He decided to push home the concerned parent theme: an attempt at appealing to her on a personal level.

'Sorry, I didn't explain myself very well. This man I'm trying to help is distraught about losing contact with his daughter. He's really worried about her. Thinks she's got involved with some criminals here in Vegas. He wants to know she's okay. This flyer is all I've got to go on, so any help you can give me would be greatly appreciated.'

Drayce watched her closely. Her eyes flicked down to the bracelet on her wrist. She leaned forwards, rested her elbows on the counter, and considered the flyer more intently.

'That's a membership booklet,' she said. 'They look like the flyers we send out, but we only give them to our members. There're a few extra pages in them with some basic membership rules. Every new starter gets one when they join up.'

'So, she was a member here?'

'Perhaps, I guess. If that booklet was hers, then yeah, sure.'

Drayce took out of his pocket the photograph Carlos had given him. He showed Adriana's image to the woman with no name badge. 'Do you recognise her?'

She frowned first at the photograph, then at Drayce. 'What are you? A private investigator or something?'

'Yeah. Or something.'

She glanced back at the photograph. There was a look in her eyes when she examined Adriana's face. Drayce thought it might be recognition.

'You know who she is,' he said.

She looked back up at him, trying to hold his gaze but failing. Her hands fidgeted, her fingers pulled at her bracelet: she was holding something back. Maybe not an ex-cop after all.

'Do you have some kind of ID you can show me?' she asked. 'Don't you need an investigator's licence or something?'

Now she was stalling for time, throwing up road blocks to avoid answering the question. Never mind, Drayce thought. It didn't matter. She'd already told him what he needed to know.

'No, I don't have one of those,' he said, slipping the photograph back in his pocket. 'Don't really need one. This is more of a favour for a friend as opposed to any kind of official investigation. I told him I was going to Vegas for a few days and promised I'd ask around to see what I could find out. Not to worry. I'm sure she'll calm down and get in touch soon enough.'

'Okay. Can I help you with anything else?'

Drayce studied the timetable on the wall behind her. A ladies-only hour on the range started at nine o'clock.

There were only two of those slots per week. A female member would make it to at least one of them, Drayce thought, if not both. He looked at his watch: 8:05 p.m. Time to kill. If he planned on hanging around to see if Adriana showed up, he figured he might as well enjoy himself. It'd make the time go by quicker, and he might bump into some members who knew Adriana and were easier to bleed information out of than the receptionist.

'Yeah, I think you can,' he said, glancing at the rack of weapons available for hire.

7

Turns out they had two ranges on site: one for tourists, the other for members. Drayce offered to pay double the rate to go on the member's range, hoping he might be able to speak to someone with looser lips than the receptionist. Ideally, he wanted further confirmation that Adriana was a member. If he'd misread the receptionist's reaction to Adriana's photo, he'd be wasting his time staking out the gun range.

The expression on the receptionist's face changed as she considered it for a moment, but in the end, she just said, 'No way, buddy. Members only means members only.'

Drayce reluctantly tripled his offer, holding the cash out in front of him as a visual stimulus.

'No need to put it all through the books if you don't want to,' he said. 'Maybe a third of this goes straight into your pocket for your kindness? I won't say anything.'

Now she was thinking it through properly. She checked over her shoulder to make sure her boss was nowhere in sight, then focused on Drayce. 'You know how to handle a firearm?'

'I have some experience.'

'Because if the members see you fumbling around on the line like you don't know what you're doing, they won't be happy.'

'Trust me, I'll be fine.'

She frowned at him, took the bills from his hand, and stuffed more than a third into her pocket before slipping the rest into the till. She held her arm out towards the racks behind her. Drayce scanned the rows of weaponry.

He chose a short-barrelled Mark 18 AR15 and a Glock 20. The AR had a simple set up: other than the Aimpoint Micro T-2 optical sight, and the angled fore-grip on the rail to facilitate a C-Clamp grip, there were no other additions getting in the way.

The receptionist led him across the shop floor, through a door marked Members Only, and into a locker room. A window provided a view of the range. Drayce examined the twelve lanes. There was only one group shooting, a trio together on the same lane. Perfect for what he was hoping to achieve.

The receptionist opened one of the lockers and took out a kit bag, from which she fished a pair of ear defenders and clear plastic safety glasses. Once Drayce had them fitted, she handed him a spare magazine for each weapon, along with two boxes of ammunition: 10mm for the Glock, 5.56mm for the AR15. He slung the AR to his torso, held the Glock in one hand, the two boxes of ammunition in the other, and pinched the spare magazines underneath his armpit. He felt like the mule in Buckaroo.

'I'll get the door for you,' she said with a grin. 'FYI: the AR's zeroed to fifty metres. Just pick a lane, stay out of the way of the regulars, and enjoy your shooting.'

'Always.'

As she opened the door, she appraised his appearance, her grin widening into a tooth-baring smile. 'Wait, I can't let you go on like that. Here, you can borrow this.' She took a tactical belt from one of the lockers and looped it around his waist. 'There's a holster on there for the Glock as well as two pouches: one for a pistol mag, another for an AR mag.'

Drayce thanked her. He holstered the Glock, took the spare magazines from under his armpit, and slid them into the pouches. As he walked through the open doorway he was greeted by the cool, air-conditioned space. A slight breeze passed over his body as the fans at the back of the range pushed air towards the extractor above the bullet trap. This was done to help expel the impurities that were released into the atmosphere with every round fired. Without it, the range would become inhospitable in a matter of minutes.

He chose a lane two down from the group of three, hoping to instigate some conversation, but reluctant to irritate them by taking the spot right next to them. He placed the boxes of ammunition down on his bench then shrugged his arms out of the AR15's sling, locked the working parts to the rear, and placed it on the bench next to the ammo. He stood there for a moment, admiring it all, feeling more than a little envious he couldn't do this in his home country. He glanced at the three men. They were middle-aged, and a little pear shaped: dads out for an evening away from their families. They had the bodies of men who worked in an office but dressed like soldiers: Crye Precision combat pants in desert camouflage and Coyote Danner boots all round. Each had spent over six hundred dollars on trousers and footwear to impersonate Special Forces on operations in the Middle East.

Ok, fellas, Drayce thought to himself. *I suppose you are in the desert. Technically.*

Their long sleeved Under Armour base layers did not flatter their physiques. They took turns shooting a long-barrelled M16 and none of them had sufficient control of the weapon. The muzzle climbed dangerously high with every trigger pull, their bursts of fire too long. They needed to have it tighter into their shoulder with a far more assertive grip on the rails. They looked as though they were just holding on for the ride.

One of them noticed Drayce spectating. Drayce flashed him his pearly whites, but it wasn't reciprocated. The guy turned his back, maybe ashamed of the way his mate was shooting, although he might not know any better. Perhaps they all thought they were marksmen.

Oh well. There's plenty of time to win you over yet, mate.

Drayce thumbed thirty rounds into each AR magazine, fifteen into the Glock mags, and slipped the spares into the pouches on his hip. He picked up the Glock first, loaded it, then released the slide forwards to strip off the top round, making it ready. He held it with both hands, compressed into his chest with the barrel facing down range. He extended it out in front of him with his arms locked straight and examined the sight picture. Equal height, equal light. Looking good.

He holstered the Glock, picked up the AR, and slung it across his chest. He checked the safety, fitted a magazine, then released the bolt forwards to load a round into the chamber. The weapon felt too short in his hands. He extended the stock out as far as it would go and pressed it tightly into his shoulder as he peered through the optical sights.

The reticule hovered in the centre of his view. He played about with it, tracking from head to torso on the paper target, the red dot moving smoothly with his movements, every millimetre of which was efficient. He glanced at the three 'operators' who were busy making noise with their M16, then focused down range and waited.

As soon as he heard a pause in the M16's rate of fire, he flicked off the AR's safety and let rip. He fired the weapon in blocks of three, consisting of a double tap to the centre mass, followed by a head shot, all done with smooth, fast, trigger pulls. He carried on until the bolt locked back on an empty breech, and in a blur of hand movements, applied the safety catch and ditched the empty magazine, before rapidly fitting a fresh one, releasing the bolt forwards, and pumping more rounds into the target.

After he'd fired another ten, he hit the button on the bench to reel the target in from fifty metres to twenty-five. As soon as it settled, he exploded back into the drills. This time, he put the red dot two inches above his point of aim to allow for the drop now the target was closer. As the second magazine went empty, he applied the safety, ditched the AR on its sling, and reached for the Glock on his right hip. He had it out and in play in a fraction of a second, compressing the pistol into his chest before punching it out in front of him and engaging the target. Once again, he played about with his point of aim, switching between body and head. Apart from his shooting, the rest of the range had gone quiet.

No sound from the M16.

Drayce counted every shot as he fired the Glock. Before he went empty, he dropped the magazine and fitted the fresh one with a round still in the chamber – a tactical reload. The whole thing was seamless, carried out with such speed and effortlessness, a bystander would barely notice the pause in the rate of fire.

Drayce could feel three pairs of eyes on him from two lanes away. His plan was working; he had their attention. He took a little extra time emptying the second Glock magazine into the target. He needed those groupings nice and tight when he reeled it in for a closer look. After firing the last round, he dropped the magazine, examined the breech, and then placed the empty pistol down on the bench, doing the same with the AR. As he hit the button to reel the target in, he heard a voice off to his right.

'Hey buddy, those are some nice drills.'

Drayce turned his head. All three Special Forces Dads were looking at him. He assumed it was the one at the front who'd spoken. His head was as round and bald as a pool ball. Drayce smiled. 'Thanks. It's nice to get some practice in. Don't get many opportunities to do this back home.'

'Oh, you're British. Cool. You here on vacation?'

'More business than pleasure to be honest with you. I work in close protection.'

That really got their attention. Their eyes perked up and all three shuffled towards him.

'So, you're what, like, a bodyguard or something?' the lead guy said as he waddled over. 'Cool. What's your background?'

'Law enforcement,' Drayce said.

'Noble profession.' He held out his hand. Drayce shook it. 'Nice to meet you. I'm Burt.' He pointed his thumbs over his shoulders. 'This here's Larry and Tom.'

Drayce followed the thumbs with his gaze. Tom was the taller of the three, peering over his two friends at Drayce. The peak of his baseball cap was pulled low down over his eyes, flattening the wisps of thin grey hair that flirted out from underneath. Larry was stick-thin with curly black hair; the opposite in appearance to Burt. The whirring mechanics of the chain and rails stopped as the target reached the bench. Drayce didn't unclip it yet. He let it hang there in full view. Didn't even look at it. His eyes were on his three new friends; theirs were on the target.

'Nice shooting,' Tom said, his voice giving away just how impressed he was.

'Thanks,' Drayce said, as he took a quick glimpse to check just how *nice* it had been. There were two distinct clusters of holes: one in the head and the other in the centre mass. Either group could have been covered by a child's yoghurt pot.

'You know,' Drayce said, disturbing their mesmerised concentration on his target. 'It's funny you should ask me about my work.'

'Why's that?' Burt asked.

Drayce took Adriana's photo out of his pocket, the more recent one, given to him by her father. 'I've been hired to find a man's missing daughter.' He held Adriana's image up so all three could see it. 'Any of you guys recognise her?'

All three studied the photograph. Burt was the first to look back at Drayce.

'Yeah, we know her,' Burt said, speaking for the entire group. 'She comes through here all the time. Never misses one of the ladies-only hours. That's when we normally see her, always with the same little handgun and never interested in shooting anything else.'

Burt paused. Perhaps he expected Drayce to say something in response, but Drayce decided to keep his mouth shut. He knew from his policing days that people often felt compelled to fill an awkward silence, sometimes with useful information. He waited him out. Seconds later, the trick worked.

'She's taken a lot of lessons from the instructors here,' Burt said, 'and I think it's her own personal weapon she brings with her. A concealed carry type thing, for self-defence. Not a bad idea, for a woman in her profession. She's probably worried about being followed home by some stalker.' He peered over each shoulder to acknowledge his two friends, a creepy smile edged across the lower half of his face. The other two smiled back, knowingly. Drayce's cold look wiped the smirks off their faces.

'What profession?' he asked.

'You mean her daddy didn't tell you? Shit, maybe he doesn't know. She's a stripper, man. Works all over the city. It's common knowledge amongst the members here. Larry saw her at a strip joint last month called Bunnies. Ain't that right, Larry?' He gazed over his shoulder at Larry, who just shrugged and nodded, leaving Burt to continue. 'Rumour has it she's not afraid to give the customers a little extra service, for the right price.' A horrible smirk infected his expression. He winked at Drayce. 'Know what I mean?'

Drayce didn't answer.

'Thought about paying her a visit myself,' Burt continued, unashamedly. 'Pretty little thing like that. Have me a real good time.'

Drayce considered the weapons on the bench, then faced the exit. It was a shame not to use all the ammunition he'd paid over the odds for, but he'd got what he wanted: confirmation Adriana was a member, always there during ladies-hour. There was no need to continue the act with these idiots. He reacted as if his phone had vibrated and took it out of his pocket.

'Sorry guys, got to take this,' he said. 'It's work. Could be important.'

They nodded as he released the tactical belt with his free hand and dumped it on the bench. He strolled towards the exit, carried on out of the range, and didn't stop until he'd crossed the parking lot and was back in the driver's seat of his Expedition.

8

Adriana was early.

Drayce recognised her as she climbed out of her vehicle – a tired-looking dark blue Toyota sedan – but he checked the photograph, just to be certain. The head and shoulders were a match for the woman walking across the parking lot. The parts of her not visible in the photograph were covered in a baggy white T-shirt and tight black yoga pants. She walked up to the entrance with a handbag over her left shoulder, just big enough to carry a pistol case. Drayce didn't take his eyes off her until she was inside and out of sight.

He decided not to follow, fearing it would arouse suspicion. The smart move was to wait for her to come back to her car. He sat there in the dark and heard his stomach rumble. He needed food, and Adriana would be a while on the range.

He drove to the nearest fast-food place and bought a double cheeseburger, chilly fries, and a big bottle of water. He pulled back into the parking lot twenty minutes later and chose a space in a dark corner that gave him a direct line of sight to Adriana's Toyota, far enough away that she wouldn't notice him when she walked back to it. He turned off the engine, ate his food, then reclined his seat and relaxed in the darkness as the inside of his mouth tingled from the spicy fries. He took a sip of water. His eyes never left the Toyota.

At half nine, Adriana left the range, walked over to her car, and drove out of the parking lot. Drayce pulled his seat upright, started his engine, and followed her. She picked up the interstate and drove north. Drayce tried to stay as far back as he could without losing sight of her for more than a few seconds at a time. Ideally, he wanted to keep at least two or three cars between them, which was fine when she was on the multi-lane interstate with lots of heavy traffic for cover, but as soon as she exited it for the side roads it became harder. A few times he had no choice but to follow right behind her, which was far from ideal, but he could only do the best with what he had. Undetectable surveillance was a hard enough task when you were part of a big team, spread across several vehicles, motorbikes and foot units. On your own it was virtually impossible.

Luckily, it appeared she hadn't spotted him. He watched her turn off the main road into the parking lot for a small apartment complex. He cruised past, only pulling over once he was out of her sight, dived out of his SUV, and ran back to the corner of the parking lot entrance, getting there just in time to see which apartment she walked into.

Her new neighbourhood looked like her old one. Every door and window had metal bars, and the walls either side of the entrance to the parking lot were covered with graffiti. Nothing artistic, just unintelligible words scrawled in a rush with black spray paint. Drayce didn't understand what any of it meant, but he suspected they were gang tags. He walked into the parking lot and got close enough to see the number on her front door:

apartment eight. He ducked out of sight around the corner of a building, made a mental note of her address, and thought of what he should do next.

He could certainly justify ending the job right there, because he'd done what he'd been hired to do. He could call Carlos, inform him of his daughter's new address, and then arrange for when and where they were going to meet so he could collect his finder's fee and go back to LA. However, making the call to her father at that point in time didn't feel right. He wanted to speak to Adriana first, because he wanted to see her up close, and look into her eyes, and be certain she was Adriana Garcia. Sure, she looked just like her from across a dark parking lot, but he needed to be one hundred per cent certain before he made the call to her worried father. He didn't want to risk giving him false hope, and he certainly didn't want to risk taking money from him for an incorrect address.

Drayce walked around the corner and knocked on Adriana's door. From the other side came the sound of deadbolts sliding out of place. Drayce practised his smile, the only method he had of making a muscular two-hundred-and-eighty-pound giant with cauliflower ears look unthreatening. When the apartment door opened, Adriana's expression told him it hadn't worked. She peered at him through the gap, the chrome glint of a fastened security chain crossing her chin. Smart woman.

'Sorry to bother you,' Drayce said in his friendliest voice.

'What do you want?'

There was music playing somewhere in the apartment. Drayce recognised it as an R 'n' B number in the charts that had been getting a lot of radio play recently. The smell of cooked food wafted through the gap between the door and the frame. It involved fried chicken and roasted peppers, so thick in the air he could almost taste it, as though it had been bubbling for hours inside a slow cooker, filling her apartment with the smell. Drayce licked his lips; somehow, the cheeseburger seemed like days ago.

'Are you Adriana Garcia?' he asked.

Despite only half her face being visible, he noticed her change of expression when she heard this stranger speak her name, a wary look morphing into one of confusion.

'Maybe. Who are you?'

'I've been hired to find you.' Adriana moved closer to the gap, presumably to get a better view of Drayce. Any uncertainty he might have had two minutes ago vanished. She was undoubtedly Adriana Garcia.

'Are you the guy who was asking questions about me at the range?' she asked.

The receptionist with no name badge, Drayce suspected. He leaned forwards. 'Yes, I am. Your father's worried about you, Adriana.'

Her face creased into an angry scowl. She glanced at the ground, deep in thought for a moment. Then, as if being released from a trance, she snapped back into the moment.

'Go away!' she said, her raised voice taking Drayce by surprise. 'I don't know who you are, or why you've come here, but you need to leave. Right now!'

Out of the corner of his eye, Drayce saw her neighbour's curtains twitch. A middle-aged guy in dirty blue mechanic overalls peered through the gap.

'Please, Adriana,' Drayce said. 'Just listen to me.' She slammed the door in his face. 'I've only come to talk,' he said to the closed door. 'Your father just wants to know you're okay.'

He gave it a few seconds, waiting patiently in the silence, then he took out the photograph he'd found in her old apartment: the one of her and her mother from a few years ago. He smiled when he heard the chain rattle against the door, thinking she'd changed her mind and was now willing to talk. A second later it flew open, no chain this time.

Drayce's smile quickly vanished.

Adriana was pointing a small black revolver at him. It was a Smith and Wesson .38 Special. A nice little weapon, held steady in the hands of someone with professional tuition under her belt, backed up with hundreds of hours of practice time.

Drayce raised his hands in the air and took a step back. 'I thought you might want this.' He nodded at the photograph in his hand. 'Looks like you forgot it when you left your old apartment in a rush.'

She didn't reply. Drayce looked past the gun and noticed a bracelet on her wrist, the same silver chain with a love heart charm she'd worn in the photo with her mum. In the bright porch lights, her tired, bloodshot eyes came into focus, beneath which were the beginnings of dark bags of skin. They weren't black eyes, swollen because of blunt trauma; they were the result of a lack of sleep. It appeared she'd spent days snatching the odd hour-long nap here and there when her body demanded it be allowed time to shut down. To say she was clearly worried about something was an understatement. Drayce had no doubt she'd been pointing that revolver at him through the door the entire time. She was a woman living in the grip of fear. Her father was right to be so concerned about her.

Drayce kept his hands in view as he slowly bent down and placed the photograph on the ground. 'Whatever it is you're afraid of, I can help.' He took another step back. 'If you talk to me, I promise we'll find a solution to the trouble you're in. Nothing's insurmountable. There's always a way out.'

Adriana walked forwards, picked up the photograph, then shuffled back into her apartment, the gun pointed at Drayce the entire time. No more words were exchanged. The message was obvious: this visit was over.

She leaned across herself and pushed on the door, swinging it slowly on its hinges. They held eye contact until it shut. Her nosy neighbour – the guy in the blue overalls – watched it all play out from his window. The chain rattled as it was slid back into place. A key turned. The deadbolt *clunked* into the frame.

Drayce dropped his hands, turned around, and walked away.

–

He sat in the driver's seat of the Expedition with the engine off, his face lit by the screen of his phone: the only source of light in the dark interior. The street lights in that part of town were as weak as cheap coffee, creating dark corners everywhere. All around him figures skulked in the shadows as local villains began their night's work. Drayce started the engine, hit the central locking, and put it in drive, just in case. He didn't want to resort to killing a man who fancied his chances at a carjacking. That would be far too much hassle.

He stared at Carlos's number. His thumb hovered over the call icon as he contemplated the various avenues the conversation might take. Adriana's reaction had unnerved him, as had the image of her tired, stressed-out face, in so much fear she felt the need to answer the door with a gun in her hands. There was now no doubt in Drayce's mind that she had some very dangerous people in her life, and after meeting her face to face, he felt as though this assignment was growing into more than just the little earner and time-killer he'd expected when he'd taken Carlos's number from Nelson.

He closed his eyes and considered what else he could do to help her. Was it worth going back and trying to speak to her again? Probably not, judging by how it had played out the first time. In which case, was there any help he could offer Carlos? If the threat to Adriana was as significant as it seemed, then it would be too much for him to deal with on his own, especially if his daughter was refusing his help.

Drayce shook his head.

What did it matter? He'd found her new address, and that was all that was required of him. He didn't know her, and therefore, it didn't matter to him that she'd got herself involved with dangerous people. That was her problem, and moving forwards, her father's problem. This wasn't personal for Drayce. She was just another troubled young woman, like thousands of others across the world. He wasn't there to save her. He'd done his job. The rest was up to her and her father.

Drayce opened his eyes and tapped the call icon with his thumb. It was answered immediately. He imagined Carlos sitting in silence in his poorly lit trailer, staring at the phone in his hand, waiting for the call.

'Hello?'

'Carlos, it's Alex Drayce. I've found your daughter.'

A sigh of relief, then, 'Where?'

The question was short and snappy, lean and with purpose.

'She's still in Vegas,' Drayce said. 'She's safe. It didn't take—'

'The address,' he demanded.

Drayce bristled. No way was he giving it up before he'd been paid. 'You'll get her new address after you've given me my money. So, are you coming to Vegas, or do I need to come to you?'

Carlos treated himself to a moment's thinking time. 'I don't trust my truck. It's old and I don't want to risk a breakdown in the desert at night. You'll need to come to me.'

'Fine, I'm on my way. I'll call when I get there and we'll meet somewhere for food. By the time I get back to Baker, I'll be starving. And remember to bring that fat roll of cash with you. You're buying.'

He didn't bother waiting for a reply. He simply cancelled the call, ditched the phone on the passenger seat, and drove back out into the desert.

9

It didn't take Drayce as long to get back to Baker as it had taken him to get to Vegas. Nobody left Vegas at night; people travelled there during the day to experience it at night. Which meant he had a clear run all the way along I-15, arriving back at Baker late that evening a hungry man.

He turned off the main road into the parking lot for the only restaurant still open, killed the engine, took out his phone, and tried calling Carlos. When he didn't get an answer, he left a frustrated voicemail informing him of the restaurant's name and telling him to get back to him as soon as possible. Afterwards, he typed out a text message, reinforcing the same points just in case Carlos didn't pick up the voicemail. As soon as he had confirmation the message had been sent successfully, he climbed out of the Expedition, put on his jacket, and walked inside the restaurant.

On first appearances, there was something of the old American diner vibe about the place. Nothing fancy, just the promise of good food at a reasonable price. He was greeted by a tired looking waitress who led him to a booth and handed him a menu. The cushions creaked as he sat down, their plastic coating crunching underneath his weight. He took off his jacket and laid it down next to him. It was late and there weren't any other customers.

It probably wouldn't be long before they'd close for the night. He hoped Carlos turned up soon. He didn't want to go to sleep hungry that evening.

'Can I get you something to drink while you decide what you wanna eat?' the waitress asked as she wiped down the tabletop with a damp cloth.

'You read my mind,' he said. 'You got a bottle of Southern Comfort back there?'

'Sure do.'

'I'll take a double, topped up with ginger beer.'

'Coming right up.'

As she walked away, he checked his phone. There was no reply from Carlos, but the message he'd sent was showing as having been read. He set his phone down on the damp tabletop with the screen up, so he'd know as soon as he got a reply. The waitress came back a few minutes later with his drink and set the glass down in front of him. She pulled a note pad and pen from her apron pocket and asked if he was ready to order. He glanced at his phone: still no reply from Carlos. Too bad, Drayce thought. He wasn't waiting any longer. He ordered a 16oz ribeye with sweet potato fries.

'How d'you want it cooking, hun?' the waitress asked.

'Medium rare, please.'

'Good choice. That steak is my favourite thing on the menu.'

'I'm looking forward to it,' Drayce said as she walked off to the kitchen.

It didn't take long for the food to arrive, and it didn't last long on the plate once it had. The waitress was right: the steak was fantastic. In the middle of his meal his phone buzzed with a message from Carlos, telling him he was five minutes away. Drayce needed a refill on his Southern

Comfort as soon as he'd finished eating, then he sat back and sipped his drink as he stared at the entrance.

When Carlos walked in, his presentation was different to earlier. He wore the same clothes, but his posture was different: straighter, prouder, more energetic. Clearly the news that his daughter was safe had perked him up. He saw Drayce immediately, approached the table, and sat opposite him at the booth.

'How did she look?' Carlos asked.

Drayce set his drink down. 'She's terrified of someone. She pointed a gun at me when I spoke to her.'

'You spoke to her?'

'Only briefly. I needed to make sure it was her. I didn't want to risk giving you the address of someone who just *looked like* your daughter.'

Carlos nodded.

'You eating?' Drayce asked.

Carlos's only response was a shake of the head.

'What about a drink?'

'What's the address?' Carlos asked, ignoring Drayce's question.

Drayce picked up his Southern Comfort, necked it, and placed the empty glass back on the table. He looked Carlos in the eye. 'Where's my money?'

Carlos closed his eyes briefly and shook his head as though annoyed with himself. 'Of course.' He reached into his pocket. 'Sorry. I'm just keen to see her again.' He took a stack of bills out of his pocket and placed it on the table in front of Drayce, who picked it up and ran a thumb through it. Straight away he knew there was too much. He counted out three hundred dollars' worth and handed the rest back. Carlos's eyebrows arched.

'I only take what I earn,' Drayce said. 'And three hundred bucks, on top of what I took earlier for expenses, is more than enough for the few hours I've spent driving around Vegas, asking the right questions in the right places.'

'Thank you.'

'No problem. What's your plan now?'

'To help my daughter any way I can.'

'Whatever she's involved in, I hope for both of your sakes she gets out of it safely.'

'So do I.' Carlos stood to leave.

'Be careful.' Drayce inspected the man's feeble figure; he did not like Carlos's chances of successfully dealing with whatever trouble his daughter had got into.

Carlos nodded. 'I will.' He offered his hand. 'Take care, Alex.'

Drayce got to his feet and shook it. 'You too.'

Carlos turned away and walked out of the restaurant, leaving Drayce behind. The waitress was busy wiping tables and stacking chairs, glancing at him every few seconds, no doubt hinting it was time for her to close the restaurant and go home for the night. He got the message loud and clear, paid his bill with a twenty per cent tip, picked up his jacket, and followed Carlos out.

The temperature outside convinced him to put his jacket back on. There was a clear sky with thousands of stars shining down on him, ensuring none of the residual heat from the day had been stored for the night. There was no sign of Carlos. Maybe he'd gone back to his trailer, Drayce thought. Or maybe off into the night, risking the journey across the desert in his rusty old Ford pick-up to speak to his daughter as soon as possible. Good luck to him, Drayce thought, as he examined the main road through Baker for somewhere to spend the night.

There were a few hotels, but they were small and not the type whose reception would be open for a last-minute booking that late. He checked his watch: quarter past eleven. It had been a hell of a day and he was tired. Didn't fancy driving back to LA straight away. It was too late and too dark to be making that length of a journey across the desert when he was exhausted. He felt it best to wait until the morning, which meant he only had one option for where to spend the night. He walked over to his SUV, unlocked it, and climbed into the front passenger seat, because there was more leg room without the steering wheel in the way. He moved the seat back to the end of the rails and tilted it as far as it would go. He didn't want to waste fuel by having the engine ticking over, so he took off his jacket and draped it over his torso to stay warm in the night. He pressed the central locking and got comfortable, turning his wedding ring around his finger as he always did right before he was about to fall asleep. He took a deep breath and closed his eyes. After a while, he subconsciously stopped turning his wedding ring, the only thing moving inside that vehicle his chest, which rose and fell with the slow, consistent rhythm of deep sleep.

10

Drayce was woken by bright sunlight streaming through the windows. He tried to stretch his body but banged his head on the roof and his knee on the dashboard. He grunted as he shielded his eyes from the glare of the morning sun that peeked over the hills in the Mojave Desert out to the east. As his vision sharpened, he saw the sunrise in all its glory: an ocean crashing waves of blood oranges and fresh lemons, a current swirling through the clouds, as though everything in the world that was beautiful and vibrant had been tossed into a blender and pasted across the sky. The gorgeous colours illuminating the landscape went some way to counteracting the horror of his nightmares.

He checked his watch: 6:30 a.m. He lay there for a minute, twisting his wedding ring around his finger, groggy and ill-tempered from an uncomfortable night's sleep. He ditched his jacket onto the back seats, reached underneath his T-shirt for the silver locket on his black leather necklace, and rubbed his thumb over the engraved name on the front.

Lily.

He opened it and admired the photograph of his late wife, taken on their wedding day. His mind hurtled back to that glorious, sublime moment in time, before darkness engulfed his life following her murder. Now he was awake and in full control of his thoughts, he was able to block out the nightmare of her death and keep the chaos at bay by holding onto that locket, allowing the memory of their wedding day to comfort him while he slowly came back into the conscious world. In a matter of minutes, he found the strength to close the locket and begin another day.

He thought of what his friend and former colleague, Julie Adler, had told him when she'd dropped him off at Heathrow airport three weeks ago.

Lily's case has been reviewed. Word in the Met is there's new information that needs following up. They're putting a team from Major Crime back on it.

His right hand clenched into a fist.

I think it has something to do with the identification of a suspect.

Maybe he shouldn't go back to London in five days' time. Perhaps he should look for another job, in another country, far away, where he couldn't be tempted to speak to the SIO running his wife's murder case. Where he wouldn't have to listen to that devil on his shoulder, telling him to tease information about the suspect from the SIO, before heading out into the city to conduct enquiries of his own that would inevitably get him into deep trouble.

He screwed his eyes shut, forced his mind elsewhere. He thought about the money he'd been paid by Nelson, the extra few hundred he'd taken from Carlos, and wondered how he might spend it when he got back to LA. He unclenched his fist and opened his eyes. It was time to get on the road and find out.

He opened the door and unfolded himself from the vehicle. He lifted his arms in the air, raised up onto the balls of his feet, and stretched his entire body, properly this time. It felt glorious. His shadow was cast long and thin across the asphalt by the low sun. Once his heels landed, he walked to the trunk and opened his rucksack, the contents of which were everything he owned. He took out the collapsible framed photographs of Lily: five of them, all linked up, side by side with hinges, the black edges and corners scratched and chipped because he took them everywhere with him. He opened them out and rested them on the trunk's lip, his eyes barely leaving hers as he unpacked his washbag and aluminium water bottle and started his morning routine.

After he'd brushed his teeth and washed his face, he glanced around and noticed how deserted the town looked. He cut a lonely figure in that parking lot at that time in the morning. It would be a while before any of the other travellers passing through Baker were up and about, ready to make the rest of their journey to Vegas or LA. The desert air still had a biting chill to it, and he knew it would be an hour or more before the sun warmed it through. Goosebumps rippled across his arms, but not just because of the temperature. A man was staring at him from the back of an old, black Chevrolet Impala, parked on the opposite side of the lot.

Not so deserted after all.

Drayce squinted and assessed the man carefully. His window was down, his arm stretched out, pointing something at Drayce across the thirty-foot gap.

A pistol.

Drayce's first reaction was to flinch his hand, because he wanted to reach for something he could shoot back with. But then he remembered he was unarmed, so his legs were next to start, his instincts telling him to move, to run, to get into cover. Then he remembered there was no cover, not unless you counted the engine block of the

Expedition, which Drayce didn't, because he'd never be able to get to the other side of it quickly enough. And then he thought it through, and realised if the man's intention was to kill him straight away, he'd already be dead, because the guy could have walked over and shot him through the window while he slept.

At the end of this split-second deliberation, he simply stood there, eyeballing the man, waiting to see what his next move would be.

Even though Drayce could only see his top half, he could tell he was a big Latino with wide shoulders and a thick neck. The arm holding the gun was thick with muscle, the sleeve of his white button-up shirt stretched tight. It was rolled up to his elbow, the tattoos on his forearm exposed, the most prominent of which was a human hand in black ink. The heel of the palm started at his elbow joint, and the fingertips stretched all the way to his wrist.

Movement caught Drayce's eye. Another big Latino, this one in a black suit, was now out of the driver's seat, stood tall while he waited for his friend with the gun to climb out. A third, wearing all black trousers and shirt, climbed out of the back and joined them. As soon as all three pairs of feet were on the concrete, they walked towards Drayce, the weapon pointing at him the entire time. They stopped well outside of his reach, an indication they might have experience at this sort of thing. The four of them formed a diamond, with Drayce at the tip.

His eyes darted around the trio. He noticed the guy in the suit also had a tattoo of a black hand, this time on his neck. It triggered something in Drayce's brain that he'd once heard, or perhaps read, about such tattoos. His memory told him it was a sign of gang membership.

The Mexican Mafia.

'You need to come with us,' the guy with the gun said.

Drayce didn't reply. He carried on scanning from one man to the other, with chaos, mayhem, and hell fire burning in his eyes. His mind spun. Why did three Mexican gangsters want to take him somewhere at gun point?

'You've got the wrong guy,' he said.

The one with the gun shook his head. 'No way are there two gringos in this shithole town as big and ugly as you.' He took a step towards him. 'Now get in the car.'

'Or what?'

'Or we make you.'

'I'd like to see that.'

The Mexicans stared at one another, as though this perhaps wasn't the reaction they'd expected. Maybe they were accustomed to more compliance from the people they kidnapped.

'Do I get a clue as to what you idiots want with me?' Drayce asked.

'We've come to escort you to the airport,' the man with the gun said.

'My flight isn't for another few days.'

'You'll get an earlier one.'

'I've planned to do some things in LA, see some sights, spend some money. I don't want to leave early.'

'It doesn't matter what you want. You've run your little errand for Carlos and now it's time for you to go home.'

The hair on the back of Drayce's neck stood up. 'Is he all right?'

Cold, emotionless eyes stared at him, their lips silent.

'What about Adriana?' he asked. 'Is she okay?'

'Don't worry about either of them,' the guy dressed all in black said. 'They're not your concern. You don't live here, Englishman.' A nod to the Impala. 'You're going home. Right now.'

Drayce eye-balled the three men. He didn't move an inch.

'Is that a fact?' he asked.

'Unless you want to do it the hard way,' the guy in the suit said.

'Remind me what that might look like.'

The three Mexicans glanced at one another again, their brows furrowed, as if to say: who does this guy think he is?

The one in the suit glared at Drayce. 'It looks like my friend here shooting you in the stomach, then us tying a rope from the back of the car to your ankles, and dragging you back to LA.'

Drayce nodded. 'The easy way it is then.'

The guy with the gun and the one in the suit escorted him to the Impala. The man dressed all in black slammed the bottom lip of the trunk up, causing Lily's pictures to catapult into the vehicle. Drayce heard a crack. Several muscle groups twitched violently. He forced himself to stay calm as the upper lip of the trunk was slammed down. The guy dressed all in black climbed into the driver's seat to follow the Impala.

The guy in the suit opened the rear door for Drayce, who glanced in the front as he got in, noting the manual handbrake in between the two front seats. He scooted over to sit behind the driver. The guy with the gun got in next to Drayce, the weapon always trained on him. The one wearing the suit resumed his place behind the wheel and pulled out of the parking lot onto the main road, the Expedition trailing closely. Drayce slipped his seat belt over his shoulder and clipped the buckle in place, observing that the other two didn't bother. He patiently waited for the speed of the vehicle to increase.

'So, what kind of trouble is Adriana in?' he asked.

Silence.

'Must be serious for you to want me out of the country so quickly.'

'You don't wanna know,' the guy next to him said. 'You're already lucky we're allowing you to leave. Shit, on another day, sticking your gringo nose in our business would see you buried in the desert.' He jabbed the gun in Drayce's face. 'So, count yourself lucky, bitch.'

They hit thirty miles an hour along the main road. Drayce took a deep breath. Dilemma: let these men take him back to LA and return to London, where he can get on with his life, leaving Adrianna and Carlos to deal with these men on their own; or stay and help.

He turned to the guy next to him.

'Your gun isn't made ready,' he lied.

The guy frowned. 'The fuck you talking about?'

'You forgot to rack the slide when you fitted the magazine.' Drayce shrugged. 'Happens to amateurs all the time.'

The driver's eyes appeared in the rear-view mirror as he assessed this new development. The expression of the man next to Drayce changed, his brain taking a U-turn, lost in a sudden fog of confusion. His skin began to glisten, panic sweat breaking out.

'Bullshit,' he said.

Drayce shook his head. 'No bullshit. I've been staring down the barrel for the past couple of minutes. There's nothing but blackness. If a round was chambered, the tip of the bullet would be visible.' Drayce smiled. 'You fucked up, amigo. Better tell your friend to pull over and let me out before I turn ugly.'

The guy fell for it. He lowered his gun to press-check the weapon, his mind sufficiently distracted.

Drayce lit the touch paper.

His hand snatched the barrel of the gun and twisted the muzzle away from him. He heard the *crunch* of the man's finger breaking as it got caught in the trigger guard, motivating the guy to lash out with his other arm, knocking the pistol out of Drayce's hand in the melee. It bounced off the headrest of the driver's seat and landed on the front passenger's seat. With the freedom to lean forwards without being shot, Drayce reached for the handbrake and yanked it up.

In the blink of an eye, the world stopped spinning, causing everything around them to immediately and violently come to a halt. The wheels locked and the tyres smoked, the energy within the vehicle's heavy mass keeping it travelling for a short distance. The momentum of the three bodily masses inside the cabin was no different; they all wanted to adhere to the laws of physics and continue moving forwards at the same rate they had been. The only difference between the three of them was that Drayce had something to hold him safely in place, whereas the gangsters didn't. He felt his seatbelt dig hard into his chest, heard the driver's face impact the steering wheel, and saw the head of the guy next to him bounce off the seat in front of him. The loud crack of small calibre gunfire erupted inside the cabin, stunning Drayce as he tried to make sense of where the shot had come from. A split second later he realised the pistol had slid off the passenger seat into the footwell and had unintentionally discharged.

Making use of the chaos in the immediate aftermath, Drayce went to grab the gun, but just as his hand was about to make it, he was stopped by the immoveable resistance of his seat belt. Frustration overwhelmed him, his face reddening with anger as he clawed his fingers towards the weapon. In the corner of his eye, he saw the driver straighten up, spit out a mouthful of blood all over his suit, and turn around to glare at him. Out of reach of the pistol, Drayce tried to feel for the buckle to release his belt as he watched the driver make a grab for the gun. With no time, Drayce abandoned the buckle and snatched the driver's belt, wrapping it around the man's neck and pulling him back into his seat. The driver instinctively brought his hands up, trying to free up enough room to breathe, the weapon now safely out of his reach.

Drayce gripped that belt as though his life depended on it.

Meanwhile, the guy next to him started to come back into the real world. Before he regained enough consciousness to be useful, Drayce took one hand off the belt and punched him in the face, causing his head to bounce off his window with a loud *crack*. Somehow, the guy managed to stay awake and slipped his hand down to his ankle, pulling a knife out of a scabbard. Drayce's eyes widened when he saw the blade and instinctively released his hold on the driver's seat belt so he could grip the man's wrist with both hands. Now unrestrained, the driver leant over for the gun. His outstretched fingertips were nearly able to reach it with some slack in his noose.

Drayce forced the knife towards the front passenger seat, embedding the blade into the leather and stuffing, giving him the leverage he needed to tear the man's hand from the grip. With the knife no longer in play, Drayce let go of his wrist and elbowed him in the face, which bought enough time for him to get both hands back on the seatbelt, reining the driver in before he managed to reach the gun. Drayce heard a loud, retching cough, followed by the panicky, spluttering sound of the driver desperately trying to breathe.

Drayce took a hand off the belt and pulled the knife out of the leather, plunging it into the thigh of the guy next to him. The scream was horrendously loud in that small, cramped space. To shut him up, Drayce took a hold of his ear and used it as a handle as he repeatedly slammed his head into the window. On the fifth hit it broke, scattering them both with tiny diamond-shaped chunks of glass. Realising he was now the only thing holding the guy up, Drayce let go of his ear, allowing his head and shoulders to slump forwards between his knees.

Drayce put a knee to the back of the seat and pulled as hard as he could on the belt, strangling the driver with all his might. Five seconds later he saw the man's flailing arms go still.

Silence swamped the car's interior, returning Baker to the calm setting Drayce had enjoyed moments before these men had introduced themselves. He released his grip on the belt and took a deep sigh of relief, letting the driver slump forwards, his head thudding into the steering wheel. Drayce freed himself of his own seat belt and checked both men for a pulse, his own heart rate galloping. Relieved to feel two distinct, rhythmic drumbeats, he wiped the sweat off his face and felt his blood pressure begin to settle. He'd already killed enough people on this trip. Didn't fancy adding to the list.

A figure came into view on Drayce's left.

The third guy was out of the Expedition, advancing on Drayce's door. Drayce let him come. As he got close, Drayce kicked the door open, slamming the top edge of the frame into the man's face. He yelped, hands cupping his nose as blood poured. Drayce got out of the Impala and closed him down, wrapping his neck in a guillotine choke. Ten seconds later he let the man's unconscious body fall to the ground.

11

Drayce's world spun, his feet unsteady as he staggered around the vehicle. He blinked sweat out of his eyes and stared at the three unconscious gangsters.

Two distinct possibilities rose to the surface of his mind: either he'd been followed by these men all the way from Adriana's place in Vegas, or somehow, Carlos had unknowingly led them to him. He thought through his interactions with the Garcias: he'd met with Carlos, tracked his daughter down, knocked on her door, and left. That was it.

So why on earth were these people so keen to ensure I leave the country immediately?

Drayce shook his head, unable to make sense of it all. They couldn't have followed him to Baker; he would have noticed. Anti-surveillance was second nature for him.

So how did they find me?

He marched to the Expedition and circled it, running his hands under the lip of the bodywork. At the rear bumper his fingertips caught something small, round and flat that didn't belong. He dug his nails under its edge, prized it off, and examined what was in his hand.

An Apple AirTag.

So they'd tracked him to Baker using this simple GPS device. But when had they planted it? The SUV had barely left his sight since renting it yesterday.

Then it hit him: the gangbangers who tried to rob him; it must have been them.

While piecing it all together in his mind, something caught his eye. It was on the ground next to the man dressed all in black: a small strand of metal that glinted in the rising sun. Drayce walked over. As he got closer, the object sharpened.

Adriana's bracelet.

He squatted down, picked it up, held it in the palm of his hand with the AirTag. It must have fallen out of the gangster's pocket as Drayce choked him out. Adriana had been wearing it when Drayce saw her last night, meaning these men had paid her a visit after he'd seen her, and for some strange reason, this animal had taken it from her.

But why?

Drayce was immediately struck by an all-encompassing concern for Adriana. He needed to find her and make sure she was all right. He tossed the AirTag on the ground, dropped the bracelet into his pocket, and retrieved the gun from the Impala's front passenger footwell – a black self-loading Ruger. If there were serious criminals coming after him, he wanted to be armed from this point on. He could see through the witness hole that a round was chambered, so he dropped the magazine and racked the slide. The bullet was spat from the ejection port, somer-saulting as it climbed in the air. Drayce caught it on its way down and examined it.

It was a .45 ACP, which would have made a hell of a mess inside that Chevy if things had gone differently. He pulled the trigger to release the spring, thumbed the round into the top of the magazine, slid it back into the grip, and tucked the weapon into the front of his beltline, all too aware of how dangerous it was to have in the front of his jeans a stranger's weapon with a bullet chambered. Criminals aren't exactly renowned for their weapon maintenance standards, so he couldn't be certain the firing pin would only be released with a deliberate trigger pull, rather than just from a bang or a jolt, as it had done when it had fallen into the footwell. He didn't fancy being castrated by hot metal at eight hundred and thirty feet per second, so while that gun was tucked in his belt, the chamber would remain empty.

He searched all three gangsters. On the guy behind the wheel, he found a wallet with a driver's licence in the name of Gabriel Herrera; on the guy in the back of the Impala, he found photo ID for a Miguel Perez; and on the man dressed all in black, sprawled out on the concrete, he found an iPhone. Illuminating the screen, Drayce lifted the man's head up by his thick black hair, using the device's facial recognition technology to open it. It took a few attempts because of how his gormless expression sagged, but eventually it came to life. He flicked through a few apps until he found Instagram. The profile showed his name was Raul Ramirez and was full of photos of him partying, taking drugs, and flaunting his cash, his entire lifestyle seemingly spent with an endless line of beautiful women, all of whom had undoubtedly been paid to be in his company. Drayce searched through the phone for any messages that might give away why the trio had been sent after him, but there was nothing. Either they communicated with their associates on a different device, or Raul was savvy enough to delete the thread after every conversation. Although, judging by his social media presence, Drayce wasn't convinced Raul was the most disciplined man in the world.

He tossed the phone on the ground, stared at the three gangsters, and considered whether it might be feasible for him to get them off the street, to a place where he could question them, but he quickly decided it would be too messy, with too much potential for carnage. He stood a better chance of finding out what was going on if he could speak to Adriana again, and this time her front door wouldn't hold him back. He'd drive right up to it, make sure she let him in, and he'd find out precisely what she was involved in, and why, after tracking her down on her father's behalf, and speaking to her on her doorstep, there were now serious criminals coming after him.

But before he left Baker, he needed to check on Carlos.

Drayce jumped into his Expedition and drove to Carlos's trailer on the outskirts of town. He stamped on the brakes next to the chain-link fence, the wheels skidding, sending plumes of dust billowing around him. He flung open the car door, heard the gate rattle against the frame as it blew in the wind. The driveway was empty. He ran to the front door and knocked loudly: no reply; tried the handle: locked; pressed his ear to the plywood: nothing.

Drayce hoped Carlos was okay, prayed he had driven to Vegas after getting Adriana's address from him last night, and wasn't lying dead in his trailer after a visit from the black hand gang.

Drayce tested the front door and felt it bend around a flimsy latch mounted next to the handle. He pushed the flex out of the bottom of the door with his foot, and the top with his hand, and slammed his hip into the lock. It popped open.

He made a hurried search of the trailer, calling Carlos's name as he went. A minute later, he breathed a sigh of relief: Carlos wasn't home. The interior hadn't changed in the slightest since yesterday. Drayce pulled the duvet off the bed and placed his hand on the mattress. Stone cold. Carlos hadn't spent the night there. Drayce hoped it meant he was still alive.

Drayce bolted out of the trailer, pulled the door to behind him, and drove to Interstate 15, racing down the slip road towards Vegas. He broke more than a few speed limits on the journey, arriving back in the city just over an hour later. He hurtled through the busy streets and turned hard onto Adriana's road. As her complex came into sight, he swore and hit the brakes, forced to pull over short of the entrance.

With what he was facing, there was no way he could drive up to her front door now.

12

Gabriel opened his eyes, a crippling headache instantly forcing them shut again. He knew he was sat in the driver's seat of their car, but other than that he was entirely confused. There was a pressure build up in his head, amplifying the ice-pick sensation in his forehead. Something was restricting his breathing. He reached up, took hold of the material wrapped around him like a python, and began to untangle it. He winced, a sharp pain screaming at him as he pulled it loose, the skin around his neck on fire. He forced his eyes open and examined the serpent in his hands: his seatbelt.

What the fuck?

The world gradually came into focus, the events that had transpired to put him in his current position forming in his cloudy mind. He flipped the sun visor down and stared at himself in the mirror. His nose was broken, face and chest caked in dried blood. His tongue touched something sharp, an alien sensation. He smiled in the mirror, purely to examine himself as opposed to a symptom of amusement; there was nothing funny about his current appearance. The jagged shards of his broken front teeth stared back at him. He lifted his chin; there were marks on his neck, friction burns, the skin red and bleeding with nasty welts forming on his black hand tattoo. He explored them delicately, sucked air through his clenched teeth as his fingertips touched the wounds.

'Motherfucker!'

The sudden pain kicked his brain into gear. Memories flooded in: the big white boy they'd been sent for; confronting him at gun point and forcing him into their car; a fight breaking out in the back; the vehicle slamming to a stop; the seatbelt around his neck, tightening, unable to breathe. Gabriel turned around: no sign of said white boy. Miguel was slumped forwards, chin on chest, covered in broken glass and bleeding from a head wound as he groaned, slowly rousing. Anger took over, rage now Gabriel's most potent sensation, blocking out the pain of his injuries.

He flung his door open and stepped outside.

Raul was sprawled out on the road, a rivulet of dried blood tracking away from a wound to his face. Gabriel scanned their surroundings before moving forwards. The white boy's SUV had vanished and the town was deserted, the hour still too early for people to be venturing outside. He walked over to Raul and kicked him in his ribs, leaving behind a dusty imprint on the man's black shirt. A low moan answered him back.

'Get up!' Gabriel ordered. He returned to the Chevy, opened the back door, and pulled Miguel out by his jacket. 'Wake up!' He slapped him across the face, twice, forehand then backhand. Miguel opened his eyes, his sagging facial muscles steadily coming to life. 'We need to get moving,' Gabriel told him. 'The Englishman can't have got far.'

Raul put his hands flat on the road and pressed his face away from the concrete, a long line of bloody mucus trailing from his nose to the ground. He wiped his face, grimaced at the pain it caused, then stood tall. Miguel stepped forwards, shakily at first, then with purpose as he found his feet. The trio stood together in a triangle, eyeballing one another as they came to terms with the disastrous turn of events.

Raul rubbed his face, grumbled as he touched his broken nose, and surveyed the scene of their botched kidnap attempt. 'His vehicle's gone.'

'Of course,' Gabriel replied as he shot Raul a dirty look for voicing such an obvious observation. 'He must have taken it when he escaped. Hurry up and get your head together. We need to track him down.'

As Raul gradually came out of his dreamlike state and back into the real world, Miguel slipped his phone out of his pocket, the sicario's razor-sharp eyes now fully back in focus. 'I'll get a signal for the AirTag to see where his truck's at.'

'Don't bother.' Gabriel stepped away from the group, bent down to the ground, and turned the small white circular tag around his fingers. 'He found it.'

'Fuck.'

'So what do we do now?' Raul asked, wide-eyed, his head now fully in the game. 'How we gonna find him again?'

'Maybe we don't need to.'

Gabriel locked eyes with Miguel. 'How the fuck you come to that conclusion?'

'He might be on his way to the airport. Shit, nine hundred and ninety-nine out of a thousand people who had just avoided a kidnapping would be running home as soon as possible.'

'And after what he just did to us, I'm thinking he might just be that one in a thousand. We can't assume he's leaving the country voluntarily.'

'What else he gonna do?' Miguel glanced from one man to the other. 'Go back to Vegas?'

Gabriel scratched the stubble on his cheek. 'Perhaps.'

'Way I see it,' Raul began, 'that's the only play we got. If he's running scared back to LAX, then we don't got nothing to worry about. But if he's decided to stick around and dig deeper, going back to Vegas is his only option. And like you say.' He nodded at Gabriel. 'He sure don't seem like the type who scares easy.' A sudden thought appeared to grip Raul, his eyes flashing to the ground, his mind lost in thought. He did a three-sixty as he scanned the dusty concrete, searching his pockets and patting himself down at the same time. 'Son of a bitch!'

'What is it?' Gabriel asked.

'Motherfucker took the slut's bracelet.'

'You shouldn't have taken it in the first place. It connects us to the scene if we're ever stopped by the police.'

Raul threw Gabriel a stern look before flashing a smile. 'You know I like to take trophies from the bitches I kill.'

Gabriel ignored that last comment and attempted to get Raul's head back in the game. 'Forget the bracelet; it's irrelevant. Time to focus: we head back to Vegas, track him down, and this time we don't give him the option of going home.'

'I hear that,' Miguel said, tentatively exploring the damage to his face. 'Motherfucker gonna pay!'

'What about Vasquez's orders?' Raul asked, a hint of nerves in the hardened gangster's voice.

Gabriel took a moment to consider Raul's concerns. 'He wanted him back on the next plane home, nice and simple, no drama. But that shit changed the second he broke free. The boss would not want him running loose in Vegas.'

'I hear that,' Miguel said.

'Okay,' Raul agreed. 'So what? We hunt him down and kill him?'

'Precisely,' Gabriel said. 'But we gotta be smart about it. The boss wants as little attention as possible drawn to this drama. I'll put another call out to the homies in Vegas. But not just Barrio. I'll get every *ese* in Nevada on the lookout for that big motherfucker, with orders to snatch him off the street, alive, by any means necessary.'

He took out his phone, glanced at the nearby buildings to check for cameras as he did so. 'Doesn't look like we'll be leaving any footage of ourselves behind, but we can't hang around any longer. Let's get back on the road to Vegas. The people in this shithole town will be out on the streets soon. We need to get out of here before we're seen.'

'Wait.' Something seemed to have suddenly come to Miguel's mind. He patted himself down, checked on the ground, then peered into the Impala. 'Shit! My pistol's gone. He must have taken it.'

Gabriel nodded at the back of the vehicle. 'Check the trunk. Make sure we still got the rest of the shit. White boy might have searched it before he left.'

Miguel turned and walked to the Chevy. Lifted the trunk. Smiled. 'Shit still here, homes.' He looked back at Gabriel. '*All* the shit.'

Gabriel and Raul joined him at the back of the vehicle. Beneath the gaze of the sicarios were three AR15s, alongside a pile of magazines and a large tin of 5.56 ammunition.

'White boy ain't gonna stand a chance next time we meet,' Raul said.

Gabriel slammed the trunk shut. 'Get in the car. Miguel, you driving us back to Vegas. I'll let the homies know the plan while we're on the move.'

They all climbed inside and moved off, heading out of Baker at speed and hurtling down I-15. Gabriel dialled the first number on his list of contacts, put the phone to his ear, and made the call that would spell the beginning of the end for the big Englishman.

13

Drayce surveyed the scene for a moment: the police tape blocking the entrance; the squad cars in the parking lot; the pressed uniforms with their shiny badges; the detectives with their notebooks; the neighbours with their long necks and curious eyes, trying to overhear what was being said on the other side of the tape.

He tried to quieten his concerned mind by telling himself it was a rough neighbourhood, so anything could have happened to any one of the residents in that apartment complex that would require a crime scene. But he didn't really believe himself when he laid it out in his mind. Experience told him he should be worried. A hot feeling of dread flushed his face and burned up the back of his neck. The police presence was clearly for the victim of some horrendous crime that had occurred overnight, and a sinking feeling in his gut told him it wasn't for some stranger.

Adriana.

He moved off slowly, circled the block, and parked the Expedition on a quiet side street nearby. He grabbed his grey ThruDark jacket off the back seat, climbed out, and pulled his T-shirt over the grip of his newly acquired pistol. Slipping his jacket on, he fastened it at the front to make sure the weapon was out of sight, then locked the vehicle and set off on foot to get a closer look at the police activity.

He approached the apartment complex the same way the nosy neighbours and passing pedestrians had, ambling up to the crime scene tape with a mixture of wide-eyed curiosity and fear that enabled him to blend in with the crowd of ghoulish onlookers. He glanced across the parking lot and saw number eight's front door was wide open. Precisely where he'd been stood the night before, more scene tape blocked access to Adriana's apartment.

Four detectives in cheap, earthy-coloured suits, their LVMPD badges clipped to their belts, stood in a semi-circle in front of a police cruiser. They were doing the usual detective stuff, chatting amongst themselves and taking notes. Two uniformed cops were stood shoulder to shoulder on the other side of the entrance tape, ignoring questions from the gathering crowds. Another detective – an athletic, red-haired female – was talking to a group of neighbours, taking notes while they spoke. Drayce glimpsed a Crime Scene Investigator leaving number eight, dressed head to toe in a white forensic suit that reflected brightly in the morning sun. The hood was pulled tightly over her scalp and she had a face mask covering her mouth. She used a gloved hand to lift the scene tape, ducked under, and exited Adriana's apartment with a stack of bulging exhibit bags wedged under her arm. She held the tape high for two ambulance workers who carried a body bag out of the apartment on a stretcher. Despite it being covered in thick black plastic, Drayce's instinct told him whose body it was.

He thought about the mafia henchman he'd left back in Baker, and assessed the high probability they were Adriana's killers.

As he began to wonder what kind of trouble Adriana might have found herself in to warrant a group of criminals killing her, he sensed he was being watched; a strange, unnerving feeling. He instinctively turned to his right and saw one of the detectives staring at him: the woman with big, red curly hair. He smiled awkwardly, turned away for a second, and then glanced back to see if she was just scanning the crowds.

No such luck.

Drayce felt frozen, confusion rooting his feet. Why had he drawn her attention? Then he spotted the reason. Adriana's mechanic neighbour was stood on the detective's shoulder, whispering into her ear. He was still wearing the same dirty blue overalls he'd been wearing when he'd spotted Drayce from his window the night before, and was pointing at Drayce with a chubby finger, his expression stone-cold serious, the way a person might look after seeing a killer.

The red-haired detective swept back her suit jacket as she might a curtain, and rested her hand on the grip of her black service pistol. The prickly heat of panic in Drayce's gut engulfed into a raging forest fire. He should have foreseen the danger of this happening. He'd been in such a rush to get back to Vegas to check on Adriana, he'd completely forgotten her neighbour had witnessed him standing on her doorstep as she pointed a gun at him. And now she'd been murdered which, in anyone's book, put Drayce way out ahead as prime suspect number one.

The detective shouted something to her colleagues. They all looked at her and then turned to face Drayce. He sighed. It seemed this once simple job was about to become even more complicated.

Damn it, Nelson.

Drayce let his arms hang loosely by his hips, his fingers spread wide, making it clear he didn't have a weapon in his hands. He had a decision to make, and he needed to make it quickly. Should he go quietly, or should he run for it? The first option seemed the most sensible in his head. He'd been a cop for eighteen years, so he knew how things would play out. The investigation would clear him eventually, because he'd done nothing wrong. If he ran, it would make him look guilty, because every cop knows innocent people don't run.

But then he thought about what he'd say in his interview, which made him think about his alibi, or more accurately, his lack of one. The waitress at the restaurant in Baker would no doubt remember serving him, but if Adriana had been killed in the middle of the night, or the early hours of the morning, then the waitress's testimony would be worthless, because in theory he would have had plenty of time to travel back to Vegas and commit the crime after his meal.

It made him feel sick to his stomach with worry, but he continued to assess it from the cops' point of view, picking holes in his story.

He considered where he'd spent the night: slouched in the passenger seat of his rented Expedition, fast asleep, with not a soul to vouch for his whereabouts. He thought back to the image of Baker: a quiet little town with not a single person out at night, and no cameras covering the streets. All of which meant he only had his word for where he'd spent the night, and his own word would mean jack-shit to the cops. They'd want irrefutable evidence he couldn't have been at Adriana's home when she was murdered, otherwise he'd stay locked in a cell, unable to do anything proactive to determine what had happened to Adriana.

And what would the cops be doing during that time? How hard would they be searching for her real killers? Maybe they'd keep an open mind and find evidence linking her real killers to the crime scene. Or maybe they'd be confident they already had their man and would hone the investigation on the objective of getting Drayce convicted, missing vital evidence that might have exonerated him.

Drayce no longer fancied his chances in handcuffs.

Then things got worse.

The hard object digging into his hip bone reminded him of the pistol in his waistline, making the internal debate instantly vanish in a puff of smoke. He had to run. Everything he knew up to this point suggested the thugs who tried to kidnap him were Adriana's killers, which meant the gun currently tucked out of sight in his waistline, covered in his fingerprints, might have been used to kill her. On top of that, Adriana's bracelet was in his pocket, which was easily identifiable to the cops because Adriana was wearing it in the photo Drayce had returned to her, which would surely still be in her apartment for the cops to find.

I've been seen arguing with the victim at gunpoint the evening before she was murdered, I'm armed with an illegal firearm which was potentially the murder weapon, and I have an item of the victim's property in my possession.

They'll throw the book at me.

The burning fire of anxiety in Drayce's gut erupted like a volcano, spewing lava through his veins as he felt his freedom slip out of his grasp. The crowd fed off the cops' energy, backing away from him with scared looks on their faces. The red-haired detective flipped the retention clip off her holster.

'Police!' she shouted. 'Stand still!'

The other detectives by the cruiser all did the same as they stepped towards him, their pistols leaving their holsters almost in unison.

Time to leave.

Drayce turned and bolted for the road, weaving through the crowd as he went. More shouts erupted from behind him, the cops' voices loud and sharp like the barks of angry dogs. Panic spread through the onlookers. The hands of a few have-a-go-heroes pawed at him as he ran past, but he just smashed straight through them, like a running back at full sprint.

As he broke free from the back of the crowd, he found himself in the middle of the road, running into the path of a white Lexus. With no time to think, he committed to his course and sprinted even harder, only just clearing the vehicle's bonnet. A long blast from the horn blared out behind him as he narrowly avoided being struck side on, but he didn't care. He was committed to escaping.

Negotiating a path through the traffic, he got to the other side of the road safely and darted to the left, the opposite direction to where he'd parked his Expedition. As it stood, there was no way they could connect that vehicle to him, so he didn't want to risk leading them back to it where they could get the registration and trace his name through the car rental company. In his mind, he stood a better chance of escaping on foot and coming back for the vehicle later, providing he wasn't caught and arrested in the meantime.

He took the next junction on the right, glancing over his shoulder. The police were crossing the road behind him, led by the red-haired detective at the front. The sight of them chasing after him knocked his adrenal glands into high gear. The marked police cruiser that had been parked in the apartment complex broke through the scene tape and came screeching out into the road with its lights flashing and sirens blaring. He couldn't stay on the road network now; he'd be caught in seconds. His only chance of staying out of handcuffs was to take advantage of being on foot.

Switching directions, he crossed the road, leapt over a chain-link fence, and ran across someone's garden. A group of men who were eating breakfast around a plastic table by their back door shouted at him as he ran past. He ignored them and pushed on. Up ahead he saw dozens of chain-link fences separating the boundaries between properties. The next minute was going to be like running the two hundred-metre hurdles. He focused on his breathing, knowing his muscles were going to need all the oxygen they could get.

The first fence didn't pose a problem at all, and neither did the one after that. The third one was covered in barbed wire, its evil looking spikes coiling around the top, forcing him to slow down and take his time. He had to be careful, not wanting to cut himself and leave behind any DNA that might help the cops identify him. With painstaking caution, he managed to hoist himself over. Dangling from the top of the fence, he risked a glance at the red-haired detective, who was still in sight.

Need to be quicker than this, Alex. No point leaving anything in the tank.

As he dropped to the ground and turned around, he stopped with an immediacy born from terror: a giant brown pit bull rushed him at full speed, preparing to attack the man who dared invade its territory. It pulled its lips back, exposing vicious teeth covered with foaming saliva.

With little time to react, Drayce threw himself back against the fence, his feet scrambling in the dirt, fighting to stay out of the animal's reach. Its teeth got to within a few inches of him, but then it stopped dead as though it had run into an invisible wall. The animal's head hovered in front of him, unable to get any closer, its teeth snapping violently as it barked, sending flecks of drool spraying in Drayce's face. He noticed the chain attached to its collar, the other end of which was anchored to a post outside its kennel, keeping it just out of reach.

With breathless relief, Drayce got to his feet and carefully ran the perimeter of the yard, making sure he stayed beyond the length of the animal's leash. He climbed a breeze-block wall at the back with the pit bull snapping at his feet, this time checking for guard dogs before he dropped down and committed to his new route.

The coast was clear. Time to press on.

When his feet landed in the neighbouring garden, he heard the pit bull focus its attention on the red-haired detective who was now approaching its territory. He hoped the sight of the snarling beast would be enough to put her off following his path, forcing her to waste time taking a different route. He sprinted through the garden and down the driveway, passing a row of beat-up old cars and a battered tyre swing. He risked a glance over his shoulder: nobody had followed him. Yet. If he could stay out of their sight for a little while longer, making a few changes in direction along the way, they wouldn't know which way he'd gone, and he'd be able to put some distance between them.

But as he hunkered down next to the side of a single-storey white house, he felt a sudden change in the air. Something was different. He heard it before he saw it: the tell-tale *thud-thud-thud* of the rotor blades getting louder and louder. He scanned the sky and noticed the distinctive shape of a police helicopter high above, flying towards the scene. His heart sank.

It looked as though his attempt to escape might have been for nothing.

–

Detective Naomi Ocean stopped running and placed the palm of her left hand against the fence, her fingers clawed in between the links to give her purchase. Her right stayed down by her side, clinging onto her Colt Delta Elite pistol. Her long frizzy red hair dangled in front of her face as she gazed at the ground, her lungs gasping for air. Her pulse drummed a beat in her neck; fat beads of sweat introduced themselves to her forehead; several strands of hair stuck to the damp skin on her face. The chain links sagged forwards with her weight, edging her closer to the pit bull. She stood up straight and glared into the dog's eyes, right into its soul.

'What you making all that noise for, you loud son of a bitch!' The dog stopped barking, let out a couple of half-hearted whines, and lay down. 'That's better. You might get away with blocking my pursuit, but there's no way I'm getting a headache because of you as well.'

She examined the pit bull's garden. Her suspect must have changed direction and climbed over the wall to the right; with that dog in the way there was nowhere else for him to go. Judging by the muscles in its neck and shoulders, and the size of its teeth, it wouldn't be safe to cross that yard in an armoured truck, never mind on foot. An animal like that would force a tank to detour.

She unclipped the radio from her belt. 'All units, suspect is now heading east. He should come out on North Bruce Street at any moment.'

A crackly reply came back from her partner, Detective Melvin Jones. 'The K9 units have just arrived, and with that big bird in the air, there's no way this guy can escape.'

Naomi raised her chin to the sky and saw what Melvin was referring to. Hovering above them was the department's twin engine Airbus H145, which had nine point six million dollars' worth of aerial surveillance, equipped with the most advanced and up-to-date versions of night vision, infra-red and thermal imaging. It was an elite hunter with a bird's-eye view, capable of tracking a small mammal from over a mile away; not something easily escapable. Long story short, their suspect was toast.

'Yeah,' Naomi said to herself. 'We got this guy. It's only a matter of time.'

'You sure that witness is right about what he saw?' Melvin asked.

'One hundred per cent,' Naomi said. 'He saw the guy arguing with our victim on her doorstep last night. Says he didn't leave until she pointed a gun at him. Now she's dead and he's running from us. I'd say this is our guy, and even if he isn't, chances are he knows something that'll help us get to the bottom of this woman's murder.'

'Roger that. We got North Bruce Street locked down. The K9s are deploying— Get back in your houses! Suspect on the loose!'

Naomi grimaced as she turned her head away from her radio because of Melvin's shouting. It would appear the universe was determined to give her a headache that morning.

'We've got visual on your location,' came the voice of the navigator inside the helicopter. 'Looks like you guys have that block surrounded. We'll begin our sweep and should have this suspect pinned down in no time.'

'Roger that,' Naomi said, smiling to herself.

Since she'd been promoted to detective a few years ago, she'd rarely had the opportunity to chase down a suspect like this. Her world now was all crime scenes, paperwork and interviews. She found herself missing the excitement of her patrol-cop days. She assessed the wall that marked the boundary at the back of the row of houses, and wondered if she could make it. It must have been seven, maybe eight feet high. The suspect had vanished out of sight almost immediately, which meant he must have climbed over it like it was nothing. From the view she'd got of him, she'd been able to tell he was a giant of a man. She promised herself she wouldn't give him an inch of wiggle room. There was no chance of him doubling back and escaping through her, and if she got him cornered, she'd take him down hard.

'You're about to lose the most important game of hide and seek you've ever played in your life, buster.'

She clipped her radio onto her belt, tucked her Colt in its holster, and walked backwards to get a run up. With her eyes locked onto the lip of the wall, she visualised where she wanted her fingertips to land.

'Ready or not,' she said with gusto. 'Here I come.'

–

Drayce crept along the side of the house and peered out onto North Bruce Street. He saw exactly what he'd been dreading: an army of police officers swarming the streets, with several patrol cars having been diverted into the area to help with the search. Two of the vehicles were dog units, the handlers of which had just deployed their Belgian Malinois dogs. The animals' noses were down, searching for scent, their eyes scanning back and forth between the streets around them and their handlers, waiting for their command. With a vicious pit bull behind and trained attack dogs ahead, the word *trapped* sprang into Drayce's mind.

He moved back into cover and tried to think of a new plan. He couldn't go forwards because his exit had been cut off, he couldn't go back because the red-haired detective was hot on his heels, and he was in danger of being spotted by the helicopter at any moment. And once that thing locked eyes on him, he might as well put the handcuffs on himself.

Pressing his back up against the wall of the house, he gazed up at the sky for any sign of the helicopter. He couldn't see it because it was now blocked by the roof of the house, but he could hear it close by. He searched for options. About five metres away was a side door. He crept along the wall and reached for the handle.

Unlocked.

Voices made him startle. They hadn't rounded the corner yet, but the cops – led by their land-shark Malinois – were fast approaching his position. They were so close he could hear the dogs panting. He opened the door just wide enough to slide in sideways and managed to close it behind him just before the cops appeared.

The sound of the helicopter was dulled by the building's insulation, but it still made its presence known above the roof. He took a step further into the kitchen, freezing when the silhouettes of two police officers jogged past a window. Much to his relief, the blinds were down, so they couldn't see him. Realising he was holding his breath, he exhaled gently and listened to the cops' communications outside. He could tell from the way they were speaking to one another they hadn't seen him slip into the house. He decided to press on.

After crossing the kitchen, he inched his line of sight around the corner of an open doorway, trying not to make a sound as he moved. He stared into a living room, in the middle of which was a coffee table with a square glass top, surrounded on three sides by large cream leather sofas pointing at a giant flat-screen TV that was mounted to the wall. There were three bowls of cereal on the coffee table, brimming with milk and multi-coloured lumps of sugar and corn starch, with a spoon wedged into each. Like Goldilocks should have known, those bowls meant he wasn't alone.

He froze at the sight of three grown men. They were stood by the front window, huddled together as they stared at the cops on the street through a thin gap in the blinds. They were dressed in scruffy jeans and T-shirts and had their backs to him, their attention entirely gripped by the commotion outside. Drayce surveyed the living room from where he was standing. There was drug paraphernalia all over the place: blackened crack pipes on burnt foil; ashtrays brimming with burnt-out joints; coke-dusted mirrors. Among all this party gear were several pistols, revolvers and nasty-looking combat knives scattered around the room, ensuring these guys always had a weapon within reach. Drayce crept back behind the door frame, closed his eyes, and took a deep breath.

He'd bought himself some time by entering the house, delaying his capture for at least a few minutes. But it had been a roll of the dice, one that now seemed to have landed him snake eyes. He was a trespasser in the home of three armed criminals, who would undoubtedly be on edge with the presence of huge numbers of police officers swarming the streets. With every step he took, it seemed more and more likely that Drayce would be left with no choice but to give himself up, forced to take his chances with the cops.

In the corner of his eye, something caught the light that streamed through the kitchen blinds. A set of keys dangled from a hook on the wall. Being careful not to step in sight of the living room, he gently and silently unhooked them, examining them in the palm of his hand. They were car keys with a garage door fob attached, and a metallic key ring engraved with the name Eleanor.

Maybe he wouldn't need to give himself up just yet.

Recalling the exterior of the house, he remembered the garage being attached to the front left side, meaning if there was an internal door to it, it would be on the other side of the living room. He closed his fist tightly around the keys to ensure they wouldn't jingle and tiptoed back to the door frame.

He was right: the door to the garage was exactly where he'd suspected it would be, and he would only need to walk a few metres into the living room before he got to it. He stared at the criminals' backs, then at the garage door, wondering if he could make it without being seen. The assortment of guns and knives in the room meant it would be a shitstorm of epic proportions if they turned around at any point. He glanced down at the car keys in his hand, knowing he had no other choice but to risk the short journey. He quickly began to visualise it step by step, forming what he'd need if he was going to get out of this situation alive, with his freedom intact.

An escape plan.

–

Naomi landed in a crouch on the other side of the wall, drew her pistol, and scanned the garden. Happy the suspect wasn't in the immediate vicinity, she moved tactically between a row of rusty cars and an old tyre swing. The house to her left was a small, white, single-storey place. She opened her arc to improve her view of North Bruce Street and caught sight of half a dozen police vehicles, a mixture of patrol cars and K9 units, lining the road. Uniformed officers were searching inside bins and underneath cars. She could see Melvin standing next to the open trunk of his unmarked police cruiser, his dark brown skin glistening, giant bald head sweating profusely, as he wrestled into body armour he clearly hadn't worn in years. He'd put on more than a few pounds since it had been issued to him. Naomi reminded herself to pester him about his diet again.

'Melvin!' she shouted down the driveway. 'Any sightings?'

He looked up from the Velcro straps he was fiddling with. 'Nothing yet. The helicopter's doing a sweep and the dogs are trying to pick up a scent.'

A handler and his Malinois appeared from North Bruce Street and jogged between Naomi and the white house, the dog's nose sniffing the ground, hunting for their suspect's scent.

'Any indications?' she asked the handler. His name badge told her his last name was Griffin.

'Nothing yet,' Griffin said. 'But we should pick up his trail pretty quickly.'

Naomi had seen police dogs working on numerous occasions during her career and knew the Malinois was favoured because of the breed's legendary drive. During her days in uniform, she'd benefitted from the dog's ability to track human scent, catching suspects who were long out of sight. She knew it took time, and the less contamination of the working area there was by other people's scents, the better. The fact it was morning meant there shouldn't have been many people in the gardens yet. She hoped this particular dog had a good nose.

An unexpected jolt on the lead suddenly pulled Griffin off balance. 'Wow,' he said. 'Okay, good girl. Seek, seek.'

The dog's body language had changed in a heartbeat, her nose working even harder as she pulled Griffin down the side of the house.

'This is good,' Griffin said. 'She's definitely tracking someone.'

The giant Malinois sniffed all the way along the wall of the white house, right up to the side door. She stopped dead, sniffing frantically around the frame and paying particular attention to the handle. She tried to push her nose between the frame and the door, whining obsessively as though she wanted to go inside.

Griffin addressed Naomi. 'You seen anyone go in or out of this door while you've been here?'

'Not a soul,' she said. 'But I only climbed over the back wall a few seconds before you came around the corner, and I didn't get a view of this door until I got close. I guess someone would have had time to slip inside if it's unlocked.'

'Only one way to know for sure.'

Naomi watched Griffin tighten his grip on the lead with one hand, before reaching out for the door handle with the other.

—

Drayce took his first tentative step into the living room. The sole of his shoe made a very slight squeak as he carefully planted his foot on the floorboards: the quiet, almost imperceptible sound of rubber pressing on polished wood. It made the hairs on his arms stand up, but the three men by the window didn't move. They were far too engrossed in the activity out on the street to pick up a faint noise coming from within the house. Drayce hoped their hypnotic mindset would continue until after he'd reached the garage.

Mid-way through his next step, he paused, hovering his foot as one in the group spoke.

'The fuck going on out there, man?' the one at the back asked, a skinny guy with short black hair, craning his neck to see above the other two.

'Shit, I don't know,' the guy at the front said, his bearded face pressed up to the gap in the blinds. 'Cops be searching for someone.'

'Think they want us?' This from the guy next to him, a worried tone to his voice. He was wearing a red baseball cap and was shaking a little, perhaps coming down from whatever he'd taken the night before. Drayce could see a pistol in his right hand and could tell straight away his grip was too tight. The guy was shifting his weight from one foot to the other, brimming with anxiety, sweeping his two friends with the muzzle as he gesticulated, his finger squirming inside the trigger guard. The guy was a negligent discharge waiting to happen.

'How the fuck should I know?' the guy with the beard replied.

Drayce watched Red Cap steady the gun, tilt it sideways, and point it in the general direction of the window. 'Well, I'll tell you something. If those motherfuckers come in here, I'm gonna kill me some pigs!'

Drayce used the idiot's loud voice as cover for his own footsteps, clearing the distance to the door. He examined the hinges: it opened out into the garage rather than the living room, which made him hope there was nothing blocking it on the other side.

Too late to do anything about it if there was.

He gripped the handle and began to twist, watching the three men intensely. Thankfully, it didn't make a sound, not even a rub or squeak as the latch bolt moved out of the frame. But then the sound of another door flinging open somewhere behind him filled the entire house with noise.

The three men by the window turned around.

The first thing their eyes settled on was the open doorway to the kitchen, because that's where the sound had come from. But it was only a split second later when they clocked the giant stranger standing in their living room, right by the door to the garage, frozen to the spot like a cat burglar caught in the act.

Nobody moved.

The brains of the three men gradually processed what their eyes were seeing. Their expressions changed, morphing into angry scowls. Shouts of 'police' roared from the kitchen. Red Cap lifted his gun in Drayce's direction.

The room erupted.

Drayce opened the door and disappeared into the garage at the same time as the cops entered the living room. He lost sight of Red Cap as he vanished into the dark space, but he didn't hear any gunfire, so assumed the guy must have lost his nerve and dropped the weapon as though it was white hot after the cops burst in.

Drayce swung the door to behind him. A giant police dog's razor-sharp teeth snapped at the closing gap. With an instinctive outburst, he managed to whack the door with the palm of his hand, slamming it shut just before the dog was able to get through and rip him to pieces.

Drayce was plunged into darkness. He heard the animal headbutt the other side, unable to slow itself down quickly enough. With no time to search for a light switch, he turned around and braced himself against the door.

On the other side he heard the cops shouting at the three occupants to get down on the ground, no doubt at gunpoint. A second later he felt them try the handle and push against him, then when they felt his resistance, kick it with all their might. Every thud rattled through his body as he held his ground. He reached out with his hands and searched the walls either side of the door. His fingertips caressed the contours of a light switch. A bare bulb came to life. It dangled from the ceiling, a foot or two above the roof of a gunmetal grey Mustang.

Eleanor.

A giant refrigerator was set back against the wall to his right, the sight of which gave him an idea. He reached for it, but his fingertips only just brushed its edge.

'Damn it!' he hissed.

The kicks on the other side of the door had taken on a predictable rhythm. He waited for a pause then seized his opportunity, lunging to within reach of the refrigerator.

He gripped it with both hands and toppled it over in front of the door. A split second later there was another kick from the cops, their power now absorbed entirely by the giant appliance instead of Drayce's back. After a deep sigh of relief, he turned to face the Mustang.

No time to waste.

He hit the remote for the garage shutters, climbed into the driver's seat, and fired up the engine. The V8 roared to life, shaking the walls of the house and drowning out the noise of the cops' continued efforts to smash the door down. He focused on the bottom of the rising shutters, the garage steadily filling with daylight as the outside world was slowly revealed to him from the ground up. First the driveway, then the street, then the tyres of the cop cars, and the boots on their feet. He saw them draw their guns, preparing for their suspect's exit.

Drayce buckled his seatbelt and selected first gear. His right foot flirted with the accelerator, sending loud pops through the exhausts as he waited for the shutters to clear the Mustang's roof. He throttled the steering wheel.

This next part was going to be interesting.

–

'Keep your hands where I can see them!' Naomi shouted. 'Nobody moves unless I say so!'

Her eyes darted between the three men over by the window, aware of the gun at their feet, rattling from side to side as though one of them had just dropped it. Behind her, Griffin kicked the door they'd seen their suspect slip through.

'The fuck going on?' the guy in the red cap said. 'Y'all can't just burst in here like that! You got a warrant or something?'

'Shut the fuck up and put your hands against the window!'

All three reluctantly turned around and did as they were told. Naomi moved forwards to take control of the gun on the floor. Afterwards, she noticed at least half a dozen other weapons scattered around the room. She glared at the three men and spoke to their backs.

'You three live here, or do I need to arrest you for burglarising this place?'

'Yeah, we live here,' Red Cap said. 'This our home. The only people trespassing right now are you and that big dude you chasing.'

Naomi frowned; she hated a smart-ass. 'If this is your home, what were you doing standing in your living room with a gun drawn?'

'Protecting our property. We got rights you know.'

'You got a permit for that pistol?'

Red Cap went silent.

'What about all these other weapons?' Naomi asked. 'You decide to suddenly get those out and scatter them around your home to defend your property against the man we're chasing?' Red Cap kept his lips still, as did both of his friends. 'I suppose you're going to tell me you've got licences for all these weapons, huh?' Her eyes caught sight of something on the arm of a sofa: cocaine paraphernalia. There wasn't much left, but it seemed the three of them had a good time last night. 'Well, well. It looks like you clowns have got some explaining to do.'

She backed up to Griffin, keeping an eye on the three men by the window, then radioed through to her colleagues outside for backup. The dog barked frantically at the door, the sound of her claws scratching the wood accompanied by the loud booming thuds of Griffin's boot as he tried to kick his way into the room.

Three patrol cops ran into the living room from the kitchen. Naomi directed them to deal with the three guys she was pointing her gun at, enabling her to turn around and help Griffin.

'Did he lock it?' she asked.

'No. A few seconds ago there was some give every time I kicked it, so it's not locked. But I heard a loud crash and now it's solid, so I think he's dropped something big and heavy in front of it to stop us getting in.'

Naomi turned back to the three occupants. 'Where does this door lead to?'

'The garage,' one of them said.

'Man, shut the fuck up,' Red Cap interjected. He turned to Naomi, a leering smile spread across his face. 'Work it out for yourself, bitch. We ain't helping Po-Po.'

Naomi turned to the three uniformed cops. 'Get them cuffed up and under arrest. There are enough felonies lying around to wipe that smile off his face for the next ten to fifteen.'

The three cops took hold of a man each and began handcuffing them. Two of them decided to go quietly until they could speak to their lawyers. A sensible decision. They obviously understood the inevitability of the process.

Red Cap didn't.

'You fucking bitch! Barking orders in my house. I orta kill you for that!'

Red Cap violently pushed his arresting officer, who staggered backwards, stumbled over the coffee table, and fell to the floor. Emboldened, Rep Cap turned to face Naomi, an arrogant smile forming below his glaring eyes.

She'd had enough of his nonsense. Time to show him who was in charge.

Like a sprinter off the block, Naomi charged at him and exploded into a double leg takedown. Her chest and shoulders made impact with his hips and thighs and she drove her head into his stomach, knocking him off balance as she simultaneously hooked her hands around the back of his knees, sending him crashing to the ground. Following through with the momentum, she wrapped an arm around one of his ankles and then got back to her feet. Without giving him a moment to comprehend what was happening to him, she turned him over and sat back, lifting her chest to apply the foot lock. He howled in pain as his ankle was stretched beyond its natural range of motion.

By this time, the felled cop was back on his feet, hurrying over to help restrain Red Cap. Only once the handcuffs were applied did Naomi release the joint lock. She stood up to the sound of Red Cap bitching about making a complaint, but there was another sound she heard that was far more important to her. A rumble like thunder had just fired up from within the garage. Picture frames on the walls started to rattle.

'What the hell is that?' she asked Griffin, but he didn't reply. He was too busy shouting into his radio, warning the cops out on the street.

'Oh shit!' Red Cap shouted, no longer concerned with complaining about Naomi. 'Not Eleanor. You can't let him take her. Please, you gotta stop him!'

Their suspect's plan quickly dawned upon Naomi.

She ran to the front door.

14

Drayce stamped his foot on the throttle and released the clutch, sending the rear wheels into a frenzied spin. The tyres spit small chunks of rubber at the rear wall of the garage as the car jolted forwards. The expressions on the faces of the cops out on the street told him they weren't ready for him. Some had made it to a good position, huddled behind their vehicles with weapons drawn, but most were still on the move, running off the driveway to the nearest point of cover. Their behaviour told him the radio call from inside the house had only just gone through, otherwise, if they'd had more time, they could have blocked the driveway with one of their vehicles to prevent his escape. Luckily for him, he had a clear path to the road.

The roof of the Mustang clipped the bottom of the shutters as it shot out of the garage, sending a flurry of sparks out behind it. Up ahead was an assault course of police cars littering the road. Drayce spotted officers braced across the hoods and roofs of vehicles, taking aim at the Mustang with sidearms and pump-action shotguns. He gripped the steering wheel to death, preparing himself for the inevitable chaos.

A *ting-ting-ting* chorus of bullets and buckshot clipped all four wheels as the cops tried to disable his vehicle. He thought he heard a couple of rounds penetrate the cabin and flinched when a round burst through the front windscreen, missing him by nothing more than a few inches. He squinted against the tiny shards of broken glass and turned his face to the side to protect his eyes.

He caught sight of the red-haired detective who'd been chasing him through the gardens. She was running out of the front door of the house he'd just left, her pistol rising on aim. For a split second he made eye contact with her, but then just as quickly broke it as gravity settled the tiny pieces of glass in the air, enabling him to look ahead without the risk of being blinded. He ignored the spiderweb cracks in the windscreen and focused on the road, negotiating a route through the hastily parked police cars. He jerked the wheel to the left to avoid hitting a cop who'd moved out of cover to take a shot, causing the Mustang to oversteer, the tyres bouncing over the cracks in the asphalt as it skidded across the carriageway.

Drayce kept his foot on the throttle, holding enough opposite lock on the steering to keep the car drifting in the right direction. The Mustang glided somewhat elegantly through the gaps between the cop cars, making it all the way to the other side of the road where it mounted the kerb and scraped down a fence at the front of a neigh-bouring property. He corrected the steering, punching up a gear as he made full use of the sidewalk where there weren't any police vehicles getting in the way. Seconds later he re-joined the carriageway and broke free from the last of the LVMPD motors, powering up North Bruce Street as fast as the Mustang would go.

Once clear of the initial melee, Drayce took a deep breath, slid the gear stick into fourth, and glanced in his rear-view mirror. The cops were all diving inside their cars and spinning around to chase after him. Remembering his priorities, he carefully patted himself down. Relieved to find no injuries, he placed both hands on the steering wheel, focused on the road, and concentrated on his escape.

Three Kawasaki Ninja motorbikes appeared from a side street, flying out into the road ahead of him. Each had a rider and a pillion, their all-black helmets with tinted visors making it impossible to see their faces. Which, Drayce deduced, was the only reason they were wearing them, considering their complete lack of other safety gear. The baggy khaki shorts and white vests they were wearing, along with gang tattoos displayed on their arms and legs, told Drayce they weren't cops.

As did the Uzi 9mm machine pistols in the pillions' hands.

One bike stayed out front, while the other two fanned out and hit their brakes, bracketing the Mustang as they came alongside. Drayce swerved from side to side to try and knock them off, but the riders were too slick. They leaned hard to the side and accelerated away from him every time he made a move. The pillions took aim and fired, not at Drayce, but at the tyres, peppering the rubber with bullets from the side and the front.

Drayce dropped down a gear and slammed his foot on the throttle, accelerating towards a bend up ahead. This time, the rider of the bike out front wasn't quick enough. Drayce caught his back wheel and sent him spinning, catapulting his pillion into the door of a parked car. The rider managed to stay with the bike as it somersaulted over a wall and crashed into the side of someone's house. As the bike on his left caught him up, Drayce swerved at it, hitting the legs of both rider and pillion. He heard a scream under one of their helmets as they lost control, the front wheel hitting the kerb, causing the bike to flip end over end, launching both rider and pillion into the air, landing in someone's garden. Witnessing the carnage inflicted on their friends, the third bike backed off.

Wanting to get away from whoever these people were and escape before the cops made any ground on him, Drayce focused on the bend up ahead, where he estimated he should be out of sight of his pursuers. But as he dipped the throttle again, he frowned: the Mustang was sluggish, suddenly refusing to accelerate as it had been doing. He stamped his right foot harder and heard a persistent thudding from the back wheels. It sounded horrendous, as though the tyres were about to be torn from the rims. He wound his window down, angled the side mirror, and saw a large flap of loose rubber slapping the wheel's arch with every rotation.

Anxiety building, Drayce knew he needed to abandon the Mustang as soon as possible, otherwise the third biker and the cops would catch up with him in seconds. He limped the vehicle along the road as fast as it would take him, continuously glancing back and forth between the road ahead and his rear-view mirror, waiting for his moment of opportunity.

As soon as he rounded the bend, out of sight of the nearest cop car, he took a right, the tyres screaming in protest, the rims leaving behind a trail of sparks that flowed over the concrete, mimicking waves in a boat's wake. He stopped the car in the middle of the road and wiped the steering wheel, gear stick and door handles with his sleeve to remove his fingerprints.

The third bike came into view as it hit the bend at speed, both rider and pillion leaning hard into the turn. Drayce abandoned the Mustang and ran up someone's driveway. The pillion took aim with his Uzi. Drayce leapt over a fence as his pursuer opened fire, spraying bullets in his direction. He landed hard on the other side, rounds peppering the ground at his feet as he pushed on, sprinting across one garden, then another, until he found an open back door to someone's house and continued through it, sprinting down a hallway, past a kitchen where a young mother and child were sat, and out the front door. A quick glance over his shoulder caught sight of two figures in black motorbike helmets chasing him with guns in their hands. He faced ahead and pushed on, crossing the street and darting through a neighbouring house, ignoring furious shouts from a man who saw him from his living room sofa as he ran down his corridor and out the back door. Gunfire erupted in his wake, bullets clipping the doorframe as he exited the house.

But those gangsters weren't the only ones chasing him down.

Drayce could hear the police helicopter in the air and had to assume it was following his every move, reminding him of the need to constantly change direction and run under cover at every opportunity to confuse the spotter. It was imperative he be unpredictable, making it difficult for them to determine which way he'd gone.

There's a reason a hare runs from a hawk in zig zags.

He leapt over a wall, crouching low to hide from the pursuing gunmen, and found himself on a road called Civic Center Drive. Sweating and panting hard, he searched for an idea as to what to do next. There was a white van parked about twenty metres up the street, the driver's door open, with nobody sat behind the wheel. The engine had been left running. He ran towards it, and as he got close, saw a delivery driver appear from a house further up the street. Drayce got to the open door just as the driver saw him, the two men locking eyes.

'Sorry!' Drayce shouted.

He climbed in and drove off, the delivery man running behind, his angry, incoherent curse words fading into the distance. Feeling better now he was back in a vehicle, Drayce drove hard down Civic Center Drive. The two gunmen appeared in his wing mirror. They took aim and fired, the rounds clipping the bodywork. Drayce weaved in and out of traffic, making himself a hard target until he was out of their sight.

Clear of the immediate danger, he breathed big lungfuls of air, trying to settle his heart rate and calm his mind so he could focus. But every time he passed a junction, he expected a patrol car to pop out and block the road, having managed to get ahead and cut off his escape, or perhaps another sicario death squad on motorbikes waiting to gun him down. This fear made him drive even faster, taking more and more risks to get through traffic and make good his escape.

He approached a set of crossroads, leaned forwards, and gazed up to the sky. The helicopter hovered above the city, still tracking his every movement. To the layman, it might have appeared to be an irrelevant little dot amongst the clouds, but Drayce knew it would be his downfall if he let it have its own way. He couldn't just keep driving north because soon he'd end up in the desert, with nowhere to hide. Vast space was not his friend. What he needed were thick, messy, confusing crowds of people, both in and around tightly packed and congested buildings. The helicopter could have all the technology in the world, but it was only as sharp as the people in it. It was time to make their job more difficult.

At the crossroads he changed down a gear, took a hard left, and powered across all five lanes of Cheyenne Ave, the van's tyres only just meeting the demands being put on them. He ignored the red lights and carried on across the next junction, narrowly avoiding a side-on collision with a truck as he took the turning for the freeway as fast as the big van would allow.

As soon as he hit the freeway, he pushed on, making use of all five lanes so he didn't have to relinquish any speed. Sweat beaded on his forehead as his brain reminded him there could be roadblocks up ahead, the helicopter's navigator no doubt feeding back his direction of travel to the swarming law enforcement, who would be doing everything they could to pin him down. But he couldn't allow himself to dwell on negative thoughts. He had no other choice but to head south to the Strip. If he didn't get out of that van and vanish amongst a crowd of people soon, it would all be over.

His relentless pace and dare-devil driving tactics meant he made it to a turning for the Strip less than a minute later. He wiped the sweat off his forehead with the back of his hand while negotiating the long sweeping bend, breathing a sigh of relief when he saw there wasn't a roadblock waiting for him on Sahara Avenue. He couldn't see a cop in sight, other than the ones in the sky, but he could hear them close by, their sirens giving away their encroaching presence.

Feeling the jittery energy that came with his adrenaline kicking up a notch, he dipped his foot on the throttle and swung a left onto Las Vegas Boulevard, catching sight of flashing red and blue lights, both ahead and behind. They were roughly a quarter of a mile away, but nonetheless, he needed to make his move. The net was drawing in; it was now or never. At the rate they were closing him down, another minute spent inside that van would mean certain capture.

At the next set of lights, he abandoned the van, once again wiping down the steering wheel, gear stick and door handle with his sleeve to remove his prints. The delivery driver had left a blue baseball cap on the passenger seat, so he slipped it on, pulling the visor as low down on his forehead as possible. He left the keys in the ignition and ran diagonally across the junction, following a path between two rows of palm trees that led to the entrance for the Stratosphere Casino Hotel.

The heavy glass doors groaned on their hinges as he pushed his way through. Once inside, he immediately felt out of place, his sweaty, panicked state at total contrast to the relaxed guests who were loitering around the entrance. He walked calmly across the lobby with his hands in his pockets, trying to look relaxed, head tilted down so the cameras wouldn't get a good image of his face. If he managed to get away from the cops' initial pursuit, he didn't want to leave behind images of his face along the trail, making their jobs easy for them when it came to investigating his movements and tracking him down.

He got past the staff at the registration desks who were too busy with guests to even glance at him. All he had to do was act as though he belonged there, until he could vanish out of sight amongst the thousands of slot machines up ahead. But before stepping off the shiny polished floor of the lobby and onto the garish red carpet of the casino, he peered over his shoulder and saw to his dismay a bright display of blue and red lights flashing wildly on the other side of the entrance doors.

Drayce cursed under his breath. He knew it was inevitable the helicopter would track him inside the Stratosphere, but what he hadn't expected was for the cops on the ground to have caught up so quickly. The entrance doors swung open, a team of uniforms hurrying inside, their weapons drawn, creating gasps and screams from the guests in the lobby.

Drayce disappeared amongst the slot machines.

15

The casino was vast. Despite accelerating from a fast walk to a jog, Drayce still hadn't cleared the slot machines minutes after entering the hotel. They went on and on in an endless display of blinking lights, every corner leading to more and more gambling opportunities. He ran past table games like blackjack, roulette and craps, then a line of poker rooms for the big spenders, and a state-of-the-art sports betting room. He focused as far ahead as he could in search of a way out, peering over his shoulder every few steps to see if the police had caught up with him yet. He couldn't see them, but that didn't mean they weren't close by. The casino might have been huge, but the floor space was still claustrophobic. For all he knew, they were right there on the other side of the machines he'd just passed, only seconds away from being able to put their hands on him. Blocking out his nerves, he ignored what was behind, and focused instead on what he was searching for ahead.

An exit.

With nothing obvious on the casino floor, he darted up a staircase, leaping multiple steps with each bound. On the next floor was a selection of bars and a glass viewing area for the Sky Jump landing pad: one of the theme park-style attractions available to customers at the Stratosphere. Drayce approached the window and tried to blend in with the onlookers as he examined the area for a way to escape. A sign next to him explained what the Sky Jump was: a controlled descent from a platform on floor 108 of the hotel, which used zip wires to drop participants eight hundred and fifty-five feet. A door to his right led out to the landing pad, at the edge of which was a bannister that would be easy enough to climb over, leaving him with a single-storey drop back down to ground level.

Achievable.

He peered at the sky and picked up the tiny black shape of the police helicopter: his main obstacle. The cops would all be inside the building by now, systematically searching the premises for him, which meant the odds said the streets would be clear, allowing him an opportunity to make a run for it – no way would the cops have enough staff to surround the entire hotel *and* search inside for him, which is where the eye in the sky began to really earn its money. Using the aircraft as visual containment was a pretty good tactic for the cops, but it came with a downside. The circling manoeuvre would unavoidably leave the pilot and spotter blind to the opposite side of the building.

Drayce waited patiently, checking over his shoulder every few painstaking seconds to make sure the cops hadn't made it to his floor yet. It seemed to take forever for the aircraft to move far enough around on its pass so it no longer had a view of the landing pad, but as soon as it had, Drayce was ready.

He turned towards the doors, but the sound of rushed footsteps made him freeze. Over his shoulder he glimpsed the sandy-coloured uniform of the first LVMPD officer to reach the top of the stairs. They made eye contact with one another, the officer stopping dead just as Drayce had, time slowing down to nothing more than a crawl as their brains processed what they were looking at.

His senses heightened, Drayce took in the smaller details of the man standing less than twenty feet away: the Marine's buzz cut hair; the black Oakley shades resting on his head; the finely pressed shirt and trousers. As more officers joined their colleague, Drayce's mind focused on more important details, like the Beretta M9 pistols holstered on their hips, and the M4 carbines slung across their torsos.

Drayce sprinted to the doors, clattering into the pane of glass. Locked. Shaking off his stupidity, he turned and ran with angry commands from the cops snapping at his heels. The bar area was his only option, so he sprinted through it, dodging the tables and chairs before diving head first over the counter, the barmaid screaming at him as he did so. His head collided with the door behind the bar, and he was immediately confronted with a wall of intense heat and noise as he crashed onto the floor of a working kitchen.

Back on his feet, he scanned for a route through the chaos, slipping past several angry chefs armed with razor-sharp knives and pans of boiling water. He found a door on the other side of the kitchen and hit it shoulder first, stepping into an empty corridor as he heard the cops enter the kitchen behind him, shouting for him to stop. He frantically grabbed at door handles as he rushed down the corridor, but they were all locked. An elevator at the other end seemed his only option, so he ran to it and pressed the call button.

Time moved painfully slowly at this point. The counter was telling him the car was just ten floors away, moving quickly, but not nearly quickly enough for his needs.

He could do nothing but stand there and wait, hoping it would get to him before the cops did. The sounds of them banging and clattering their way through the kitchen made him glance over his shoulder. One of them shouted for someone to get out of their way, his voice just the other side of the door. Any second now and they'd have Drayce in sight. He looked back at the counter: two floors away.

Come on, come on, come on.

'Police! Show me your hands!'

Drayce let out an angry groan. He could see the officer's reflection in the shiny elevator doors, his pistol up to eye level, hovering just below the tidy Marine's haircut. Drayce calmly raised his hands.

'Do not move!' the officer shouted. 'Wait for my next command!'

Drayce watched him take a couple of steps forwards to allow room for his colleagues to join him in the corridor, but then they all disappeared as the elevator doors opened wide. Not one to miss an opportunity, Drayce stepped into the car, making sure he kept his hands in full view of the cops.

'I said do not move!' the cop screamed.

'What are you going to do?' Drayce asked with a peek over his shoulder, the doors closing behind him. 'Shoot me?'

There was a second's hesitation before the cop broke into a sprint, holstering his pistol and reaching for his Taser. He fired, but was too far away: the barbs bounced back when they reached the end of the cord. In a last ditch attempt to stop the doors from closing, the officer dived for them, a single arm stretched out to block them: a close one, but not close enough. Drayce heard a dull thud on the other side.

Safe to drop his hands, he hit the button for floor 108. He had an idea for how he was going to get out of that building without wearing handcuffs; an insanely reckless one, but at this point he'd run out of options. The force of the car's momentum pressed into the soles of his feet as he was propelled upwards. Less than a minute later the car came to a gentle stop and the doors opened. He tilted his shoulders sideways and slid through as soon as the gap was wide enough, marching across the gift shop and past the line of customers who were queuing for the chance to jump off the side of the hotel.

Drayce quickly realised there was no time to waste. The staff were glued to their radios, eyeing him as he walked past, as though they'd just been told a suspected killer was in the room.

'Hey,' he heard from somewhere off to the side. 'You in the grey jacket. Stop!'

Drayce ignored the staff member's voice and instead focused on what was at the front of the queue of customers: a metallic booth leading out to the steel struc-ture that housed the platform from which they would jump. A young guy, college age, was hooked up, standing right on the edge of the platform, ready to go. He appeared fit and strong, as though he could handle the terror of someone joining him for the ride.

A loud *ping* motivated Drayce to leg it. Another elev-ator to his left had just received a car from the lower floors, an army of LVMPD uniforms spilling out as soon as the doors opened, several of whom immediately locked eyes on Drayce and shouted for him to stop. He noticed panic spreading amongst the line of customers as they clocked on to the cops' attempts to chase him down. Ahead of him, the member of staff out on the Sky Jump ledge clearly had no idea what had ignited within the building. He had his back to them all, gusts of wind drowning out the noise of the commotion as he counted to three for the jump. When he got to two, Drayce slipped past him. Instead of saying three he shouted 'hey' as he saw Drayce run onto the platform, just as the college kid moved to the edge, tilting face down towards the Vegas streets eight hundred feet below.

Drayce ran with his arms stretched out in front of him, trying to grasp onto the kid's harness. But he was too late. His fingertips missed by mere inches as the kid made the leap and dropped out of sight.

With no time for second guesses, Drayce summoned his courage, along with the remaining power in his legs, and did something only a mad man would do.

He jumped.

16

The terror was phenomenal, as was the regret. As soon as his feet left the ledge, Drayce was falling to his death. The college kid's harness pulled tight against his torso, the slack taken up in the safety cables, causing his descent to become controlled. Drayce, on the other hand, was still having his considerable weight pulled back to earth by gravity with no restrictions, meaning he closed the gap between them in a matter of seconds.

Drayce's chest slammed into the kid's back, the air leaving his own lungs with the same sound as a football player being tackled. For a terrifying moment his fingers couldn't find a grip, sending a bolt of fear through him at the thought he might just slide down the kid's body and continue falling to the concrete several hundred feet below. But then, miraculously, his fingertips snagged the harness, allowing him to cling on and join the kid for the ride.

Hotel windows rushed by, and powerful gusts of wind whipped at their clothing as they plummeted down the outside of the building. Drayce could see Vegas in its entirety: the roads, billboards, hotels and casinos, stretching all the way to the desert and mountain ranges. If it wasn't for the helicopter banking around the hotel, and the long line of cop cars extending out from the

Stratosphere's entrance, it would have been one hell of a view.

The journey took fifteen seconds. Drayce let go moments before they reached the pad, breaking his fall with a forward roll, before running towards the edge of the balcony. He slapped the palms of his hands onto the top bar of the bannister and swung his legs over to the other side. He hung for a moment, trying to calculate the best route to the street; with only five metres or so of thin air below him, he needed to be careful: a broken ankle would really spoil his efforts to remain a free man. He shuffled along until he was dangling above the roof of one of the parked cop cars, reducing the distance he would drop to a manageable three metres or so. Bracing his feet against the wall, he pushed himself off and let go of the bannister.

A dull metallic *clunk* erupted below him as he landed, denting the roof either side of the emergency light bar. After creating two small craters underneath his feet, he buckled his knees and dropped into a roll to help absorb the impact. Not being a parkour enthusiast, the landing wasn't particularly graceful. His lower back glanced off the light bar and he rolled off the vehicle, clattering through the side mirror and hitting the road with a bodily thud.

Groaning like an angry bear, he slowly got to his feet, the blunt trauma of the landing resonating across various parts of his body. Before he'd even stood up straight, he heard brakes squeal, his head snapping up to see a vehicle's front grill racing towards him. With no time to get out of its way, he dived onto the hood and rolled up to the windscreen, his back cracking the glass with the impact, before being thrown back down the hood onto the concrete as the vehicle came to a stop.

His body on fire, he somehow managed to get to his feet again, using his fingers to climb up the grill. He glared through the windscreen at the driver, his angry expression soon melting into one of shock as he realised who he was staring at.

17

Naomi couldn't believe her luck when it happened. After all, how often does your fleeing suspect fall from the sky and land right in front of you?

She'd arrived at the hotel later than her colleagues because she'd had to retrace her steps back to the crime scene to retrieve her vehicle. Frustrated, she'd screeched onto the entrance road in a foul temper, convinced she'd be way behind in the chase, fully prepared for missing out on all the glory.

How wrong she was.

The eye contact between them lasted for nothing more than a moment of incomprehension, followed by recognition, all of which passed by in total stillness as they stared at one another, neither of them daring to move. Like a rabbit breaking free from the spell of the mesmerising headlights in front of it, the suspect suddenly ran, firing Naomi into action as she reached for her door handle.

He moved surprisingly quickly for a man who'd just jumped from a balcony fifteen feet high before being hit by a car. Naomi shouted at him to stop before she'd even exited her vehicle, immediately identifying herself as a police officer. But it made no difference. The guy was on his toes, sprinting down the boulevard as fast as his legs would carry him.

Naomi flung open her door and ran after him, sprinting between the two lines of palm trees, trying to keep him in sight for as long as possible to reduce the chances of him vanishing again. Up ahead the road forked. He took a left and disappeared out of sight behind the hotel's building line. The fear of losing him a second time gave Naomi a fresh pair of legs, filling her with adrenaline and enabling her to up the pace. But as she reached the corner there was no sign of him at all. He'd disappeared.

'Shit!'

She continued along Main Street for a couple of hundred yards until she ran out of steam, slowing to a jog, then a walk. Before long she came to a stop, bending over at the waist and resting her hands on her knees as she tried to breathe. After a few seconds' respite, she forced herself to stand tall so she could fill her lungs properly. She brushed her hair out of her face and unclipped her radio as she prepared to transmit an update. Her colleagues in the hotel needed to know what was happening.

'Suspect sighted, heading north on Main Street,' she managed to say in a breathless whisper. 'He's on foot and I've lost sight of him. I need more units out here on the streets.'

Melvin was the first to respond. 'I'm with SWAT. We're about to exit the front of the Stratosphere. Watch yourself with this guy. Dude's crazy. He just jumped off the top of the tower with no harness.'

'What? That can't be possible.'

'I just watched him do it. Grabbed on to some other guy for the ride. Don't give this guy an inch, Puddle. Keep your eye on him but wait for backup before you move in for the arrest. Lord knows what he's capable of.'

Naomi winced at Melvin calling her Puddle. It was a nickname she hated, but it had stuck nonetheless, ever since she'd been through detective training school. The reason it had stuck was probably because she openly hated it so much, pulling a face every time she heard it. Cops are like that: bite at something that annoys you and you can guarantee they'll keep poking you with it. She'd tried turning the other cheek to show them it didn't bother her, but that wasn't really her style. She made a mental note to remind Melvin of her feelings when she saw him later.

Putting her radio away, she wiggled her toes inside her shoes. They were leather slip-ons with a small heel: good for looking smart and professional at crime scenes; not so good for a foot chase. She could feel something on the side of her foot that felt like the beginnings of a blister. She sighed, grumbled a bit, then turned around on the spot, searching for her suspect.

Traffic was backing up towards the junction, so she walked down the line, checking to see if he was crouched down, hiding out of sight between vehicles. When that didn't turn anything up, she focused on a group of people across the road. They were having their pictures taken next to a City of Las Vegas sign, grinning amongst the statues of giant dice, a roulette wheel, and stacks of chips that had been built where the road forked. They were obviously tourists, and without exception they were dressed in shorts, T-shirts and baseball caps. Without a shadow of doubt, none of them was her suspect.

She turned sharply to her left, her heart rate spiking. Something big was moving quickly in the distance, darting between parked cars in the lot at the back of the Stratosphere. The figure was the right height, right build, and was wearing the right clothing. He was moving much faster than anything or anyone around him, the kind of speed at which an athletic person runs when their freedom is at stake.

Naomi forgot all about her burning lungs, tired legs and painful feet, and went after him with everything she had. In and out of her view, he darted between palm trees and parked cars, and through a long line of tall coaches with blacked-out windows. She ran between two buses being washed by their drivers, her feet splashing in the pools of soapy water that had accumulated on the concrete. As she emerged from the end of the line, she cursed her luck: he was no longer in view. The only other people in the vicinity were a heavy concession of valets, coach drivers and delivery drivers, along with a few hotel workers mingling near a fire exit as they enjoyed a cigarette break.

Thinking it unlikely her suspect would re-enter the hotel, Naomi jogged away from the building line towards his most likely route. She noticed wet footprints leading out of the soapy puddles, marking out a path. Whoever had left them had big feet, long legs, and had been running fast.

The footprints faded as they led into what was known locally as Naked City. Naomi found herself surrounded by apartment buildings with bullet holes in the walls, and small houses in such bad shape they almost looked derelict. Sinister curls of barbed wire looped around the tops of their small, fenced-off plots, graffiti tags marking nearly every sign.

As the footprints diminished to nothing, Naomi came to the mouth of a deserted alleyway next to an abandoned construction yard. The alleyway was long and thin, so there was no way he could have made it all the way to the end before she got there, which meant he was still in there somewhere, hiding from her.

Standing still to catch her breath, she passed an update on her position to her colleagues and was immediately reminded by Melvin to wait for backup before going any further. She drew her pistol and held it in the compressed position in the centre of her chest, ready to have it out on aim in a split second if needed.

For the first time since arriving there, she noticed just how quiet the area was. There were no sirens, and no sign of the helicopter. She now felt truly alone against a suspect who may be responsible for the violent death of a young woman. She press-checked her pistol, just to be certain a round was chambered.

Taking a cautious step forwards, Naomi was presented with an array of potential hiding spots. To her right was a pick-up truck with an exposed bed. Up ahead to her left was a stack of cardboard boxes with a dirty old sheet draped over the top, which appeared to be temporary accommodation for one of the city's homeless citizens. Even further into the alleyway were three dumpsters, discarded from the last refuse collection in a staggered line, their metallic edges jutting out at haphazard angles.

Naomi was sure their suspect was there somewhere, but she also knew she could be wrong. Backup was still a few minutes away, and if she waited for her colleagues to arrive before she cleared the alleyway, and it turned out their suspect was still on his toes somewhere, they would have lost him, potentially forever. She couldn't allow that to happen, which meant she couldn't afford to wait for backup to arrive. She needed to clear the alleyway herself.

She approached the pick-up truck with her pistol just below eye level, moving as quietly as she could, each step taken from heel to toe until she was within reach of the exposed bed. Her pistol on aim, she stepped onto a rear tyre and gripped onto the side of the bed, lifting herself high enough to see inside.

Nothing.

Naomi moved to the cabin. The windows were tinted, which unnerved her. She tried the handle: locked. No way could he have found the keys and secured himself in there before she came around the corner. She moved on.

The stack of cardboard boxes with the dirty sheet draped over the top were set back slightly from the main thoroughfare of the alleyway, tucked into a four- by five-foot recess in the fence line. She approached with caution, arcing around from roughly ten feet away to open her view through a small gap in the sheet. It was dark inside, with no sign of life, but that wouldn't do. She needed to be sure.

'Police!' she shouted. 'You in the boxes. Come out, hands first!'

No response.

'I know you're in there,' she bluffed. 'Get out here with your hands where I can see them.' Still nothing. 'I'm not going anywhere until you come out and speak to me.'

Something moved within the boxes, a person rummaging around inside a small space full of all their worldly possessions. The dull noises that clothing and blankets make when they're moved out of the way were accompanied by the harsher metallic sounds of tin cans and pots and pans being knocked aside. Naomi knelt, her finger resting on her Colt's trigger.

A scruffy figure appeared, cautiously pushing his head through the gap in the sheets. She couldn't see much of him but could tell he was terrified. He had just one hand up.

'I need to see your other hand,' Naomi said.

'I can't,' he replied with a shaky, mumbling voice. 'I need it for my stick.'

'What kind of stick?'

'One to help me stand upright.'

'A walking stick?'

'Yes, ma'am.'

Naomi sighed. 'Okay, come out with your stick. But make sure you do it real nice and slow.'

He took her last word seriously; she felt as though she was watching him through a slow-motion camera. Once he'd eventually cleared the sheets and was stood up with his walking stick, she got a good look at him. His skin was blackened with dirt, the state of his clothes giving her the impression he'd worn them for the last couple of decades but had never washed them. They hung off his emaciated frame in the same way they would a wire coat hanger. The flesh around his lips sunk in towards his mouth as though he had very few teeth left. Track marks peppered both forearms and his neck. Naomi suspected his groin and both his feet would likely be covered as well. He was so weak he was struggling to stay standing. His left ankle was badly swollen, likely due to an abscess, Naomi thought, brought on by an infection caused by using dirty needles.

This man was definitely not her suspect.

'Officer, I… I…'

'Relax,' Naomi said, lowering her pistol. 'It's not you I'm after. I've chased a suspect down this alleyway. You see anyone come by here in the last minute or so?'

'No, ma'am. Not a soul.'

With few teeth in his mouth, his lips smacked against his gums when he talked, making it hard for Naomi to understand what he was saying.

'You say you've not seen a soul?' she asked.

'That's right, ma'am.'

'Not got anyone else in there with you?'

'No, ma'am.'

'Stop calling me ma'am,' Naomi said as she stood back up. 'Just do me a favour and lift those sheets so I can see inside the boxes. I need to be sure before I move on.'

The guy was hesitant. He gave Naomi the impression he wanted to do what she was asking of him, but something was holding him back.

'Listen,' she said. 'I'm not interested in whatever drug paraphernalia you might have in there. I have bigger fish to fry right now, so as long as you're not hiding a fugitive, I'll be on my way.'

He reached back with his free hand and did as she asked. Naomi switched on the torch mounted to the bottom of her pistol and moved sideways, opening her view. It seemed less chaotic than she'd expected. There was storage to the right-hand side, bedding at the far end, and a cooking stove mounted near to the opening. Happy she'd seen it all, she thanked the man, turned around, and focused her attention on the dumpsters. She followed a similar procedure as with the pick-up truck: lifting herself up over the side with her pistol out front. Once she'd cleared the first two, she had a horrible feeling she'd missed something.

Was I thorough enough with the homeless man's shelter? Should I have found a way to check inside the pick-up truck's cabin even though it was locked?

These insecurities prevented her from venturing any further into the alleyway. She needed to double check.

As she pivoted, she caught a glimpse of someone hunched over by the cardboard boxes, as though he'd just appeared from within the shelter. As he stood up straight, she got a full appreciation of just how big he was, his physique emphasised by the skinny comparison of the homeless man he was stood next to, as though they were demonstrating two different stages in the evolution of man. Underneath his grey jacket was a solid torso, above blue jeans on bulging legs. After a split second, the figure's description registered properly in her brain and her senses kicked up a gear, her training bringing her pistol up in an instant.

18

Drayce had known it was risky to make his move while the detective was still in the alleyway, but he didn't have a choice. There would be a hundred cops closing in on his location. They'd contain the area and search every square foot. If he didn't leave before they got there, he would certainly be caught. But despite that inevitability, he wished he'd given it another minute before climbing out from underneath the blankets in those boxes.

'Police!' he heard the detective shout from behind him. 'Turn around! You're under arrest!'

The officer's voice was sharp and angry, full of hard-boiled authority. There were years of experience in that voice, Drayce knew. He heard no hint of a quiver, or any sense of self-doubt. He watched the homeless guy scurry back inside his cardboard shelter. He didn't blame him for not wanting to get caught up in this arrest. It had been good enough of the guy to help him hide, even though it had cost Drayce a twenty-dollar bill. If at any point there was an indication he was going to get into trouble for harbouring a fugitive, Drayce decided he'd tell the cops he threatened him, or overpowered him; something to make sure the guy didn't get into trouble for helping him out.

Drayce raised his hands in the air even though she hadn't told him to, simply because the detective's tone suggested it might be a good idea. He turned around slowly, keeping his chin tucked in to conceal his face with the peak of his cap. Even before he set eyes on her, he knew she'd be pointing a gun at him.

'Take it easy, big guy,' she said. 'Nice and slow, keeping your hands where I can see them.'

He lifted his chin slightly once he was facing her to give him a view of what he was up against. The breeze caught her hair, sending giant red curls wafting across her green eyes and pouting lips, dancing as though it was alive, with a mind of its own. She probably woke up looking that good, unlike most others, who'd have to hand over half a month's wages to a designer hairdresser to get the same appearance.

He'd been right about her athleticism. She reminded him of the CrossFit type, honing her physique with a finely tuned mixture of strength and endurance, forced out by a punishing work rate. No wonder she'd caught up with him.

He'd been right about the gun part too; she was indeed pointing one at him. There was no use trying to escape this time, he knew. Her stance, her posture, the steely look in her eyes, were all marks of an experienced professional. It was time to stop running and take his chances in jail. For the first time in a long time, he was going to do as he was told. Almost.

'Get down on your knees!' she yelled.

'I'd rather not.'

His response appeared to throw her off track.

'Listen dipshit, I'm a police officer pointing a gun at your chest, and you're a murder suspect under arrest. You'll do as you're told.'

'I didn't kill anyone. You're wasting your time chasing the wrong guy.'

She huffed a sarcastic laugh. 'Want to know how many times I've heard that same bullshit from proven killers?'

'More than a few I'm guessing.'

'Well, you'd guess right, genius. Now do as you're told and get down on your knees.'

Drayce smiled. He liked her already.

Sirens bellowed from somewhere in the distance, getting closer. It wouldn't be long before the alleyway was swarming with guns and badges.

'Listen,' he said. 'I'm not running anymore, and I will come quietly, but I don't kneel for anyone.' He glanced over his right shoulder towards the mouth of the alleyway, directly towards the sound of the approaching police cars. Any second now, he thought. They must only be a couple of streets away. He turned back to face the detective. 'So if you want to wait until those sirens get here before you come any closer, that's fine. But I'm not kneeling. Not now, not ever.'

Her expression told him she'd thought through everything he'd just said, relenting to the fact his mind would not be changed. She appeared comfortable with his non-compliance, knowing she wouldn't have to cover him with that pistol alone for much longer.

Drayce heard tyres screech to a halt behind him. The detective's head turned slightly towards the mouth of the alleyway. He didn't turn around to look, but he could tell her backup had arrived. He tensed his arms and shoulders, prepared for a bit of rough handling. Kneeling or not, it was time for the handcuffs to come out.

Except something was wrong. The detective's expression didn't paint the picture of help having arrived. The shock on her face slowly turned to fear as the muzzle of her gun pivoted sideways towards the mouth of the alleyway.

Drayce turned around to see what the detective was pointing her gun at. The vehicle was a blue Toyota Previa: a seven-seater minivan used predominantly by soccer mums to ferry their kids around. Some of the body-work had faded to a mint-green colour, the edges around the wheel arches showing signs of rust. The paintwork on both the roof and the hood had faded in the sun over time. There were dents so big Drayce could make them out even from twenty feet away. The bumpers were black plastic and they were badly scuffed. It was perhaps the least intimidating car on planet earth, under normal circumstances.

But these weren't normal circumstances.

Parked side-on to the alleyway with the sliding door wide open, a guy in the back caught Drayce's eye. He was sitting on the bare metal floor, the rear seats having been ripped out. He had the sliding door jammed open with his foot so it wouldn't shut in front of him and block his view, which is the last thing this guy would want, considering he was aiming a sub-machine gun into the alleyway.

Another two men leaned into view, either side of him, holding similar looking weapons. Drayce thought they looked familiar. Something about their clothing registered in his memory, triggering alarm bells.

A yellow jacket and a blue bandana.

He examined the guy in the middle again, the leader of the four would-be robbers from the previous day, smiling over his sub-machine gun. His lips dished an order out. Goldtooth was in the driver's seat. He peered over his shoulder to respond. The three in the back all nodded their heads.

Drayce didn't move a muscle.

Goldtooth stamped on the throttle and swung the Toyota into the alleyway. Drayce leapt back against the fence to get out of its path. It skidded to a stop, the wide-open door lined up directly in front of him.

Drayce stared down the barrel of a gun.

A Taser appeared over the leader's head, two red dots dancing around Drayce's chest. A loud pop resonated in his ears a split second before he felt two razor-sharp punches in his chest, right in the middle of the gap between his jacket lapels, the barbs puncturing through his T-shirt and embedding themselves in his skin.

He collapsed on one knee, partially paralysed by the electric current. Realising two barbs weren't going to be enough to deal with a man of Drayce's size and strength, Yellow Jacket shot him again with the Taser, this time in his hip and thigh. With the current now passing through a much larger portion of his muscle mass, Drayce was left with no choice but to collapse to the ground with a *thud*.

Hands were on him in seconds, hooking his arms and dragging him to the vehicle. He tried to fight them off, but his body wouldn't work. The Taser was scrambling his central nervous system, blocking the message from his brain to his limbs, turning him into a rigid, motionless, defenceless being. He didn't even feel his shins clatter against the sharp edge of the minivan floor, the hard metal scraping down the bone as it took all three men to drag him in.

A bullet hit the front windscreen. Goldtooth returned fire at the detective a split second later, the exchange nothing more than muffled background noise to Drayce, amidst the electric agony pulsing through him in waves, as though his nerve endings were being scalded with boiling water. His captors pinned him face down to the floor of the minivan with their hands and knees. Blue light flickered through the back window. Voices barked at each other above Drayce's head, panicking about the arrival of the detective's backup.

Goldtooth accelerated away with the side door still wide open. They flew down the alleyway, bullets clipping the bodywork as the red-haired detective opened fire. Drayce began to take stock of his situation once he'd stopped shuddering with convulsions. They were moving at speed, Goldtooth making overtakes and hitting corners far faster than the vehicle was designed for. Wind howled through the open door. Drayce growled through clenched teeth as his face rattled against the metal floor, like a captured lion waking up from sedation.

The men holding him down stunk of bad breath and body odour. Drayce observed a bag of plastic cable ties on the floor at the back of the vehicle, plainly to be used to restrain him fully. He heard sirens behind them as the cops gave pursuit through the Vegas streets. One of the men kneeling on him yelled at Goldtooth to go faster, but judging by the way they were all being thrown around inside that cramped space, Drayce didn't think it was possible.

The worst of the pain had stopped now an electrical current was no longer passing through his central nervous system. Exhausted from the ordeal, he could feel the four giant barbs embedded in his chest being pushed deeper as he was pinned to the floor face down. It took all his discipline, but he managed to relax from head to toe, as though he was completely out of it: a limp, lifeless mess, with no fight left in him. He felt one of them climb off him – Yellow Jacket, reaching for the cable ties.

Mistake.

Drayce came alive, hurtling up and snapping the wires trailing from his chest and hips. He spun onto his back, grabbing hold of the leader and Blue Bandana by their throats. They clawed at his hands, desperately trying to create room to breathe. Behind them, Yellow Jacket saw the melee, ignored the cable ties, and pulled the Taser's trigger. Drayce heard a loud crackle of electricity, a worried look manifesting in Yellow Jacket's eyes as he wondered why it wasn't having the same effect as before.

In an explosive, violent shove, Drayce threw the two men at Yellow Jacket, the three of them cracking the back window before collapsing to the floor in a heap. Amidst the chaos of tangled limbs, they all reached for their guns. With the threat ramping up, Drayce drew the pistol from his own waistline, racked the slide, and took aim. Everything slowed down. He monitored their reaction, hoping they'd see sense. The leader had his hands on the grip of his sub-machine gun, Blue Bandana his, Yellow Jacket pulling a pistol, trying to aim it past his two friends. None of them were backing down. The sub-machine guns swung up on aim, past the point of no return.

Drayce had no choice.

He double tapped each of them in the head, their bodies slumping lifelessly, guns clattering harmlessly onto the metal floor. He got to his knees, leaned between the two front seats, and pressed his pistol to the side of Goldtooth's head. The hot barrel made the guy wince.

'How many cop cars are following us?' Drayce asked, pushing the weapon harder against his head to remind him of the situation he was in.

'None,' Goldtooth replied, shakily. 'We lost them a few streets back.'

Drayce scanned the road. 'Where are we?'

'Lewis Ave. Downtown.'

'Pull over. Right there, next to that yellow fire hydrant.'

Goldtooth did as he was told. As soon as the vehicle was stationary, Drayce did a quick check of the surrounding area and, happy there was no police presence, turned his attention back to the driver.

'Turn off the engine and hand me the key.'

Goldtooth's nerves caused a delay as he fumbled with it, his jittery fingers struggling to take hold. When he finally pulled it free from the ignition, he handed it over, and in exchange, Drayce tossed two zip-tie restraints into his lap from the bag in the back.

'Tie your wrists to the steering wheel,' he ordered.

Only once Goldtooth was properly restrained did Drayce lower the pistol. He dropped the magazine, racked the slide to eject the chambered round, then thumbed it into the top of the magazine. He pulled the trigger to ease the springs, then replaced the magazine into the grip of the weapon. With the pistol once again in a safe condition, he tucked it back into the waistline of his trousers and covered the grip by pulling his T-shirt down. He collected the discharged casings, jumped out onto the pavement, opened the driver's door, and checked the plastic ties. Too much room left. He pulled them as tight as he could.

'Shit, man!' Goldtooth exclaimed. 'The fuck you doing? That hurts!'

'Consider yourself lucky. Your friends back there would give anything to feel the pain you're in.'

Goldtooth glanced in the mirror. The whining stopped.

Drayce watched the streets. Other than the occasional passing vehicle, it was quiet, which meant he could probably do this next bit without drawing attention. He noted a deserted alleyway leading off from where the hydrant sat: a good escape route if he needed to vanish quickly.

'I guess you know what happens now,' he said. A stubborn face glared back at him. 'Or maybe not. In which case I'll give you a hint.'

He started moving before he'd even finished the sentence, hooking his left fist into Goldtooth's solar plexus, soft and flabby against his knuckles. The air left Goldtooth's lungs with a *whoof*, the breakfast vacating his stomach with a *splash*. It made a horrible mess of the dashboard.

'That's as friendly as I'm going to be from now on,' Drayce said. Goldtooth heaved as he tried to get his breath back, his broken ribs from their earlier encounter now a shattered mess. 'Explain to me what's going on.'

'Fuck... You.'

Drayce hit him again, causing him to cough so violently it sounded as though he was going to tear his abdomen.

'One of your gang put an AirTag on my vehicle,' Drayce said. 'Now you've kidnapped me off the street, mid-arrest. What's going on?'

'Suck a dick, *puta*!'

The next punch was a straight right to a different section of his ribcage, a *crack* resonating under the force of the blow.

'I can carry on like this for a long time, but I don't want to. What I want is for you to tell me who tasked you to put that tracker on my ride and grab me off the street, and why.'

Goldtooth fought to control his breathing. 'I can't… they'd kill me.'

Tears ran down his cheeks. A pang of empathy caught Drayce by surprise, but he shrugged it off and hit Goldtooth again, same place as last time. Breathing was becoming a serious issue for him. A couple more hits and he'd explain everything.

Drayce froze mid-punch, his fist paralysed.

A black Impala screeched onto the street.

–

'There he is!' Miguel said, pointing at the gringo over the top of the steering wheel.

'Keep it smooth,' Gabriel told him as he aimed the AR15 through his open window. 'I'll drill that piece of shit from here.'

The white boy saw the gun aimed his way and ran for the alleyway. Gabriel tracked him with his carbine as he pulled the trigger, bullets spitting from the muzzle. But the big man went out of sight before a round landed, the last of Gabriel's shots clipping the corner of the wall he'd just vanished behind.

'Fuck!' Gabriel shouted. 'Get us over there. We can go after him: it's wide enough for this car.'

Miguel accelerated past the Toyota and swerved hard into the mouth of the alley, the back end of the Impala swinging wide, clipping a row of dustbins before deflecting to the other side where it glanced off a telegraph pole. As Miguel straightened it out, Gabriel saw their target thirty metres ahead, running hard, glancing over his shoulder every few bounds.

'Put your foot down!' Gabriel roared, his blood up, red mist descending. 'He ain't getting away from us this time.'

Gabriel felt his back press into his seat as Miguel floored it, rapidly closing the distance between them and their target. Gabriel rested his AR's railing on the dashboard, flicked the setting to full-auto, and fired through the windscreen. The first bullet punched a hole in the glass that the others quickly followed through, a maze of cracks snaking out from its centre. His target dodged from side to side, zig-zagging his way down the alley, the sparks of Gabriel's rounds flinging up from the concrete as they ricocheted past him. The AR bucked relentlessly as it cycled through the magazine, the muzzle spitting flames through the hole in the windscreen that the shots had created, tiny shards of glass spraying back at Gabriel as it disintegrated, forcing him to close his eyes, his aim becoming worse as a result. Miguel held an arm up, protecting his eyes so he could still see to drive. Within seconds the magazine went empty, the bolt locking back on an open breech. Gabriel lowered the weapon and checked ahead.

Their target was still on the move.

'*Puta madre!*' Gabriel yelled. He kept his eye on their target as he reloaded. 'Run this piece of shit over,' he told Miguel. 'He's blocked on both sides by walls and fences; he's got nowhere to go.'

Miguel selected a lower gear and pressed his foot all the way to the floor. They lurched forwards, hurtling towards the gringo. Raul had put himself in the middle of the backseats, a hand on the driver's and front passenger's headrests, leaning forwards with a big grin on his face as he stared through the cracked windscreen.

'Smash that *puta* to pieces, Miguel,' Raul said with glee.

The Impala's front grill hurtled towards the man they were chasing, the gap closing every second.

Fifteen metres.

Ten.

Five.

Miguel held the steering wheel rock steady and closed his eyes, bracing for the impact.

—

Drayce heard the gearbox kick down, the exhausts barking loudly as the vehicle raced after him even faster than before. He didn't need to look over his shoulder to see what was happening. They had failed in their efforts to shoot a moving target while on the move themselves, and now they were simplifying their tactics. The ground shook, the vehicle's engine roaring as it rocketed towards him like a missile. Drayce had seconds before he was flattened.

He glanced at a wall to his right, locked eyes on the lip, and darted towards it, leaping as high as he could. The ball of his right foot gave enough purchase on the breeze block to catapult his fingertips within reach of the top. The sicarios swerved after him in an obvious attempt to crush him against the wall. He clamped onto its top with both hands, pulled himself up, and lifted his legs as high as he could to clear his limbs of the speeding motor.

Sparks flew as the Impala collided with the breeze block and scraped its far side along the wall, its roof missing Drayce by mere inches as it passed underneath him. Capitalising on his momentum, he swung his legs up and over the wall, disappearing out of sight on the other side.

–

'Did we get him?' Raul asked, craning his neck out the back window, no doubt hoping to see the gringo's mangled body splattered in the alleyway. 'Yo! Did we get him or what?'

'Nah, we missed him,' Miguel replied with a shake of his head. 'Motherfucker moves like a gazelle.' He glanced at Gabriel. 'You want to go back for him?'

The sound of sirens a few streets away answered the question, but Gabriel responded anyway. 'Keep driving. Too much heat to stick around.'

Miguel nodded as he flew the Impala out of the alleyway at the opposite end and joined East Bridger Ave at speed, tyres screeching as he took a left and then a right, racing up 10th Street away from the sound of the rapidly increasing presence of law enforcement.

Gabriel noticed the sound of his breathing, fast and heavy, face hot with anger, his heart thumping in his chest in the aftermath of the adrenaline dump. He breathed deeply to help calm himself, his eyes never leaving the rear-view mirror, staring hard in the direction the Englishman had run, his knuckles white as he throttled the grip of his AR. 'We'll catch up with him soon enough.'

19

Naomi walked under the Stars and Stripes, which waved proudly in the desert breeze from its position at the top of the flagpole, and resisted the urge to kick open the entrance doors to the Las Vegas Metropolitan Police Department headquarters. She stomped up the stairs to her office and snatched the jug of hot coffee from the percolator stand, its tar-black liquid sloshing inside as she hurriedly poured herself a cup. Once empty, she refilled it, replaced the jug, and took a seat at her desk.

She shared her office with a dozen other detectives, most of whom were also filtering through the doors with solemn faces after losing their murder suspect. It was your typical squad room, full of your typical cop stuff. The coffee supply was substantial because they consumed it in the way athletes did water. At one end of the room the framed commendations on the walls were mixed with cut-outs from both local and national newspapers, reporting on various big cases they'd solved. At the other end was a cork board, pinned to which were printouts with images that represented misdemeanours committed by team members. If you found yourself depicted on that board, it meant you'd done something stupid that needed ridiculing. For the perpetrator, it acted as a light hearted reminder of their stupidity; for the team, it was a source of amusement and morale. On the board now was a cartoon of a uniformed cop running after a suspect, coffee and doughnut in hand as he struggled to keep up, along with a photograph of a squad car, crushed into a cube after being written off in a clumsy crash during a pursuit.

The room was a big, open-plan space, without any partitions between the desks. The type of homicide crimes Naomi and her team took on, needed fast-moving, dynamic investigations, where communication was essential and time of the essence. They didn't want to be blocked off from their colleagues. They needed to be able to see one another, and shout instructions at one another, and throw memory sticks and mobile phones and other devices across desks between one another. It wasn't a cold case department, where they might seek solitude for days or weeks on end, cocooned from the world behind their desks while they examined old case files and forensic reports. Far from it. The team Naomi was a part of dealt with the golden hour of a murder investigation: the time when evidence was fresh and the killer was most likely to be caught.

Without question, Naomi loved her job. The only downside was most murders were committed at night, which meant she could be called in to work at any hour, just as she had at 5:00 a.m. that morning, waking her from her much needed slumber. She knew herself to be many things, but a morning person was definitively not one of them.

Kicking off her shoes, she lifted a foot to examine where it felt as though she had a blister coming. An angry red patch had formed on her heel, the skin ballooning. Cursing the shoes she'd chosen in her rush to get ready, she threw them under her desk, took a pair of black trainers out of her bottom drawer – kept for just this sort of emergency – and slipped them on instead.

The doors to the office crashed open. Melvin walked in with a group of colleagues. He took off his suit jacket, threw it over the back of his chair, and glanced at Naomi. The first sound to pass his lips wasn't a word, it was more of a grunt, as though expelling some of the tension from the chase across Vegas they'd just lost.

'What a morning,' he said. 'I wonder what else can go wrong today.'

Naomi stood up, walked over to where he was standing, and slapped him across the back of his head. The sound echoed across the room, like a hardback book had landed from a great height onto polished wooden floorboards.

'What the hell?' Melvin said, rubbing the back of his head, a pained expression on his face.

'Don't even think about acting stupid with me. You know exactly what you've done to deserve it. You know I hate that nickname.'

'Jeez. It's only a joke. You could have just said something.'

'I find interactive teaching methods last longer. And don't be such a pussy. You'll need to toughen up if we're going to get back on the trail of Adriana Garcia's killer.'

As she collapsed back into her chair, she heard someone call out from across the room.

'Speaking of which, why don't you explain to everyone how you lost a suspect who you had cornered at gunpoint in an alleyway. How does that even happen?'

Naomi didn't need to turn her head to know who'd spoken. The voice belonged to Detective Nicolas Wilson. He was sat at his desk, which Naomi had made sure was on the other side of the room to hers. He leant back in his chair, put his feet on the table, an arrogant smile spread across his weathered, unshaven face. His shaggy grey hair appeared to have never been washed, as did his clothes: a brown suit and tie over a white shirt, dappled with stains, the most obvious of which were the patches of yellow sweat marks peeking out from underneath his armpits. He was a worthless member of the team in Naomi's opinion, but he certainly had a high opinion of himself. The two printouts currently pinned to the cork board were inspired by his ineptitude. In her book, he couldn't be trusted. He was always out to try and make himself look good to the commanders, often at detriment to his colleagues. He didn't care about anyone but himself. Not the victims; not the community. It was all about him and his precious career. Naomi was the exact opposite: she couldn't care less about her career. It was all about the job for her, which she did for the victims and their families, no one else. Consequently, she had no time for Wilson, and on most days had the energy and self-restraint to ignore his ignorant jibes.

Today wasn't one of those days.

She crossed the room before he could even get his feet off the desk.

'First of all, it's whom,' she hissed. 'Secondly, what on earth would you know about what happened in that alleyway?' She leaned over his desk, her lips mere inches from his dumbfounded face; she could smell a mixture of beer and gum disease on his breath. 'At least I was right on his tail. Where were you? At the back of the pursuit the whole time. Staying safe, like always, huh Wilson?'

Wilson's brain finally kicked into gear. 'Right on his tail? I seem to remember you were the last officer to turn up to the casino, and then, by some stroke of luck, the guy literally lands in your lap.' An arrogant smirk materialised off the back of that last word. 'And you still couldn't get the guy in handcuffs.'

Naomi reached for his lapel, tempted to collar-choke the son of a bitch.

'Ocean! What in God's name is going on in here?'

Naomi reined her hands in and turned around to face their boss: Sergeant John Pikard. He was stood in the doorway to his office, which opened out into the main squad room. He only just fit within the frame, but not because of his height. He was only five foot three inches tall, but he had to buy the biggest belts he could find, and still had to buckle them on the hole closest to the end. It was a running joke on the team because all he ever ate at work was salad. Naomi struggled to imagine what he must eat at home.

'I...' Naomi uttered. 'I was just...'

'About to assault one of my detectives by the look of it.' He stepped to one side and held the door open. 'In my office. Now.'

She trudged across the room through a gauntlet of smirks and sniggers. Pikard swung the door shut behind her, then sat down at his desk. Naomi stayed standing.

'Take a seat,' Pikard told her.

'I'd rather not.'

'Excuse me?'

'I have a busy day ahead. We've got a suspect to track down. I don't have time to sit around.'

'But you do have time to bicker with a colleague?'

Naomi sighed. 'Just say what you have to say and let me get on with my job.'

Pikard stiffened. If it had come from anyone else, he'd have hit the roof; from Naomi, he was accustomed to it. They all were. Naomi knew he valued her as an investigator too much to ever contemplate kicking her off the team. Not that he would ever admit it.

'Let's get one thing straight,' he said. 'I only put up with your bullshit attitude because you get results, but when you let your anger get the better of you and go to put hands on other team members, you put me a step closer to kicking you back downstairs where you can be someone else's problem while you walk a beat in uniform.'

Naomi kept her mouth shut.

'Got it?' Pikard asked.

She reluctantly dragged her three-letter reply past her lips. 'Yes.'

Pikard settled. 'How are you after this morning?'

'Fine.'

'You sure? You don't need to put on the tough-gal act with me.'

'I said I'm fine. He got away. What more is there to say?'

Pikard nodded. 'Remind me how this guy came to our attention.'

'One of the neighbours heard a commotion late last night. When he looks out, he sees our victim standing on her doorstep, pointing a gun at some guy. He was big and she clearly felt threatened by him and wanted him to leave, which he does, somewhat reluctantly in our witness's opinion. Then another neighbour, who suffers from insomnia, hears two loud gunshots in the middle of the night. She's certain they came from the direction of number eight, so she calls 911.

'When units arrive on scene, they find the front door to number eight locked, and after containing the building, gain entry from an insecure back door, smashed open prior to their arrival, presumably by the offender. They search the apartment and find our victim in her bed, two bullet wounds to her head, and no sign of any suspects. Then we get called out to begin the investigation and I speak to the neighbour who saw the argument on our victim's doorstep. He starts to give me a description of the guy, then fumbles his words and points to the crowd at the edge of the crime scene. He tells me the guy's standing right there, so I call out to the team, and as soon as we move towards him, he turns and runs.'

'So if he's our guy, that means he came back to the murder scene the morning after committing the crime, and just stands there watching the investigation play out. What kind of a crazy son of a bitch does that?'

'The same kind who's willing to shoot a defenceless woman dead in her own bed. We've had it before. Arsonists and murderers wanting to see the police activity in the immediate aftermath of their crimes. They get a kick out of it.'

'Sure, with the serial killers, and the perverts. But this doesn't feel like that. No struggle, not woken up by the killer to hear her emotional final words, just two bullet wounds to the head while she sleeps. I dunno, Naomi. That sounds more like a professional hit than a passionate one.'

'Maybe,' she conceded. 'But one way or another we need to track this guy down and bring him in for questioning.'

'Agreed. Where d'you wanna start?'

'I'll need the footage checked from every camera, both public and private, that he would have passed on the route he took from Adriana's street to the alleyway where I lost him.'

'Already being done. I've got a dozen cops from the Area Command combing that route as we speak.'

'Good. That should give us a decent image of him if we decide to go public.'

'Where do you think he made the call to get picked up? Melvin said he escaped in some Toyota full of other gangbangers.'

'He's not a gangbanger, John. The guy's British, I think. Maybe Australian.'

'How the hell do you know that?'

'I talked to him.'

Pikard's eyes widened. 'You've spoken to our suspect?'

'Yeah, in the alleyway.'

'What did he say?'

'That he didn't kill anyone, and would come quietly but wasn't going to kneel for me. And he didn't escape with those gang members. He was abducted by them.'

'You get a look at them?'

'A bit, but it all happened so fast. From their tats they looked like they were with Barrio Naked City.'

'You remember them from your time on the Gangs Vice Bureau?'

'You bet I do. They're a fearsome bunch. Didn't recognise this group, but I've been out of it for a few years. Faces change quickly in that game. Only a select few survive long enough to be OGs.'

'What are your thoughts regarding their motive for grabbing this British guy at gunpoint?'

'My instinct tells me it was probably revenge for Adriana's murder. Maybe she was related to someone in the gang, or was dating someone in the gang, and they wanted to get hold of him and exact their revenge before we arrested him.'

'Maybe. Ballsy move though, with so many cops around.'

'Very.'

'We need to find that Toyota and ID these gangsters ASAP, before they bury our suspect out in the desert.'

'Agreed.'

Pikard reached for the phone on his desk. 'I'll put a call through to your old unit. It seems we might need to work together on this one. I'm getting the sickly feeling something bad is going down in our city.'

'Me too. Not like we shouldn't be used to it though. They don't call it Sin City for nothing.'

Before Pikard had even pressed the first button, the phone rang.

'If this is the Gangs Vice Bureau calling me,' he said, 'I'll be spooked.'

Naomi smiled. 'You not believe in coincidences?'

'No such thing.'

He put the phone to his ear, said hello, but then didn't say a whole lot else. He just listened. Then there were some *mmms*, and *ohs*, and other noises that told Naomi he was hearing something both surprising and pleasing. After a minute, he said, 'Wait where you are. I'm sending someone to you.'

'Who was that?' Naomi asked once the call ended.

'Area Command. They've found a Toyota Previa on Lewis Ave.'

'Let me guess: it's been bleach-bombed and abandoned?'

'Far from it. There are three dead Barrio City gangsters in the back, and a driver who's been beaten to a pulp, with his wrists tied to the steering wheel.'

'Wow.'

'That's exactly what I just said in my mind. What in the name of all that's holy is going on here? We get a murder, a positive ID on the suspect, and then the kidnapping of that suspect all before my first coffee of the day. And now the kidnappers' car turns up with three of them dead. Who the hell is this guy you were chasing? I mean, what type of a man can win that kind of a fight, when he's outnumbered four to one against a gang of armed criminals?'

Naomi stood up and marched out of the office. She'd had enough of the talking; time for some action.

'Where you going?' Pikard yelled after her.

'Lewis Ave,' she called back. 'I have a feeling the survivor might be able to answer your last question.'

20

Drayce peered over his shoulder to check for cops. He was on Charleston Boulevard, heading east. A young couple crossed his path as they approached a Home Depot. The woman gave him a funny look, wary and disapproving. Her eyes focused on his chest, reminding him of the four barbs from the Taser. He inspected them: little patches of blood had spread out from each wound. Probably a good idea to get those out, he thought. He'd need a change of clothes anyway, now he was on the run.

He bought some alcohol wipes and plasters from a drug store and continued to a clothing store further along the boulevard. Before going inside, he walked to the alleyway at the back where he was out of sight of the road and the sidewalks, checked for cameras, and removed the pistol from his waistline. Being careful not to get blood on it, he used his T-shirt to remove his fingerprints, just in case circumstances dictated he couldn't return to collect it. Happy it couldn't be traced back to him, he stuffed it out of sight in a dumpster, threw in the used bullet casings he'd collected from the Toyota, and left the alleyway.

Drayce didn't want to stroll in with a firearm tucked into his trousers. Staff in clothing stores often inspected a customer's waistline the moment they walked in, to help judge what they'd try to sell them. If a gun caught their eye, it might elicit a few questions. Maybe even a 911 call. Best to avoid that.

He covered the bloodstains with his jacket, grabbed a pair of navy chinos, a light blue shirt and a dark blue baseball cap, then disappeared into a changing cubicle. He pulled the barbs out, stripped off his clothes, and cleaned the puncture wounds to his torso, hip and thigh. Once he was satisfied they wouldn't get infected, he slapped plasters over them and dressed in his new clothes. The barbs were rolled into his old T-shirt and jeans, which he bungled under his arm as he walked out of the cubicle to pay.

He left the store confident he had the appearance of a different person, dumped his old T-shirt and jeans in a bin, but kept hold of his undamaged ThruDark jacket, an essential garment after sunset. He walked up the street and ducked into a pancake house. After the morning he'd had, he needed food and coffee.

He found an empty booth in the back corner that was perfect: only a couple of steps to the kitchen door, which led to a rear exit – useful if circumstances demanded he leave quickly and quietly out the back. He perched himself on the edge of the vinyl-covered seat with a view of the entrance and decided not to scoot across to the window, where he wouldn't be able to get to his feet in a hurry if needed.

The waiter was on the ball; a steaming black cup of Joe was placed in front of Drayce in no time at all. First impressions were good: the steam told him it was hot enough, and the colour told him it was strong enough. As the liquid settled, he noticed his reflection in the jet-black surface. A worried face stared back at him.

His nerves made the surface of the coffee tremble. He drank quickly, half a cup enough to still the tremors.

Thoughts spun furiously in his head. In the heat of the chase, he'd been calm, his mind focused. In the back of the minivan, held captive by those villains, the need to concentrate on his survival had kept the panic at bay. But now that he'd escaped the initial threat and had time to think things through, anxiety crept in. He rubbed his eyes, tired from the adrenaline, pulled his necklace out from underneath his shirt and held the locket. Several dangerous questions revolved in his mind, like bullets in a spinning cylinder during a game of Russian roulette.

Who are these people coming after me? My interactions with Adriana were momentary at best. We spoke a handful of words, she pointed her gun at me, and I left. How could that possibly give these people a reason to hunt me down?

Drayce considered how deep Nelson was involved in this mess. After all, he was the one who had provided Drayce with the number that had thrown him headfirst into this carnage. Was Nelson somehow involved with the people who had killed Adriana? Drayce knew the Mexican *federales* had a reputation for being infested with corrupt officers. Did Nelson have ties to the people who were coming after Drayce? Had he set him up for some reason?

Drayce took out his phone and tried calling Nelson, wanting to put some pressure on him with questions about his motivation for pushing Drayce to take this job on. But there was no answer. Drayce put his phone down and rubbed his face with both hands.

If he wanted to answer these questions, he knew he needed to work out why Adriana was killed. But how was he supposed to do that whilst on the run from the police, in a foreign city, having to stay low at every available opportunity?

He drank the second half of his coffee, feeling overwhelmed by the situation, and decided to call Carlos. No answer. Drayce was worried about him. Had these people gone after Adriana's father as well as her? He thought about the AirTag on his truck. Did that lead them to her? He'd parked a distance from her address, but it would have narrowed down their search area considerably.

Feeling overwhelmed with guilt that he may have unintentionally helped Adriana's murderers find her, he waved the waitress over for a refill and a food order. He'd need the energy for the work he planned to put in: gathering clues; identifying leads; examining evidence. He had to find her killers and make them pay. It was the least he owed her.

Three cups of coffee and two breakfast sandwiches later, he decided to start by visiting Bunnies: Adriana's last known place of work.

He searched for the address on his phone and discovered it was a good distance across town. Knowing he was vulnerable to being spotted on foot, the idea of getting his rental vehicle back sounded appealing, but it was parked just a couple of streets away from the murder scene, which would still be swarming with cops. He tried to focus on the positives, such as the fact the police hadn't seen him get out of the Expedition, and with no cameras covering the area where he'd parked it, it meant the cops had no witnesses or other evidence to link him to it, meaning they wouldn't even have it on their radar. As a result, he knew it should still be parked exactly where he'd left it, safe and sound, waiting for him to return and collect it. If he could get to it without being seen, he had himself a set of wheels.

Drayce froze.

A big silver Ford Interceptor with bull bars fixed to the front grill pulled into the pancake house's parking lot. Drayce didn't need to inspect the livery to know who was in the vehicle: Nevada Highway Patrol. The driver and front passenger would both have Glock .40s on their belts, loaded and made ready, along with AR15s and combat shotguns within easy reach, with full mags of 5.56 ammunition and a couple of dozen twelve-gauge cartridges containing solid lead slugs.

Drayce held his breath.

A second NHP vehicle pulled in after the big Ford, just a few seconds behind, smaller, faster, and lighter than the first. A Dodge Charger, Drayce knew. It had dark blue bodywork with yellow State Trooper badges. Both drivers were too calm and collected for this to be part of an arrest strategy. Rather than screeching up in a cloud of tyre smoke, they took their time finding spaces and backed their motors up in between the lines, all nice and tidy. Meeting up for coffee, Drayce guessed.

He released his breath.

As the troopers climbed out of their motors and began the usual shit talking and chain yanking amongst themselves, Drayce worked it out. These guys were law enforcement, but they weren't LVMPD, who had chased Drayce across Vegas. They would share stuff with other departments and ask them to keep an eye out for their suspect, of course, but that would come later. They wouldn't be too quick to shout to another department about how they'd lost a murder suspect; that sort of thing was embarrassing. The guys approaching the pancake house probably knew nothing about a well-built, six-foot-six murder suspect on the run in the city. They'd just met up in Vegas for their morning coffee. Nothing to worry about.

Still, Drayce thought as he grabbed his jacket and stood up from the booth. *Probably best if I don't hang around to test that theory.*

As the troopers took off their hats and sunglasses and walked through the front entrance, Drayce had already cleared the kitchen and was out on foot in the rear alleyway. He slipped his jacket on, recovered the pistol from the dumpster, tucked it back into his trousers, and looped around to the sidewalk, tilting his cap down. His back to the pancake house windows, he made eye contact with no one as he walked away, planning precisely how he was going to get his Expedition back safely.

21

Naomi pulled onto Lewis Ave and parked at the back of a long line of patrol cars. There must have been a dozen scattered around the street, some still with their light bars flashing blue and red, with most of the cops out on foot, just standing around, not doing a great deal. Naomi sighed, climbed out of her motor, and walked up to the uniforms who were crowding the Toyota. She scanned faces for someone she recognised.

A big recruitment drive over the past few years meant there were a lot of newbies in the department these days. To Naomi, they had the fresh young faces of kids who should still be in school. She was only thirty-five, but stood amongst these twenty-somethings, she'd never felt older.

'Who's in charge here?' she called out to the sea of polished boots, pressed uniforms and shiny body armour, all of which presented as though it had come straight out the packaging that morning. They turned to face her with blank expressions, but she didn't repeat herself. Instead, she simply pulled open her jacket, revealing the detective badge clipped to her belt, and the Colt holstered to her hip.

'Sergeant Hamilton, ma'am,' one of the officers said.

Great, Naomi thought. *For the second time today, someone thinks I look old enough to be called ma'am.*

The officer who'd spoken fumbled with a roll of scene tape, his head swivelling left to right as he tried to decide where the cordon should go. He had the soft complexion of a boy so young he hadn't started shaving.

'Fifty metres,' Naomi said.

'What's that, m—'

'Don't you dare call me ma'am a second time.' She pointed her finger at him. 'I've got at least ten years before you have any right to use that word to refer to me. And I said fifty metres, everywhere the public have access, which means Lewis Ave in both directions, and includes this alleyway here.' Her finger moved to where it began at a yellow fire hydrant. 'Block the road with patrol cars, the pavements and alleyway with scene tape, and don't let anyone through unless I say you can. Got it?'

The officer nodded and scurried off. The rest of the group stayed where they were, mesmerised by the angry detective.

'Where's Sergeant Hamilton?' Naomi asked.

Her expression made it clear she didn't want to ask again.

'I'm right here,' came a voice through the crowd of officers, who parted to allow the sergeant through.

Naomi knew Sergeant Joshua Hamilton well. He was a good man: hardworking and conscientious. An old sweat with eighteen years of service, he'd spent his entire career with a firm moral code. He might have been the only person at the scene she had respect for, but that didn't mean this encounter would be friendly. They rarely were when Naomi was working a case.

As Hamilton cleared the crowd, his expression matched the scowl on Naomi's face. He'd experienced her temper more than a few times.

'I thought that was your voice, Naomi,' Hamilton said. 'Pikard called back to tell me you were coming, and I've had a smile on my face this big ever since.'

Naomi gazed past his thick black moustache to his mouth. Whatever that shape was, it certainly wasn't a smile.

'Why isn't a cordon set up yet?' she asked.

'We were just...'

'Not quickly enough you weren't. Where's my suspect?'

'The survivor's in a patrol car.'

'Survivor?' The disapproval in her voice was blatant. 'Really?'

'I'd say that's an apt description, considering what happened to his friends.'

'Whatever. From here on out, he'll be referred to as a suspect. *My* suspect. Where is he?'

'Over there.' Hamilton pointed to a lone patrol car across the street.

Naomi marched in its direction and Hamilton followed, his legs struggling to keep up with her pace.

'Has he said anything?' she asked.

'Not a word. You know how it is with the gangs. They always keep their mouths shut.'

'What about IDs?'

'None have any on them, so we won't know who they are until we've run their prints and DNA through the system.'

'Makes sense. Wouldn't be smart to carry anything with your name and address on if you were planning to abduct another criminal.'

'You know who he is yet?'

'Not yet,' Naomi snapped, not wanting to discuss the man she'd let get away. 'What about the three bodies? What do we know about them?'

'Nothing yet. We've locked the vehicle down for forensics, and it's not as though we can go through mug shots to ID them. Their wounds are devastating. They were all shot in the face twice, and it looks like the second round passed through the entry wound that the first created. That means a double tap.'

'I know what that means,' Naomi said as they reached the other side of the street.

'Well then, *Detective*, you'll also know it means we're dealing with a serious threat here. This suspect of yours was outnumbered four to one when he was taken, and just minutes later he shot three of them dead and beat the fourth to a pulp. As soon as you get any leads, we need to know about them, for the safety of my officers out there looking for this guy.'

Naomi opened the rear door of the patrol car and climbed inside next to the suspect. He was curled up on the other side of the seat, clutching his ribs, clearly in pain. She turned back to Hamilton. 'You'll be told what you need to know, when you need to know it.'

She slammed the door shut, leaving Hamilton muttering angrily on the sidewalk, and stared at the two uniformed cops in the front seats. She caught the eye of the driver in the rear-view mirror and flashed her badge.

'I need to speak to my suspect in private,' she said with authority.

'Yes, ma'am,' the driver replied.

Goddamn kids, Naomi thought, as they both climbed out and shut their doors behind them, sealing her in with her suspect.

To begin with, she didn't move a muscle, and neither did the suspect. The stillness was palpable; the silence intense. She wanted him to feel the weight of her presence, so she just sat there, jacket swept to the side, not saying a word, her shiny detective's badge and Colt making the introduction for her. The world outside was nothing more than a series of muffled, indecipherable noises, vibrating through the glass and bodywork. The engine was off, which meant there was no air blowing through the vents. Consequently, it was warm in there, which made it a little claustrophobic, especially for a man restrained in his seat with his hands cuffed behind his back, staring into the eyes of a thirty-year prison sentence.

Good, Naomi thought. *I want him uncomfortable.*

He was younger than she'd expected: nineteen, maybe twenty – a man, but only just. Not many gang members survived to see old age, but this kid was kidnapping people at gunpoint uncommonly early in his career. He stunk as though he hadn't showered in a month. Big round droplets of sweat carved a route down his face and dripped off his jawline. Naomi knew this was the product of fear, not heat. It was stuffy in there, but it wasn't hot enough to make a Barrio City gangster in a T-shirt sweat. This guy lived in a shitty part of the desert, probably in a rundown apartment with no air conditioning. He'd be accustomed to heat, familiar with discomfort, but he hadn't been in the game long enough to become hardened to the fear associated with having a three-decade prison stretch in his future. This was a whole new territory for him. Time for Naomi to exploit that fact. She prepared the bait on the hook.

'You know what you are, kid?' she asked.

He didn't move an inch. He was facing away from her, his body curled up tightly, his words muffled against the fabric of the door.

'I need to see a doctor,' he managed to say.

'You're a statistic,' Naomi said, ignoring his request for medical attention. 'Another miserable statistic in a world full of miserable statistics. Another poor boy grown into a poor man, destined for a violent life. At some point you were seduced into crime, or forced into it through necessity. I don't care which. Take your pick. Whichever makes you feel better.'

She scrutinised him. The hostility and hatred towards her came off him in waves.

'Without knowing it, you've led your whole life according to the statistics,' she said. 'The statistics that say boys from your neighbourhood are less likely to go to college, less likely to get a well-paid job, more likely to drop out of school, to be introduced to illegal drugs at a young age, to commit crime, and far more likely to serve time in prison.' She let that last word hover in the air for a moment. Its presence filled the interior of the car. 'You've let it go too far to get out of this situation completely unscathed, but I can offer you a way to break the statistics that have dominated your life up to this point.'

She noticed his head turn slightly towards her, as though considering a nibble on the hook she was dangling.

'What's your name, kid?' she asked.

Silence.

'Look,' she said. 'I'll find out sooner or later. I know your prints and DNA will be on file, so where's the harm in telling me now, instead of me finding out later?'

Another moment of silence. Then, 'Felipe. My name's Felipe.'

'Okay Felipe, let me tell you a little bit about what I know: you haven't done time yet, I can tell. What are you? Eighteen, nineteen years old?'

'Eighteen.'

'Okay, so up to this point, I'd say your experiences of the justice system have been juvenile and community based.' She leant closer to him. 'Well not anymore, Felipe. Now you're an adult, committing big boy crimes, in the big boy league, and that means big boy prison.'

His eyes widened. He was shaking. Her pressure tactics were working. Time to offer the lifeline.

'But it doesn't have to be that way,' she said. 'You can break the cycle. You don't need to become another statistic. I can offer you a way out of this mess.' She paused, letting those words echo inside his mind. 'But I need something from you in return. I need you to be honest with me. Tell me who that man in the alleyway is. Tell me why you and your friends grabbed him. Tell me who made you do it, because I sure as hell know it wasn't your idea. I need you to tell me these things so I can get to the bottom of that woman's murder.'

Felipe turned to Naomi and focused on her properly for the first time, his eyes wide and glassy.

'What you talking about?' he asked with a tremor in his voice. 'What woman?'

Naomi leant closer to him. 'Are you telling me you don't know anything about what happened to her?'

'Who?' he asked, tears building as his emotions got the better of him. 'Who the fuck you talking about? I don't know anything about no woman's murder. I was just told to drive the car. I don't know nothing else.'

Naomi examined him carefully. Either he was telling the truth and his emotions were real, or he was the best actor on planet earth. The latter wasn't a realistic possibility.

She jabbed a finger at him to emphasise every word. 'If you don't start talking then I promise there are a whole team of detectives who will try and link you to this woman's death.'

'Listen lady, I swear I don't know what the fuck you're talking about!'

Tear drops broke free and scurried down his cheeks, joining forces with the beads of sweat. Naomi stayed silent, unsure whether she should divulge the victim's name at this stage. She had Felipe on the hook, it was just a question of what it would take to reel him in. She studied his pleading expression and thought she'd get the most honest reaction from him now, rather than in a few hours' time, when it was revealed to him in an interview room, after he'd had an hour's consultation with his lawyer.

'Her name was Adriana Garcia,' she said, watching his reaction carefully. The look of confusion was unmistakeable. There wasn't even a flicker of recognition. The emotions displayed were raw and honest; he had no idea who Adriana was. Which meant Naomi's initial suspicion that he and his three friends were trying to abduct her suspect as revenge for Adriana's murder, was inaccurate. Now she didn't know what to think.

'She was murdered last night,' she said. 'We believe the man you tried to kidnap might have had something to do with it.' She leaned even closer to him, their noses inches apart. 'I need to know precisely what you know, so I can rule you out of the murder investigation and catch this guy.'

'All right,' he said with quivering lips. Naomi prepared herself. She'd seen this kind of thing hundreds of times before. He was about to offload everything, the burden too much for his young shoulders to carry. 'We put a tracker on the guy's car.'

'Why?'

'Orders.'

'From whom?'

'I don't know. Diego handled all that. I just did what I was told.'

'Who's Diego?'

He jerked his head at the Toyota across the street. 'One of my homies. Motherfucker dead in the back of that ride.'

'Describe him.'

'He's like, thirty years old or some shit. Strong-looking dude. Always got a bunch of jewellery on.'

'What about his tats?' she asked.

'The fuck you wanna know that for?'

'Just answer the question.'

Felipe thought about it for a second. 'He got a tear drop under his left eye.'

Naomi considered the horrific facial injuries Hamilton had described. 'What else?'

Felipe's eyes rolled up as he recalled the memory of his friend. 'He had dice on the back of his left hand.'

'Okay. So how did Diego handle these orders?'

'Huh?'

'You said he was the one who handled it. Did he do it by phone or in person with whoever gave the orders?'

'Phone.'

'When?'

'The first time was yesterday.'

'The first time?'

'Yeah.'

'What were the logistics of it?'

'Huh?'

'How did you know where to plant this tracker?'

'They sent a photograph of the guy to Diego's phone, and told him what car he was driving around in.'

'Who did?'

'I told you, I don't know!'

Naomi sighed. 'What about the instructions? Were they sent to Diego as messages or did they call him up?'

'Both.'

'Did you see or hear any of the conversation?'

'I didn't see any of the messages, but I was there when Diego took the call. I could only hear Diego's side of things, but it seemed to be real important that we got the tracker on this guy's car as soon as we could. They wanted to know where he was going.'

Naomi had the distinct impression the kid was telling the truth. 'Talk me through how it went down.'

'Diego told me to drive to some apartment block. Said they told him the guy might go there. That's when we found his truck parked up. We was just going to stick the tracker to it and bounce, but motherfucker came back. We had to act like we was gonna rob him, you know, to give us an excuse for being huddled around his truck and shit.' Felipe rubbed his ribcage. 'Dude beat the shit out of me, took my knife, and held it against Diego's neck.'

'Then what?'

'Shit, we got up out of there.'

'You backed down?'

'Hell nah! I told you, the robbery was just an act. The tracker was already on the truck, so we'd done our job. It was time for us to leave.'

'Tell me about the second call.'

'Diego got that today, first thing this morning. They told us to find the guy again. I don't know why. Maybe the tracker didn't work or some shit. So we get back out on the road and start searching again. Didn't take too long. Diego got a bitch who work in the city offices. She told him what traffic cameras the truck was hitting, and pretty soon we got behind the motherfucker. Followed him all the way to your crime scene. Watched you chase him across the city. You were all so busy running after him, and he was so focused on escaping from you, none of y'all noticed us following in the background. All we had to do was pick our moment.'

'And you chose the alleyway?'

Felipe shrugged. 'Made sense. It was only you and him, and we knew we could outgun your ass.'

Naomi frowned. 'I need to know who gave Diego those orders.'

'I already told you I don't know who they were. I don't even think Diego knew. We was just doing as we was told.'

'What was in it for you?'

Felipe frowned. 'What d'you think? Money, bitch. Dude on the phone told Diego we get ten large for planting the tracker, then another twenty if we catch him before you arrested him.'

Naomi nodded. 'Who do you guys normally take orders from?'

'Huh?'

'You're just a local street crew, right? Selling drugs on the corner with kids for runners? Who would give you orders to do something this serious?'

Felipe pressed his lips together. His body language changed, as though he was trying to shrink within himself, a turtle sensing danger and retreating into his shell. He didn't want to answer that last question. But it didn't matter. Naomi was sure his reaction to what she was about to say would give her all the answers she needed.

'An order that serious must have come from people with real weight behind them.' She looked at him closely and prepared to drop the bomb. 'A cartel, perhaps?'

Felipe slumped in his seat and pressed himself into the door. The kid wasn't a poker player. Naomi knocked on the window to get one of her colleagues to open the door for her. She climbed out and was just about to shut the door behind her when Felipe spoke up.

'You gonna have a busy day, *puta*!'

Naomi glared at him. Hard. 'Well look who's found his big boy voice.' She bent down to stare at him through the open door. 'A busy day you say? And why is that?'

'White boy got a green light on his ass. Plenty more out there looking for him, not just Barrio. Every Latino click in the city out for a piece of that guerro.' He smiled, a gold tooth shining bright. 'There's gonna be war in the desert tonight.'

Naomi didn't like the look on his face, not one little bit. She stood tall and slammed the door, drowning out his laughter. There was no point in interrogating him any further. He'd already given her plenty to work on, and besides, she doubted he knew much more than he'd already divulged.

She marched across the street to the Toyota, ignoring Hamilton's watchful eyes, who had seen her get out of the patrol car from his position at the far end of the cordon. He set off towards her, so she picked up her pace, pulled on a pair of forensic gloves, and got to the Toyota while he was still a good thirty metres away. Working quickly, she opened the trunk and leaned inside to examine the bodies. A potent stench of warm, congealed blood wafted over her face. After a quick scan of their hands, she spotted the dice and searched through Diego's pockets. She found his cell phone and dropped it inside a plastic evidence bag, then shut the trunk and turned on her heels.

'Hey!' Hamilton shouted as he got to within a few metres of her. 'What do you think you're doing, Naomi?'

'Gathering evidence!' she called back without even turning around. The plastic bag dangled from her hand as she held it up for him to see. He shouted something else at her, but she couldn't hear what he was saying. She climbed into her car, his voice blocked out as she closed the door, started the engine, and drove back to the office to find out exactly what Diego had been told to do.

And by whom.

22

Keen to conduct some anti-surveillance, Drayce navigated a long route on foot to get back to the Expedition, walking three sides of a square and cutting down alleyways and side streets to avoid the main roads. Just before his final approach, he sat on a park bench for ten minutes and checked in every direction for signs he was being followed. Happy he wasn't, he exited the park and made his way to the street where he'd left the rented SUV, arriving at just after noon.

He didn't want to just walk up and climb in. Too risky. He might not have been seen parking it, but he knew how resourceful and dynamic American law enforcement were, and how much technology they had at their disposal. It was unlikely they had enough information at this stage to identify him, but if they did, they would definitely have linked him to the SUV he'd hired out.

The same was true of the criminals who were on his tail. If they could get a tracker on his vehicle once, they could do it again. Consequently, he couldn't be certain there wasn't an observations team – cops or criminals – watching the truck to see if he came back to it. He needed to approach it with caution, and ideally, he needed to test the water. Much safer to know the depth before you dive in head first.

If someone has got eyes on the Expedition, how can I expose them without exposing myself?

He stayed at the top of the street, cap tilted low as he leaned against a palm tree and squinted at the Expedition. He took out his phone and searched the internet for the number of a tow company that would give him the response he wanted.

'Yeah?' came a raspy male voice on the other end of the line. Drayce could hear chewing, wet and noisy, disgusting so close to the microphone.

'Hi,' Drayce said in his best American accent, his voice taking on the tone of a friendly, concerned citizen. 'I was wondering if you could help me.'

The man grunted with indifference, a mouthful of God-knows-what still masticating inside his mouth.

'There's this SUV parked on our street,' Drayce said. 'It's a big black Ford Expedition. The thing is, it's been here for a couple of weeks, hasn't moved an inch. I've been up and down the entire street and it doesn't belong to any of the neighbours. I think it's been abandoned.' Drayce heard the guy shuffle around on the other end of the line and imagined him quickly packing his lunch away as he realised the potential of this call. 'Trouble is, I don't want to bother the police with something like this. They're too busy with more important things for me to be hassling them about an abandoned vehicle.'

'No, no,' the man said, his voice now sharp and urgent. 'Don't call the police. You've done the right thing, calling us. We can get it recovered in no time at all. Just give me your address and I'll come straight to you.'

Drayce gave him the street name.

'I'll head to you right now,' the man said. 'I'm ten minutes away.'

'Oh, thank you, that's really kind of you.'

'What did you say the licence plate of the vehicle was?'

'I didn't. Sorry, I forgot to write it down. It's a black Ford Expedition, the only one on the street. You can't miss it. Thanks for your help.'

Drayce cancelled the call and put his phone back in his pocket. He'd chosen a dubious tow company with bad reviews: in his experience, they tended to be the ones who were more willing to do whatever it took to make the most amount of profit with the least amount of effort. A reputable tow company would most likely have advised him to call the police about a suspicious vehicle abandoned on the street. A less than reputable tow company, as demonstrated, would see the financial potential of towing away a vehicle that wouldn't be missed, enabling them to acquire an asset for free that nobody would ever come looking for.

Drayce spent the next ten minutes propping up the palm tree as he waited for the tow truck, enjoying a rest in the shade. He heard it before he saw it, its noisy diesel engine kicking out black smoke as its bulky red mass drove past him and pulled up in front of the Expedition. The driver climbed out of the tow truck and walked over to examine the prize, leaving his engine running. He was a strong, thick set man with thinning brown hair, grown long in a failed attempt to cover his encroaching baldness. His trunk was the size of a barrel and strained the zips on his green overalls. A logo was sown onto his chest pocket. He walked around the Expedition, examining every inch of it, then retraced his route back, stopping a couple of times to cup his hands over the glass and peer through the tinted windows. It was hard for Drayce to tell from where he was, but he got the impression the guy was happy with his find.

Drayce watched him turn on the spot a few times as he surveyed the houses that were in his view, presumably to see if the caller was going to come out and speak to him. When no one did, he walked back to his tow truck and climbed onto the ramp. He likely planned to sell the Expedition by the end of the day, or perhaps wanted it stripped down for parts, meaning there was no time to hang around. Drayce watched him work switches on an electric control panel to lower the ramp at the back. He took hold of the hook on the end of the cable that he would use to drag the vehicle on board, and hurried down the ramp towards the front of the SUV.

Drayce assessed his surroundings: there was nothing moving. If the police, or the criminals, had surveillance on the Expedition, by now they would have done something to stop a crucial lead from being towed away. But there was no intervention taking place. Nobody ran over and waved a gun or flashed a badge. There were no lights or sirens, or an undercover attempt to send someone to claim ownership. The street was silent. Testing the water had worked. Drayce moved the pistol from the back of his waistline to the front, then pushed himself off the palm tree.

It was time to get his vehicle back.

Drayce approached the recovery guy, who was facing away from him as he unravelled black ratchet straps that he would use to secure the wheels. Drayce coughed. The guy stopped what he was doing and turned around, giving Drayce a better look at the logo sewn onto his chest pocket. It was a cartoon replica of his red tow truck, below which was a name badge. Earl was noticeably startled and a little frightened, the way you'd expect a person to present when they've been caught breaking the law.

'What are you doing with my vehicle?' Drayce asked.

Earl's response was delayed, clearly not sharp enough to quickly come up with a plausible lie. He fumbled as he tried to think of something. The words stumbled out of his mouth incoherently.

'I… urgh… I got a…'

'This isn't a towing zone, and there are no signs warning of parking restrictions.'

'Listen, I got a call about it.' Earl turned defensive, a sting of anger in his voice. 'A resident on this street made a complaint about it being abandoned.'

'So where are the cops?'

'Huh?'

'Why are the police not here if it's suspicious? They should be checking to see if it's been reported stolen or used in a crime and then abandoned. It's not for you to just come along and tow it away, hoping no questions will be asked.' Earl's face turned bright red; he knew he'd been caught out. 'Luckily for you, I've had a really bad start to my day and just want to get out of here, so unhook my vehicle and I'll be on my way.'

'Now, just wait a minute.'

'No.' Drayce lifted the front of his shirt to reveal the back strap and grip of his pistol. 'I won't.'

Earl locked eyes on the menacing black shape that protruded from Drayce's waistline. He glanced at his truck's cabin. Probably had a firearm stashed in there, Drayce thought. It would make sense for him to carry one on the job. Towing vehicles would undoubtedly instigate regular confrontations. He was probably cursing himself for not carrying it on his person. When his eyes flashed back to the grip of Drayce's pistol, his expression said it all: the SUV wasn't worth it. In less than a minute, Earl had unhooked it, lifted the ramp, and slung the cable and straps away. Without another word, he drove off, leaving a cloud of black smoke behind as he escaped as swiftly as his truck would allow.

Drayce unlocked the Expedition, threw his jacket on the back seat, and climbed in behind the wheel. He put Bunnies' address in the navigation system and checked his messages: still no reply from Carlos. He tried calling him again, but it wouldn't even connect. Carlos's phone was now turned off. Not a good sign.

Drayce fastened his seat belt, started the engine, and drove off. He pulled the peak of his cap down to obscure his face to other motorists as he drew the pistol from his beltline and tucked it in between the cushions on the passenger seat, muzzle first, with the grip sticking up, so he could grab it in the blink of an eye if needed.

While he figured this mess out, he wanted that gun within reach.

23

Naomi got back to the office just after noon. Wilson was still at his desk, killing time with busywork while everyone else was out on the streets, chasing down enquiries. He'd managed to convince Pikard to put him in charge of an LVMPD homicide social media account, to update the public on serious investigations, and for witness appeals. But Wilson used it as a personal ego trip, flooding it with photographs of himself posing at crime scenes and other embarrassing nonsense. Naomi could see he was posting something now, no doubt about the Adriana Garcia case. She wanted to go over and say something but decided to hold her tongue and walked straight to her desk instead. He looked up and glared at her as she crossed his line of sight. She returned the gesture by flashing her best *fuck you, pal* face and continued to her desk.

The first job on Naomi's list was to phone the Digital Investigations Bureau. She wanted the cell phone she'd seized from Diego's pocket to be thoroughly examined, which would normally take weeks, maybe months. In a case involving multiple homicides, she would get bumped to the top of the list, but even so, it would take too long. Luckily for her, she had a little something in her back pocket to make sure the device was scrutinised as soon as it landed on their desk. She picked up the handset and dialled the extension.

'Digital Investigations Bureau, Lianne speaking.'

The voice was bubbly and cheerful. Wouldn't last long.

'This is Detective Ocean – Homicide,' Naomi said. 'I have an urgent enquiry regarding a cell phone that needs to be done right away.'

'You know the drill. Fill out the forms and submit them once you've booked the exhibit in, and we'll get to it as soon as we can.'

Naomi sighed. Not good enough.

'Put Reese on the phone,' she said with not an ounce of decorum.

'Excuse me?'

'Put. Reese. On. The. Phone.'

'I don't know who you think you are, but you can't—'

'Listen, I know he's there, and I'm sure you're eager to get rid of me, so do yourself a favour and let him deal with my attitude.' A moment of quiet contemplation passed over the line. 'Trust me, Lianne, it's the quickest, easiest way to stop me being your problem.'

A heavy sigh whistled down the line. 'Hang on.'

Naomi heard a clunk, some shuffling, then the nervous breathing of a man with an elevated heart rate. She waited for him to offer the first word.

'Hello?' came a frightened, cautious voice.

'Hey stud,' Naomi said. 'Remember me?'

She sensed fear emanating from him as her voice registered in his memory.

'What do you want?' he asked.

'I have a cell phone I need you to look at. It's in relation to a homicide committed in the early hours of this morning, followed by a kidnapping and multiple homicides a short time ago. Real important stuff. There will undoubtedly be communications on that phone that will break the case wide open, so it needs doing right away.'

'I can't.' The quiver in his voice reminded Naomi of a broke man explaining to the bailiffs why he can't pay his debt. 'You know the score: stuff gets prioritised. We already have exhibits from three other homicides at the top of the list. You've got to wait your turn.'

Naomi shook her head. 'Oh, Reese. How quickly you forget.' She listened to the silence on the other end of the line. 'Don't you remember the Christmas party?'

A few months back they'd bumped into one another at a work's festive do, held at a cop bar in the city. Reese was drunk and forgot his manners. He put his arm around Naomi and dropped his hand down to her backside while they were queuing at the bar. In return, she elbowed him in the face. He'd needed the rest of the holiday period off, allowing time for his nose to get reset and the bruising to go down enough for him to show his face at work. Naomi had considered that to be the end of the matter, but didn't see why she couldn't use it to her advantage now. She put her lips close to the handset and purred down the line.

'Don't think I won't speak to your supervisor about what you did, asshole.'

'You broke my goddamn nose,' he hissed quietly, presumably so the others in his office couldn't hear. 'I could press charges.'

Naomi chuckled. 'Against a woman you sexually assaulted, who has police colleagues as witnesses, proving her actions were totally justified as self-defence? Good luck with that.'

There was a pause as the reality of his situation hit home.

'The fuck d'you want?' he asked.

'I want you to put all your other commitments on hold for the rest of the day and get me what I need from this phone.'

Reese hesitated. Naomi imagined he was considering what she'd said, weighing up his limited options, and if he had half a brain, discarding all but one.

'Bring it to me,' he said, his half a brain making the right decision. 'I'll get it done.'

Naomi smiled. 'Good boy. I'm on my way.'

She hung up, grabbed the exhibit bag, and stood to leave the office. After taking only a couple of steps from her desk, she noted something new on the cork board: a fresh printout, pinned to its surface, put there whilst she'd interrogated Felipe. She walked up to inspect it more closely, but she already had a good idea who the target of the abuse was. There was only one person who'd messed up so far that day. Her anger built as the picture came into focus.

A cartoon image of a female cop stared back at her, red-faced and panting as she failed to keep up with a suspect who was laughing as he ran away. The cop was in uniform, and the suspect was dressed in the classic burglar outfit: black and white striped top, a black domino mask on his face, and a swag bag over his shoulder with a dollar sign on it. Someone had used a black Sharpie pen to write Naomi's badge number on the cartoon cop's shoulders. There was only one person who could be responsible for putting it up there, because there was only one person who'd been sat in the office all morning while everyone else was out chasing down leads.

She turned to Wilson.

Instinct told her to let him have it. A pure blind rage compelled her to rip the image off the board and ram it

216

down his throat, wiping that self-satisfied smug expression off his face. But she chose square breathing instead: a calming technique she'd been taught a couple of years ago on an anger management course her lieutenant had made her go on, after she'd threatened to shoot a colleague who called her *sweet cheeks*. She'd been exaggerating when she'd made the threat. Kind of. But they'd made her go on the course anyway, and the breathing technique was the only useful thing she'd taken away from it.

She ignored Wilson and strode to the staircase doors. It was called being the bigger person. She'd seen others do it but had never understood the concept. Wasn't really her style. She preferred fighting in the trenches to taking the high ground, but knew she needed to tame her temper, and now was as good a time as any to work on it. She managed to walk past him without even glancing his way. A feeling of pride bubbled inside her. She made it to the stairs.

Almost.

Out the corner of her eye, she detected the snigger on his face, which sealed his fate. No amount of square breathing was going to keep her anger in check now.

Oh well, she thought. *Sometimes you've just got to be who you are.*

'Hey, dickhead,' she snarled as she slammed her fists onto his desk. He leapt back, startled, as though a Rottweiler had just jumped up and snapped at his face. The grin vanished. 'Try getting some work done instead of leaving it all to the rest of the team.'

'What's up, Naomi?' The smile returned. 'Can you not take a joke?'

'Only when they're funny.' She pushed off his desk and stood tall. 'And he may have got away, but at least I was out there, in the arena, putting the work in. Who are you chasing from behind this desk?'

Naomi turned and marched away, a long way from the high ground, but feeling pretty good, nonetheless.

'That's quite the nerve I hit,' he called after her, visibly pleased with himself. 'I'll remember that for the future, next time I want to push your buttons.'

'The only thing you need to remember is to take that picture down before I get back,' she said as she pushed open the double doors that led to the stairs. 'Otherwise, we'll discover how far up your ass I can stick my pistol whilst still able to pull the trigger.'

She heard him stand up out of his chair. 'And just you remember what happened the last time you threatened a colleague. You got away with an anger management course last time, but when I tell Pikard about this latest—'

Mercifully, the sound of his voice was cut off as the doors swung shut behind her.

24

Naomi dropped Diego's cell phone off with Reese, then drove to the crime scene at Adriana Garcia's home. The buzz from earlier had all but vanished. Most of the investigators were out conducting enquiries assigned to them by Pikard, and the locals were back in their homes, already bored with the drama on their street. Left behind were two officers guarding the scene – one front, one back – along with Melvin and a CSI. Melvin's car – a Buick Lacrosse in metallic silver – was parked in the lot, a couple of spaces from the CSI's van. Naomi parked between the two and walked to the front door.

She hadn't spent long at the crime scene that morning before she'd found herself chasing after a suspect, but even during the short time she'd been there, she'd gained a good understanding of what had occurred when Adriana had been murdered.

Theft had been ruled out as a motive because it didn't appear Adriana owned anything of great value. The apartment was neat and tidy, so the killer hadn't performed an untidy search of the premises. And it would have needed to be messy, in Naomi's opinion, because the 911 call had come in seconds after the murder weapon had been fired, meaning the killer wouldn't have had time to carefully search the property and escape before the cops arrived. The best he could have done was ransack the place looking for something worth stealing, but he clearly hadn't done that, because the house was immaculate. Everything they knew up to this point indicated he smashed through her back door while she was sleeping, rushed to her bedroom, and shot her twice in the head, before fleeing the scene via the same route.

An execution, in anyone's book.

Naomi nodded to the cop stationed at the front of the house and parted her jacket to show him the detective's badge on her belt. She snapped on a pair of blue forensic gloves as she walked inside, struck once again by how clean and tidy the place was. This wasn't a crime of passion. It hadn't been committed by a jilted lover, or a jealous stalker. It had all the hallmarks of a professional hit; the kind of thing serious criminals did to one another. However, from what had been gleaned so far, Adriana Garcia was most definitely not a serious criminal. Far from it.

So, what did she get herself involved in that led to her being murdered in this brutal fashion?

A motive, Naomi thought as she reached the bedroom. *We are desperately in need of a motive.*

The door was ajar, providing her with a partial view into the room. The bottom corner of a bed was just in sight. She could see the CSI stood next to the bedside table, labelling little plastic bottles of swab samples. She spotted Naomi out of the corner of her eye, which darted to her detective's badge. They nodded a silent greeting to one another before the CSI got back to work. Naomi pushed the door open with a gloved hand, slowly revealing the full extent of the horrific scene.

The headboard was splattered with dark blood, almost black in colour now it had congealed and dried. A gruesome outline had been left in the mattress and bedding, marking where Adriana's body lay before she was transported for an autopsy. The pillows had soaked up most of what had seeped out of her head wounds, and the mattress had absorbed the rest. Naomi took a deep breath and stepped into the room.

She didn't get far before she had to stop, her senses absorbing all the finer details. Shards of skull and blobs of scalp decorated the headboard. A pungent smell of decomposing brain matter hung in the stale air. Clumps of hair were matted to the blood-soaked pillow. Naomi stood as still as a rock. The horror, sadness, and wasteful-ness of it all made her feel sick to her stomach. She was glad that, even after all her years of policing, scenes such as this still prompted a strong emotional reaction within her. She was terrified she'd reach the day when they didn't.

A touch on the shoulder startled her. Melvin appeared dishevelled and exhausted. His suit jacket was missing and his shirt sleeves were rolled up, his tie pulled loose with the top two buttons undone. In one hand a legal pad lay open, the notes scruffy, almost indecipherable, as though he'd dipped a spider in ink and let it run riot over the pages. In his other hand he clutched a small, pink cardboard box. Like Naomi, he wore blue forensic gloves, and held the box as though it contained something precious. Her gaze dropped below his shiny bald head, once again glistening with sweat, and examined his clammy complexion, blem-ished and pitted, betraying his dreadful diet. She again reminded herself to pick a good moment to hassle him about eating more healthily.

'What's up?' she asked him.

'This is *what's up*.'

He took out his phone and showed her the screen. It was the department's X account. A photograph of the police tape at the edge of the crime scene had been posted recently, along with an explanation as to how the case was progressing.

'Wilson?' Naomi asked, although she knew the answer.

'You guessed it. He came down here for all of ten minutes, took that photo, then left.'

'Goddamn worthless SOB!' Naomi took a deep breath. 'I take it you've been busy here, then, if that jerk-off didn't stick around to help.'

'You could say that. Don't think there's much more to go on until the forensic report comes back.'

'Talk me through it.'

Melvin closed his notebook and pinched it underneath his armpit. He pulled a handkerchief out of his pocket and wiped his forehead. 'Adriana hadn't been here long. She moved to this apartment two days ago and lived alone. Her landlord doesn't know where she moved from, or why she moved. Said he doesn't ask new tenants those kinds of questions. I get the impression he's just happy to fill the place and have some rent coming in. No background checks were done, and no references needed. She just paid a small deposit and then had to cough up rent money at the beginning of every month, all of it in cash. Worked better that way for both of them, apparently. Landlord prefers cash, presumably for tax reasons, and Adriana was a stripper, so cash was the easier option.'

'A stripper, huh? What else do we know about her?'

'Not much so far, although we're working on it. The apartment isn't much of a clue. The furnishings belong to the landlord and there aren't many personal items, even fewer that might have sentimental value.' He held out the pink cardboard box. 'Apart from this.'

Naomi glanced at it, but her eyes soon returned to his, the unspoken question obvious between the two seasoned detectives.

'Don't worry,' Melvin said. 'It's already been swabbed for DNA and dusted for prints.'

Naomi took it from him and carefully lifted the lid.

'Found it under her bed,' Melvin said.

Naomi examined the contents. She moved a few things around, took the odd item out to get a better look, then replaced the lid and handed it back to him.

'Interesting,' she said. 'Anything else?'

'She has her clothing in the wardrobe and drawers, and her make-up in the bathroom. Other than that, not much. Seems she was a girl all alone in this city.'

Naomi nodded at a cardboard gun box by the CSI's feet, taped up with an exhibit label on it. There was a small plastic window that showed the weapon strapped to the inside of the box with cable ties. 'That her firearm?'

'Yep. It's a Smith and Wesson .38 Special. First responders found it on her nightstand with the grip facing the bed. It was fully loaded.'

Naomi raised her eyebrows. 'Must have been scared of someone for her to keep a loaded gun by the bed like that.'

Melvin nodded. 'Someone like the guy on her doorstep last night, who she was seen pointing it at?'

Naomi bobbed her head from side to side as she contemplated that idea. 'Maybe.'

'Well, something had her worried. She slept fully clothed and even had shoes on her feet, presumably so she was ready to either run or fight if this person came back. But she didn't get the chance to do either. She was shot face down on the bed, her left arm reaching across for the revolver on her nightstand, her fingers only a couple of inches away from it when the first bullet hit her in the back of her head. She was dead at that point, but the fucker put another one in her skull just to be sure.'

Melvin put down his note pad and the pink box, tore off his gloves, and rubbed his face with both hands.

'You're tired,' Naomi said. 'Go get yourself some coffee and a bite to eat.'

'I will, later. How'd you do over on Lewis Ave?'

'Not bad. I got the driver talking, but the other three weren't up to much. They'd all been double tapped in the head.'

'Jesus.'

'Yeah, they got what was coming to them all right. But they were just stupid little street corner punks doing someone else's dirty work for them. Whoever's behind all of this is far bigger and badder than those four idiots. I've got one of their phones being worked on by a guy in digital investigations as we speak, so I should have their paymaster's messages by the end of the day.'

'That quick, huh?'

Naomi smiled. 'You know me. I can be very persuasive.'

Melvin chuckled. 'You got that right.'

Naomi turned away from the horror scene on the bed. She'd seen enough. 'What else can the neighbours tell us?'

'Nosy guy a few doors down says the strip club she worked at is called Bunnies. He let it slip when I was talking to him.' Melvin smirked. 'Wouldn't go into too much detail about how he knew. His wife was in the next room. I think he was worried she'd overhear.'

Naomi pinched her lips and felt the skin on her nose wrinkle. 'That's men for you.'

'Hey, don't paint us all with that brush.' He wiggled his wedding ring to emphasise his point. 'I happen to love my wife.'

'Fine. *Some* men.'

'Better.'

'Anything else for us to go on?'

'Not a thing unless forensics give us something.'

'Huh, yeah right. Don't hold your breath on that one.' She felt the eyes of the CSI in the room zone in on the side of her face. Naomi had forgotten they weren't alone. To redeem herself, she blurted out, 'I mean, not if our suspect is as professional and experienced as he appears to be. Nothing to find if there was nothing left behind.' She turned away from the CSI's glare and silently mouthed the word *awkward* at Melvin. He failed to hold back his grin. They came to a subliminal agreement and stepped out of the bedroom.

'We need to track this guy down,' Melvin said once they were in the hallway. 'And quickly.'

'Yes, we do, and we've got every cop in Vegas looking for him, as well as Highway Patrol now providing spotters and roadblocks on all the major routes in and out of the city. Nothing more to be done in that regard. For now, we need to learn more about Adriana.'

Naomi's phone rang. She took it out and caught Melvin's eye. 'It's Pikard.'

'Better answer it. Don't want to keep the boss waiting.'

She tapped the screen and put it to her ear. 'What can I do for you, Boss?'

'You can stop threatening Wilson for starters.'

Naomi winced. 'He came to see you?'

'Took me a solid half hour to convince him to let me handle it, rather than file a complaint with Internal Affairs. What the hell are you doing threatening him like that, Naomi? You should have better things to do.'

'And he should be too busy to be putting pictures up about me on a day like today, when we're all hands to the deck trying to locate a young woman's murder suspect.'

Pikard sighed. 'He gone back to not pulling his weight?'

'He improved for like, a month, after your last talk with him. But he fell back into his old ways weeks ago.'

'Why haven't you said anything?'

'Because like the rest of the team, I'm too busy, John.'

'All right, I'll make it clear to Wilson he needs to get up to speed or he's gone. In the meantime, be professional around him. No more threats.'

'Deal,' Naomi said, rolling her eyes at Melvin, who appeared both confused and intrigued about what she was discussing.

'How did you get on with Hamilton at the Toyota scene?'

'Not bad,' she replied. 'I'm having a phone down-loaded. Should know more when I get the results.'

'Sounds promising. Where are you now?'

'The scene at Adriana's apartment.'

'I spoke to Melvin recently and I don't think there's much more we can do there. Best to leave the CSIs alone to do their job. I want you to go to this Bunnies place Melvin told me about. See what they can tell you about our victim.'

'I'm on it. I'll call you with an update later.'

'Speak soon.'

Naomi ended the call and paced to the front door with determination.

'Where you going?' Melvin asked as he jogged after her, hobbling as though his knees hurt.

'Bunnies. Pikard figures it's the best place to get to know more about Adriana, and I agree.' She peered over her shoulder as she stepped outside. 'You coming?'

'You bet your ass! I'm sick of being cooped up in this horror show.'

They walked to the parking lot, stopped in front of Melvin's Buick, and stared at one another as though they were both waiting for something.

'You driving?' Melvin asked.

'No, you are.'

Melvin sighed. 'Fine. But only if you promise we'll stop for food. I'm starving.' He extended his arm. 'Shake on it?'

Naomi considered his outstretched hand. 'Okay. I'll call an informant of mine on the way who knows everything and everyone involved in Vegas's club scene. See if he can tell me anything about Bunnies that might be useful before we march inside.' She went to shake Melvin's hand, but at the last second pulled it back. 'But you're only coming with me to Bunnies if you agree to eat from somewhere healthy.'

Melvin appeared hurt. Feeling a pang of guilt, Naomi hurriedly said, 'It's only because I care about you. If you want to have a retirement to enjoy with Tina and the kids, then you need to change your eating habits.' She smiled at him in the hope he'd realise she was only looking out for him.

'Don't do that,' Melvin said. 'Your face isn't used to it. It's creepy.'

Naomi laughed as she held her hand back out. 'Do we have a deal?'

Melvin seemed to give it a moment's thought, then he shook on it. 'Deal.'

'Good.' She walked to the passenger door. 'Now get this car unlocked. I want to get to Bunnies. Someone there must know what Adriana was so scared of. Chances are she confided in someone, and we need to identify that someone and put pressure on them.'

'What do you mean when you say *pressure*?' Melvin asked as he unlocked the door and climbed behind the wheel.

Naomi took the seat next to him. 'Don't get your panties in a bunch. We're just gonna talk to them.'

'That's precisely what I'm worried about.' Melvin started the engine and pulled out into the road. Naomi noticed his grip on the steering wheel tighten. 'I've seen how things escalate when you *talk* to people.'

'Relax. What could possibly go wrong with a simple conversation?'

Melvin sighed. 'The last time you said that, we needed SWAT to rescue our asses.'

'You talking about that hostage thing a few years back?'

'You know I am.'

'Please. I had everything under control until those knuckleheads gatecrashed the party.'

Melvin chortled despite his nerves. 'Just promise me you'll stay calm at this Bunnies place.' He patted his large belly with the palm of his hand. 'I'm built for loving, not fighting. And remember, they're not forced by law to answer our questions, so if we're going to get anything out of them, we need to be friendly. Okay?'

'Okay.'

'Promise?'

'I promise.'

Luckily for Naomi, Melvin couldn't see her right hand, down by the side of her seat, the index and middle finger hugging tightly as they crossed over one another.

25

Drayce drove past Bunnies, took the next exit, and parked in the customer lot for a busy recreational vehicle rental place on the other side of the multi-lane highway. He turned off the ignition and examined the environment with nothing but the clicking sounds of the engine to keep him company.

A good view of Bunnies across the highway enabled him to assess the place, his Expedition camouflaged amongst the giant rental vehicles. Bunnies had its own lot – which was surprisingly busy considering the time of day – but he'd ruled out parking there. If things turned sour and he needed to make a run for it, he didn't want anyone to identify what vehicle he was using. He needed to keep the Expedition a secret. Not only would the cops find out who he was if they saw him in it – he'd given the rental company his real ID – but it was also the only transport he had that enabled him to get around Vegas undetected.

Bunnies wasn't a big shiny 'gentleman's club' like the ones on the Strip. It was in the north of the city, in a relatively quiet part of town; just a single level, off-white building on a dusty plot alongside the Boulder Highway. There was awning over the entrance doors that had once been black, stained and torn in places, and whatever had been used to render the outside of the walls was crumbling off in big chunks. There was a sign in the lot that had neon tubes over the seven letters of BUNNIES, below which a sign read: GIRLS! GIRLS! GIRLS!

Judging by the rest of the venue, Drayce suspected more than a few of those letters wouldn't light up when night fell. He wondered which ones would be broken, and what it would spell in the dark as he grimaced at the sight of the place. It was seedy and disgusting, the building so old and tired it was as though it had been one of the first things to be built in Vegas and nobody had ever cared for it. He felt uneasy at the thought of a young woman like Adriana undressing on a stage in such a place, egged on by a crowd of leering men. He averted his eyes, unable to look at it any longer.

His gaze instinctively dropped to the grip of his gun, which poked out from between the passenger seat cushions. Did he need it, or didn't he? Being armed had saved his life more than once, but introducing a gun when unnecessary made a difficult situation a dangerous one. If he didn't take it with him, it wasn't an option, and he wouldn't be tempted to put holes in people, bringing the city's law enforcement screaming back into the equation.

Drayce took off his cap and laid it over the weapon.

He climbed out of the Expedition, locked it, and set off on foot to Bunnies. He had to wait until there was enough of a gap in the traffic for him to sprint across the highway's four lanes to the central reservation, where he then had to pause again until he could dash across another four lanes. Once safely on the other side, he marched across Bunnies' parking lot and underneath the shabby sun-bleached awning to the entrance doors. As he stepped inside, his mind conjured up images of the creatures he might find in a strip club in the middle of the day. At this point, his decision to leave the gun behind started to feel like a big mistake.

26

'Plant protein snack bar?' Melvin said as he leaned out of the driver's window and gazed up at the sign. 'What could you have possibly found for me to eat in a place called that?'

Naomi climbed back into her seat and slapped a tubular shaped object wrapped in paper onto his lap. 'That's a Lean Carb Burrito. It's got grilled chicken, brown rice, beans, avocado, and lettuce. Full of goodness, which is precisely what you need.'

They were parked in a busy retail park, facing a strip of nine shops, of which the snack bar was one. Melvin eyed the place suspiciously.

'I'm supposed to trust a restaurant that serves food next to a swap meet and a tyre garage?'

'What's the matter?' Naomi frowned at him. 'Not up to your usual standards? Would it make you feel better if I dunked it in batter and deep fried it?'

'At least my usual spots have—'

'Just shut up and eat your damn lunch. You're in danger of sounding ungrateful.'

Melvin picked up the tube and unwrapped it. Naomi watched him examine it as a vegan might a steak.

'I've changed my mind,' he said.

Naomi bit a big chunk off the end of hers. 'Too late. I can't take it back, so that's all you're getting.'

Melvin turned it over in his hands, as though expecting it to become more appealing if he gave it time. Seeming to conclude it hadn't, he stared at Naomi.

'What did you get?' he asked.

'The same, but with extra chicken.'

Melvin appeared hard done by. 'How come you got extra chicken for you, but not for me?'

Naomi swallowed her mouthful and looked across at him. 'I need the protein. I went training last night, so I've got muscles to repair.'

'Still going along to that jiu-jitsu place, huh?'

'Yep.' She took another bite, unashamed at speaking with her mouth full. 'Three times a week.'

'What's it called again?'

'10th Planet,' she mumbled through the masticated chicken, rice and vegetables tumbling inside her mouth.

'Stupid name.'

Naomi stopped chewing and glared at him. He always got like this when he sulked after she'd convinced him to try something healthy for lunch. After a few seconds of the hard stare, she swallowed, and spoke like a mother to a pouting child.

'I should probably warn you, I'm starting to lose my patience. For the last time, eat your damn lunch. It's good for you, and that was the deal we made. Of course, you could always turn down my generous offer and go to Burger King instead, but then you wouldn't be coming to Bunnies with me to make enquiries. Instead, you'd be taking me back to my car and returning to the office to see what bullshit jobs Pikard has got lined up for you.' She turned away from him. 'Your choice.'

As Naomi tucked back into her burrito, Melvin contemplated his own. He took a small bite. His eyes lit up.

'Huh. It's not that bad.'

'See, I told you I'd make a healthy eater of you one day.' She smiled at him. 'Next on the list is for me to drag you along to 10th Planet, have you busting some moves on the mats.'

'One step at a time.'

They ate in silence for the next few minutes. Naomi thought about Adriana and contemplated what banal reason her killer would have for taking the young woman's life. As a police officer, Naomi had spent years witnessing pointless tragedy inflicted on people's lives by others. It was this that had formed her cynical outlook on the world. She longed for change, for her world view to be restored to the optimistic haven it had once been, but she knew her police service had opened her eyes to a world that was hard to forget. There was no shutting Pandora's box.

'Think you'll ever settle down?' Melvin asked.

The question shook Naomi out of her thoughts, its blunt delivery having shocked her. She stared at him.

'Where'd that come from?'

Melvin shrugged. 'I got bored sitting here in silence.' He paused a beat, summoning some bravery, perhaps. 'You're thirty-five now, missy. Ain't getting any younger.'

Naomi resisted the urge to punch him in the throat when she saw the smirk on his face and realised he was trying to stoke a reaction from her.

'You don't get me that easily, buster.' She turned her attention back to her burrito. 'I've known you too long.'

He chuckled. 'Fine. But seriously, far be it from me to tell a feisty single woman she needs to meet a man.'

Naomi pulled her fist back and jerked her head in Melvin's direction, mimicking preparations for launching an attack. Melvin flinched, Naomi's swift, instinctive change of body language evidently noticed by him. She relaxed. A grin bloomed on her face at the sight of her friend's reaction.

'Wow,' Melvin managed to utter as he leaned into his door to get out of her reach. 'Take it easy. You know, it'd be good for you to be nicer to people sometimes. Let them see what *I* see. That way, you might not scare off every suitable bachelor who comes along. You might meet someone. You might fall in love. Which is pretty fun, by the way. Look at me and Tina. Neither of us were this happy before the day we got married.'

'And Tina would echo that sentiment would she?'

'Of course. Look at me. I'm adorable.'

Naomi laughed. 'Stupid asshole.'

A figure in Naomi's peripheral vision caught her attention. She snapped her head to the side to examine the man properly through the window. He wore black jeans, a grey hoody and pearly white Air Jordans, so fresh they might have only come out the box that morning. She wrapped up her burrito and placed it on the dashboard.

'There's my guy,' she said.

Melvin followed her gaze. 'Where? The dude stood out front of the swap meet?'

'That's him.' She opened her door.

'Want me to come?'

'No, you stay here. He trusts me, and he's a good guy. Having a cop he doesn't know stood in the background might tighten his lips.'

Melvin nodded, but cracked his door a fraction, which Naomi knew was just in case he needed to back her up.

Meetings such as this had a horrible habit of going south from time to time.

She climbed out and marched up to Jackson. He was in his mid-forties, six foot tall and muscular, his head of Afro hair plaited into corn rows. His teeth were unnaturally white, bleached on a regular basis by one of the many obscenely expensive cosmetic dentists in Vegas. Nowadays, he lived in jeans and sneakers as he enjoyed a comfortable contrast from the two decades he'd spent wearing flashy suits and painful shoes while running some of the biggest and best nightclubs in the city.

Until his world was turned upside down.

Three years ago, his only son Demetrius was shot dead outside a club run by one of Jackson's competitors. Desperate for justice, Jackson was mortified when not a single witness came forwards, despite the front of the venue being packed with queuing clubbers. Even the nightclub management were obstructive, refusing to hand over vital CCTV evidence to police until a warrant was obtained, giving the killer time to vanish into hiding. It was only down to Naomi's dogged investigative strategy that saw the killer – a local gang member – forensically linked to a suspicious vehicle seen conducting reconnaissance in the days preceding the shooting, resulting in gunshot residue being found splattered up the inside of the passenger door, and shell casings in the footwell with his prints on. A city-wide manhunt had ensued, resulting in his arrest. The intended target had been one of the doormen, who had thrown the killer out the previous weekend; Demetrius had been tragically caught in the crossfire. Jackson had been profoundly grateful for Naomi's efforts, and had passed information to her about every dodgy activity he'd heard of ever since. Which from a man who knew everyone worth knowing in Vegas, made him the perfect police informant.

'How's it going?' she asked.

Jackson flicked his head up at her and half smiled. 'Good. You?'

'Never been better. Thanks for agreeing to meet with me.'

Jackson stuffed his hands in his pockets. 'No problem. Sorry I couldn't talk over the phone; I was with some people who are best off not knowing I'm friendly with the local PD.'

'That's okay. I appreciate your time.'

'So what can I help you with?'

'I'm investigating the murder of a young girl. She worked at a strip club on the outskirts of the city called Bunnies.'

The face Jackson pulled told her he knew where she was referring to.

'What can you tell me?' she asked.

'Nothing first-hand, only what I hear. It's a shithole of a club, way below the league I've always worked in. Run by a pompous son of a bitch called Conrad McAuley, who treats the girls like garbage and considers them his property. You know the type of asshole: a dozen sexual harassment lawsuits dodged by paying off the complainants. His head barmaid's his right-hand gal. Jeanette somebody. Known to drink drive home nearly every night if that's something you're interested in?'

'I'll pass it on to the local patrol teams and the traffic department. Anything else?'

Jackson checked over each shoulder. 'Word is he pimps the dancers out.'

'Seriously?'

Jackson shrugged. 'Just what I hear.' He leaned closer. 'Think he's got something to do with your victim's murder?'

'I doubt it. But I'm hoping I can find out more about her from him. I'm going to head to Bunnies now and question him. What kind of welcome do you think I'll get?'

'Hostile, I'd say.'

'He dangerous?'

Jackson frowned as a huff of air blew past his lips. '*Pfft!* The only thing dangerous about Conrad McAuley is how dangerously stupid he is. Might have a gun on site, though, so take care.'

'Thanks. I will. Anything else about this guy I should know before I go confront him?'

'Yeah, wear sunglasses. The man wears shirts so bright they make your eyes hurt.'

Naomi chuckled.

'How's life treating you?' Jackson asked.

'Same old bullshit—'

'Just a different day.'

They smiled at one another.

'I saw the plant you left at D's grave,' Jackson said. 'Gave it a drop of water.'

'They last longer than flowers.'

'Yes, they do.' He locked eyes with her, pupils glistening. 'Thank you.'

Naomi stepped forwards and hugged him. 'Thanks again for meeting with me.'

'Any time. You take care out there.'

'Always.'

The embrace over, Jackson clenched his hand into a fist and held it out. Naomi bumped it, turned, and walked back to the Buick.

'How'd it go?' Melvin mumbled through half a mouthful of burrito as Naomi climbed in, shut her door, and watched Jackson saunter off to the other side of the retail park.

'As expected, I suppose. He knows a little bit about Bunnies, but nothing in depth. The owner is a guy called Conrad McAuley, who sounds like your typical scumbag, but he's nothing for us to worry about. Rumour has it he pimps out the dancers, though, so we need to be prepared to put some pressure on him if he doesn't want to talk to us willingly – the thought of our young murder victim working for a man like him makes my spider senses tingle. And he might have a gun at the venue, so let's be switched on at all times once we cross the threshold.' She turned to Melvin. 'Deal?'

'Deal.'

Melvin dropped the remainder of his burrito into his mouth, scrunched up the wrapper and threw it over his shoulder onto the backseats, having patently enjoyed a meal that wouldn't add to his bad cholesterol. Naomi felt pleased with herself.

'Not so bad after all, huh big guy?'

He licked his lips. 'It was edible.'

'Good.' She swiped her burrito off the dashboard. 'Now that you've got two hands free, let's get to Bunnies.'

'You not want to wait until you've finished your lunch?'

'Nah, I'll eat the rest of it on the way. Let's get there. I'm itching to speak to McAuley to see what more we can learn about Adriana.'

Melvin started the engine and checked his phone. 'Google says we're ten minutes away in current traffic.'

'Great, let's get moving. I've got a feeling there's something waiting for us at this place. Something that'll help us bust this case wide open.'

27

Bunnies was somehow both gloomy and bright. Blinding red lights illuminated the dancers in the windowless venue, but the rest of the place was lit by little more than dim table lamps, underlighting the ghoulish faces that stared out from the darkness. Drayce felt his shoes stick to the floor with every step as he walked past a sign advertising two for one on drinks. He thought this went some way to explaining how busy it was. Not being the type of man who enjoyed spending time in strip clubs, he'd always assumed it to be a strictly nocturnal habit. But as he walked the floor, he saw that despite it being one o'clock in the afternoon, Bunnies was nearly full, mostly of groups of men who appeared to be on vacation, and lonely truckers who wanted to ogle at naked women while they ate lunch. Drayce sighed as he took a seat at the bar.

'Excuse me,' he said to the barmaid, loud enough for her to hear him over the music. She stopped drying glasses, flicked her long black hair out of her face, and ambled over to him. She was somewhere in her late twenties, with a skinny body, but thanks to modern medicine had a chest size that would compete with the biggest and best of them. She was wearing a red corset, cinched tightly around her torso, accentuating her investment. Her lipstick matched her attire, as did her long nails, which dug into the counter as she gripped its edge with both hands and leaned towards him.

'What can I get yer?' she asked.

'I'm not drinking.'

'You know we got two for one until—'

'Yeah, I saw. I'm here to speak to your manager.'

Worry afflicted her expression. 'Is there a problem?'

'No, not yet. I'd just like to speak to him. It won't take long.'

The barmaid eyed him with suspicion, no doubt thinking: is this guy going to be a problem? Because I don't want to be taking a problem to my boss. She took in his size, and more importantly, his features. She appraised his cauliflower ears, calcified over years of grappling, and the deformed knuckles on both hands, more so the right, because that was the fist that delivered his power. He smiled at her, but it only seemed to make her even more suspicious of him. She turned around, walked away, and with her back to him, said, 'Wait here. I'll go get him.'

She disappeared through a door marked Staff Only. She'd obviously decided her boss would want to know about a huge stranger asking for him. Drayce spun around on his stool, reclined against the bar, and turned his wedding ring around his finger as he watched the place.

A bouncer was sat in a chair next to the curtained doorway at the end of the stage, right where the dancers would appear from and disappear to. Drayce guessed there might be enough trouble in Bunnies during the hours of darkness, when Vegas really came alive, to warrant a few extra pairs of hands. But any trouble during the day was nothing a single bouncer couldn't handle. Simple economics. You pay for more security at night when you need them, and less during the day when you don't. So the meathead protecting the access point to the dancers was all the manager had to protect him.

Drayce assessed the challenge.

He was big, obviously; size would be one of the few requirements for a bouncer in a Vegas strip club, along with a healthy propensity for violence. He had greasy black hair, swept back over his scalp. His face was as red as the barmaid's corset, forced into an angry scowl. Steroids were responsible for both, Drayce suspected, the additional hormones ramping up his blood pressure and shortening his fuse. He wore light blue jeans, black boots and a white polo shirt with the word SECURITY printed in big black letters across the chest. The cotton stretched tightly over his torso, strained from a level of mass only achievable with pharmaceutical help. The muscle fibres in his face and neck twitched as he ground his teeth together, suggesting there might be some amphetamine in his system as well. Drayce knew the concoction would make him jumpy and paranoid, which for someone his size, would be a dangerous and formidable thing, especially when a stranger walks in and starts asking difficult questions of his boss. Drayce rolled his shoulders to loosen the muscles. Just in case.

He heard a door swing open behind him and spun around on his stool. The barmaid was back, this time with company. The man she was with was a balding middle-aged gentleman, who might have had a gym membership but never used it. A thin gold necklace was visible between the open collar of his pink shirt, which was tucked into a pair of tight white chinos, held in place by a leather belt with a giant gold buckle front and centre. The tassels on his snakeskin loafers peeked out from beneath the hems of his trousers. He'd rolled his sleeves up to show off his gold watch, undoubtedly. Clearly a man who liked attention.

In his hand he clutched a smart phone, his concentration on the screen. He tapped out a message as he walked along the bar, the opposite side to Drayce, and stopped when he got level, keeping the counter in between them. A sensible decision. The barmaid stood off to one side and watched the interaction from a safe distance. Pink shirt dropped his phone in his chest pocket and rested his hands on the edge of the bar.

'I've been told you want to speak to the manager,' he said.

'That's right,' Drayce replied as he assessed the man's expression. The frown, the curled top lip, the puffed-out chest; he didn't catch a friendly vibe off him.

'Well, here I am.' The manager spread his arms out wide. 'What d'you want?'

Drayce knew he needed to be guarded with what he said next. News travelled fast, so there was a chance this guy already knew about Adriana's murder. But maybe not. Perhaps the cops would manage to seal the news until they had a suspect in custody. Drayce decided it was best for him to withhold his knowledge of her murder.

'I'm here about Adriana Garcia.'

'Who?'

'Don't be like that.'

'Like what?'

'A liar. I know she works here.'

Drayce studied him carefully, observing no reaction to his use of the present tense in reference to Adriana. It appeared her manager didn't know she was dead.

'Okay, yeah, she works here,' the manager said. 'What's it to you?'

'I work for Adriana's father. She's gone missing and he's worried about her.'

The manager stared daggers at him. 'So what you bothering me for?'

Drayce resisted the urge to drag him across the bar and slap the tone out of his mouth. 'I thought I'd come by to see if you could tell me something that would help me find her. Her dad wants to know she's okay.'

He shook his head. 'Can't help. Ain't seen her in days.'

'That not concern you?'

He shrugged. 'Normal behaviour. Stupid bitch turns up to work when it suits her.'

Drayce's blood angered. The pressure built in his head, his pulse throbbing in his neck and forehead. 'When was the last time she showed up for work?'

The manager's frown deepened. 'You got some ID you can show me?'

'No. I was relying on your better nature. I thought you might care that one of your employees has gone missing.'

He shrugged again. 'It would appear not. And I'm done talking to you, so if you ain't drinking, or paying for a dance, then why don't you get the fuck out of my club?'

Interesting. Drayce knew acts of aggression of this sort were usually in response to fear. But of what? He clasped his hands together on the bar and interwove his fingers, making it clear he was going nowhere. He stared into the manager's eyes. The anger was only skin deep. Lurking underneath was terror. He knew more than he was letting on.

Drayce called upon the accuracy of his short-term memory, pictured the manager just before he'd walked along the bar, and zoomed in on his phone, his fingers dancing energetically across the screen, as though he'd felt the need to send a message once he'd seen Drayce in the flesh. Drayce now gazed at the same phone, sitting in the manager's top pocket. The manager seemed to read Drayce's thoughts, but he was too slow. Drayce gripped his pink shirt, pulled him halfway across the bar, tore his phone from his shirt pocket, and tilted the screen towards his face.

'The fuck you doing?' the manager asked in a panic.

It was an iPhone, one of the latest models, so Drayce knew it would have facial recognition software. Sure enough, a split second later the screen opened, giving him access to the man's digital world. He pushed him back over the bar, where he clattered into the bottles mounted on the wall behind him.

Drayce opened the messaging app.

His mouth went dry.

28

Drayce leapt to his feet as though the stool was white hot. He read the message again.

It's him. He's here.

There was nothing else in the thread, the conversation regularly deleted, Drayce suspected. He concentrated hard on memorising the recipient's number, then tossed the phone to the ground and stamped on its screen with his heel. Anger burned through him. The manager knew something, maybe everything. A flutter of nerves told Drayce his adrenaline had kicked in. His face flushed. He could feel his heart beating in his chest. He clenched his hands into fists and scowled at the manager, the racks of clean glasses and bottles of spirits clinking as he cowered against them. The barmaid held her eyes on Drayce and sensibly retreated, slowly, as a hiker backing away from a grizzly would. She slipped through the door behind the bar. Drayce let her go. She wasn't important.

The manager was.

He waved his arms as he frantically beckoned someone over.

Ah, Drayce thought. *The bouncer. Of course.*

Drayce peered over his shoulder at the swollen gym rat, who stood up out of his chair and walked over, eyeballing Drayce every step of the way. The bouncer moved across the club like a shark amongst the shallows, full of intent.

When he was a few metres away, he stopped. His expression suggested he now understood what he was up against. Drayce turned back to the manager, who crept towards the door to join the barmaid. Drayce pointed a finger at him.

'Don't move,' he said.

The manager stopped instantly, as though he'd run into a pane of glass. He regarded the bouncer pleadingly, stuttering his words. 'Dddd… do something then, George! What do I pay you for, huh? Kk… kick this guy's ass!'

Drayce faced George, who hadn't moved an inch. His hands were balled into fists, the muscles in his forearms rippling as he tensed his grip. He considered Drayce as though he wanted nothing more than to beat him to the ground and throw him out to the gutter. But as most of those who'd fancied their chances over the years had found, a close-up appreciation of the threat had forced George's self-preservation to kick in. Drayce decided to give the guy a chance.

'Think this through,' he advised him, loud enough for his voice to carry the six-foot gap over the noise of the music. 'I'm not like the punters you throw out of here.' Drayce stood square on to him, feet shoulder width apart, his hands hung loose by his hips; relaxed, but ready. They locked eyes. 'I'm a completely different animal.'

George examined his challenge from head to toe. He stepped forwards: his first mistake.

'Be careful,' Drayce warned. 'It won't go the way you think.'

George took another step. Which made sense to Drayce. The man's choice was to have a fight and throw this stranger out or lose both his job and his reputation; no kind of a decision for a seasoned bouncer.

Drayce considered how the next few seconds were expected to play out. George had decided to take a couple of steps forwards to deal with his boss's problem, and then he'd take a couple more, Drayce knew, at which point he'd throw some punches and drag Drayce out of the club, just as he'd done to a thousand customers over the years.

Drayce had some decisions of his own to make. George would soon be within reach of his fists, and within easy, comfortable reach of his feet. But as skilful a kicker as Drayce was, he wasn't much of a fan of throwing them in tight, congested, close-quarter situations like this, with tables, and stools, and podiums, and poles, and people, all milling about the place, ready to get in his way. Not to mention the huge arms growing out of his target, both of which could easily grab hold of one of his legs and throw him down to the sticky, beer-soaked floor, where he'd be stomped to death.

Drayce watched George take another step, time slowing down as his senses kicked up a gear. George's back foot hovered in the air for a moment, swung forwards, and moved ahead of his planted foot. His fists came up, ready to attack Drayce the moment both feet were firmly rooted to the ground again.

No time to waste.

Drayce moved like a charging bull, chin tucked in, driving the tip of his kneecap into George's groin so hard it might have ruptured his bladder. George winced and buckled forwards, his head landing in Drayce's guard. Drayce gripped his ears, rocked back, and head butted him square in the face.

Tens of thousands of years of evolution had hardened the forehead into a thick slab of bone, intended to protect the brain from a frontal attack, but unwittingly creating a decent weapon in the process. George wobbled on his feet, his entire world shaken to its core. Drayce clinched his neck and yanked him down, face-first, bouncing his head off the floor like a medicine ball. It made a worrying sound.

Drayce straightened himself out, breathing deeply, the remnants of the adrenaline dump making his hands tremble. The dancers no longer danced; the customers no longer leered. Everyone watched him with understandable concern. He faced the manager, who was frozen to the spot on the other side of the bar, his mouth wide open in shock. Drayce bent down to George and checked him over. There were no soft spots on his skull, and he was breathing, so other than some bruises and a nasty concussion, he'd be fine. Probably. Drayce put him into the recovery position and fronted the manager again.

'Who did you send that message to?' Drayce asked. The manager's lips quivered but no words came out. 'Your protection is no longer with us.' Drayce nodded at the giant snoring mass curled up on the floor, moved to the bar, and leaned over it. His fierce eyes glared at the man he was talking to. A bottle smashed on the floor as the manager melted further into the wall. 'It's just you and me.'

The door behind the bar flew open. The manager glimpsed it, then focused back on Drayce, a new-found confidence in his expression. 'Not exactly.'

Drayce clocked the barmaid the moment she appeared, a pump-action shotgun cradled in her arms.

–

'Hey, G!' Raul said, reaching between the front seats from the back of the Impala as he pushed his phone in Gabriel's face. 'I just got this. From the manager of the strip club.'

Gabriel took the phone from him, bored after visiting a long list of associates, trying to get as many people as they could out on the streets searching for the Englishman. He read the four-word message. His heart rate spiked. 'Shit!'

'We going, right?' Raul asked, wide-eyed.

Gabriel scanned the road ahead. 'Where we at?'

'The 612, heading south,' Miguel replied from behind the wheel.

Gabriel felt his excitement increase. 'Put your foot down and take a left onto the 582. If we hurry, we can be there in ten minutes.'

Miguel did as instructed, the needle on the speed dial steadily ramping up.

Gabriel turned to face Raul. 'Check your piece. I want us ready for this motherfucker the minute we get there.'

Raul sat back in his seat and grabbed his carbine with a smile on his face. Gabriel lifted his AR15 from the footwell and pulled the charging handle back a quarter inch, grinning at the sight of a steel casing nestled in the chamber.

29

Melvin turned off the Boulder Highway into Bunnies' parking lot and switched off the radio, uttering a sigh of relief. Naomi frowned at him.

'Hey,' she said through a mouthful of burrito. 'I was listening to that.'

'Billy Joel? Really?'

'Better than that jazz nonsense you waste your time with.'

'There's nothing wrong with jazz.'

'Sure, just like there's nothing wrong with tinnitus. Give me a break, would you? I'm trying to finish my lunch.'

Melvin pulled into a space and cut off the engine. 'You finally done with that thing?'

She dabbed her mouth with a napkin, the delicacy at odds with the savagery she'd displayed while eating. 'Yep.'

'About time. What you say we go see what the management at Bunnies has to tell us about our murder victim?'

'Right behind you.'

They walked towards the entrance together. Naomi observed the state of the building as she dodged the clusters of weeds growing out of the cracks in the parking lot concrete.

'Nice place,' she said, with every ounce of sarcasm she could muster.

Melvin nodded. 'Adriana definitely wasn't living the Vegas dream she probably had in mind when she moved here.'

'You got that right. I wonder what beer they serve.'

She noticed Melvin's expression out of the corner of her eye.

'Come on, Naomi,' he said. 'You can't be serious.'

'What?'

'We're on duty, working a case, and we're about to question a bunch of people who worked with our victim. We've got to be professional.'

'Just a light one.' She flashed him her puppy dog eyes. 'That burrito has made me thirsty.'

Melvin sighed. 'Goddamn it.'

'What? You going to tell on me? You going to rush back to Pikard like the school snitch running to teacher?'

Melvin let out a stifled laugh. Naomi punched him on the arm and smiled. 'Relax, big guy, I'm kidding.'

'As long as you're relaxed, I'll be relaxed. Remember what I said about being nice to these people.'

'Uh-huh, yep. I'll be super nice. You know me.'

'Yeah, I *do* know you. *That's* why I'm anxious.'

'Sounds like you're the one who needs a beer, mister.' They walked under the shadow of the tattered black awning. 'Or maybe a joint. Something to chill you out.'

She reached for the handle, but just before her fingertips got to it, the door swung open. She darted to one side, keen to avoid the crowd of people running out, all with frightened expressions on their faces. Most were obviously customers, but there were also a few half-naked dancers among the crowd, their arms crossed over their chests, eager to cover their modesty in the cold light of day. Some were screaming, but most were silent, their faces ghostly white, desperate to get away from something inside the club. Naomi asked what was going on, but they were all too panicked to answer, running as though their lives depended on it. Seconds later the crowd thinned out, leaving Naomi one side of the entrance, Melvin the other. Their eyes met, the same level of confusion etched on both of their faces.

'The hell was that about?' Melvin asked.

'No idea,' Naomi said. 'Let's go find out.'

She took her badge off her belt and clipped it to the chest pocket of her jacket where it was prominent. Melvin did the same. Naomi gestured she would go in first and took a step over the threshold. As her foot landed, a thunderous *boom* inside the club made her shudder. Her hand snatched her pistol from its holster, a tingle of fight or flight adrenaline rippling out from her core to the surface of her skin.

—

The *crunch-crunch* of the barmaid chambering a cartridge was all it took to snap Drayce out of his state of incomprehension and hurtle him into action. The stage was the nearest point of hard cover. He pumped out three hard strides and dived across its surface, clattering into tables and chairs on the other side just before the first shot rang out.

The ground shook as the barmaid sent a cluster of buckshot into the stage structure, right where Drayce had just been. Breathing hard, he flattened himself on the floor, no longer caring or even noticing the sticky residue underneath him. As he tried to form a plan, the weapon erupted a second time, the buckshot thudding mercilessly into the stage floor just above his head. He peeked at the curtained exit from the stage: his only means of escape that didn't involve sprinting across open ground. He stayed low as he crawled and heard the manager shout at the barmaid.

'Get after him!'

'What if he's got a gun?'

'He's not got a gun!'

'How do you know?'

'He'd have shot back by now if he did. Just get after him. You've got a shotgun for Christ's sake.'

That's it, Drayce thought to himself. *Argue amongst yourselves while I find a way out of here.*

He crawled faster, another shot landing behind him, shredding the scattered table and chairs he'd clattered into. Where the stage met the wall, he stopped and looked up at the stage exit above him, hoping it would lead to a way out of the building. To reach it, he would have to climb onto the stage, exposing himself to the barmaid's shotgun for a couple of seconds. He turned back the way he'd come and locked eyes on the corner of the stage: the spot from which the barmaid would appear if she decided to chase him down and finish the job. She could come into view any second now and he had no means of defending himself. A feeling of regret washed over him.

Armed is always better than unarmed, he remembered telling himself.

He pictured the pistol underneath his cap on the passenger seat of the Expedition and realised now why it had felt like a mistake to leave it behind.

You go against your gut for the first time in a long time and look what happens. Well done, genius.

Another blast from the shotgun, closer this time, throwing debris from the ruined stage into Drayce's face. He scanned the club for something to improvise with. He needed a distraction: something to tear the barmaid's attention away, allowing him to get up onto the stage and through those curtains before she could get a clear shot at him. He heard footsteps at the end of the stage. She was coming for him. He grabbed a chair, preparing to fight for his life, despite the futility.

But then, at precisely the right moment, he heard a couple of distractions walk through the front door.

–

'This is Detective Jones,' Melvin said into his radio. 'We got shots fired inside Bunnies strip club, Boulder Highway, about a hundred metres north-west of the exit from Interstate 515. We need backup ASAP!'

Naomi led the way, pistol out in front in a two-handed grip, both eyes open as she gazed over the top of the weapon. Melvin was right behind her, his revolver pointing south. Another two shotgun blasts stunned the pair of them. Naomi paused in the entrance foyer; before she rounded the corner and stepped into the main room, she needed to be certain they weren't the ones now being shot at.

Voices echoed in the main room: a man and a woman, arguing. Naomi pushed off with her back foot and pivoted around the corner. A dark-haired lady in a red corset caught her eye. She had a shotgun in her hands, the weapon aimed at a stage that snaked out into the middle of the room as she stared angrily at a man behind the bar. Naomi allowed her focus to dart away from the threat, assessing the stage as quick as a flash, but she couldn't see who the woman had been shooting at. What she did notice was an unconscious male a few feet away, curled up in the recovery position. Naomi couldn't see any gunshot wounds, certainly not from a shotgun. His eyes fluttered as he gradually came around from whatever had put him down in the first place.

Naomi appraised the man behind the bar, his panicked expression worsening when he saw Naomi and Melvin. The woman with the shotgun reacted to the abrupt change in his body language and turned towards the entrance.

'Police!' Naomi shouted. 'Drop that weapon, now!'

The woman did as she was told, literally; the big shotgun clattered to the floor right in front of her feet. They both put their hands in the air, their arms ramrod straight. Evidently in shock, their eyes widened like deer caught in headlights.

'Both of you get over here, now,' Naomi shouted. 'And keep your hands up.'

They hurried, the guy hustling out from behind the bar. Once a few feet away, Naomi roared at them again.

'Face down on the floor!'

They dropped to their knees and tentatively lowered their top halves, making sure their hands stayed in sight. Melvin secured the shotgun while Naomi kept her pistol trained on their two suspects, being mindful of the stage area where another threat may lurk. She knelt next to them.

'Who were you shooting at?' she asked the woman. She poked the man in the back of his head. 'And who were you telling her to shoot at?'

The woman's head tilted slightly towards the stage. The man lying next to her pointed his finger in the same direction. Naomi stood up, her watchful eyes scanning the area they'd indicated. This time movement startled her. A man appeared with his back to her. She aimed her pistol at him.

'Police!' she shouted. 'You on the stage! Stand still!' To her surprise, the figure complied. 'Turn around! Do it, now!'

The man slowly pivoted, his face gradually coming into view. As more of him was revealed, she began to mistrust what her eyes were telling her. Goosebumps rippled across her skin, excitement rushing through her. She wanted to run up to him, handcuff him, and arrest him on suspicion of murdering Adriana Garcia. Instead, she did the only thing she could do at that moment in time, the only thing her mind and body would allow under the shock of it all.

She froze.

Her suspect saw her reaction, and whilst keeping his hands in view, took a single step backwards, and vanished through the stage exit.

–

Drayce ran down a corridor with several doorways leading off it. He frantically opened each one as he went past, searching for his earliest opportunity to get out of the building. The first couple led to dressing rooms, with lights, and mirrors, and racks of different outfits for the dancers to wear, but no windows. He could hear the red-haired detective's muffled voice shouting at him to stop from somewhere on the other side of the stage curtain. With a breathlessness that comes with running for your freedom, Drayce pushed on, scanning every nook and cranny for an escape route. Then he saw it: a pair of fire exit doors at the end of the corridor.

Bingo.

As he ran to them, he passed an open doorway to a room that looked different to the others: an alternate layout, with peculiar decor, for a blatant purpose. It was fitted with a giant mattress covered in red plastic that filled the entire floor space. The walls and ceiling were also red. The only window in the room had been blacked out with wooden boards nailed across the frame. The lighting was dim and the bulbs were surrounded by red shades. Piled in the corner of the mattress were bottles of lubricant and boxes of condoms. It didn't take much imagination to figure out what that room was used for.

Drayce risked a quick glance over his shoulder, relieved to see no sign of the detective. He kicked the release bar on the fire exit doors at full stride, the dull metal clattering against the crumbling plaster on the outside wall, and skidded to a halt outside, dust pluming around him as he squinted against the desert sun.

He was in another area of the parking lot, somewhere off to the side of the building. After twenty feet or so of cracked concrete there was a stretch of dusty desert and then a big multi-lane expressway, on the other side of which were residential streets, with cars, and houses, and other things to either hide behind or escape in. With at least a hundred metres of open ground to cover before he could get to those, he ran the risk of being caught out in the open when the police helicopter arrived on scene. He didn't want to be chased by that thing again, certain he'd exhausted all his luck by getting away from it the first time.

Knowing he wouldn't escape by running off in that direction, he turned left, away from the front entrance parking lot where more cops would be arriving soon, and followed the building line, full pelt. He scrambled over a chain-link fence, cursing as his shirt tore on the barbed wire that coiled around the top. He hit the ground with both feet and leapt back on his toes, sprinting towards the Boulder Highway, on the other side of which was the RV rental lot with his Expedition, and the Ruger, both waiting patiently for him to return.

As he cleared the building line, he hit the strip of desert that separated Bunnies from the highway. With each stride he kicked up small clouds of dust behind him, until the soles of his shoes hit the first lane of asphalt. There wasn't time to wait for a safe gap; he careered across all four lanes without even checking for traffic, staring straight ahead, not daring to look at what might be coming his way. His ears ignored the terrifying sounds of horns being leaned on, and tyres locking up, the rubber squealing as passing vehicles nearly lost control all around him.

Miraculously, he made it to the central reservation safely, his feet skidding on the loose stone surface as he finally came to his senses and realised the danger he was causing. Affording himself a quick glance to the right, he spotted a gap in the traffic and went for it, barely breaking stride as he sprinted across another four lanes.

The perimeter of the RV rental place was marked by a chest-height white wall. Drayce's hands slapped against the top edge as he hoisted himself over, wincing as his ribs landed on the rocky border of the RV parking lot on the other side. He crouched low, allowed himself a couple of seconds to catch his breath, then followed the wall line, moving away from the spot where he'd climbed over. He worked his way into a deep squat and placed his hands flat against the wall. He needed to peer over to make sure he wasn't still being followed, but first he listened.

There were no further sounds of screeching tyres and roaring car horns to indicate the detective had followed him across the highway, which meant she either hadn't seen which direction he'd run off in, or wasn't as crazy as him, and was unwilling to risk her life to get across the busy road. Unless of course, being local law enforcement, she knew of another, quicker, simpler way of getting across. He'd been running so fast, so focused on where he was trying to get to, he hadn't once bothered to look over his shoulder. For all he knew, the detective might have followed him the entire way, and was, at that very moment, forming up on the other side of the brick wall with her partner, their guns drawn, ready to leap over to arrest their prized murder suspect.

Holding his breath, Drayce flexed his pumped leg muscles and pushed up out of the squat, raising his eyeline to the top of the wall, hoping he wasn't about to stare down the business end of that red-haired detective's pistol for the third time that day.

–

Naomi felt a moment of trepidation as she approached the curtains with her pistol, her survival instincts telling her there was a killer on the other side. But just like with every other terrifying moment during her long career in the police, she pushed the fear aside and moved forwards.

The curtains wafted across her figure as a cape in the wind might, introducing her to the world on the other side of that stage. She found herself in a corridor, leading off which were doorways to rooms full of mirrors, bright lights and racks of skimpy outfits. She kept her gun up, aiming it into each room as she went past. The layout in the last one concerned her, filling her head with numerous avenues of enquiry now that it was obvious their murder victim had worked in a brothel.

Naomi didn't want these thoughts to distract her in the middle of a pursuit, so she focused on the wide-open fire escape doors she was now approaching: the first escape route their suspect would have come across. She ran outside, scanning the area for him.

Nothing.

She assessed the geography, aware he would have been presented with few options. He hadn't run off in a direct line from the fire escape, because if he had, he would still be in sight; there was simply too much ground to cover before he would have reached suitable terrain in which to hide. Right wasn't much better. It led back to the main car park, which was precisely where their backup would be arriving any second now. She turned left: the only viable option for him once they were boiled down.

She followed the building line, gun up on aim as she rounded the corner. A fence up ahead, six foot high, made of chain link with coils of barbed wire looped around the top, had something caught in it, wafting in the breeze. She holstered her pistol, hooked her fingers in between the links, and lifted herself up for a closer look. It was a piece of cloth, small and frayed at the edges, as though it had been ripped off a light blue cotton shirt.

Just like the one she'd seen their suspect wearing.

Excitement flushed through her now it was confirmed she was on his tail. She took off her jacket, threw it over the coils of barbed wire, and hoisted her body up and over the fence. Leaving her impaled jacket behind, she ran towards the highway and drew her pistol again as she pivoted around the corner of Bunnies. She opened her mouth wide, ready to shout at their suspect that he was under arrest.

-

'Drive right up to the building,' Gabriel instructed Miguel as they swerved into Bunnies' parking lot. 'We go in guns up and shooting. I don't wanna give the gringo a chance to escape again.'

Miguel raced up to the black awning, the tyres squealing as they locked up, the vehicle skidding to a halt. All three men climbed out of the Impala and ran to the front entrance doors, the stocks of their carbines pressed into their shoulders and their fingers on the triggers.

-

'Stay down!' Melvin shouted at the manager and the barmaid, both of whom were squirming on the ground. 'Neither of you are getting up until our backup arrives!'

'This is bullshit!' the manager shouted back. 'Your partner's gone after the real threat. We're the victims here, dumbass!'

Melvin parted his lips to put the guy in his place, his tongue halted by the sound of the front doors crashing open. Keeping his gun trained on the two suspects, he glanced towards the entrance, expecting to see a swarm of uniforms filing into the club. This thought brought with it a sense of relief.

The relief vanished the moment he saw the three armed men.

Instinct and training kicked in immediately. Running for cover, he simultaneously aimed his revolver at the three figures, loosing off all six rounds as he dived for the Staff Only door. He hit it shoulder-first, sliding along the tiled floor into cover as bullets from the three gunmen slammed into the walls and clipped the doorframe.

–

'Who the fuck was that?' Gabriel asked the manager and barmaid in between firing rounds through the swaying Staff Only door.

'He's a cop!' the manager replied. 'There's another gone through the curtains, chasing the big limey you told me to look out for.'

Gabriel turned to Miguel and Raul. 'You pair hit?' They both shook their heads. 'Good. Go after them. I'll deal with the cop who just shot at us.'

Miguel and Raul ran through the curtains, carbines up on aim, as Gabriel reloaded his AR and moved to the Staff Only door.

–

Naomi rounded the corner, pistol up, lips pursed, ready to bark her orders.

There was nobody there to shout at.

She ran to the edge of the asphalt and rotated on the spot, pointing her pistol in every conceivable direction. The air displacement from passing vehicles blew sand and grit in her face, making her squint as she tried to seek out his movements. But there was no sign of him. Her chin tilted up to the sky. She took a deep breath.

And screamed.

Some of the noise was drowned out by the traffic roaring past, but it was still loud enough to make her own ears ring. She felt the heat radiating off her reddening face, and the swell of her veins that now bulged out from her forehead and neck, as every measure of frustration that had built up throughout the day was released. Once her scream died, she holstered her pistol and turned back to Bunnies.

Two men with guns appeared around the corner of the building.

She dropped to the ground as she drew and fired, her rounds skimming the wall line, missing the pair by inches. They evidently had experience in gunfights, because they instantly skipped back into cover behind the corner of the building. She pulled the trigger again, intending to use containing fire to keep them there while she moved herself into cover. But nothing happened. She tilted her pistol: the top slide was locked in place, jammed by a casing in the breech. Her heart leapt into her mouth. Keeping her eyes on the building line, she ran through her emergency stoppage drill, tapping and racking the weapon, but still the obstruction remained. She flattened herself out as low as she could, pressed the magazine release catch, racked the slide three times to clear the casing, and reached for a fresh mag.

The pouch was empty.

Her fingers stroked thin air where her spare should be. It must have fallen out as she'd climbed over the fence, she guessed. Just as she went to retrieve the partially loaded magazine she'd dropped on the ground, the gunmen appeared. Panic set in, unarmed and defenceless as she was, lying in an open area with no cover.

They both aimed their guns at her.

'Miguel and Raul,' Drayce said to himself as he watched the men stalk the detective. Then, sarcastically, 'I wonder what's brought you here.'

Drayce knew they must have been on the receiving end of the message the manager had sent and made their way straight to Bunnies to have another pop at kidnapping him. He watched it all play out on the other side of the highway for as long as he could, hoping he wouldn't need to intervene, but there was nothing else for it. He risked giving his position away, jeopardising his own freedom, but there was no way on earth he was going to witness a cop be shot dead in front of his eyes. He'd rather spend the rest of his life in prison.

Miguel and Raul approached her side by side in a tactical V formation, separating further from each other as they closed her down, making it harder to hit them both in quick succession. Using the top of the wall as support for his forearms, Drayce aimed the Ruger at Miguel on the left. He must have been seventy metres away: a hell of a distance with a pistol. Drayce locked his arms out, took a deep breath, held it, and calmed his entire body as he settled his sight picture on the man's centre mass and patiently waited for a long enough gap in the traffic. A lorry sped past, blocking his view for a heart-pounding second. His line of sight cleared. He gently rolled the trigger back.

Crack!

Miguel's upper body spun, the bullet hitting him in the shoulder. Raul noticed his friend get shot and mercifully ignored the red-haired detective, gazing warily across the highway in Drayce's general direction as he no doubt tried to spot where the round had come from.

Drayce didn't waste any time. He smoothly pivoted to the right, settled the iron sights on him, and fired, the round clipping his ribs, making him buckle to the ground. With no idea where the threat was, they both turned and ran for the cover of the building. Drayce let them go as he tucked out of sight behind the wall, hoping the detective hadn't seen him.

–

Melvin crawled along the floor on his back, putting distance between him and the bullet-riddled door as he swung open his revolver's cylinder, pointed the muzzle to the ceiling, and lifted it up quickly as he tapped on his forearm with his other hand, the sudden jolt enough to spit out all six empty casings. They rattled on the tiles as he hurriedly pulled a speed reloader from his belt and slotted six fresh bullets home.

Footsteps at the door made him stop.

He flicked his wrist to slam the cylinder back into the weapon, cocked the hammer, and took aim between his bent knees. A figure's shadow appeared, long arm in hand as it approached the doorway. Melvin estimated where the gunman was, took aim at the wall, and fired a single shot.

–

'Fuck!' Gabriel shouted as he leapt back, a bullet having just punched through the wall ahead of him. He aimed his AR at where he guessed the cop was, about to spray bullets through the partition that separated them, only to be distracted by Miguel and Raul as they ran through the curtains back into the club.

'The fuck are you pair doing?' Gabriel asked. 'I told you to go after them.'

'We got shot,' Miguel replied, a hand pressed to his bloody shoulder.

'Couldn't get a spot on the shooter, so we had to drop back.' Raul cradled his ribs, plainly injured. His black suit had a dark sheen to it where blood had seeped through. 'We'd have been killed for sure if we hadn't.'

Gabriel looked back at the Staff Only door, considered charging in as a three-man team, but soon discounted it when he heard sirens in the distance. He turned and marched to the entrance doors. 'Come on. We're leaving.'

The three gunmen sprinted back to their car.

–

Naomi rolled onto her back and sat up, staring across the highway. There was no sign of the Englishman, but she was sure he was the one who had fired those shots, undoubtedly saving her life. Panting heavily, she stood up, put her hands on her thighs, and bent over, staring at the dusty ground, her mind lost in the enormity of her near-death experience. Sweat dripped off her nose and landed on the dry earth between her feet. Not far down the highway she heard sirens start up, the repetitive drum beat of the police helicopter closing in from above. She stood up straight and watched their arrival on scene.

'Little late to the party, guys.'

30

Drayce was pleased to see the red-haired detective get to her feet safely, plainly uninjured. She stared across the highway, searching for him, he presumed. She appeared angry, which was something Drayce understood. It's never a rewarding feeling to lose a suspect, especially the same one you lost earlier that day. But hopefully she'd appreciate the help he'd given her, even though he was certain it wouldn't slow her pursuit of him in the slightest.

As carefully as he'd peeked over the wall, Drayce just as carefully lowered himself down. He leaned against it and observed the RV rental company's parking lot. The front corner of their office building poked out from behind the roof of the vehicle closest to him. Judging by what he'd observed of his surroundings when he'd originally parked up, his Expedition was approximately ten spaces over to his left, which was roughly a six-second sprint if he needed to get there quickly, or a thirty-second walk if he didn't want to draw attention.

The sound of sirens, approaching at speed from the highway, made him get right to it.

He stayed low to start with, crouching as he moved away from the wall line to avoid being spotted by the detective. Before he appeared from between the RVs and came into sight of the rental office, he stood tall and walked out into the open, using the big vehicles as cover from the highway. He tried to appear relaxed and resisted the urge to run, which was difficult with the sound of the helicopter in the sky, and the buzz of the police presence surging across the highway. He took out his Expedition keys and unlocked it on the approach, wanting to get out of sight of the helicopter's bird's-eye-view camera before it began its sweep of the area.

'Hey buddy,' he heard someone call out. 'Excuse me, pal.'

The voice was behind him, somewhere over by the entrance to the rental office, full of fake cheer and insincere friendliness: the tone of your typical salesman. Drayce cursed under his breath; attention was the last thing he wanted. He ignored the man as he tucked the front of his shirt into his trousers, trying to hide the missing strip that had torn off on the barbed wire. He was hoping the salesman would get the message and give up, but then he heard the guy's footsteps escalate to a jog, and Drayce knew he wasn't going to get away that easily.

'Hey,' the salesman said as he appeared over Drayce's right shoulder. 'How's it going?'

Drayce didn't slow down as he turned to the guy. He was probably in his fifties, his pale complexion indicating he spent most of his time indoors. He wore a short sleeve white shirt, the rental company's logo on the chest pocket, which had three cheap pens clipped inside, the lids evidently gnawed on, judging by the teeth marks. Ink stains he'd plainly struggled to wash out, merged clumsily with the logo.

'I'm good, thanks,' Drayce replied, clipping the sentence short to emphasise he was in a hurry. He bore down on his SUV, opened the driver's door, climbed in, and slammed it shut without missing a beat. The salesman stepped in front of the vehicle, waved through the windscreen like a relentless idiot, and smiled a big, fake grin of such magnitude it was evident he'd been practising it every day for the last thirty years. Drayce felt his teeth grind together.

'Hey,' the salesman said, his voice stifled by the glass. 'I saw you come in earlier and tried to find you. You been looking around?'

Drayce reluctantly buzzed his window down, giving in to the man's persistence. 'My wife and I were thinking of renting something big while we're in town.' He rested his left hand on the door, his wedding ring in view, adding a layer of authenticity to the lie. 'It's a big place you've got here. Lots to choose from.'

'Yes, there is. Nice accent by the way. Where you from? Australia?'

'Sure.'

'Nice! What you doing over here in the good ol' US of A? Vacation time?'

'Yeah.' Drayce glanced briefly at the police vehicles in Bunnies' parking lot. 'Something like that.'

'Well, you know what's better than a road trip in an RV during your vacation?' He paused for dramatic effect. Drayce reached for the window button. 'Nothing! That's what!'

A dot in the sky caught Drayce's attention as it hovered above Bunnies. It moved across the highway in their direction. He tried not to look concerned about it in front of the salesman, but the guy must have picked up on something he'd seen in his body language.

'Yep, they're after somebody all right. Must be something big n'all. Don't see 'em making that kind of an effort for a dancer's tip jar going missing.'

The salesman laughed at his own joke. Drayce moved his left arm slightly, covering the torn spot on his shirt that peeked out of his waistline.

'I best head off,' Drayce said as he glanced at his watch. 'My wife will kill me if I'm late back. She gets easily stressed when we're abroad.'

The salesman held up his hands in mock surrender, the well-practised grin still spread across his face. 'No problem. You take my card. My name's Phil. You ask for me when ya'll come back here for your RV. Because you will come back. We got the best prices and the highest standard vehicles in all of Nevada.'

Phil slipped a card from his pocket and held it out. Drayce took it from him.

'Thanks,' Drayce said.

'No problem.'

As Phil pulled his hand back, Drayce saw his eyes drop to the cap on the passenger's seat.

'Hey, nice cap. What team is that?'

Without waiting for permission, Phil reached through the window to pick it up and find out for himself. Drayce's heart skipped a beat as he remembered what it was covering. His big hand clamped down on it just in time.

'It's not a team cap,' Drayce said, his knuckles white. 'It's just some cheap thing I bought to keep the sun out of my eyes when I'm driving. Look, I really do need to get back to my wife. I lost track of time while I was looking around your yard. She'll be getting worried about me.'

'No problem.' Phil backed away from the window, the grin now fading as he no doubt realised a deal was not happening. 'I feel your pain. My old lady's a real ass-kicker

273

too. You have a great day, and remember to ask for Phil when you come back for your RV.'

'I will. Thanks, Phil.'

Drayce backed out of the space and turned around. As he drove away, he checked the rear-view mirror and saw Phil staring at the police helicopter in the sky, before gazing across the highway at the hive of patrol cars in Bunnies' parking lot, no doubt wondering what all the excitement was about.

Well, you were right about one thing, Phil, Drayce thought, as he drove out of the rear exit onto the side streets and weaved a route in the opposite direction to Bunnies. *They're after someone for a lot more than stealing a lousy tip jar.*

31

The uniformed cops who'd rushed to the scene charged around like a bunch of kids who'd heard the chime of an ice cream van in August. Commands were yelled into radios and tyres screamed out of the parking lot as they chased down one sighting after another, every single one of which had so far turned out to be nothing.

Naomi, on the other hand, had barely moved a muscle. She'd learned her lesson: this suspect was too fast and dynamic to catch that way. However, just because she wasn't running around like a headless chicken, it didn't mean she'd given up. Far from it. As a seasoned detective, she was accustomed to playing the long game, and knew if she worked hard and followed the leads, the chance of their suspect evading capture and seeing the light of tomorrow through anything other than jail bars, was about as good as a gambler's chance against the house during a long weekend at the Bellagio.

There would only be one winner in the end.

She stood with Melvin at the back of his Buick and faced the open trunk. Perched on the tailgate were the manager of Bunnies and the barmaid, both hand-cuffed to the rear. The manager's name was Conrad McAuley; the barmaid's Jeanette Brown. Neither had said a word since they'd been given their Miranda warning. Strictly speaking, they shouldn't be questioned about the suspected offence for which they'd been arrested until they were at the police station and had been given the chance to consult a lawyer.

Naomi didn't have time for that.

'Okay, listen in, dipshits. We want to know who you were shooting at and why. And we also want IDs for those Mexicans who turned up all guns blazing.'

They focused on their feet, lips tighter than a sailor's knot. Naomi took off her torn jacket that she'd recovered from the barbed wire fence when she'd gone back to collect the pistol magazine she'd dropped, casually hooked the collar with her finger, and swept it over her shoulder.

'We can play this game all day long,' she said. 'And if you think holding out for a lawyer is the way to play this, go ahead and try. That procedural bullshit might have worked in the past.' She knelt and stared into Jeanette's eyes. 'When you've been trying to dodge your drink driving case.' She switched her gaze to Conrad. 'Or perhaps your sexual harassment lawsuit.' She stood up and glared at the tops of their heads as she spoke. 'But believe me when I tell you, this shit you now find yourselves in is a whole different world. The rules of the old game don't apply here, folks. That guy you were shooting at? We have an alternate rule book for questioning that kind of suspect.' She paused for a few seconds to add weight to what she was about to say. 'Along with *anyone* we think he may have conspired with.'

Jeanette met Naomi's eyes with glazed terror in her pupils. She turned to Conrad, whose face suggested he was silently pleading for her to keep her mouth shut. Jeanette was sweating, her body temperature rising from the stress of holding it all in, like a volcano wanting to erupt. Naomi had seen it a hundred times before. Wouldn't be long now.

'He made me do it!' Jeanette blurted out.

Conrad's eyes widened.

That knot wasn't so tight after all, Naomi thought.

'It's his gun,' Jeanette continued. 'He told me to scare that guy off with it.'

Conrad's face darkened. 'You bitch! Shut the fu—'

The back of Naomi's hand silenced him in an instant. Melvin scanned the parking lot, happy to see no one had witnessed it. Conrad hung his head as a drop of blood fell from his busted lip and landed on the cracked concrete between his feet.

'You hit me,' he said in amazement.

Naomi stepped towards him; it was enough to make him flinch.

'A slap will be the least of your worries if you interrupt her again, *bitch*.' Naomi turned back to Jeanette. 'You were saying?'

Jeanette took a deep breath. 'Okay, so this guy comes into the bar – the one you've been looking for – and he says he wants to speak to the manager. So I go tell Mr McAuley, and before he goes out to speak to the guy, he takes me into his office to have a look at him on the cameras. Which makes sense, right? I mean, you wanna get a look at the guy before you go face to face with him, especially a guy who might be there to cause problems. Well, as soon as I point this guy out on the screen to Mr McAuley, he looks worried. I mean, he clearly knows who this guy is, it's written all over his face. Then he gets this big shotgun out from under his desk and starts loading it up. When it won't take no more, he sets it down on his desk and tells me to take him out to this guy, and then to come back and watch from the monitor. He said if George… Oh, George! Is he all right? That guy you chased away knocked him out cold.'

'He's fine,' Naomi snapped. 'Paramedics are treating him.' She paused for Jeanette to continue her story. 'You were saying?'

Jeanette's focus came back. 'Right. So, Mr McAuley said if George can't deal with the guy, then I was to come out with the shotgun and…'

Jeanette glanced at Conrad.

'And what?' Naomi said.

Jeanette broke free from Conrad's gaze. 'And shoot the guy.'

'Goddamn it!' Conrad said through red teeth and bloody lips. 'You stupid little whore!'

Naomi considered hitting him again, but decided it wasn't needed. She caught the eye of the nearest uniformed officer, loitering by the crime scene tape at the entrance to Bunnies.

'Officer!' she yelled, beckoning him over with her arm. She grabbed Conrad by his shirt and lifted him to his feet. 'Please take this gentleman back to the station. He's under arrest for conspiring to commit murder, so he's not to have anyone informed of his arrest until I say it's okay. And that includes a lawyer. Understand?'

'Yes, ma'am,' the officer replied.

Naomi cringed. Four people in one day. Goddamn rookies.

'You keep your fucking mouth shut!' Conrad shouted to Jeanette as he was led away, his voice fading as he was dragged over to a marked patrol car and bungled into the back seat. 'You'll get us both killed, you—'

His voice was cut off abruptly when the officer slammed his door shut. Naomi faced Jeanette. 'Ignore him.' She smiled at her. 'You're doing well. What else can you tell us?'

'Okay,' Jeanette said. 'So, I did come out with the shotgun, and I did fire some shots, but I only did it to keep Mr McAuley happy. I was just trying to *look* the part, you know?'

Naomi nodded her head as though she understood her mentality, but all she was thinking was how stupid that excuse would sound in a judge's ears.

'I wasn't aiming at the guy,' Jeanette said. 'Not really. I just wanted to make it look like I was. I didn't want to upset Mr McAuley by hiding out in the back, like I wanted to. He's got a nasty streak in him when he gets mad.'

'I'm sure,' Naomi said. 'Tell me about the three Mexicans.'

Jeanette broke eye contact. 'Oh, I don't know who they were.'

Her first lie, Naomi thought.

'All right.' Naomi flicked her head at Bunnies. 'Tell me what goes on at this place.'

Confusion flashed across Jeanette's face. 'What d'you mean?'

'That room in the back, behind the stage. What's it used for?'

'The dressing rooms?'

'No,' Naomi said, a hint of impatience creeping into her voice. 'Not the dressing rooms. Further down the corridor. The one with the red walls and the plastic wrapped mattress covering the floor.'

Jeanette's gaze fell to her feet. 'Oh. That room.'

'Yeah. That room.'

Jeanette tentatively made eye contact with Naomi. 'I've never really had anything to do with that room. That's Mr McAuley's thing. All I've ever done is serve drinks.'

And blast buck shot at strangers, Naomi thought.

'But you must know what goes on back there,' she said.

Jeanette went silent.

Naomi bent forwards at the waist, her face inches from Jeanette's. 'Don't treat me like I'm stupid.'

'I'm not,' Jeanette said, eventually. 'Yeah, I know what goes on in that room. The dancers aren't just dancers. Mr McAuley has them doing… other stuff.'

Naomi leaned a little closer. 'We know what goes on in there, Jeanette. It's pretty damn obvious, but we need to hear it from you. So, please tell us, in plain English, and don't worry about hurting our sensibilities. We've both seen things that'd keep you awake for months.'

'They're hookers,' Jeanette said. 'After they get done dancing, they go back to those rooms with customers and fuck for money. That plain enough for you?'

Naomi stood up straight. This girl was too easy.

'Next question: how well do you know Adriana Garcia?'

'I knew her pretty well, I guess.'

'When was the last time she worked here?'

'I don't know. A few days ago, I guess.'

'That normal, is it?'

Jeanette shrugged. 'Girls come and go. The money's good, so some work hard for a few months, stack up the cash, then you don't hear from them for a while. They're not the nine to five types.'

'Anything happen the last time Adriana worked a shift here? Anything that might make her run away and not want to come back?'

Naomi studied Jeanette's reaction closely: a hand came up to her cheek and stroked it with the back of her fingers. Her eyes darted high and right, avoiding contact with Naomi. There was a long pause before she gave her answer. Naomi had witnessed suspects give off the same indicators a thousand times.

She was about to lie again.

'No,' Jeanette said. 'Not that I can think of.'

Naomi caught the eye of another uniformed officer who was stood next to her patrol car, talking into her radio.

'Little help!' Naomi shouted.

The officer ran over.

'Detective Ocean – Homicide,' Naomi said. 'Please take Miss Brown into custody. Find her our dirtiest, skankiest cell to sit in, preferably one she can share with a few of our smelliest, most unpleasant customers, while she thinks about the answers she's just given me.'

'Hey!' Jeanette said as the officer took hold of her and lifted her to her feet. 'I told you what I know!'

Naomi ignored her as she was led away. Once she was out of earshot, Melvin stepped up close.

'What was that about? You had her talking.'

'She just lied to me, and there's no point listening to lies. She can sit in a cell until she wants to tell me the truth.'

'What exactly did she lie about?'

'About those Mexicans; she knows who they are. And about Adriana's last night working here. Something

281

happened, and Jeanette knows what that something was. And then there's the other thing.'

'What other thing?'

'When I asked her 'how well do you know Adriana Garcia', she replied, 'I knew her pretty well.''

'So?'

'Come on, dumbass. Work it out. I used the present tense; she used the past tense. Which tells me she knows Adriana is dead, and I'm thinking she maybe knows why she was murdered. We just need to sweat it out of her.'

Melvin nodded. 'Okay, sounds promising. A little thin, but promising.'

'Thin my ass.'

Naomi saw Wilson appear through a crowd of cops at the entrance to Bunnies.

'Ah shit,' Naomi whispered under her breath. 'I do not have the patience to deal with this prick right now.'

'Hey,' Wilson said, holding off out of Naomi's reach. 'Pikard wanted me to update you guys on what's going on inside the club.'

'Pikard's here?' Melvin asked. 'Must have missed his motor amongst all these cop cars.'

'We came together in my car. We were in the office when we heard your call on the radio.'

'You were in the office?' Naomi said. 'Big surprise there.'

She noticed Melvin throw her a look that told her to leave it.

'You want to hear what we found or not, Puddle?'

'Of course we do,' Melvin said as he flung out an arm to hold Naomi back.

Wilson ignored him and stared at Naomi. 'How about you? Want to know what I found while you were out here with your thumb in your ass, feeling sorry for yourself because you lost our suspect twice in the same day?'

Naomi pushed Melvin's arm out of her way and stepped forwards.

'I can see you two are getting along, as always,' Pikard said, halting Naomi in her tracks. They all turned to face him. He focused on Wilson. 'You tell them yet?'

'No, sir,' Wilson replied. 'Not yet.'

'Well get to it. We don't have all day, and Adriana's killer is still out there.'

Pikard's words made Naomi feel a pang of guilt for having lost the suspect a second time, even though that clearly hadn't been his intention.

'We've been checking the cameras,' Wilson said to Naomi and Melvin.

'And?' Naomi asked.

'And it's all recorded and accounted for, going back weeks and weeks, except for six hours last Friday night, which have been deleted.'

'Does it show Adriana working that night?'

'Yep. It shows her arriving at work, the first couple of hours of her shift, and then it just goes black and kicks in again six hours later when the place is all closed up.'

'And no sign of Adriana in any of the footage after that gap?'

'Doesn't look like it. It would appear Friday was her last night working here.'

Naomi felt her excitement building; they were getting somewhere. 'So, during her last night working at this place, something happened that was so bad it needed to be deleted from the camera footage.'

'That's how it sounds to me,' Melvin said.

Naomi jogged around to the passenger door of his Buick. 'Come on!'

'Where are you going?' Pikard asked.

'Yeah, where *are* we going?' Melvin asked as he opened the driver's door.

'To the jail block to interrogate Jeanette and Conrad. We need them to fill that six hour gap for us.'

'You might have some luck with the barmaid,' Pikard said. 'But her boss? Forget about it. He ain't saying nothing to nobody until he's spoken to a lawyer.'

'He can have his lawyer.' Naomi climbed inside the vehicle, leaned across, and spoke to Pikard through the open driver's door. 'Doesn't matter. Jeanette will tell us everything. She doesn't have it in her to hold out. Then we can use the information she gives us to pressure Conrad into crumbling.'

Melvin sat in the driver's seat and started the engine. 'Sounds like a plan.'

Wilson bent down and peered at them both through Melvin's open door. 'What about me?' he asked.

'Get on your little social media blog, you kiss ass!' Naomi shouted across the front of Melvin. 'And tell the world Ocean and Jones are one step closer to justice for Adriana Garcia.'

Melvin stared at Wilson while Naomi laughed, a reluctant grin on Pikard's face as he sauntered back to the crime scene in the club. Wilson's mouth flapped as though he wanted to think of a good comeback, but his brain just wasn't producing the goods in time. Melvin shrugged, shut his door, then drove away with a smile on his face.

32

It's him. He's here.

The words echoed in Drayce's mind as he drove west through the city, the hills of the Red Rock Canyon carving a path through the sky in front of him. A retail park to his right, with adverts for a cell phone store and a coffee shop, gave him two good reasons to stop. He turned the Expedition into a parking spot as isolated as possible and switched off the engine. His head fell in his hands.

It's him. He's here.

Questions hurtled around inside his mind like a swarm of bees. He took his phone out and tried calling Nelson again: no answer. Then he rang Carlos, but it wouldn't connect. Carlos's phone was dead. Drayce wondered if the same was true for him.

Drayce forced his mind to organise the information at his disposal. The motive of the cops was simple: Drayce had been identified as the last person to be seen with Adriana before she'd been murdered, and during that encounter she'd been seen to point a gun at him. Naturally, until they could prove otherwise, the cops liked him as a suspect. But who were those gangsters so desperate to take him for themselves that they were willing to intervene in a police arrest? Had he witnessed something as he'd tracked Adriana down to her new address that was worth taking such risks to kill him?

He thought back to last night, on Adriana's doorstep, staring down the barrel of the gun in her outstretched hand. He replayed the entire encounter in his mind, frame by frame, but nothing stood out to him. No clues, no hints. Nothing.

It's him. He's here.

The manager of Bunnies — Adriana's former boss — appeared to be linked to the people who wanted to get their hands on Drayce. He'd contacted them, whoever *they* were, telling them the man they were after was in his club. And what about that room in the back of Bunnies? The club wasn't just a strip joint.

Is that at the core of all this? Did something happen to Adriana there that terrified her enough to make her move apartments and start answering the door with a loaded gun in her hands?

What Drayce would give to be alone with that manager for just five minutes. With enough encouragement, Drayce was sure the man would tell him exactly who was after him, and why. Trouble was, there hadn't been the chance to ask him many questions, after being chased out by his homicidal barmaid, and then by that red-haired detective.

So, what to do now?

Bunnies would be swarming with cops, so he couldn't go back there any time soon to pick up where he'd left off with the manager. And besides, that guy would no doubt be in handcuffs and on his way to a jail cell by now, along with his barmaid.

Who else can I speak to who'd have the answers I'm looking for? Maybe the person who might have already questioned both the manager of Bunnies and the barmaid?

There was nothing else for it. It might be a crazy move, but he'd hit a brick wall, and had nowhere else to turn.

A quick search on Google found a direct non-emergency number for police dispatch in Vegas. Remembering a logo he'd seen at the entrance to the retail park, he scanned the row of shops. He could now see the same logo mounted above a set of glass doors. It was an animated image of a mobile phone with lines juddering out from it to give the viewer the impression it was ringing. He climbed out of the Expedition, took off his torn blue shirt, and slipped on a clean white T-shirt from his rucksack. He pulled the cap down on his head, stuffed the gun into his waistline with his T-shirt pulled down over it, and walked to the phone store.

He kept his head down, bought two of the cheapest Tracfones they sold, and paid in cash. Armed with his new burner phones, he walked to the coffee shop and bought a ham salad sandwich, a beef and mustard sandwich, a bottle of water and a latte. Back in the driver's seat he threw off his cap, opened the first packet of sandwiches, and started eating, unboxing one of his new phones and fitting the SIM card between mouthfuls. He started the engine and plugged the phone's cable into the vehicle's USB port to give it some charge. Whilst the device sucked up some energy, he polished off his lunch. When his latte was half drunk, the phone's display was showing fifteen per cent battery.

Time to make the call.

'Las Vegas Metropolitan Police Department. How can we help you?'

'I need to speak to a detective in Homicide.'

'What's your name, sir?'

'Not just any detective, a specific one.'

'Sir? I asked what your name was.'

'She'll be late twenties–early thirties, in good shape.'

'What is the nature of your call, sir?'

'About five foot ten, lean and muscular. Oh, and she's got big red curly hair.'

'Sir, I need to know—'

'No, you don't. What you need to do is find the homicide detective with big red hair, the one who's investigating Adriana Garcia's murder, and get her on this line within the next five minutes. Otherwise, I'm putting the phone down and she'll have lost her only chance to speak to me.'

There was a moment's silence on the line before the call handler responded.

'And who might *you* be?'

'I'm the man she's been chasing all day. I'm her murder suspect.'

33

'Did you see that jackass's face?' Naomi said.

Melvin was still smiling. 'Yeah, I saw.'

'That felt *so* good.' Naomi had her seat tilted back and her feet propped up on the dashboard, her hands behind her head, smiling as she tapped her feet together. 'I love getting one over on that selfish son of a bitch.'

The smile on Melvin's face slackened. 'I can see you're happy, but can you please contain yourself enough to not put your dirty shoes on my clean car.'

Naomi stuck her tongue out at him. 'Relax. They're not dirty. I won't leave a mark. And you should be as happy as me right now. If we didn't visit Bunnies when we did, none of this would have come to light. That barmaid is going to talk, just you wait and see. We may not have cracked this case yet, but we've certainly put a great big dent in it.'

'Be that as it may, it doesn't change the fact your shoes are going to mark the dash. So please,' he swiped at her knee, 'put your feet down.'

Naomi pulled her leg back and smiled. 'You're gonna pay for that, big guy.'

Naomi poked him in the ribs to make him laugh. She went to do it again, but he leaned away, pressed up against his door, and tried to fend her off with one arm. She reached for the lapels on his suit jacket to mimic a stranglehold, the interior of the car full of laughter. The chirp of Naomi's phone made them stop.

'Saved by the bell,' Naomi said.

'Had you right where I wanted you.'

With her middle finger in the air, Naomi put her feet back up on the dashboard and answered the call.

'Detective Ocean here.'

'Detective, this is Carla from dispatch. We've got a caller who wants to speak to you. Well, we *think* it's you he wants to speak to. We've contacted Homicide Supervision and you're the only one who matches the description he gave.'

Carla's voice sounded frenzied. It made Naomi sit up straight and pay attention.

'Okay,' Naomi said, hesitantly. 'Put him on.'

'Wait. There's something you need to know first. This guy said he's the one you've been looking for. He said he's your murder suspect.'

Naomi nearly dropped her phone. 'What?'

'You've been chasing him all day, so he says.'

Naomi was starting to feel lightheaded. 'What else did he say?'

'Nothing. You're the only one he'll speak to.'

There was silence for a few seconds while Naomi punched Melvin on the arm and mouthed the words 'pull over'. The look on her face must have told him the call was serious. He did as he was told.

'Detective?' Carla said. 'You want me to patch him through?'

'I need you to run a trace on the call.'

Melvin shut off the engine and leaned over to listen in on the conversation.

'A trace?' Carla asked. 'You'll need a warrant and someone from tech support to make that happen, Detective. And I hate to rush you, but he said he'd hang up if you weren't on the line in five minutes, and that was four minutes ago.'

'Shit! Okay, put him through.'

Naomi felt everything around her slow down as she listened to the clicks and crackles down the line. Seconds later there was nothing but silence. She listened hard and thought she could hear someone breathing.

'Hello?' she said.

'Who am I speaking to?'

'You first.'

'That's not how this works. Want to know why?'

'Shoot.'

'Because if this isn't the red-haired detective who's been chasing after me all day, this is going to be a short conversation.'

'Well, I do have red hair, I am a detective, and I have been chasing after an Englishman all day long who's wanted for the murder of Adriana Garcia. So, I guess this might not be all that short of a conversation.'

'Good to hear.'

'What's this call about? You want to hand yourself in?'

Melvin's eyes went wide, as though the caller's identity was just dawning on him. He turned sideways and moved to the edge of his seat, staring intently at Naomi as she spoke.

'Because if you do, we can arrange that right now,' Naomi said. 'Make sure it happens nice and safely, rather than waiting for SWAT to corner you somewhere. Might not go the way you want if that happens. It's best we come to some kind of arrangement. Being on the run can be dangerous.'

'I appreciate your concern, but no, I'm not calling to hand myself in. I'm calling because we need each other's help.'

'Really? How so?'

'Despite what you believe, I didn't kill Adriana Garcia. I want to find out who did, but that's a little difficult when I'm having to put so much effort into avoiding you and your colleagues. On that basis, I propose we exchange some information. I'm sure it would help with your enquiries if we talked about how I came to be at Adriana's front door last night, and I'm sure if you tell me what her manager has told you, we could start interlocking pieces of this puzzle. I think if we worked together, we'd have a better chance of finding her killer.'

Naomi couldn't stop herself from laughing. 'You must be one crazy son of a bitch if you think there's any chance of that happening.'

'Even after I saved your life earlier?'

Naomi went silent. She'd never admit it to him, but she did feel as though she owed him for that one.

'Doesn't count for much, I'm afraid,' she lied. 'You're still a murder suspect. *My* murder suspect.'

'Bit harsh, but all right.'

'Why don't I propose the only sensible option on the table: you go to the nearest police station and hand yourself in. That way, you won't run the risk of being gunned down in the street by SWAT when you run out of places to hide.'

'I didn't kill her.'

'That's what they all say.'

The line went silent. Naomi wondered whether she should change tack and perhaps be a little friendlier to try and bring him on side, but just as she was contemplating how she might do that, the Englishman spoke again.

'Okay, I'll start, as an act of good faith. Then we'll see where we stand and go from there. Sound good?'

Naomi smiled. 'Real good.'

'I was employed by Adriana's father to find her. She was avoiding contact with him after an argument, and he was worried about her because she'd got involved with a bad crowd. I tracked her down to her apartment and tried to convince her to talk to him.'

Naomi chuckled.

'What's so funny?' the Englishman asked.

'I have so many issues with what you've just said.'

'Talk to me, then. I'm telling you the truth, so whatever issues you have can be explained.'

'Let's start at the point where you tracked Adriana down to her apartment. She aimed a gun at you when she answered her door. Is that something she would do as a matter of course? For a stranger? I don't think so. She recognised you from whatever hell you put her through at Bunnies last Friday, and she was terrified of you.'

Melvin waved his arms and mouthed something at her. His lips were puckered like he was playing an invisible trombone. It looked like 'noooo', as though he was silently stretching the word out for emphasis, clearly worried about her revealing too much of what they knew to their suspect. Naomi ignored him. She needed to keep this guy talking. The more he said, the bigger the chance of him tripping up and incriminating himself.

'No,' the Englishman said. 'She didn't recognise me. She couldn't have. We'd never met before. My guess is she thought I'd been sent by the people who were after her. The same people who gave her reason to answer her door with a loaded gun in her hand. And I'm guessing from your last comment it has something to do with her place of work.'

Shit, Naomi thought. Maybe I *have* said too much.

'You might think you have an explanation for what happened at her front door,' she said, 'but I promise you can't explain my next issue with what you've said.'

'Hit me.'

'You say you were hired by her father out of concerns he had for his daughter.'

'That's right.'

'When?'

'Yesterday.'

'Impossible.'

'Why?'

'Because her father died ten years ago.'

34

Drayce stared out of the Expedition's front window with his eyes glazed over, unable to speak, unable to blink, unable to move even an inch while he processed what the detective had just told him.

After a few seconds he managed to say, 'You're lying.'

'No, I'm not.'

'Prove it.'

'I don't need to prove anything. I know what facts we've already uncovered from our investigation, and I know Adriana's father died over a decade ago.'

'You're bluffing.'

Denial, he thought to himself. Don't be so stupid. Focus on the facts.

'I'm not bluffing,' she replied. 'Now, do you maybe want to rethink your little story about how you came to have a gun pointed at you on Adriana's doorstep last night?'

'I've told you the truth, and I need to know how you're so certain Adriana's father died ten years ago. It's important. I need to know what those facts are that you mentioned.'

'Dream on.'

'Listen,' Drayce said. There was real urgency in his voice. 'You need to work with me on this. There's something deeply sinister going on, and if you want to get to

295

the bottom of it sooner rather than later, then please, help me. Why are you so certain he's dead?'

Silence down the line.

'I need to know,' Drayce pleaded. 'I need to hear it if I'm to believe it.'

Still nothing.

'Fine,' he said. 'Then there's no point in us talking. Five seconds and I hang up.'

He started counting in his head.

'We have his death certificate,' she said.

Drayce closed his eyes, scrunching the lids up tightly, his jaw clenching as he bit down in anger.

'We have Carlos Garcia's death certificate,' the detective repeated when Drayce didn't respond, presumably because she was unsure if he'd heard her.

You stupid idiot, Drayce thought to himself. *You stupid, stupid idiot.*

He punched the steering wheel with the palm of his hand. The detective obviously heard it because she asked if he was all right with what sounded like genuine concern. Drayce took a couple of deep breaths to settle himself down.

'I'm fine,' he said. 'What else can you tell me?'

There was some hesitancy from the detective, but just when Drayce thought she wasn't going to tell him anything more, she spoke.

'She'd kept some of his stuff: personal items, things of sentimental value. They'd obviously been very close when she was a child. My partner found a little pink cardboard box under her bed that was full of photographs of the two of them, along with an old driver's licence of his that we could match to the photographs. There was a remembrance pamphlet in there from his funeral, along with his death certificate which we matched to the one the city has on record. He died from a heart attack ten years ago. Her mother died when she was even younger. She was put into a children's home until she ran away as a teenager. If I were to read between the lines, I'd say that yes, Adriana had been circling amongst bad crowds for a long time before her death. But it wasn't because of an argument with her father a few days ago, it was because both her parents were dead by the time she was nine years old.' The detective stopped talking for a moment, probably wondering if she'd said too much, Drayce thought. 'If you're telling the truth, Mr Englishman-who-was-hired-to-find-Adriana-Garcia, then whoever you were hired by, was most definitely not her father.'

Drayce sat in silence for a moment. He took it all in, fanning the anger igniting within him. Adriana had a similar start in life to him: her parents died when she was a child, casting her into an unbearable solitude, followed by what would undoubtedly have been a thoroughly miserable time in an orphanage. He could certainly relate to that. He pictured her face when he'd been stood on her doorstep, telling her he'd been sent by her father to find her. What he'd taken to be anger at the time was now so obviously confusion. He'd got it all so wrong. He'd been led into a trap; lied to by a man who'd pretended to be Adriana's father. Drayce felt his nails digging into the palm of his free hand, heard the plastic casing on the phone start to crack in the other. He forced himself to relax.

'Thank you,' he said. 'I've been lied to, and I intend to find out why. I meant what I said: together we *will* find out who murdered Adriana. I can feel the fog starting to clear.'

He thought about the phone number he'd memorised, the one the manager at Bunnies had sent a message to, warning the recipient that Drayce was at his club.

'Do you have a pen and paper?' he asked.

'Sure. What you got for me?'

Drayce read out the digits from memory. 'That phone number is connected to all this somehow. Look into it. Do you have a direct line I can call you on? I don't fancy going through your call centre again if I need to speak to you in a hurry.'

The detective read it out for him without any hesitation.

'Thank you,' he said. 'I'll call you when I know more.'

He hung up.

In a few minutes he'd tracked a route to his next destination using his own phone, avoiding any likely checkpoint sites the police might have set up on the main highways and expressways. It looked as though he'd need to drive through the mountains, which might take longer, but would certainly be a lot safer. Setting his phone on the dashboard, he took the SIM card out of the burner phone and stripped the battery off the back. He stuffed his pistol between the passenger seat cushions, covered the grip with his cap, and began to drive out of the parking lot, holding the burner phone pieces in one hand as he steered with the other.

He pulled over next to a bin, buzzed down his window, and threw the dismantled burner phone and SIM card into the trash. He balled up his torn blue shirt and threw that in as well. After he'd buzzed the window back up, he unpackaged the second burner phone he'd bought, fitted it with a fresh SIM, and plugged it into the car's USB port to charge the battery.

With his mind full of angry questions, he headed for the winding mountain roads of Red Rock Canyon, the ragged edges of which were once again golden under the setting sun. He checked his phone, which showed the route to the destination where he hoped to find some answers.

A little trailer home in Baker, California.

—

'Wait! Don't go!' Naomi said desperately. 'Shit. He hung up.'

'Good,' Melvin said.

The word sounded sharp and bitter in Naomi's ears. 'What do you mean by that?'

'You were giving away things that should've been held back for when we finally get this guy in an interview room.'

'I said what I needed to say. Nothing more; nothing less. I was getting somewhere with him. The longer I could keep him talking, the better.'

Melvin threw his hands up in exasperation. 'But why tell him all of that stuff about Adriana's father, and about the box we found under her bed?'

'I was trying to trip him up on a recorded line, to expose his lies. As it turns out, what I think I've done is expose someone else's lies to him.'

'What do you mean?'

Naomi tapped a rhythm against the dashboard with her fingers, releasing some nervous energy. 'He said he'd been hired by Adriana's father to find her. Said her and her father had an argument, then she went missing. Said he was hired by her father to track her down just yesterday.'

'Impossible.'

'That's precisely what I told him. And that's the lie I think I've exposed to him. The lie told by whoever was pretending to be Adriana's father.'

'This case just gets stranger and stranger. What did he say about our eyewitness who saw our victim pointing a gun at him last night? Which, for the record, is something else I think should have been saved for when we're sat looking at this guy from the other side of an interview table, rather than just speaking to him on the other end of the phone.'

'He said they'd never met before then,' Naomi replied, ignoring Melvin's criticism. 'He assumed Adriana believed he'd been sent by whoever it was she was living in fear of. Which you've got to admit is a plausible theory, when you consider what we now suspect about her last working night at Bunnies.'

Melvin nodded, slowly and carefully, as though agreeing with his partner despite himself. 'What did he say just before he hung up?'

'He said he'd been lied to, and he intended to find out why. He said that together we *will* find out who murdered Adriana. He said he could feel the fog starting to clear and that he'll call when he knows more.'

Melvin sighed loudly as he rubbed his forehead. 'Why is nothing in this job ever simple?'

'Tell me about it.' Naomi stopped drumming her nails against the dashboard and reached for her seatbelt. 'Come on, let's get moving. The manager and his barmaid have got some questions to answer, and I'm dying to be the one to ask them.'

Melvin started the engine and headed off back to the station, where they could begin prepping for the interviews. As he settled within the flow of traffic, he said to Naomi, 'So this guy – our suspect – is still adamant he didn't kill our victim?'

'Yeah. One hundred per cent.'

'And he claims the only reason he's involved is because some guy pretending to be her father paid him to find her?'

'Yes. And after listening to him, after hearing it in his voice, you want to know something, Melvin?'

'What?'

'I think I believe him.'

35

The interview room was soulless.

It had been designed that way on purpose, Jeanette suspected. The police didn't want her to be distracted from her new, inescapable reality. It was becoming clear she would be allowed nothing but the company of her own imagination to pass the time; an imagination that would inevitably torture her by replaying the events that had created her horrible new reality, compelling her to relive it all, forcing her into the vulnerable state every interrogator wants their suspect to occupy.

The walls were plain white, undecorated, the carpet tiles dark brown with no pattern. There were four chairs in the room, each frame constructed of wood, the seats beige vinyl. They were bolted to the floor, two either side of an off-white table, in the middle of which was a black metal handle that Jeanette was handcuffed to. To her right was a black box to record everything that was said. She searched for some kind of stimulus to stop her dwelling on the trouble she was in. Found nothing. Just her own thoughts to immerse in; dangerous company for a woman in as much trouble as her.

She wiped her sweaty hands on the tabletop and glanced at the soundproof door, wondering if those two detectives were on the other side, preparing to enter, to begin the questioning that could quite easily lead her down a path to prison. She thought about the time she'd just spent with her lawyer. She couldn't afford her own, so she'd been appointed one; some dumbass at the bottom rung of the ladder, she suspected. By the time he'd seen the other suspects on the jail block and got to her, he gave off the vibe he'd rather be anywhere else. She remembered sighing with disappointment the moment he'd walked in. He was probably in his mid-fifties, which for a moment sparked some positivity within her. But upon closer examination, she realised his were the weary, disillusioned fifties of a loser, not the wise and experienced fifties of a man who had excelled in his career. He had the weakened body of a man who ate shit and barely moved. His grey suit looked thirty years old and hadn't been of good quality when originally purchased. When he'd sat down next to her and introduced himself, he hadn't appeared to be particularly interested in her demise. He'd listened, she'd grant him that, and he'd taken a few notes, which he'd scribbled down in a rush on the top corner of a yellow legal pad. But after fifteen minutes he did no more than calmly advise her to refuse to answer any questions; guidance delivered in the same carefree and mundane manner Jeanette imagined he might convey to his daughter, if he had one, when he was counselling her on which flavour ice cream she should choose.

Go for the strawberry, honey.

Having barely paid attention, he'd clicked his pen, closed his notepad, and walked out of the room to speak to the detectives.

Fifteen minutes, Jeanette thought, angrily. About a minute for every year of prison time she was facing. It didn't feel like enough.

After his bleak consultation, followed by a fleeting breath of poor legal advice, the idea of keeping her mouth shut didn't sit well with Jeanette. But it wasn't just about her conscience; it was also about her rationale. It didn't make sense for her to take the blame for something she'd taken no part in. What went on after hours at Bunnies had nothing to do with her; she'd barely even set foot behind those stage curtains. She served drinks, nothing more, and only at the bar and around the tables, never backstage. And it was backstage those detectives were interested in, that was for sure. It was what went on in that room behind the curtains that they wanted to know about.

Jeanette thought about Adriana; tears formed in her eyes unexpectedly.

Last Friday night had changed everything. The screams, the blood, the sheer violence and chaos of it all. Jeanette had denied it to herself at the time, but secretly she knew the police would come knocking at some point. They weren't stupid, and Conrad was. In his arrogance he thought it could all be smoothed over and kept a secret. He thought everything would just carry on as normal, as though nothing had ever happened.

'Huh,' Jeanette huffed to herself, as she thought of how ridiculous that notion was. 'Things will never be normal again.'

She looked around the room, reminding herself of her current predicament – her new reality.

What kind of incentive do I have for keeping my mouth shut?

To protect Conrad, perhaps?

Hell no, I don't think so.

She laced her quivering fingers together, the metal cuffs rattling against the tabletop, as she wondered what those detectives might call her. An accomplice, perhaps. A willing accomplice who *knew* what Conrad McAuley was up to and sought to protect him from the police. That's what they'd shout at her across this table if she tried to play them for fools. That's what they'd accuse her of. And was she supposed to just sit there and say nothing to that? She shook her head.

Not a chance.

She had at times *suspected* what went on behind those curtains, but she'd never *known*. Not for sure. Not until last Friday night, when that gang of Mexicans had walked through the doors, changing their lives forever.

She shut her eyes tightly and dropped her head to her hands.

Suspicions are easy to turn a blind eye to, she thought. *We've all done it. It's human nature. I just need to convince those detectives of that. I need them to picture themselves in my shoes, working for that bastard; scared out of my mind, most of the time. I need them to feel sympathy for me, and nobody feels sympathetic for someone who refuses to answer questions, do they?*

So that was it then. Decision made. Whatever had happened backstage last Friday night; whatever those Mexicans had done; whatever that big stranger had come to see Conrad for; whatever the police were after Conrad for; whatever type of monstrous people he'd got himself involved with, it was all down to him to deal with, not her. Not Jeanette Brown: the barmaid who turned a blind eye through fear. There was only one thing Jeanette needed to do.

She needed to tell the truth about last Friday night.

The sound of the door opening dragged her away from her thoughts and back into the room. She lifted her head from her hands and opened her eyes. The two detectives had walked in, the same two as before, who'd shown up at Bunnies when she'd had a shotgun in her hands. They sat down opposite her without saying a single word. Her lawyer was right behind them. He got hit with the door they hadn't bothered to hold open for him, frowning as he stumbled into the room and manoeuvred himself into the seat next to Jeanette. He didn't say a single word to her. He just put his notebook down on the table and checked his watch, probably worried about what time he'd be home for his dinner, instead of worrying about his real priority: the legal defence of his client. Jeanette glared at him with barely restrained contempt.

'Don't get too comfortable,' she said. 'You won't be sat there long.'

The others in the room stiffened, unsure as to whom she was speaking. However, as soon as her lawyer locked eyes with her, he knew exactly to whom those words had been directed.

'What?' he asked.

'I don't need your representation, for what it's worth, so please leave.' She turned to face the two detectives opposite her. 'The quicker he goes, the sooner I can tell you everything I know.'

The big male detective was out of his seat surprisingly quickly for a man of his size, Jeanette thought. He opened the door and took hold of the lawyer by his arm, leading him out of the room and down the corridor, faster than the lawyer was expecting, it seemed.

'You don't need to manhandle me,' Jeanette heard him protest as his voice faded. 'I can find my own way out.'

Before the door had even shut on its own weight, the big detective was back in the room. He reclaimed his seat and nodded towards his colleague, who hit a button on the small black box to start recording. They both opened their notebooks and looked across at Jeanette, pens in hand.

'Whenever you're ready,' the female detective said. 'In your own time.'

Jeanette filled her lungs, huffed out a big sigh, and told them everything.

36

When Drayce finally made it to Baker, he filled up his Expedition at the gas station, then pulled up in front of the country store and killed the lights and engine. He sat in the darkness, still but for the movement of his hands as he rubbed his tired face.

The route he'd taken had been a long one. He'd left Vegas on the 160, but had soon turned off when he spotted a large cluster of glass and metal, somewhere in the distance, glinting in the dying sun. Worried it might have been a police checkpoint, he decided a diversion was necessary. The Expedition's tyres kicked up sand as they rolled off the asphalt, and headed south on a remote desert road that appeared as though it might come to a dead end at any moment. Luckily, he hit asphalt again, and eventually came to a small community called Goodsprings, at which point he headed west, aiming for the state line with California with nothing but the full beam of the SUV's headlights to guide him through the pitch-black desert.

He'd found the state border just the other side of somewhere called Sandy Valley, where he'd then headed south, hoping to pick up the I-15 far past any other check points that may have been set up on the outskirts of Vegas. The view during the journey, which he knew without doubt would have been glorious in the day, had been painfully non-existent in the darkness. All he'd had to look at was an illuminated strip of grey road as far as the beam of his headlights, with two yellow lines painted down the middle of it, and a long procession of dried out bushes and cacti peeking into view on either side. Not once did he come across another car on those back roads. It had felt like hypnosis, slowly dragging his eyelids down. After nearly three hours of driving, dog tired from the monotony of the journey, he'd been relieved to hit I-15, where he'd picked up the pace, heading west towards Baker.

Outside the country store, he stopped rubbing his face and checked his watch. It had just gone ten o'clock in the evening. He tossed the baseball cap onto the back seat, pulled the pistol free from the cushions, press-checked it to ensure the chamber was empty, and stuffed it into his belt. The burner phone went in his pocket.

As he opened the door and climbed out, he shivered in the cold night air, motivating him to reach back inside for his jacket. He shrugged it on and zipped it up at the front, making sure it blanketed the grip of his pistol from anyone's view.

It would have been quicker to drive directly to the trailer, but after finding out he'd been lied to, Drayce wanted to leave some distance between the Expedition and the trailer. He hoped by making his way to the confrontation on foot, it would give him a greater chance of catching the man who'd pretended to be Carlos Garcia by surprise. He stuffed his cold hands into his trouser pockets and walked to the end of the short stretch of shops and restaurants in Baker, then dashed across the boulevard to take a more direct route. He wanted to get there quickly. He wanted answers.

It wasn't easy in the dark, but eventually he found the right trailer: a white box with a raised porch in the middle of a sandy lot, right on the corner of a set of crossroads, surrounded by a chain-link fence. With no street lamps, all Drayce had to go by was a sliver of moon, and the yellow ambient light cast from neighbouring properties. He walked around the network of dirt roads, circling the trailer from a distance.

Fail to prepare, prepare to fail.

After everything that had happened to him, he wanted to take precautions to make sure there wasn't a SWAT team, or a gang of villains, set up around the corner, waiting for him to show up. Once happy the roads were clear, he focused on the trailer.

It appeared nobody was home, the place in total darkness, the driveway empty. Not to worry though, Drayce thought. He would still find a way in and search through the man's possessions. There might be something in there to shine a light on his real identity.

Drayce pushed open the gate in the fence and approached the porch. The blinds were all closed, no sight or sound of life inside. He climbed the steps, taking care not to make too much noise until he was in position. He tested the door to establish where the lock was placed, then stood back and kicked it. Overkill. The hinges tore from the frame, the lock obliterated as the entire door flew inside. Loud cracks from the splintered wood and ruptured steel rang out into the still air. Drayce waited for a response; he didn't get one. No lights, no sounds, no footsteps.

He entered the trailer.

The interior felt different. He flicked the light switch. Nothing. Sighing in the darkness, he moved deeper inside and forced himself to focus on the positives: lights drew attention; the dark was camouflage, keeping his presence hidden.

He stepped over the broken door and began the search.

Gradually his eyes adjusted, allowing more details to emerge. He walked the same route he'd walked the day before, through the kitchen and into the living room, and began to realise why it felt alien. There was a hollow echo, absent during his first visit. He checked every room, each one the same. The tables; the sofas; the chairs; the television; the bed; even the pictures on the walls.

They were all gone.

The trailer was empty.

Drayce froze in the middle of the abandoned living room. An eerie feeling rippled across his flesh. A familiar scent registered. He lifted his chin, inhaled deeply: burnt tobacco. He clenched his fists, prepared for a confrontation he knew wasn't possible. He'd searched the trailer; he was definitely alone. His nostrils flared. The smell hung in the air and clung to the walls, a sweetness to it that evidenced it had recently been lit.

How close had he been to witnessing the trailer's evacuation?

Minutes, perhaps?

As he contemplated his poor timing, something in the corner of the ceiling caught his eye: a little black dot about the size of a quarter, a shine to its surface making it stand out in the dim light. He moved forwards carefully and quietly until the dot came into focus, but he still couldn't make out what it was in the gloomy darkness. When he touched it with his finger it felt smooth and hard, like glass. Strange. Why would there be a little dot of glass in the corner of the room? His suspicions worried him. He did the same with the area around the dot, poking it with his fingertip; it all felt normal: the rough, flimsy surface of a trailer's walls. He went back to the dot. It was slightly raised from the surface of the wall, so he pinched it with his index finger and thumb. A plastic casing surrounded its circumference.

An anxious storm rumbled in Drayce's chest.

He pinched even tighter, pulled, and after some initial resistance felt it come free. A rustling sound accompanied it. There was a wire leading into the wall. He examined the little electronic device, squinting in the darkness as he rolled it in his hands. The feeling he was being watched gathered pace within him.

And that's when it dawned on him.

He was staring into a camera.

His anxiety got traction and ran away with itself. He could feel sensors mounted below the lens, spaced out to form an arc covering the entire room. The camera hadn't been there the day before – there was no way it would have skipped his attention – which meant it had been installed *after* the trailer had been abandoned. All of which begged the question: why fit a camera with motion sensors inside an empty home?

To warn someone if you came back, Drayce told himself with sobering clarity.

Hands sweating, he glared into the lens and wondered who was staring back at him. A moment later it fell from his grasp, his attention torn away.

Tyres skidded to a halt at the front of the trailer.

37

Drayce moved to the nearest front window and reached for the blind. Before his fingers made it, he was forced to shield his eyes against a fierce glare. Floodlights lit up the front of the trailer, as bright as the midday Nevada sun. He dropped to the floor, chest down: an instinctive reaction to reduce the size of the target he was presenting. He drew his pistol, racked the slide, and aimed it at the front doorway.

Nothing happened.

He crawled towards the nearest window. Reached up to the blind.

A gunshot from outside made him snatch his hand back. The round punched through the thin wall of the trailer and whizzed over his head. A high-powered semi-automatic rifle, Drayce knew. The frequency of the shots would only be limited by the speed at which the shooter could move his trigger finger.

Unlike what came next.

Another gunman opened up with a full auto, peppering the front of the trailer with high velocity bullets. Drayce pinned himself to the floor, flattening his body as round after round of hot lead tore through the flimsy fabric around him. He retreated as he glanced at the front door frame: certain death. He considered the trailer's back windows, but ruled those out as well. He was sure there wouldn't be anyone waiting out back for him – not with the amount of gunfire heading in that direction – but to climb through one of those windows he would need to stand up, putting his head, arms and torso in the line of fire.

A hissing sound registered amongst the chaos. It was coming from the kitchen. Instinct told Drayce to cover his head. A split second later he felt a rush of air pass over him, feeding the giant ball of fire that had just erupted, its flames licking the ceiling as it progressed through the doorway. A severed gas pipe was all that was left of the cooker, spitting fire like a dragon as it writhed in mid-air. Drayce's hair singed from the unbearable heat. Smoke filled the void above his head, its black essence creeping slowly but surely down towards his lungs. A bullet must have hit the pipe, rupturing it enough to leak and catch fire. It felt like the end of the world, a hell on earth consuming the trailer. There would be gas tanks around the back, or perhaps underneath the floor, mounted within the crawl space. He couldn't afford to hang around until a bullet hit one of those. Survival would be impossible if he was still inside the trailer when they exploded. He squinted against the filthy black smog, desperately thinking of a way to escape.

Debris rained down on him as the entire structure began to fall apart. The heat was unbearable. Big, evil, chesty heaves rocked his chest, his body trying to keep out the poisonous air. For a second time he contemplated the back windows, wondering if he would be able to get up and jump through quickly enough, but the bullets from the front were still coming. There was always one shooter shooting while the other reloaded, giving them constant firepower.

Well, if up isn't an option, then I guess it's got to be down.

Aiming his pistol at the floorboards he fired several shots, creating a hole big enough to dig his fingers in and prize two boards apart, ripping one free, then another, and another. After tossing the fifth piece of wood to one side, he now had a hole wide enough for his shoulders. Blinded by the smoke and sweating from the heat of the fire, he tore the insulation and dropped headfirst into the crawl space beneath, flames scorching his heels as he vanished.

In his desperation to escape the fire, he hit the ground face-first and scrambled through the dirt with barely enough room to move through the claustrophobic space. He spat out a mouthful of sand he'd taken on board during the landing, struggling to draw breath as he moved away from the fiery hole above him. Mercifully, the air down there was much cooler and far less polluted, the smoke failing to have built up enough to reach the crawl space. With the pistol still in his hand, Drayce looked towards the front of the trailer, and even though he was tempted, he ruled out engaging with the shooters. He was armed with a pistol; they with automatic weapons. He was on his own; they had numbers. He would be shooting blindly intoflood lights; they had their whole killing ground lit up. It would have been suicide.

Coughing violently, he crawled towards the back of the trailer while he used his empty left hand to fish his burner phone out of his jacket pocket. He dialled the detective's number and put it on speaker phone as he crawled. Splintering wood cracked from above. As soon as he reached the back wall of the trailer, he kicked the bottom lip. Nothing. On the second strike, something smashed through the floor above and clipped his shoulder, causing him to drop the phone. He glanced over to see a big joist of burning wood lying next to him. A flurry of embers rained down on him through the newly created hole above his head. Shielding his eyes, he stared up through the gap, right into the inferno. More cracks, sudden and alarming, popped off around him like firecrackers. The structure was losing its integrity. It could give way at any moment. If he didn't escape soon, he was going to be buried alive.

Survivor's adrenaline powered him on like a man possessed. He smashed a giant hole in the back panels with his feet and clambered through, pistol first, sweeping the weapon across the back yard as he broke free and scanned for signs of a threat.

As suspected, there was nobody there, but as he could no longer hear any shooting from the front, he knew it wouldn't be long before the attackers began a sweep of the perimeter. He needed to get out of there. Fast. He leapt up, rooting his feet after just the second bound.

The phone.

He turned around, dropped down to his knees, and peered through the hole he'd just created, trying to see if he could reach through with his bare hand. No chance. The fire was everywhere, consuming everything. Black smoke billowed out, the heat burning his face just by being that close. He coughed violently, eyes streaming with tears. In a last-ditch attempt at communicating with the detective, he shouted out his location, hoping she'd answered.

Gun in hand, he stood up and ran away from the burning trailer, his bleary eyes checking all around for shooters, before he scrambled over the rear fence and vanished into the darkness.

38

Naomi dropped her notepad onto her desk and fell into her chair. Melvin settled alongside her, his backside perched on the edge of the table, eyes boring into the face of his watch.

'Three hours we've been in that room with Miss Brown,' he said. 'Man, she sure knows how to talk.'

'Lucky for us,' Naomi said as she flicked through the thick wad of notes she'd taken during the interview. 'She's given us everything. The entire story.'

Melvin grinned at her. She couldn't keep the smile from her face, either. She noticed a big white envelope, wedged under Melvin's left ass cheek. She reached over and pulled it out from beneath him. It had a yellow Post-it note stuck to the front. Scribbled with a black Sharpie were the words: Now we're even.

Naomi hurriedly tore open the flap.

'What you got there?' Melvin asked.

Naomi held up an index finger to silence him. She reached inside the envelope and removed the contents. There were maybe a dozen sheets of paper, which together compiled a report as to what Reese had found on the phone seized from Diego's dead body. She speed-read it, flicking from one page to the next as she hunted for the important parts. A phone number featured regularly throughout the messages. As she read through them, something became abundantly clear: Felipe had been right; Diego had been communicating directly with the people who wanted to get hold of the Englishman. And there was something about the number that caused alarm bells to ring in Naomi's brain. She frantically searched through her pockets. Seconds later she found it: the scrap of paper on which she'd scribbled the number the Englishman had given her. She held it up to the report, alongside the number from which Diego had received his instructions.

They were the same.

'Are you okay?' Melvin asked. 'It's just, you've gone a real funny colour.'

Naomi stuffed the note back in her pocket. 'I'm fine. Just give me a minute.'

She worked her way through the conversation thread. Diego had been given strict instructions to locate the Englishman and take him to the person on the other end of that number. The target wasn't to be killed, not until he'd been delivered to the man giving the orders, of whom there was nothing within the messages to help identify. But then she read further into the report and found the number these orders were coming from had been linked through an intelligence source on the Federal database. The DEA had intelligence to show the number was used by people working for a man called Luis Vasquez: the leader of a Mexican cartel. Vasquez was suspected of being responsible for orchestrating more than a hundred murders, both north and south of the border with Mexico. As a result, Vasquez was wanted by the Feds, number one on their list. Naomi devoured the report until she came to a photograph that had been sent to Diego's phone. She stopped dead.

The Englishman.

There was no mistaking the man she was looking at. It was definitely him, taken without him knowing, judging by his body language, as he was walking away from a trailer in one of the small communities out in the desert. Naomi started to piece what was in front of her to everything she'd just found out in the interview with Jeanette Brown. Slowly it began to come together. And then it all just clicked, as though someone had flipped a switch to make her understand everything. She thought about the Englishman telling her he didn't kill Adriana Garcia, after which she'd told Melvin she thought she believed him. Well, after listening to Jeanette Brown in that interview room, and reading the report sent by Reese, she didn't just *think* she believed him.

Now she was certain she did.

'Well?' Melvin asked, snapping Naomi out of her thoughts. 'You gonna tell me what all that paperwork is?'

'Not yet.'

She stuffed the sheets back into the envelope and put it on her desk. The sound of the double doors swinging open made her turn her head: Wilson had just walked into the office. He was trying to look their way without making it obvious and was doing a poor job of it. He dropped a thin stack of paper next to his keyboard, which probably consisted of witness statements he'd taken from customers at Bunnies, then strolled in their direction, slowly, as though he really didn't want to, but couldn't help his curiosity. He opened his mouth on the approach.

'How did you get on back there?' Naomi asked him, beating him to the punch.

'Not great. There isn't much consistency between the witnesses, and most of them were drunk when it all happened. The only recurring description is of a big, giant, gorilla of a man. Not the best evidence I've ever gathered, that's for sure.'

'What about the CCTV you mentioned earlier?' Melvin asked.

'It's all here.' Wilson held up a flash drive.

'What does it show?' Naomi leaned forwards, rising out of her seat an inch or two, relishing the chance to see the footage. 'I'm guessing it's pretty good. There are quite a few cameras in that club.'

'Yes, there are.' There was hesitancy in Wilson's voice.

'I'm sensing there should be a "but" at the end of that sentence,' Melvin said.

Wilson reached across and plugged the flash drive into Naomi's computer. 'Have a look for yourself.'

It took a few seconds for the files to load, but once they had, Naomi was ready, clicking furiously at the icon to open them. Melvin stood and turned around so he could see the screen. A second later a window sprang open, split into a grid system containing a dozen viewpoints.

'So these are all the cameras in the club?' Naomi asked.

'Yep.' Wilson said. 'Every single one. Hit that button there and they'll play at the same time. That way you can follow the guy across each square of the grid, watching his movements throughout the venue.'

Naomi considered berating him for pointing out the obvious, but she bit her tongue. She didn't want him to pout and pull the flash drive out, like a sulky child picking up the ball and walking out of the playground.

'Where does this "but" come into the equation?' Melvin asked.

'Just hit play and watch it,' Wilson said. 'You'll see.'

Naomi did just that.

It started out pretty much exactly as she imagined it would. Each square showed a stereotypical strip club scene: drinkers, dancers, disco lights. There was no sound on the footage, but Naomi could tell there was music playing loudly just by the rhythmic way in which everyone was moving. Her eyes flicked across each square until she found the camera that pointed at the entrance. A big guy in a blue shirt and navy chinos walked in.

'Is that him?' Melvin asked. 'Hard to tell.'

It *was* him, Naomi thought, and it *was* hard to tell. Mostly because the angle meant they couldn't see his face. There wasn't much to go on other than his height and his build. She followed him across the grid as he walked through the lobby and up to the bar.

'Damn, he's good,' she said.

'Yes, he is,' Melvin agreed.

'He's kept his head down and angled his face away from every single camera he's walked past. It's remarkable.'

'And it continues to be remarkable,' Wilson said. 'I've watched the entire incident, several times over, and at no point is there a decent image of his face. It's the same case with the cameras in the Stratosphere. Looks like he's taken care whenever he's been near a camera in this city. Which means, as it stands, the only way we can identify what he really looks like, is from your memory.'

Naomi glanced at the envelope on her desk. She said nothing.

'Now it's my turn,' Wilson said. 'What did the barmaid tell you?'

'What didn't she tell us, more like,' Melvin said with a smile.

'Really? It was that good?'

'Put it this way,' Naomi said. 'If she's telling the truth – and with the interviewing experience we both have, we're convinced she is – then we know why Adriana Garcia was killed.'

Wilson's lips rapidly parted for his next question but were stopped dead in their tracks by the sound of Naomi's phone ringing.

'Sorry,' she said, pulling the device from her pocket while trying not to smile at the torment she was putting him through. 'Got to get this. Might be important.'

She answered the call with her usual, clipped, 'Detective Ocean here,' but there was no reply. On the other end of the line there was nothing but chaotic background noise: crackling and rumbling and God knows what else. But then she heard something she recognised.

Gunfire, and lots of it.

And something else: a voice, English accent, shouting out an address.

Naomi grabbed a pen and scribbled it down onto a scrap of paper. She shouted a panicky 'hello!' down the line to try and get a response from him and could feel both Melvin and Wilson staring at her with concern, but her efforts didn't instigate a reply. All she could hear was that awful noise, as though the world had entered an apocalypse on the other end of the call. Soon there was nothing but silence as the line went dead.

She dropped her phone into her pocket as she stood up and glared at Melvin, contorting a worried expression to tell him everything he needed to know. She grabbed the scrap of paper with the address on it at the same time as Melvin took his car keys out of his pocket.

They barged past Wilson and ran for the doors.

39

Resting had been a mistake, Drayce realised. Even if it had only been for a few mere seconds, collapsed on his knees amongst the rocks and sand, unable to breathe. His throat was agony from the smoke inhalation he'd suffered, and he could barely open his eyes. When he did manage to, his surroundings were lit by nothing more than the stars in the sky, with the faint glow of the burning trailer a few hundred metres behind him. He was alone and half blind in a featureless desert landscape, almost entirely consumed by the darkness as he was hunted by an unknown formidable team of gunmen, acutely aware his surroundings were void of anything he could use to navigate his escape.

Escape. Was that even possible? If it wasn't, then he was a dead man, destined for a violent, lonely death out in the desert, never to learn the identity of the man responsible for Lily's murder. He couldn't allow that to happen. He reminded himself of what his friend Julie Adler had told him about the police's identification of a suspect. He couldn't die not knowing who had taken Lily from him. He had to survive this ambush, despite the odds, and return to London to seek justice for his wife.

He coughed up a mouthful of God knows what and spat it onto the ground where he knelt. Attempting to clear his vision, he rubbed his tearful eyes with his fingers, trying to remove some of the carbon, acids, chemicals, metals, and other polluting particles the smoke had deposited in them. These incapacitating factors had made resting seem like the sensible thing to do.

Until a bullet flew by.

He heard it cut through the air a split second after the crack of the weapon, which meant they were close, less than a hundred metres at a guess, and no doubt closing him down quickly. Without the debilitating symptoms of smoke inhalation to hold them back, they would be fast and efficient with their movements, and would no doubt know this terrain far better than Drayce did.

He stood up and staggered forwards. Another round whistled past his left shoulder. They were even closer now, probably nearer to fifty metres than a hundred; hellishly fast progress over rough terrain. Drayce's heart sank when he heard the engine notes of big heavy vehicles rumbling behind him as they chased him down, making him break into a run despite the burning feeling in his chest and throat. He hoped he might come across a large rock formation that would force them to abandon their vehicles and get out on foot, giving him a chance to extend his lead and lose them in the dark wilderness.

But that hope soon vanished.

Their headlights caught up with him, lighting him up from behind, a long silhouette of his fleeing figure cast in front of him. The ground shook with the encroaching presence of the vehicles that were pursuing him. Through his blurry vision he examined the newly lit landscape ahead: nothing but flat desert, as far as those powerful lights could reach. He remembered hills in the distance from his visit to Baker in the daylight, but they would be a long way off on foot. In his immediate vicinity the ground was littered with rocks no bigger than the palm of his hand, scattered among the shin-high shrubs and small trees that made up the arid vegetation.

As the headlights got closer, more of the landscape was revealed. None of it looked promising. There was nothing to level the playing field, nothing substantial to force them to abandon their vehicles, and no hard cover. Everything was vast, flat and open; nowhere to hide, and no means of escape.

Drayce was entirely at their mercy.

Lit up like a firing range, a flurry of bullets peppered the area around his feet, kicking up dozens of tiny clouds of dust, giving him no choice but to come to a stop. He turned around and brought his pistol up, taking aim at a tight cluster of bright lights heading his way. He pulled the trigger, again and again, fast and relentless. Two of the lights disappeared. When the top slide locked back, he dropped the weapon at his feet and stood his ground. No way was he getting shot in the back as he ran away. If this was it, he would make sure he was staring them down when he took his last breath. Sweat poured down his face as he anticipated the red-hot punches of bullets tearing through his flesh.

The tight cluster of lights separated, flanking him on both sides until they'd cut off his route and had him surrounded. Every single vehicle in the big circle turned to face him, blinding him as they came to a stop. He rotated on the spot, examining the threat in its entirety.

He was being dazzled by hunting lights, mounted to the roof bars of six different pick-up trucks. There appeared to be four per vehicle, two of which were broken from the shots he'd fired. Thousands of lumens rained down on him. He held a hand up in front of his squinting eyes to shield them from the hellish light and tried to make out the details of who and what had surrounded him. After the chaos of gunfire, there was now just the persistent mechanical rumble of the convoy that encircled him.

The doors opened.

Shadowy figures moved beneath the light bars. They walked into the open ground, three men from each vehicle, each of them cradling a long weapon. Drayce clenched his fists and held them up in a guard, turning on the spot to face them as they closed him down.

But it was no use.

There were too many.

As his attackers got close enough for him to see their faces, he noticed the plate carrier body armour, the tactical rigs with several magazine pouches on their torsos, and the substantial firepower in their hands. He wanted them to get close enough for him to be able to grab onto a barrel and disarm one of them, but he couldn't help but have his back to the majority, meaning he would be cut down a split second after making his move. He continued turning on the spot, trying to predict their movements, ready to go down with a fight. Fast-moving feet scuffed the ground behind him a split second before he felt an unforgiving thud to his head.

Everything went black.

40

Naomi and Melvin drove the entire journey west in silence. They were at the back of a five-vehicle convoy, each one flashing blue and red emergency lights. There was no need for sirens; the darkness of a desert night was absolute. They could quite literally be seen for miles around, like a long line of fireworks snaking through the desert.

They averaged one twenty on the interstate, flew through the Highway Patrol's checkpoints, and made it to Baker fifty minutes after Naomi had received the call. The fifth car in the convoy, Melvin tried his best to keep up with the four armoured Ford Rangers, which had three SWAT operatives in each, all of whom were armed to the teeth and as well trained as a person could be. Naomi had managed to scramble them in a matter of minutes as she'd left the station, thinking if she'd heard what she thought she'd heard on the other end of that line, she would need their help. She glared through the front windscreen as she thought about the gunshots and the sound of the Englishman's voice, frantically shouting out the address they were all now racing towards.

Something in the distance caught her attention.

'Is that what I think it is?' she asked Melvin as she pointed through the front windscreen.

'How am I supposed to know what you're thinking?' Melvin said as he turned off the interstate and flew onto Baker's streets behind the SWAT vehicles. 'I'm not a mind reader.'

'Why you got to be a smart-ass at a time like this?' She punched him on his arm and pointed through the window again. 'Just look over there and tell me what you think.'

Melvin winced at Naomi's rock-hard knuckles, then looked in the direction she was pointing. His mouth hung open. 'Oh shit. That is not good.'

'Looks like you *can* read minds after all, because those were the exact words in my head.'

Roughly three hundred metres ahead of Naomi's finger was the hazy yellow glow of a house fire. They followed the SWAT vehicles to the address, and just as suspected, they found themselves parking right outside the burning home. The shell of a former trailer, black and charred, that had crumbled in on itself into a bed of embers and withering flames, was all that remained. The SWAT team disembarked their vehicles and fanned out to put cover in every direction with their assault rifles. The powerful torches fixed to their weapons' railings beamed out from each position, lighting up the area around the trailer. Plumes of smoke wafted between them as they used hand signals to communicate with one another, only calling out to Melvin and Naomi once they were certain the immediate area was safe.

'I'd say we're definitely in the right place,' the SWAT commander said to Naomi as she climbed out of her vehicle. He was a short guy with the stocky build of a man long accustomed to hard physical work, and wore black fireproof overalls underneath a ballistic plate carrier, designed to protect his vital organs from gunfire. He had over half a dozen fully loaded magazines tucked into pouches on his torso, and a utility belt fastened around his waist that was full of kit, with a thigh holster for his pistol. In his hands was a customised assault rifle with an M4 platform. The only part of his face she could see were his eyes, the lower half covered by a protective shield. On his head was a Kevlar helmet with night vision mounted to the top. Naomi examined the others in the team; they were all kitted out in the same way. She was glad she'd brought them along.

'What makes you say that?' she asked.

'Take a look around your feet.'

Glinting in the commander's torchlight were hundreds of spent cartridges in the dirt, most nine mil, some a lot bigger.

'This many rounds fired means we're dealing with people who are armed with fully automatic weapons. These casings are all over this trailer's front yard. There was a big team of shooters here, Detective.' He looked up at Naomi. 'Just who the hell is this suspect of yours?'

'We don't know.'

'Well, I'd say he may have bitten off more than he can chew.'

Naomi didn't reply. She examined the burning trailer and wondered if they'd find the Englishman's body in there, a man whom she now believed to be innocent, potentially killed just for being unlucky enough to stumble into the drama of another world.

'We're too late,' Naomi eventually said. She kicked the dirt and brass in frustration. 'Fuck!'

'Maybe not!' Melvin shouted.

Naomi turned to him. He'd walked around the perimeter of the trailer, following the curve of spent cartridges. She jogged over to join him.

'What makes you say that?' she asked.

He shone his little pocket torch down at the ground.
'Look.'

Naomi followed the faint beam of light. It took her
a few seconds to spot what he was trying to point out,
but then the blur of dirt and sand came into focus and
she started to see the details. There were deep, wide tyre
tracks snaking off into the surrounding desert.

'Holy shit,' she said.

Melvin moved the beam of light along the tracks for as
far as the little torch would allow, creating shadows within
the shallow depressions in the sand. 'There's a lot of them:
several vehicles or more at a guess.'

'The SWAT commander says we're definitely dealing
with a large team armed with fully automatic weapons.'

'Well, I think we know which way they went.'

'Hey Commander!' Naomi shouted as she turned
around. 'You got room in your vehicle for two more?'

'Sure,' he said as he walked over. 'Why'd you ask?'

'Because it's four-wheel drive and we need to follow
these tracks.' She nodded at Melvin's Buick. 'And I'm not
sure our vehicle's up to it.'

The commander nodded, then spoke into his radio,
sending the rest of his team running back to their trucks.
Seconds later his driver pulled up alongside the three of
them.

'Get in,' he said.

Naomi and Melvin climbed into the back, the
commander into the front. Once seated, the commander
spoke into the team radio.

'Everyone, kill your lights: the emergency lights, the headlights, everything. We don't know what we're heading towards, so I want us to decide when we make our presence known. We'll work from our night vision.'

A second later their world fell into total darkness. Naomi heard goggles click down over the eyes of the men in the front seats, and then they were away, engine roaring as they hurtled forwards into the night, the suspension rocking as the tyres thumped over the rocky, sandy ground. Even though she knew the driver could see everything, Naomi was still terrified, and had to shut her eyes and pretend the headlights were on as they hurtled into the unknown.

Less than a minute later, she felt her seat belt push into her chest as they slowed down.

'You see that?' The driver asked the commander.

Naomi couldn't hold it in. 'See what?'

She felt the truck come to a stop and then heard the commander turn around in his seat as the two front doors opened.

'Stay here until I tell you it's safe,' he said.

'Wait.' Naomi heard them climb out of their seats. 'What is it? Have you seen someone?'

Naomi opened her eyes just as the two front doors slammed shut. She scanned their surroundings through every window, trying to make out what it was they'd seen, but it was no use. There was only a sliver of moon in the sky, and only a handful of stars. As soon as they'd taken a couple of steps away from the vehicle they disappeared into the darkness, with not even the silhouette of their bodies to track. All she could do was sit there in the back seat of that Ranger, gun now in hand, anticipating the dazzling muzzle flash of the SWAT team engaging with a threat. After thirty seconds had ticked by like minutes, Naomi spotted the outline of a figure approaching the front passenger door.

'Who's that?' she asked Melvin. 'One of our guys?'

'Can't tell.'

Naomi brought her pistol up, just in case, but lowered it again when the door opened and she saw who it was.

'Jump out,' the commander said. 'You're gonna want to see this for yourselves.'

Naomi holstered her pistol and leapt out of the truck. When her feet hit the sand, the headlights of every SWAT truck came on, lighting up the surrounding area like the sun had just fallen from the sky. She shielded her eyes with her hands until they'd adjusted to the glare, then followed the commander as he walked forwards into the light.

'What did you see?' she asked.

'I'm about to show you. Here. Look.'

The area lit up around them was the size of a football pitch. Naomi followed the end of the commander's finger. He was pointing to the ground.

'See the track marks?' he asked.

She nodded. They were all around them, imprints in the sand from multiple vehicles, swept out in a giant circle as though whatever had created them had surrounded something.

Or some*one*.

'Can your officers see where they lead to?' she asked the commander.

'I've got them checking the tracks, but it could be that they headed back the way they came after they got this far. There might be tracks on top of the tracks we followed. A hard thing to spot if there is.'

'If that's the case it means they were long gone before we even got to Baker,' Melvin said angrily.

Naomi locked eyes with him. 'Which means I was right.'

'About what?'

'What I told you at that burning trailer,' she said solemnly. 'We're too late.'

Melvin marched off towards the SWAT team.

'Where you going?' Naomi asked.

'To join the search.' He peered over his shoulder and waved for her to follow him. 'Come on. It's not over until it's over.'

She set off, pounding through the sand to catch up with him, the commander by her side.

'Over here!' a SWAT officer shouted. 'We got something!'

Everyone broke into a run.

'What is it?' Naomi asked.

'Tracks.' The young officer pointed at a long line of tyre marks that broke off from the circle and stretched further out into the desert, disappearing into the darkness at the end of their torchlights.

'We better get back to the vehicles and catch up with these sons of bitches,' Melvin said, chest heaving to catch his breath. 'Seems we're not too late after all.' He smiled as he turned to Naomi. But she wasn't there to smile back.

She was already rushing headlong back to the SWAT team's Ford Rangers.

41

When Drayce first woke up, they were lifting him into the back of a truck. It had been as brief as the flashbulb of a camera, a snapshot of the metallic sides of the vehicle's bed, captured in his vision as he'd regained consciousness, before he was hit over the head again to send him back to sleep.

The second time he awoke, his consciousness lasted a while longer, his head bouncing off the black rubber matting that covered the bed's floor as the vehicle rumbled over bumpy ground. He'd stayed awake right up until the vehicle stopped, the tailgate dropping a few seconds later to the sight of masked gunmen, a glimpse of poorly lit desert behind them. It wasn't the same area as before – they would undoubtedly have driven a good distance away from Baker – but the terrain was still the same: sandy, rocky desert ground, strewn with arid vegetation, lit by nothing more than truck headlights, with not a solitary sign of civilisation on the horizon. After pulling him out of the pick-up's bed and beating him over the head for the third time, his brain hadn't needed much encouragement; it had quickly shut itself down in the blink of an eye to protect itself.

The third time he came around, his face was in the dirt, sand in his mouth, throat so dry it felt as though he'd swallowed shards of glass. He'd obviously taken a beating while he'd been out, because everything hurt. Not just his head, from being clubbed unconscious, but also his legs, chest, back and face. He could feel blunt trauma and lacerations all over his body, the pain of which stepped forwards now he was conscious, screaming at him, demanding attention he couldn't give them. His brain tried to prioritise them, but with his hands and legs tied, there was no way he could tend to them. He just had to lie there, squirming in agony, totally helpless, wishing he was still unconscious so he didn't have to live through this torment.

Then he heard voices. Close. Everywhere.

A crowd of gunmen surrounded him. They spoke Spanish to one another. A shimmering haze of foreboding tension hung in the air, their words barked angrily. He couldn't understand a word they were saying, but their tone was frightening, even for a man like Drayce.

It made him ignore his suffering and switch on.

His locket was still around his neck, his wedding ring on his finger, providing him some relief; if it came to it, he wanted to die wearing them. Boots came into view through the dazzle of the trucks' headlights. He winced, expecting another beating, but all he felt were two pairs of hands grip him tightly underneath his armpits and lift him to his knees, the men grunting with exertion. Someone else took a handful of his hair from behind and raised his head, before gripping him under his chin and forcing him to look directly at a particular vehicle. Drayce wasn't sure if it was fear, or the chill of the desert at night, but he started to shake. More gunmen moved around his peripheral vision to form a tight semi-circle with Drayce in the middle. Everyone faced the same vehicle.

The doors opened.

Two men stepped out: one from the driver's seat, the other from the back. The driver was the first to walk forwards into the light. He looked like all the others in the mob: casual clothes underneath body armour, with a big handgun holstered on his belt. The guy from the back was different. Headlight beams slowly travelled up his body as he walked forwards. Drayce sensed an aura about him, as though he was the man whom all this muscle and fire power was here to protect. The first of his features to reach the lights were the snakeskin boots on his feet, then the pair of tailored white trousers on his legs, followed by the red silk shirt on his torso. Drayce saw a big gold watch on his left wrist, peeking out from beneath the cuff of his shirt. It was covered in clusters of expensive stones that blinged in the trucks' headlights. He took a few more steps forwards, bringing him fully into the light.

Drayce saw his face.

But not for the first time.

42

It was as though he was staring at a different person from the man he'd met in that Baker trailer home, the one who shook his hand and asked for help to find his troubled daughter. It wasn't just his hair that was different, no longer grey and dishevelled, now neatly cut and dyed jet-black. Nor was it the expensive clothes he was wearing. It was his entire persona: the way he walked; the way he carried himself. In the trailer he'd been skulking in the shadows, hunched over, frightened and feeble; now he was stood tall, his body appearing stronger, more muscular than before, and had marched out of the darkness and into the light as though in command of everything and everyone around him.

Drayce glared at the man who'd pretended to be Carlos Garcia. His anger built. The man came to a stop a few feet short, perhaps nervous about getting within reach, despite having little reason to be. He was surrounded by enough muscle and firepower to deal with anything Drayce could offer at that moment in time, battered and bruised, unarmed and on his knees.

The man behind Drayce let go of his chin and hair, but the two either side kept hold of his arms. He blinked hard, trying in his concussed state to keep everything in focus. After a few seconds he met the eyes of the man in the red shirt, but he didn't say anything, because he didn't want to communicate with words. He just knelt there, showing him the cold, unrelenting eyes of a man who wanted to kill him.

'You're probably thinking I owe you an explanation,' the man said, his deep, gravelly tone no longer spoken in an American accent; now it had a strong Spanish rhythm – his real voice.

Drayce didn't reply.

'It's understandable that you don't want to talk to me. You've been through a lot since we last spoke. Your silence is undoubtedly a symptom of your rage.'

The fingers on Drayce's right hand flinched as the old hunter-gatherer part of his brain fired signals down his spine without asking his frontal lobe for permission, calling for him to get a weapon in his hands and begin the violence. But he didn't. His prefrontal cortex had kicked in just in time, demanding he stay still, on his knees, listening to what the man in the red shirt had to say.

'I feel I owe it to you to explain what all the misery you've been through today has been for. So let me start from the beginning.'

'Your name,' Drayce said, in the shaky, quivering voice of a man right on the brink of losing control.

'Excuse me?'

Drayce locked eyes with him. 'I want your name.'

The man gazed down at his snakeskin boots as he thought it through. 'Why not? It's not as though it matters now.' He lifted his chin to Drayce and smiled. 'It's not like you'll ever be able to reveal my identity to anyone. Not once this conversation is over.'

He nodded at the two men pinning Drayce's arms. They spun him around. Drayce saw a mound of earth with a shovel sticking out the top, just a few feet away, right next to a hastily dug hole about six feet long and three feet wide.

A shallow grave.

His shallow grave.

'My name is Luis Vasquez,' the man in the red shirt said. He walked into Drayce's view and stood next to the grave. 'I'm sorry I lied to you before, but at the time I had nowhere else to turn. You must understand: I did not choose you. This is nothing personal. You came to me, remember? It could just as easily have been that associate of yours. What was his name? Nelson something, right? Then it would be him who was here now, knelt in front of his own grave. But it wasn't him, was it? It was you who came. Fate brought you to my door, and unfortunately,' he lifted his arm towards the grave, his hand open, as though standing aside for someone at a doorway, 'this fate was destined for whoever came knocking on my door yesterday.'

The prospect of an imminent death filled Drayce's body with an absurd amount of adrenaline. He was struggling to stay still, striving not to fight, battling not to unleash the rage building within him. The micromovements this energy caused made his locket bounce against his chest with the rhythm of a ticking clock. He thought again of Lily, of what Julie Adler had told him. Had the police really identified her killer? He couldn't die here, in this godforsaken desert. He had to beat these men, despite the odds, and make it back to London in one piece so he could find out what the police had discovered. A surge of energy pulsed through Drayce's body.

'Let me start from the beginning,' Vasquez said, 'so at least you can die knowing what you've died for.'

Drayce's shaking was worsening, the symptoms of his adrenaline adding to the effects of the cold, causing the grip of the men who were holding him to become even tighter in response.

Vasquez took a packet of Marlboro Reds from his trouser pocket, tapped it, and pulled a cigarette out with his lips. One of the gunmen came over to light it for him. He sucked in a big lungful as he dropped the packet back in his pocket, then he pinched the cigarette from between his lips and spoke through a haze of smoke.

'I'm a wanted man, Alex. Have been for many, many months.'

He placed the cigarette back between his lips and pulled on it as though he couldn't get it down him fast enough. As he continued to talk, smoke escaped from his mouth with every word that was spoken.

'Police, DEA, FBI. They don't agree with how I make a living for myself.' He glanced around his men, smiling. They all smiled back. 'For years they've built cases on me, swapping and exchanging information between one another, and now they think it's time to put me in prison for my crimes.'

The tip of the cigarette crackled as Vasquez inhaled another lungful of smoke, the air hissing as it was sucked between his teeth, before being blown up into the dark desert air.

'This sort of response from law enforcement is a well-known occupational hazard for men in my profession. Ever since I received news of my wanted status, I did what all men in my profession inevitably resort to at some point during their lives: I went into hiding. Last Friday night was the one hundredth night I'd spent inside that shit excuse for a home: that miserable fucking trailer in the middle of the desert.'

As his cigarette burned down to the filter, he regarded the grave as though he was considering flicking it in there, before coming to his senses and handing what remained of it over to one of his men.

'A man like me can never be too careful. Leaving something like that behind with my DNA on it would be enough to tie me to your dead body – if by some miracle your body is ever found – adding another murder charge to the long list the Feds already have against me. No point making their job any easier than it needs to be.' He sighed. 'If only I'd been more careful. If only I'd been strong enough to keep control of my mind.' His eyes dropped to his feet and he slowly shook his head, as though disappointed with himself. 'My urges.'

He put his hands in his pockets and locked eyes with Drayce.

'I know what you're thinking, Alex. What could possibly have led to me losing my mind? I'll tell you. For one hundred days my skin did not touch sunlight. For one hundred days I had nothing to look at but the walls of that trailer. I lurked in the shadows like a vampire, had all my food and water, everything I needed, delivered to me at night by my people. I feared going out in case the cops saw me and recognised me, the blinds closed so there was no chance of anyone seeing me through a window. It was like prison. I thought, why the fuck have I given myself this sentence? What is the point of evading capture if all you do is create your own prison on the outside?'

Vasquez stepped closer and squatted down in front of Drayce, who said nothing, his body quivering against his instinct to kill every man in the vicinity.

'There is no point, is there, Alex? So as a man who felt like a prisoner, I decided to escape. On the one hundredth day of my self-inflicted sentence, I ran from that trailer. And guess where I went?' He stood up out of his squat and lifted his hands in the air. 'Vegas baby!'

The gunmen laughed; Drayce didn't move a muscle.

Vasquez lowered his arms and tucked his hands back in his trouser pockets. 'I had my people drive me into Vegas, and I did what every prisoner does upon his release. I partied like a motherfucker!'

More laughter rippled throughout the group of gunmen.

'Of course, I was risking everything,' Vasquez said. 'It was a mistake; I understand that now. I could have been recognised at any moment.' He shrugged his shoulders. 'But at the time, after spending so long in that trailer, the urge was too strong to resist. After a few hours on the Strip, my friend Tiago,' he held out his arm as a way of pointing out Tiago in the group. He was Vasquez's driver: a short, fat man with black hair swept to one side. 'He tells me we need to move on. Warns me we need to go somewhere quieter. Too many cops on the Strip. Too much risk. But I tell him this is Vegas! I wanna see some strippers!' He smiled again. 'We take a drive and Tiago walks me through the doors of a little club called Bunnies.' He bent at the waist, leaning towards Drayce. 'Do you see where this story is heading?'

Drayce did, but he didn't say so. He wasn't sure he was capable of coherent speech. His jaw was clamped shut, his two rows of teeth biting hard against one another. He was putting all his effort and concentration into restricting the urge to fight, because he knew it would do nothing more than begin a chain of events that would result in him being shot dead seconds after he'd made his first move.

'I find myself in this little strip club,' Vasquez continued. 'I'm drinking, I'm watching the dancers, I'm having a good time. But then I see this one girl I really like. I call her over, but she won't come, so I decide to go to her.' He grinned at Drayce. 'It's the mixture of cocaine and alcohol, Alex; it makes me crazy. Another dancer struts over – her name was Kelly Carter, I later discovered – and stands in between us, defending her friend. The bouncer sees me trying to climb onto the stage and approaches our table.' He threw his hands in the air. 'Ah! Such drama. My people reach for their guns. The manager, fearful his security is going to try to put hands on the most dangerous cartel leader in the country, rushes over and ushers the bouncer away. He tries to calm me down. Tells me I'm safe in his venue. I'm among friends, he says.' Vasquez paused for a moment and smiled at Drayce. 'Then he invites me behind the stage curtains.' His insidious smile crept wider across his face. 'This, he tells me, is where the real fun happens.'

43

Drayce's body began to act independently of his own rational thought, his muscles flexing despite him demanding they be patient. The two men holding him must have felt him tense up. They tightened their grip, hurting him as they dug their fingers into the painful blunt trauma injuries on his arms. Then a third man got involved, slapping Drayce across the back of his head, causing everything in his vision to go dizzy. He cursed himself for being so stupid, forced himself to settle down, used his self-discipline to demand his body appear weak. This wasn't a time to portray strength; he needed them to believe he was a broken man, to increase the chances of them making a mistake. He turned his wedding ring around his finger, his body finally getting the message and relaxing. He felt the grip of the hands that were on him ease just slightly.

'I chose the dancer I wanted to take backstage with me,' Vasquez said, 'the same one I told you I liked the look of.' He smiled that big sinister smile again. 'I think you might have met her, Alex. Miss Adriana Garcia.'

Drayce wanted to leap up and punch his teeth down his neck, but he held onto his discipline, constantly turning his wedding ring around his finger to keep him calm.

'The manager took the two of us to this room and...' He paused to lick his evil, grinning lips. 'Well, you're a grown man, Alex. I think you can guess what was going to happen next.'

The gunmen laughed, a pack of cackling hyenas. Drayce turned his head, unable to look at Vasquez any longer without attacking him. A split second later he felt hands on his head, forcing him to look at their boss. He had to breathe through his nose because the guy behind him now had one hand on his crown, and the other on his chin, clamping his jaw shut as he held his head in place like a vice.

'I wanted to get straight down to business,' Vasquez said. 'I told the bitch to get naked, but she just stood there, arms folded. Couldn't even look at me. She was scared; I saw it in her face. Then her friend Kelly bursts into the room, glaring at me like she hates me. She tells me to leave her friend alone and takes Adriana by the arm to lead her away. The manager rushes in behind Kelly, furious with her, and apologises to me for the interruption. To show them all who's boss and bring these bitches in line, I stepped forwards and drew my arm back to hit Adriana, but Kelly stepped between us, protecting her friend. She blocked my punch and kicked me in the shin. At that point, it all turned crazy. I start fighting with Kelly, but she was one tough cookie. She hit me with a fucking lamp!' He pointed to the cut on his temple, now cleaned and sealed with steri strips. 'I had to think on my feet when you questioned me about this.

'After that fucking bitch Kelly hit me, I lost it. I drew my gun, there was a struggle, and it fired. Kelly collapsed, hands clutching her chest. Adriana screamed and dived onto her friend, trying to stem the bleeding.' Vasquez shook his head. 'But it was no use. The manager panicked, initially, but once things calmed down, thoughts of his

345

own welfare kicked in and he assured me everything would be all right. He said he'd shut the club while my people cleaned up, told me he'd help hide the body, and promised me his staff would stay quiet. But Adriana does not look as though she will stay quiet, scowling up at me as she knelt beside her friend's dead body, her hands coated with Kelly's blood. She looks angry and fearful. Angry because she just watched me kill her friend; fearful because she knows who I am. And believe me, Alex, I know anger and fear. I know what they lead to. Angry people seek revenge. Those in fear desire to talk.' He paused his speech as he ran the fingers of both hands through his black hair. 'So, Adriana needed to die as well.'

Drayce examined Vasquez with his eyes half shut. The man took a few steps forwards, putting him within reach. Drayce considered it, momentarily, certain he could get his hands on Vasquez for a few seconds before one of the gunmen shot him. And that was all he'd need. Just two or three seconds to whip his arms out of the grasp of the men either side of him and place them onto the head of the man in front of him, breaking his neck in a single, violent movement. But it only ever went as far as a consideration. He kept his arms where they were and stayed relaxed, waiting, hoping for a better opportunity. One that wasn't suicide. One that would give him a chance of escaping his captors and returning to London to discover who'd killed Lily.

'I tried there and then,' Vasquez said. 'I called one of my men into the room to control her, but she pulled a gun from her bag, shot him, then ran out of the club and vanished into the night.' Vasquez squatted down again, this time only a few inches in front of Drayce's face. The top few buttons of his shirt were undone. Drayce could see a small black tattoo on his muscular chest, almost hidden amongst the grey hairs. It read: *El Jefe*. The boss.

'So now I have a real problem,' Vasquez said. 'Not only have I killed a woman, but there is now a witness out there in the world. I needed to act quickly. I got her address from the manager and made him tell me everything he knew about her. He mentioned her dead father, Carlos. Said she talked about him all the time to Kelly. They were evidently a father and daughter who were close to one another, once upon a time.'

Vasquez's eyes burned into Drayce's, waiting for a reaction. Drayce didn't give him one, didn't move a muscle, just stared back, his breathing reminiscent of a bull waiting to charge the matador.

'I ordered my people in Vegas to kill Adriana,' Vasquez said. 'But she was clever. By the time they got to her apartment, she had already moved. Probably ran home and packed her things straight from the club. Which meant the entire city needed to be searched. My first thought was to use my own people, but in the end, I decide not to.' He considered the group of gunmen as he spoke. 'As committed, violent and intimidating as they can be, sometimes, they are not as professional, or as discreet as they need to be. And to track down a young woman hiding in a civilised city, I needed someone who could find her quickly and quietly, without any drama. Tattooed *eses* attract too much attention. What I needed was a professional, who could ask the right questions, in the right places, and not make people suspicious.' He shrugged. 'Fate chose you, Alex.'

Another cigarette found its way between his lips. Tiago walked over and lit it. Vasquez took a big lungful of smoke then blew it in Drayce's face.

347

'I played the role of the concerned father who wanted to find his daughter,' Vasquez said. 'I took Adriana's photograph and birth certificate, both of which she'd left behind in her apartment in the haste of fleeing, and used them to trick you, Alex. I dressed in baggy clothes to hide my physique, to become the weakened middle-aged father I wished to depict, broken by the worry and anxiety his daughter's reckless behaviour was causing. And you fell for it. You played your part perfectly.'

Tears filled Drayce's eyes as he realised how much involvement he'd had in Adriana's death. If it wasn't for him, she might have stayed hidden. She might have survived long enough to find the courage to go to the police about what she'd witnessed. She might still be alive. He felt responsible; awash with guilt. But most of all, he felt hatred for the man in front of him, who'd tricked him into finding her. A man like so many Drayce had locked horns with in his life, playing God with others as though they're beneath them; their futures, their souls, their very lives unimportant. Drayce closed his eyes, forcing a single tear down his cheek, and concentrated on the feeling of his wedding ring turning on his finger.

'Once my people had killed her, I could turn my attention to you,' Vasquez said. 'You didn't know who I was, so you weren't an imminent threat to me, but you still needed to be taken care of. You'd seen my face, and you knew where I'd been hiding. If the police got their hands on you, that might be enough to cause me problems. The subtlety required to quietly track down a witness was not required for you, and because you didn't know who I was, I could afford to be louder with my efforts to find you. I used the photograph taken on our first encounter, captured by one of my men with a long-range camera as he lay in the desert and watched you leave my trailer.'

Vasquez paused, presumably expecting some sort of reaction from Drayce. But he didn't get one. Drayce kept his eyes closed and turned his wedding ring around his finger to remind him why he needed to survive this encounter.

'I had your image sent to my contacts in Vegas,' Vasquez continued, 'with instructions for them to hunt you down and bring you to me. You see, I couldn't just have you gunned down in the street, Alex. Think of the trouble your friend Nelson could have caused for me if he'd seen your name as a murder victim on a news report. I'd spoken to him, remember? I'd given him the address for the trailer. He might have felt the need to come forwards as your employer, which would undoubtedly have led to questions being asked of your recent work. And that would likely have sent the police to my temporary home in Baker, maybe before I'd had a chance to move on. I wanted to make sure you vanished, with no chance of your body being discovered.' He laughed. 'But as it turned out, you ended up coming back and falling right into my hands. Thank you for that.'

'Who pulled the trigger?' Drayce asked.

'Excuse me?' Vasquez said, clearly startled by Drayce's abrupt question.

'The gun that killed Adriana.' Drayce opened his eyes and stared into Vasquez's dark soul. 'Who pulled the trigger?'

Vasquez smiled. 'You've met him before.' He pointed to the man holding onto Drayce's right arm. Drayce gazed up and recognised him instantly: Raul Ramirez, who peered down his nose at Drayce and grinned. Drayce promised to himself he'd wipe it clean off the man's face the first chance he got.

'So, there you have it, Alex.' Vasquez said. 'Now you know everything, and the time has come for me to find a new place to hide, and for you to say goodbye to this world.'

Drayce watched his opportunity vanish. Vasquez walked around his kneeling body, well out of his reach. Drayce heard him march back to his vehicle, his footsteps fading. The man gripping onto Drayce's head let go, and the two men holding his arms began to tug him forwards.

With his fear mounting, and his options fading, they dragged Drayce's knees to the edge of the hole and dumped him headfirst into the grave.

44

Drayce only just managed to get his hands out in time. His palms and forearms hit the dirt with a dull thud, protecting his face. A plume of dust rose, forcing his eyes shut. He coughed violently and spat out the sand that had blown into his mouth. From above came the sound of engines revving and tyres grinding in the sand. Moments later the noise of the vehicles faded away. With the headlights gone, it was almost completely dark. He rolled over onto his back in the cramped space. The hole wasn't deep enough, maybe only a couple of feet. Had they filled it in as it was, he would still have been able to feel fresh air with his chest.

Fierce glare from a torch beam forced him to shield his eyes. Between his fingers he saw two pairs of boots perched on the edge of the grave: one directly ahead; the other on the left side. Drayce tracked up their bodies to their faces and instantly recognised them: Miguel Perez, and Adriana's murderer: Raul Ramirez. They were dressed differently, the pair now in jeans, T-shirts, and desert camo body armour. The bruising around their facial injuries was peaking. Miguel's left leg appeared to be padded out underneath his trousers, no doubt from the thick bandages that now protected the knife wound. The way in which Raul held himself suggested he had a stiff, rigid neck from the guillotine choke Drayce had applied, and his nose was bulbous because Drayce had rammed the Impala's door in his face. Drayce knew that under their clothing would be more bandages over the gunshot wounds he'd inflicted upon them at Bunnies. In one hand, Miguel held the torch; in the other, a shovel. Both men scowled at Drayce.

'The hole's too small,' Miguel said as he shone the beam around the grave.

'Nah,' Raul replied, whom Drayce noticed had an AK47 in his hands. 'The hole is not the problem. It's the guy. He's too big.'

They both laughed. Drayce stayed quiet, thinking through his options.

'Not so tough now, hey gringo,' Miguel said. 'Here.' He threw the shovel into the grave. It landed on Drayce's legs.

'The fuck you doing, man?' Raul asked.

'It's no problem. If he fucks around, just shoot him. Besides, I'm not digging anymore dirt. Let this *puta* dig his own grave.'

Drayce took hold of the shovel.

'Yeah!' Raul shouted. 'Dig your grave, *pinche pendejo*!'

Drayce carefully got to his knees and lifted the big tool in front of him. The spade end was made of shiny metal. He tilted it until Miguel was in the reflection, but he was met with nothing but glare from the torch. Tilting it the opposite way, he saw Raul, and clocked that there was no sling securing the AK to his body.

Drayce shut his eyes, slowly got to his feet, and tightened his grip on the shovel.

'He said dig, you stupid fucking gringo,' Miguel said.

With his eyes shut, Drayce's sense of hearing was heightened. He planted his feet, cocked his hips, and marked in his mind the angle from which those words had just been spoken, his eyes still closed, keeping his whole world as black as the night.

'You deaf, *puta*?' Miguel asked, the torch quivering in his hands as his anger got the better of him.

'Start digging!' Raul ordered, 'or I'll shove this gun up your—'

The last word of that sentence was replaced by the sound of a steel shovelhead breaking the man's jaw, the *crack* of the impact ringing out into the quiet desert air. The force of the blow knocked Raul down instantly, his body melting to the ground. On the return swing, Drayce swiped the shovel at Miguel, connecting with his arms, the torch slipping from his limp grasp into the pile of earth next to him, plunging their surroundings back into darkness. The entire outburst of unbridled violence from Drayce had taken less than a second to execute. He dived backwards over his left shoulder as he tumbled out of the grave. Raul, clinging onto consciousness but blinded by the darkness, had no option other than to roll onto his side and spray bullets at the grave where he thought Drayce remained. The assault rifle blasted the open pit with 7.62 rounds, each muzzle flash lighting up the immediate area like the flash bulbs of a hundred cameras.

Safely out of the firing line, Drayce waited for the shooting to stop, and opened his eyes.

Having protected his natural night vision, he could now see his surroundings far clearer than his enemy. As Raul got to his feet, Drayce leapt upon him, gripped the barrel of the AK with his left hand, and pushed it away from him as he punched Raul in the gut with a straight right. As Drayce pulled his fist back, he tapped it underneath the barrel to tilt it up high, reached underneath for the stock, and yanked it down to break Raul's grip. With the weapon now in his control, he slammed the muzzle into Raul's bladder, dropping him like a rock again. A cloud of dust plumed as he hit the dirt hard, but he recovered quickly, scrambled to his feet, turned, and ran away. Drayce shouldered the AK as he pivoted to Miguel, who was reaching for the gun in his waistline, the whites of his eyes visible in the darkness as he drew it and homed in on Drayce.

The report from the AK in Drayce's hands resonated across the desert as he gunned Miguel down. The noise echoed back seconds later, the soundwaves having hit some nearby mountain range. Drayce turned away from the dead man and over at Raul's fleeing figure. The bright muzzle flashes had diluted Drayce's night vision, but he could see enough of the man to know of his intentions: he was sprinting for their truck, no doubt in a bid to escape, or perhaps reach a satellite phone or a radio in the vehicle to warn the others they needed to come back. Drayce fired, but Raul dived just as he pulled the trigger, the round kicking up sand a few metres beyond him. Realigning the sights on Raul's prone figure, Drayce fired again.

Nothing happened.

Drayce tilted the weapon: the bolt was locked back, magazine empty. Raul seemed to notice, his face beaming as he realised Drayce was out of ammunition, giving him an improved chance of escaping. Raul leapt back to his feet and sprinted for his ride. Drayce ditched the AK and gave chase, leaping over the grave in a single bound as he pursued Adriana's killer. Raul hit the driver's door at speed, his palms slapping against the bodywork as he came to a stop and desperately yanked the handle. Drayce was several metres away, legs and arms pumping, closing fast. He watched Raul climb in and slam the door shut, the engine instantly firing up and the headlights illuminating, telling Drayce the keys must have been left in the ignition. He cursed under his laboured breathing as the truck moved off and forced himself to put everything he had into these last few feet.

He didn't like his chances.

The truck was picking up speed, working up the gears. Drayce couldn't let Raul get away and warn the others, leaving him stranded in the middle of nowhere, lost, with a team of heavily armed sicarios racing back to encircle him and finish the job. He had to stop Raul, leaving Drayce with the element of surprise intact as he went after Vasquez. But the pick-up was gaining speed and would soon be going too fast for Drayce to catch up. It pulled away, getting ahead of him. No way could he get close enough to open a door now. There was only one thing for it. He lengthened his strides, like a long jumper approaching the sand pit, and dived for the rear bumper.

45

Drayce's hand hit metal with a hard *slap*, far enough down his palm to enable him to wrap his fingers around the bumper. He held on for dear life, legs hauled through the sand and rocks as he was dragged along for the ride. The truck sped up, the desert floor whizzing underneath him, sharp rocks and jagged bushes tearing at his clothing and skin. His shoulders felt as though they might rip out of their sockets any moment. He tensed every muscle in his upper body, gritted his teeth, and strained to pull himself closer, clambering up the metal licence plate and light clusters to the open bed one hand at a time. Mercifully, his fingers found the top of the tailgate and he was able to heave himself up and over, landing with a *thud* on the bare metal floor.

He glared into the truck's cabin, his eyes locking onto Raul's in the rear-view mirror. Raul returned the look with a confused stare, visibly bewildered that Drayce had managed to get aboard. He took his right hand off the steering wheel and fumbled with something.

A radio handset.

Shit.

Drayce ran at the rear cabin window, his feet unsteady with the bed moving beneath him. Raul noticed and wrenched the steering wheel one way, then the other, throwing the vehicle into a slalom. Drayce staggered, struggling to keep his balance. He stumbled sideways, careering perilously close to the pick-up's edge. At the last second, he managed to kick off the side panel and redirect himself to the cabin. He hit it with the kind of force a man his size is capable of when they're barely in control of their movements. His ribs hit the edge of the cabin with a *crunch* and his knee struck the window, smashing the glass into a thousand tiny shards. Gripping onto the roof bars to hold himself steady, he kicked the rest of the glass out and slid inside, landing in the passenger seat, right next to Raul, who regarded him sternly, his face contorted into a snarl, shoulders and hair covered in broken glass, thumb stabbing ferociously at the radio's transmit button to warn the others. Drayce swiped it out of his hand just in time, the device plummeting into the footwell, and punched him square in the side of his head, causing Raul's face to bounce off his door's window from the force of the strike. Still conscious, Raul instantly rocked back and threw a punch at Drayce, his knuckles connecting with Drayce's forehead. Raul pulled his fist back and groaned, his hand undoubtedly injured, but such was his desperation to win the fight that he threw another punch with the same hand, this time catching Drayce on his cheekbone, causing him to fall back, his shoulder blades hitting the passenger door behind him with a *thud*.

Drayce sat up, dazed and confused, blood trickling down his face from a fresh cut under his eye. Raul had switched hands to steer, his injured one now cupping the wheel gently while he reached under his seat with the other, fiercely rummaging around for something. He smiled as his fingers caressed what he was looking for. A second later he pulled his arm out.

A pistol.

Drayce instinctively kicked out, his foot glancing Raul's arm, knocking the weapon's aim away from him, the gun fortunately discharging into the windscreen rather than Drayce's face. He went to sit up properly so he could fight Raul more effectively, but the sicario whipped his arm around, pistol-whipping Drayce across his skull. He was thrown back again, hitting the passenger door for a second time. His heart stopped for a terrifying moment as the latch gave way and the door opened from the force of the impact, having evidently not been shut properly. Drayce held his breath as he swung both arms out wide to stop himself from falling under the wheels to his death. He managed to wedge himself in the frame to halt his descent, but then he saw Raul taking aim, lining up a shot on his flailing figure.

Too far away to kick him again, Drayce grabbed hold of the passenger door and swung out on it, his feet colliding with the desert floor, catapulting him back up like a ragdoll as he held on for dear life. Raul's gun fired, the bullet missing Drayce by inches. The door hinges reached their limit and swung Drayce back the way he'd come. He tucked his knees in to his chest as he was launched back into the cabin, his feet clashing with Raul's gun-wielding arm with enough brute force to cause Raul to lose control of the weapon. It flew out of his hand and rattled against the dashboard, before plummeting into the footwell.

On his back in the passenger seat, Drayce kicked out again, the sole of his boot bashing the side of Raul's head, causing his skull to crack the driver's door window. Raul moaned loudly, a torrent of blood pouring down his face, his eyes rolling back into his head as he slumped forwards, unconscious. Drayce sprang up and gazed out the windscreen, conscious the truck was now hurtling uncontrollably through the desert at speed. He grabbed the steering wheel and focused on the visual limit point provided by the headlights. A cluster of rocks appeared, each one the size of a family home, the truck bearing down on them, the collision sure to be fatal if Drayce didn't do something. He jerked the wheel, throwing the back end out as the vehicle swerved a wide arc. He shut his eyes, certain he wasn't going to make it. But when he opened them a split second later, he'd missed the rocks by no more than a hair's breadth. He straightened the truck out, reached across Raul's body for an AK propped in the footwell, and used its stock to gradually press the brake pedal, bringing the truck to a steady halt.

He opened the driver's door, kicked Raul's body out of the truck, and shuffled over until he was behind the wheel. Raul stirred, gradually coming round from his knockout. Drayce pulled the AK's bolt back a quarter inch to check a round was chambered, then aimed the gun at the head of Adriana's killer.

'Hey, Raul!' he called out from above, gazing down at the man from over the iron sights of the assault rifle.

Raul was sprawled out on his back, barely conscious, a layer of gritty sand stuck to his bloodied face. He murmured something unintelligible as he sat up, his eyes glassy, jaw slack, gradually coming back to the real world enough to understand what Drayce was about to say.

'For Adriana,' Drayce said.

The AK bucked violently in his hands, the bullet hitting Raul's face just below his septum, mushrooming as it drilled a hole through his head the size of a quarter, splattering what it didn't vaporise across the sand behind him.

Raul's body slumped back to the ground.

Staring down at the dead body of her murderer, Drayce thought of Adriana, and contemplated everything she might have become if she'd been given a better chance in life. He pictured her smiling face on the photograph he'd found of her and her mother and was overcome by the sickening waste of it all. He shivered in the cold night air of the desert that breezed through the cabin, told her he was sorry, then shut the door so he could go after the rest of the men responsible for her and Kelly Carter's death.

Drayce stripped the magazine from the assault rifle and pressed on the top round with his thumb. Judging by the resistance in the spring, he estimated it was three-quarters full. With a capacity of thirty rounds, that put his current arsenal somewhere in the region of twenty-two bullets. He slammed it back into the receiver and scanned the horizon for Vasquez and the rest of his men. His eyes caught sight of the convoy, a slithering line of tail lights in the distance.

Vasquez had a squad of killers; Drayce had an AK and a truck.

Twenty-something bullets against a dozen heavily armed criminals.

Should be enough to get the job done.

46

The truck wasn't fast, but it made good progress over the bumpy desert ground. Drayce knew the convoy would be taking care over the terrain, being sympathetic to their gas tanks and suspension, thinking of the long journey they had ahead of them to get their boss across the country to another safe house, in another state.

Drayce had no such concerns.

The quandary he was currently trying to solve as he chased down their tail lights, was how to force all five vehicles to stop, and deal with every single gunman on his own. As he got within fifty metres, he searched the dashboard, and eventually found the controls that operated the hunting lights on the roof.

He set his eyes on the trucks ahead and flipped the switch.

–

When Vasquez heard the gunshots that indicated his men had killed Drayce, he tapped his pack of cigarettes and pulled one out with his lips. Tiago must have seen him do this in the rear-view mirror, because he took one hand off the steering wheel and both eyes off the rest of the convoy up ahead, while he rummaged around in his pockets for his lighter. A moment later he reached back with his right arm, lighter in hand, ready and waiting. Vasquez leaned forwards and touched the tip of his cigarette to the dancing flame.

As Tiago put the lighter back in his pocket, something else caught his eye in the rear-view mirror. He seemed concerned. Something was wrong.

'Boss,' he said to Vasquez. 'The other truck's trying to catch us up.'

Vasquez turned his head and stared out the back window, squinting against the blinding glare of the flashing hunting lights.

'The fuck they doing?' he asked.

'Perhaps Drayce told them something before they killed him. Could be important.'

'Then why not use their radio?'

Tiago shrugged. 'Maybe the batteries died.'

Vasquez considered Tiago's observations as he stared at the flashing lights. He picked up his radio handset. 'Miguel? Raul? You guys done already?' No response. 'Speak to me if you hear this message.' Still nothing. He turned to Tiago. 'Perhaps you are right. Tell Gabriel and the others to stop and see what their problem is. We'll carry on and they can catch us up.'

Tiago radioed through to the rest of the convoy, passed on Vasquez's orders, and overtook the long line of vehicles. Vasquez saw them come to a stop through the back window and park side by side in a long line. He pulled a lungful of smoke from his cigarette and focused ahead, pushing a flutter of concern out of his mind for what might have occurred at the gravesite.

–

Every single gunman in the other vehicles climbed out of their trucks, assault rifles in their hands, and stared into the lights that had chased them down.

'What they doing?' Gabriel asked his men.

'Fuck knows,' came someone's reply.

The truck had maintained its distance from them, stopping at the same time they had. The hunting lights were still on, the beams no longer flashing.

'Maybe they've broken down?' another sicario offered.

'It was working a few seconds ago,' Gabriel said.

'Tyres burst all the time on this kind of ground. I'm amazed we haven't had one sooner.'

'Anyone see who's driving?' Gabriel asked.

A chorus of responses in the negative came back at him.

'Tell them to turn the fucking lights off,' Gabriel said. 'And find out what they're doing.'

'Hey!' one of the gunmen shouted as he walked forwards and made a throat cutting action. 'Kill the lights!' No change. 'Hey!' he shouted again, louder and angrier. 'I said turn off the li—'

A crack of gunfire silenced him. Gabriel felt something splatter over his face, a metallic taste suddenly registering on his lips. He watched his associate's body melt to the ground as everyone around him shouldered their weapons and returned fire, shooting blindly into the night. Gabriel snapped out of his shock and hurriedly did the same. Another volley of gunshots came back at them, this time from another position, their attacker having moved within the cover of darkness. An unrelenting hailstorm of lead tore through the men around Gabriel, the high velocity rounds punching straight through their bodies and slamming into the vehicles behind them.

Within seconds, the chaos ended. Out of bullets, Gabriel summoned the courage to examine his surroundings. They were all dead, lying motionless in expanding pools of blood that seeped into the sand beneath them, the entire grisly scene illuminated by the hunting lights.

Gabriel was frozen to the spot, unable to move. Terror coursed through him. It had all happened so quickly, so ferociously, his brain struggled to take it all in. He wanted to run, but he couldn't; his legs wouldn't do as they were told. So he just stood there, waiting for a bullet of his own. But when something did appear from the blackness, it wasn't a bullet. It was something else.

Some*one* else.

–

Drayce stepped into the glare of the hunting lights, AK shouldered, the barrel aimed directly at Gabriel's head. He stopped ten metres away, feet planted, left ahead of right, knees bent with his weight balanced in a shooting stance. He said nothing, just stared into Gabriel's eyes from over the top of his weapon. Gabriel opened his mouth to speak.

'I—'

The first bullet hit him in the throat, exited out the back of his neck, and slammed into the body work of the truck behind him. The second took the top off his head, removing his scalp of neatly trimmed, jet-black hair, and spreading it across the hood of the vehicle.

Drayce watched Gabriel's body fall backwards like a felled tree and hit the sand without a glimmer of life in it. He searched the line of dead sicarios; two were missing: Vasquez and Tiago. He scanned the dark horizon. A single pair of tail lights bobbed in the distance as they made their way across the desert. Drayce went to give chase, but something else caught his eye, forcing him to stop: a different convoy of headlights, way off in the distance, getting closer by the second.

More sicarios?

Drayce had to get to Vasquez and Tiago first; he couldn't allow them to regroup with more gunmen.

He turned away from the line of bodies and ran back to the truck.

47

Naomi jerked forwards, her seatbelt locking in place as she strained her eyes, trying to identify the lights in the distance. After following the tyre tracks for over half an hour, with nothing to illuminate the pitch-black desert in front of them due to the SWAT team's use of night vision to guide them, the brightly lit bulbs had grabbed her attention the moment they'd blinked over the horizon. Eventually, the cluster separated into two and she realised they were headlights, moving steadily across the landscape, away from the direction in which the tracks led. She patted the SWAT commander on his arm and pointed past his face.

'See that?' she said.

'I do. Just the one vehicle?'

'It would appear so. I can only see one so far.'

'Anyone this far out into the desert at night is certainly up to no good.'

'Absolutely.'

'You want to continue following the tracks or shall we intercept it?'

In her mind, Naomi ran through the likely outcomes for both options in a fraction of a second. 'Intercept it. It must be something to do with our guy. And tell everyone to turn on their headlights; I want to see how they react to our presence.'

'Roger that. The helicopter's five minutes out, and it's game over for these guys once it gets here; there's nowhere within a hundred miles where they can hide from that thing.'

'That bird sure owes me a result after the day we've had together.'

The driver switched on the headlights as he and his commander both lifted their NVGs. The commander turned to the driver. 'Cut them off. And step on it.'

They veered off course and headed straight for the lone vehicle, their engine roaring.

–

The shock of unexpected gunfire made Vasquez drop the stub of his cigarette into his lap. He drew air sharply through his front teeth as he batted it into the footwell before it burned his clothes, sending a streak of ash across his trousers. He turned in his seat and stared through the back window, his eyes searching the darkened landscape in the direction from which the sound had come. Muzzles flashed in the distance like a dozen fireflies, the barks of the assault rifles dulled through the glass. He felt his heartrate increase, a slight tremor introducing itself to his bottom lip. He snatched his radio off the seat, put it to his lips, and pressed the transmit button.

'Gabriel! What is happening?' No response. 'Is it Drayce?' Nothing but a burst of static as he took his finger off the button. 'Speak to me, Gabriel!'

As the last muzzle flash erupted in the darkness, Vasquez tossed the radio onto the seat, his face taut with anger.

'What should we do, *Jefe*?' Tiago asked.

Vasquez turned back around and met Tiago's eyes in the rear-view mirror, his driver desperate for leadership. Vasquez considered their options, but what choice did they have other than to continue? It was clear Alex had escaped his execution, somehow, and was now engaging with a substantial team of Vasquez's men. What would adding two more to the mix bring?

'Drive faster,' he replied. 'They have probably already killed him, but if not, they soon will have. He is only one man.'

The engine roared as Tiago followed his boss's instruction. Vasquez slouched in his seat, closed his eyes, and put his head back, trying to stay calm. But it was no use; an energy buzzed within him that he knew wouldn't subside until Alex was dead. He opened his eyes and saw something in his peripheral vision.

Headlights, a whole motorcade's worth, heading directly for them.

'Boss?' Tiago was staring at him in the rear-view mirror again, this time with even more worry in his expression than before. 'You see this?'

'*Si*,' Vasquez managed to say, his eyes never leaving the lights.

'What shall we do?'

Vasquez's lips moved, but the words didn't materialise, his mind lost in the spiralling events.

Who's driving those trucks? he mused, trying to make sense of the emerging chaos. *What the fuck is happening?*

'*Jefe!*'

Vasquez shot Tiago a look, a flash of anger at being spoken to in such a direct way bringing his focus back into the real world.

'Drive as fast as you can,' Vasquez said as he snapped out of his trance, picked up an AK47 from the footwell, and racked the bolt. 'I'll deal with whoever's in those trucks.'

–

'They're speeding up,' the SWAT driver said.

'Think they're reacting to us?' Naomi asked.

'Almost certainly,' the commander responded. 'Which means we've got a pursuit on our hands.' He turned around in his seat. 'Make sure you're buckled up and holding onto something. Asking ain't gonna be enough; it looks like we're gonna have to *make* this vehicle stop.'

Naomi checked her seat belt and held onto the handle above her window. 'Switch on the emergency lights. If they think we're a rival gang, they'll open fire for sure; if they know we're cops, at least we'll stand a chance of avoiding a gun fight.'

The commander pressed the button, their entire surroundings instantly flashing blue and red.

–

Drayce had eased off compared to when he'd first got in the truck and chased down Gabriel. He'd heard more than a few worrying sounds and didn't want to risk damaging the suspension, or breaking a drive shaft, or an axle, leaving him stranded in the desert, with nothing to do but watch Vasquez and Tiago make good their escape. But a change in risk assessment was necessary as he watched the gap between his truck and Vasquez's lengthen by the second. He dropped down a gear and accelerated, wincing as the tyres hit bump after bump along the uneven desert floor, the truck bouncing up and crashing back down again every few seconds, like a speed boat riding waves in a heavy storm.

Despite the rough journey, Drayce kept his eyes on Vasquez's tail lights. They were getting closer. Slowly but surely, he was catching them up. He lifted the AK, put the stock in his shoulder, and rested the barrel on top of the steering wheel. As soon as he was close enough to guarantee his shots would be accurate, he'd let rip at their truck.

Something distracted him, tearing his attention away from the vehicle he was chasing. Blue and red lights came to life on the fleet racing towards Vasquez, putting an entirely different meaning to that convoy's purpose. They weren't backup for Vasquez, as Drayce had initially thought; they were cops, a big team of them by the looks of it.

It seemed the red-haired detective had answered his call after all.

But this revelation brought little relief with it. Vasquez and Tiago both knew Drayce's name, so if the cops got to them before Drayce did, they would be arrested and might tell the police who he was, guaranteeing Drayce would be unable to leave the country, hunted down and arrested within days.

He stamped his foot to the floor and hurtled through the desert like the goddamn Road Runner.

–

A raging panic coursed through Vasquez as the red and blue lights came to life. He lowered the AK he'd aimed at them out the side window, a dusty wind blowing across his face.

'*Policia!*' he shouted at Tiago.

'*Si, Jefe.*'

'How can it be?'

'Drayce must have contacted them somehow.'

Vasquez punched the seat in front of him. '*Hijo de puta!*' He swiped the radio off the seat and put it to his lips. 'Gabriel! Where is Drayce? Is he dead? Tell me you killed the fucking dirty rat!'

'Still alive and kicking, I'm afraid,' came the reply in an English accent.

Vasquez couldn't speak, his mouth hanging open, jaw slack, his voice lost in astonishment.

'Gabriel wasn't looking too healthy when I left him, though,' Drayce continued. 'And neither were the rest of your men. Hard to look vibrant when the contents of your skull are smeared across the sand.'

'Where are you, you piece of shit?'

'Look behind you.'

Vasquez did. A truck was following, thirty metres or less, and gaining quickly. The headlights flashed twice.

'You can't get rid of me that easily, Luis.'

Vasquez felt his face flush, a giant vein in his forehead throbbing. 'I will kill you, you son of a whore!'

The words spoken back were calm and measured. 'Not if I kill you first.'

With a hearty roar, Vasquez threw the radio across the cabin, shouldered his AK, and opened fire through the back window.

–

The burst of flames from Vasquez's AK was the first indication Drayce had that he was being shot at. He heard the crack of the rifle at the same time as he swerved, the rounds peppering his windscreen on the passenger side. He swung the wheel back the other way as Vasquez fired again, the bullets slamming into the engine bay and ricocheting under the vehicle's floor. Drayce flinched as a round deflected upwards and entered the cabin, bringing razor-sharp chunks of metal from the vehicle's bodywork with it. It all screeched past his thigh and continued up, the round missing his shoulder by inches, the fragmented metal shards passing right in front of his face. He hurriedly patted himself, relieved to find he hadn't been hit.

A pause in gunfire allowed Drayce to settle the truck on a constant trajectory. He steadied his AK back on top of the steering wheel, aimed where he knew Vasquez was seated, and fired short bursts at him. He saw a flash, caused by the rounds hitting the rear window, the glass exploding into a thousand pieces seconds later. But they'd landed too far high and left, guaranteed to have missed Vasquez, who would undoubtedly be cowering down in his seat. Drayce took aim and fired again, keeping the bursts to three rounds to control the recoil. He saw sparks where rounds clipped the tailgate, certain to have altered the bullets' course of direction, meaning he'd once again missed Vasquez.

Drayce changed his point of aim and fired at the driver. He saw bullet holes appear in the windscreen, so he knew the rounds were travelling through the cabin, but although their truck slowed, it didn't stop, meaning the driver hadn't been fatally injured. Drayce took aim again and pulled the trigger. Nothing. He tilted the rifle and saw the bolt had locked back, the breech empty. He impatiently searched the parts of the cabin he could reach for spare magazines but found none, so tossed the AK into the passenger footwell and put his foot down. The police were closing in fast, blue lights everywhere, reflecting off everything as their entire motorcade fanned out to surround them. Drayce had to do something, and if he was no longer armed, then he'd need to think of something else to use as a weapon.

He dropped down a gear, floored the accelerator, and went to overtake Vasquez's truck. He saw Vasquez rear up from his seat, his face a hateful, snarling beast, gun in hand, sticking the weapon out of the broken rear window to take a close shot at Drayce. The gun settled as Vasquez took aim, guaranteed to hit Drayce at that distance. Drayce stared down the barrel, expecting the last thing he'd see on earth to be the flash of that weapon's muzzle.

At the last second, he swerved into Vasquez's truck, hitting it hard on its rear quarter. The back end swung out, putting it into an uncontrollable spin. Drayce tried to correct his own steering, but the impact was too much. The tyres lost grip on the loose sand and he too spun out, both trucks whizzing through the desert like tossed coins. Quick as a flash, Drayce saw Vasquez's truck flip over, tumbling end over end, headlights illuminating the ground then the sky repeatedly, kicking up giant clouds of sand, dirt and rocks with every bounce. The wheels of Drayce's vehicle dug into the sand. He felt it tip sideways, before his senses were overwhelmed as it rolled like a barrel cascading down a hill. The windows shattered, tiny particles of glass swirling through the cabin. His seatbelt locked tight against his chest as he shut his eyes and held his breath, lost in the chaos, praying for it to end before he was killed.

-

373

'Oh shit!' the SWAT driver said. 'What the fuck are they doing?'

'It looks like they were fighting among themselves,' the commander said. 'One slammed into the other, and it was definitely on purpose.'

Naomi leaned forwards between the two front seats, eyes squinting to sharpen her focus on the wreckage, broken headlights casting fractured light across the desert, both vehicles having settled upside down.

'I think my guy did this,' she said, her eyes lighting up. 'I think he's in one of those trucks.' She turned to the commander. 'Tell your men to surround the two vehicles immediately.'

He relayed the message over the radio instantly. Seconds later the SWAT trucks had encircled the crash site in its entirety, cutting off all escape routes. They all alighted their vehicles, guns up on aim, and approached the battered trucks.

–

Vasquez awoke upside down, head throbbing. He hadn't been out long, he was sure of it; just momentarily stunned from the crash. He tasted blood, felt shards of glass in his mouth, some loose, others burrowed into his gums. Blood dripped from a head wound, pooling on the truck's ceiling below him as his seatbelt held him in place. The pressure in his head was immense. He spat out the chunks of glass rolling around his tongue and surveyed the cabin. A dark red splodge stained the B-pillar: the point where his head had made impact during the crash, he realised. He glanced to the front of the truck, saw Tiago slumped forwards in his seat, unrestrained by his belt.

'Tiago,' Vasquez said, his voice a hoarse whisper. 'Tiago? You hear me?'

There was no response from his driver. Vasquez unclipped his seatbelt, groaned loudly as he fell and hit his injured head on the roof. Struggling to move, he managed to manoeuvre himself enough to crawl head first out of a window. Shuffling to the driver's door, he flung it wide open.

'Tiago!' he called out as the man's worryingly contorted figure came into view. But his driver couldn't respond. They'd disabled the airbags shortly after purchasing the trucks, understanding the issues that would arise if they ever needed to smash into a police car that was pursuing them, or ram their way through a police roadblock. But it had now cost Tiago his life. Having not bothered to wear his seatbelt, and with no airbag to cushion him, his face had taken the brunt of the impact during the crash, its entire bone structure smashed against the steering wheel. The man was completely unrecognisable. A steady stream of blood ran up his forehead, through his hair, and dribbled onto the roof like an open tap. His neck was disfigured, cocked awkwardly at an unnatural angle. Vasquez turned away, ignoring his dead friend as he prioritised his own survival. He had to escape, on foot if necessary.

But first, he had to make sure Drayce was dead.

Voices made him startle. A group was gathering close by, speaking in hushed tones, boots trampling through the sand as they darted across the desert, getting closer with every step.

The police.

Vasquez stripped the body armour off Tiago's corpse, fitted it onto himself, then reached back into the truck for his AK. He dropped the empty magazine and reloaded with a fresh one from the front of Tiago's plate carrier body armour. Either Vasquez was escaping, or he was going down fighting. Under no circumstance would he be taken prisoner.

He slowly got to his knees, headrush making his feet unsteady as he rose to a crouched position and used the truck for cover. But then he heard more movement coming from behind him and realised he was surrounded. Which meant there was nothing else for it. He'd have to break through, hoping to kill enough of them to enable him to vanish into the darkness.

He stepped out from the cover of the truck and opened fire.

–

The SWAT team took point, Naomi and Melvin just a few short steps behind. From over the shoulder of the officer in front of her, Naomi saw a man's figure dance into view from behind one of the wrecked trucks, his frame silhouetted by the glare from the broken headlights. Everyone reacted as soon as he presented himself, the torch beams mounted to the Picatinny rails on the SWAT officers' carbines instantly pivoting to him. Their extensive training, sharpened to a razor's edge over decades of experience, meant they registered the threat immediately. As the first round from the man's assault rifle burst free from the barrel, all twelve officers opened fire simultaneously, his body shuddering every time a bullet punched through his flesh, his torso riddled with a hundred lumps of brass-jacketed lead in under two seconds, giving the impression he was being electrocuted. The man's trigger finger remained under tension, the muzzle of his weapon rising to the sky from the force of the discharges, spitting flames to the gods. His body armour did its job, but with futility; dozens of bullets landed above and below the protected areas, tearing through his neck and groin, severing major arteries. His face contorted into a vision of suffering, eyes wide in terror, jaw locked open in a final gargled scream. He collapsed to the ground, the dust pluming beneath him soon dampened by his pooling blood.

'Everyone good?' the commander called out. Affirmative responses echoed back at him.

The SWAT team cleared the first truck, confirmed the driver was dead, and moved to closely contain the other. The commander glanced at the man they'd just shot dead as they pushed past.

'Holy shit!' he exclaimed. 'That's Luis Vasquez.'

Naomi's head whipped round at the mention of his name, the phone number in Reece's report launching to the forefront of her mind. 'You sure?'

'One hundred per cent. We've been searching for him for weeks, kicking down doors all over the city. DEA knew he was hiding locally but just couldn't pin him down. There was even a sighting of him just a few days ago on the Strip, the cocky bastard.'

Naomi barely broke her stride as she marched past Vasquez's body, mangled and sprawled out in the sand, his shirt and trousers punctured with bullet holes, gold jewellery dripping in crimson, eyes stuck open in horror, any semblance of evil power he had once wielded now vaporised to nothing following his violent death. Her attention moved to the other truck, also on its roof just a few feet away. The SWAT team, having already contained it, sent three men to the driver's door: one to open it, a cover officer to point a weapon inside, and another for support. Naomi was tight on the third man's shoulder, peering at the narrow sliver between door and pillar, wanting in on the action as soon as it opened.

The officer gripped the handle as he glanced at his colleague providing cover. He nodded. The door flew wide, the interior brightly lit by the carbine's torch. Buzzing with adrenaline, Naomi leaned around the guy in front of her and peered inside.

Her heart sank.

The driver's seat was empty.

48

Five days later

Drayce walked into a bar a short walk from LAX and took a seat at a table in the corner, eyeing up a bottle of Southern Comfort. He wasn't a big drinker, but he needed something to take the edge off what remained of his injuries. Having escaped the crash site without any broken bones, he was now left with nothing more than residual blunt trauma, presenting as an all-over soreness that stretched from his feet to his forehead. He winced slightly as he sat down and, in his mind, said *suck it up*, reminding himself that he'd felt worse after hard workouts in the weights room or on the jiu-jitsu mats.

When the waitress came over, he ordered a double Southern Comfort, topped up with ginger ale, no ice. When that had gone, he ordered another. After the first sip of the third, he took the burner phone he'd bought that morning out of his pocket and dialled the red-haired detective's number. It took her five rings and three sips to answer.

'Detective Ocean here.'

'Hey, Detective.'

There was a moment of silence, which Drayce took to mean she was processing his voice, his accent, and everything this call meant.

'You're still alive then, huh?' she said.

'Feels like it.'

'Not that I didn't already know that.'

'Of course.'

'But it's nice to be certain. Know what I mean?'

'Absolutely.'

Another moment of silence introduced itself to the conversation. Drayce used it to take another sip of his drink. He waited until he'd placed his glass back on the table before he spoke again.

'You traced the call all right, then?'

'Didn't need to. I heard you shout out the address.'

'I take it you followed the tyre tracks out into the desert?'

'You know we did.'

'Do I?'

'Yes, you were there.'

'Was I?'

The detective sighed. 'You're not funny, and you're not clever.'

Drayce smiled. 'Aren't I?'

'Quite the mess you left out there.'

'Did I?'

'Enough! We both know what you did.'

'It's not what you know, Detective. It's what you can prove.'

'And how do you know what I can and cannot prove?'

'Let's just say I was careful while I battled my way through that drama. Careful with forensics, careful with CCTV. You don't even know who I am, and I doubt you have enough to find out. Memory is a tricky thing and notoriously unreliable. Some of your colleagues may have seen partial aspects of my face, from awkward angles when

I've been on the move, but you're the only one who's had a good look at me. And as a cop, you know how unreliable the memories of witnesses are. Give it another a day or two and you won't even be able to picture me in your own mind. Sure, you could get an artist to create a drawing while you've still got some recollection of me, but let's be honest, we both know that image would turn out looking so generic it'd be totally useless. Face it, you've got nothing on me.'

'I wouldn't be so sure of that.'

'We'll see. But let's forget about what you might be able to do and focus on what you want to do. I've been keeping a close eye on the news. I know you've charged the manager and the barmaid at Bunnies, and I know they're going to prison. What's more, I know what happened there that put a target on Adriana's back. I know she was a witness to the murder of Kelly Carter, and I know who the murderer was. By now I'm sure you do too. Which means you know the truth: I didn't kill Adriana.'

'I know.'

Drayce paused. He hadn't expected that response.

'Good to hear,' he said.

'I know you didn't kill her, but most of what's left of the people who did is still soaking into the Californian desert.'

'I can't take full credit for the last guy.'

The detective practically jumped down the line. 'He posed a threat to the SWAT team. They had to—'

'I know they did,' Drayce said, butting in to put a halt to her defensiveness. 'You don't need to explain it to me.'

The detective took a moment before she continued. 'Not including Luis Vasquez, we're talking about thirteen murders. Sixteen if you count the bodies you left behind in that Toyota in Vegas. Those are serious crimes. Serious enough for a federal manhunt to catch the killer.'

Drayce took a sip of his drink. 'If you want to come after me, that's up to you, but first you've got to find out who I am. Then you've got to track me down. Good luck with that.'

'You seem pretty sure of yourself.'

'I've been in this game a long time. Plus, I think I've worked you out.'

'Oh really?'

'You've been chasing me since you first spotted me in that crowd of people outside Adriana's home, and I think we've got to know each other a bit during that game of cat and mouse.'

'Well go right ahead, Mr-know-it-all. Tell me all about myself.'

'I can tell you're one of the good ones. You don't see what happened to those men out in that desert as anything other than what it was.'

'And what was it?'

'Retribution. A long time coming, judging by what the press have been saying about them. Especially Vasquez. I read all about him in the LA Times the other day. Sounds as though your SWAT guys finally delivered what had been coming to him for a long time. So come after me if you want, but we both know you'd be better off chalking it up as a win. The deaths of those men aren't tragedies like Adriana's and Kelly's. The world's a little better without them. A little safer.'

'Sounds like nothing but a load of die-hard vigilantism to me.'

'Maybe. But you know it's the truth. Sometimes, people need to die for what they've done.'

On that note, Drayce finished his drink, stood up, and strolled out of the bar into the sunshine. Out on the street, he walked in the direction of the airport. He thought of Lily. It was time for him to go back to London, to deal with someone else who deserved to die for what they'd done.

'Did the manager of Bunnies tell you everything that happened that night?' he asked.

'No, but the barmaid did.'

'So you know what happened to Kelly Carter?'

'Yes, I do. It's all on the file. The same file that would have gone to court if there was anyone still alive to charge.'

'Guys like them own the prisons,' Drayce said. 'The world's better off with them where they are.'

'Anything else you want to say before I get back to tracking you down?'

'Is it true what the papers are saying about where Adriana's body is going to be buried? Some place called Woodlawn Cemetery?'

'Yes. A charity for victims of crime did some crowd-funding to pay for her funeral. Same with Kelly. She didn't have any family either.'

'You manage to recover her body?'

'We did. The barmaid told us everything in the hope of getting a reduced sentence from the judge. Vasquez's people put Kelly's body in a freezer at Bunnies, with a plan to come back and...' The detective's voice faded out. 'You don't want to know the details.'

'You're right, I don't.' Drayce considered his last question as he walked past the LAX sign, mounted in the grass verge in big white block letters. 'Are they nice spots they've got at Woodlawn?'

'Yeah. It's pretty.'

'Good to know.'

'You thinking of making it to their funerals?'

'Doubt it, but I'll put Woodlawn on my list of places to see on my next trip to your city.'

'Be sure to give me the heads up. I'll meet you there with a SWAT team and an arrest warrant. We can all go for coffee. I know a great vending machine at the county jail.'

Drayce smiled. 'Goodbye Detective.'

He stripped the battery off the burner phone and tossed it into a trash can without even breaking his stride. As he reached the airport and marched into departures, he immediately forgot about everything he'd done during his time in the States, relegating it to the dark corners of his mind. Instead, he thought about London: the investigation into Lily's murder, reopened after all these years. He thought of what he'd said to Julie Adler a few weeks ago, when she'd told him a team had been put back on the case. His initial gut feeling was that he should stay away, frightened of what he might do if he got too close, but now he wasn't sure. Should he keep his distance from his wife's murder investigation and let the professionals handle it, or should he get involved? He'd been tossing it around in his mind ever since, trying to decide what was for the best. He felt his locket gently rock against his chest to the rhythm of his gait. His thumb moved to his wedding ring, turned it gently around his finger. His stride lengthened; his pace quickened. He was eager to check in, to get through security, to board his plane and get back to London.

He'd made up his mind.

–

Naomi put her phone down on her desk and picked up the sheet of paper with the Englishman's photograph on it. She couldn't explain why, but she hadn't shown it to another soul. Hadn't even told anyone she had it. The only people who'd seen it were her and Reese, and he lacked the context needed for him to know who it was an image of. He'd just pulled it off that phone along with everything else and forwarded it to her. He wasn't an investigator, so he didn't understand the significance of it. Which meant she was the only person in the world who did, and that made her the person who could decide whether the Feds would ever find the man who'd shot dead thirteen cartel members, leaving their bodies scattered across the desert.

She knew what she should do, but there was something holding her back. It was the thought of what those men had done: what Vasquez had done to Kelly, and what he'd had done to Adriana. Naomi didn't like the word evil; she rarely used it, even with all the horror she'd witnessed throughout her career. However, in these circumstances, it felt a good fit.

She glanced over at the copier, knowing she should scan the Englishman's image and send it to the Feds. But when she stood up, photograph in hand, she didn't walk in that direction.

Instead, she headed for the shredder.

Acknowledgments

My thanks go first and foremost to my agent, Kate Barker, as recognition for her relentless hard work behind the scenes as she champions my writing, and tirelessly negotiates the foreign rights and film/TV rights for my books, giving this newbie writer the chance of making even more of his dreams come true. Huge thanks to my editor, Kit Nevile, and everyone at Canelo, for another round of hard work to get the second Alex Drayce thriller into the hands of readers. And that brings me to you, the reader, to whom I owe the greatest thanks. Without you to complete the picture, writing would inevitably have a hollow and lonely feel to it; with you, it's more like a community, making all the hard work and sacrifice well worth it. If you enjoyed *On the Run*, and find yourself with a few minutes to spare, please consider leaving a review with your chosen bookseller; good reviews are hugely important to new authors such as myself, and I would love to read through and see what you all thought of it.

Special thanks go to all the reviewers and bloggers out there who took the time to read my first novel, *Nowhere to Hide*, and said such wonderful things about my writing, along with all the authors who have welcomed me with open arms. In particular, my thanks go to Graham Bartlett, Surjit Parekh, and Awais Khan, for the kindness and support they've shown me.

And finally, another quick message to you, the reader. I assume the fact you're here means you enjoyed *Nowhere to Hide* enough to come back for another adventure. I sincerely hope you enjoyed *On the Run* every bit as much, and if that is the case, and you had as much of a blast as I aimed for you to have, then make sure you join me for the ride in the third book, *Worth Killing For*. I promise you're going to love it.

All the best,

Max.